Shadow of the Queen

Scott Finley

ISBN: 979-8-9907909-0-2

This novel is a work of fiction. Though actual locations may be mentioned, they are used in a fictitious manner and the events and occurrences were invented in the mind and imagination of the author. Similarities of characters to any person, past, present, or future, are coincidental.

Cover by Rossano Designs

Acknowledgments

The great ocean liners from the golden age of trans-Atlantic travel are history now, save for the *Queen Mary* and *United States*. The *Queen Mary*, launched in 1936, has been since 1967 the property of the City of Long Beach, California where she serves as a floating hotel and convention center. The latest information on this historic ship, including shipboard events and event and hotel booking, can be found at www.queenmary.com/.

The *United States* was launched in 1951 and withdrawn from service in 1969. Various plans emerged over the years to return her to some sort of service, but at the time of this writing, she is destined to be sunk and turned into an artificial reef off the shore of Destin-Fort Walton Beach in Florida. Her two iconic funnels have been removed to act as part of a new visitor center at the location chronicling the fastest North Atlantic liner of all time.

The names of those other ships now gone forever evoke a grander and more elegant time when passengers dressed for dinner and socialites and social climbers aspired to sit at the Captain's table – the *Olympic*, sister ship to the ill-fated *Titanic* and *Britannic*, the *Mauretania*, the *Ile De France*, the *Normandie*, the *Queen Elizabeth*, the *Aquitania*, the *Leviathan*, the *Rex*.

With one notable exception – the *United States* – these grand liners were all of European construction. The United Kingdom, France, Germany, and Italy all had their ships on the North Atlantic passenger route, but no matter the nationality, they did have one fatal item in common: the rise of trans-Atlantic passenger jet service. The jets put an end to the ships as a means of routine transport back and forth across the Atlantic, though Cunard's *Queen Mary 2* continues to offer 7-day trans-Atlantic sailings along with her regular cruise ship schedule.

In doing research for this series to construct the fictional *Queen Victoria*, the flagship of the equally fictitious Stoddard Lines, a number of resources were consulted. Among them, *Queen Mary*, by James Steele, 1995; *Liners, the Golden Age*, by Robert Fox, 1999; *Record Breakers of the North Atlantic*, by Arnold Kludase, 2000; *The Fabulous Interiors of the Great Ocean Liners*, by William H. Miller, Jr., 1985; *Ocean Steamers*, by John Adams, 1993; *The Golden Age of Ocean Liners*, by Lee Server, 1996; *Pride of the North Atlantic*, by David F. Hutchings, 2003; *Images of America: RMS Queen Mary*, by Suzanne Tarbell Cooper, Frank Cooper, Athene Mihalakis Kovacic, Don Lynch, John Thomas and the *Queen Mary* archives, 2010; *Cunard White Star Quadruple Screw Liner Queen Mary*, reprint of souvenir issue of *The Shipbuilder and Marine Engine Builder*, 1936; *Queen Mary: Her Early Years Recalled*, by C.W.R. Winter, 1986; *The Cunard Liner Queen Mary*, by Ross Watton, 1989, and *Superliner SS United States*, by Henry Billings, 1954.

For a more in-depth look at life at sea and on a luxury liner, *The Sea My Surgery*, by Dr. Joseph B. Maguire, 1957; *A Million Ocean Miles*, by Sir Edgar T. Britten, R.D., R.N.R., Commodore of the Cunard White Star Line, 1936; *The Ile De France*, by Don Stafford, 1960; *The World's Greatest Ship: Leviathan* (six volumes), by Frank O. Braynard, 1974-1983; *Maiden Voyages*, by Siân Evans, 2020; and last but certainly not least, *The Only Way to Cross*, by John Maxtone-Graham, 1972.

There are any number of excellent biographies of Dame Agatha Christie, the best-selling novelist of all time. Her works remain in print to this day, have sold literally billions of copies, and are continuously made into television programs and major motion pictures. Go to www.agathachristie.com for a world of information on all things Agatha.

A debt of grateful thanks is owed to my good friend and *New York Times* author Marie Bostwick who continuously cheered me forward; *The Book Club for Troublesome Women* is her latest, following a lengthy string including *Esme Cahill Fails Spectacularly, The Restoration of Celia Fairchild, The Second Sister* (made into a Hallmark movie) and *The Cobbled Court* series; *New York Times* and *USA Today* author Julie Kenner, whose latest is *The Tower,* part of one of her over twenty (and counting!) series she writes; Rachel Rossano, whose latest is *Rumpled Rhett* as well as *Novels of Rhynan, The Theodoric Saga* and others; Daniel Penz, Emmy-award winning voice over and technical artist; Bill McCurry, *Death's Collector* series; *USA Today* author Shanna Hatfield whose latest is *Garden of Her Heart,* and who has written more romance than Shakespeare; and to website designer David Bolgiano for deftly guiding me through the publishing forest. Finally, thank you to my barrister and other half, Gabé.

My goal is to immerse you in a North Atlantic shipboard crossing on a fabled luxury liner; to that end I hope to have succeeded.

Welcome aboard the *Queen Victoria,* and don't turn your back on anyone.

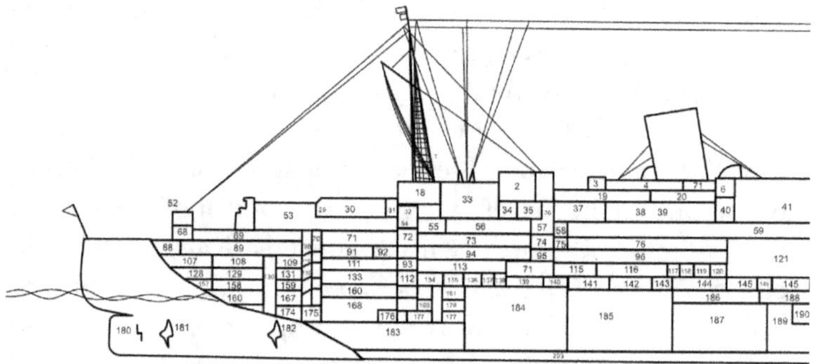

KEY TO THE SECTIONAL PLAN OF THE QUEEN VICTORIA

Sports Deck

1 Main Mast
2, 3, 4, 5, 6, 7 Ventilators
8 Staircase
9 Space for Deck Sports, Promenade, and Deck Tennis Courts
10, 11 Tank Room
12 Directional Aerials
13 Semaphores
14 Searchlights
15 Chart Room
16 Wheel-house and Bridge
17 Captain's and Officers' Quarters

Sun Deck

18 Veranda Grill
19 Engineer Officers' Accommodation
20 Engineers' Ward Room
21 Cinema Projection Room
22 Engineers' Quarters
23 Gymnasium
24 Lift Gear
25 Wireless Receiving Room
26 Staterooms and Suites
27 Forward Staircase and Lifts
28 Staterooms and Suites

Promenade Deck

29 Cinema Projection Room
30 Tourist Smoking Room
31 Pantry
32 Tourist Entrance
33 Smoking Room
34 Pantry
35 After-end of the Long Gallery (Port Side)
36 Staircase and Lifts
37 Ball Room
38, 39 Cinemas
40 Stage of Lounge
41 Lounge
42 Chair Stowage
43 Writing Rooms
44 Entrance
45 Main Hall and Shopping Centre
46 Drawing Room
47 Altar
48 Children's Playroom
49 Forward Staircase and Lifts
50 Cocktail Bar and Observation Lounge
51 Promenade

Main Deck

52 Docking Bridge
53 Tourist Lounge
54 Tourist Staircase and Lifts
55 Tourist Writing Room and Library
56 Staterooms and Suites
57 Staircase and Lifts
58 Store Room
59 Staircase and Lifts
60 Main Staircase and Lifts
61 Furniture Store
62 Staterooms and Suites
63 Forward Staircase and Lifts
64 Third-Class Garden Lounge
65 Cargo Hatch
66 Fore Mast
67 Crow's Nest (Electrically Heated)

'A' Deck

68 Cinema Film Store
69 'A' Deck Tourist Lounge
70 Tourist Entrance, Staircase and Lifts
71 Suites and Bedroom Accommodations
72 Staircase and Lifts
73 Staterooms and Suites
74 Staircase and Lifts
75 Switch Room
76, 77 Staterooms and Suites
78 Staircase and Lifts
79 Purser's Office
80 Staterooms and Suites
81 Forward Staircase and Lifts
82 Third-class Hairdressers
83 Third-class Entrance
84 Third-class Smoking Room
85 Fore Hatch
86 Rope Store
87 Forecastle and Anchor Capstan

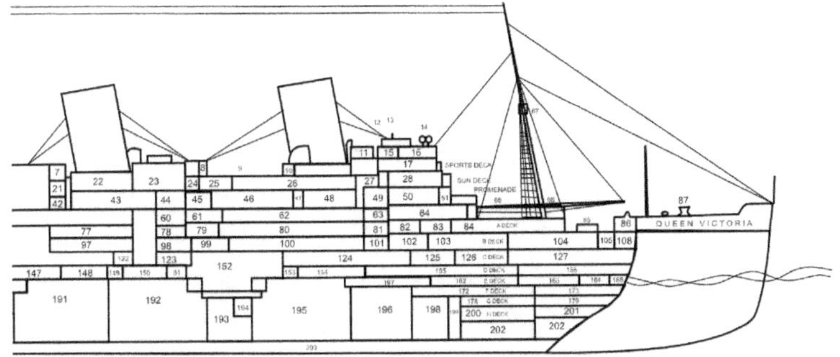

KEY TO THE SECTIONAL PLAN OF THE QUEEN VICTORIA

'B' Deck

88 Crew
89 Suites and Bedroom Accommodations
90 Staircase and Lifts
91 Suites and Bedroom Accommodations
92 Hairdresser's
93 Staircase and Lifts
94 Suites and Bedrooms
95 Staircase and Lifts
96, 97 Staterooms and Suites
98 Staircase and Lifts
99 Hairdresser's and Beauty Parlor
100 Staterooms and Suites
101 Forward Staircase and Lifts
102 Third-class Children's Playroom
103 Third-class Lounge
104 Mail-handling Space
105 Capstan Gear
106 Crew

'C' Deck

107 Crew
108 Capstan Space
109 Bedroom Accommodation
110 Staircase and Lifts
111 Suites and Bedroom Accommodations
112 Staircase and Lifts
113 Tourist Dining Saloon
114 Baker's Shop
115 Vegetable-preparing Room
116 Kitchens
117 Grill
118 China Pantry
119 Bar
120 Private Dining Room
121 Restaurant
122 Private Dining Room
123 Foyer
124 Third-class Dining Saloon
125 Third-class Entrance
126 Third-class Accommodation
127 Capstan Gear and Crew Space

'C' Deck

128 Crew
129 Suites and Bedroom Accommodations
130 Baggage Lift Well
131 Suites and Bedroom Accommodations
132 Tourist Staircase and Lifts
133 Suites and Bedroom Accommodations
134 Ales and Stout
135 Stores Entrance
136 Ice Cream, Butter, and Milk
137 Fruit-ripening Room
138 Fruit Stores
139 Vegetable and Salad Room
140 Fresh and Frozen Fish
141 Butcher's Shop and Meat Store
142 Poultry and Game, etc.
143 Bacon and Eggs
144 Grocery Store
145 Hospital
146 Dispensary
147 Printer's Shop
148 Third-class Accommodation
149 Oil-filing station
150 Third-class Accommodation
151 Dressing-rooms of Swimming Pool
152 Swimming Pool
153 Kosher Kitchen
154 Third-class Kitchens
155 Third-class Accommodation
156 Crew

'D' Deck

157 Crew
158, 159, 160, 161 Suites and Bedroom Accommodations
162 Third-class Accommodation
163 Mail Discharge Room
164 Specie Room
165 Crew

'E' Deck

166 Tourist Baggage Room
167 Bedroom Accommodation
168 Tourist Swimming Pool
169 Beer Stores
170 Lift Well
171 Wines and Minerals
172 Garage
173 Registered Mail

'F' Deck

174 Baggage
175, 176 Mails
177 Linen Store
178 Baggage
179 Mail Space

Machinery and Hold

180 Rudder
181, 182 Propeller Starboard Side
183 Shafts and Shaft Tunnels
184 After Engine Rooms
185 Forward Engine Rooms
186 Fan Rooms
187 No. 5 Boiler Room
188 Air-conditioning Plant
189 After Turbo-generator Room
190 Power Station
191 No. 4 Boiler Room
192 No. 3 Boiler Room
193 Forward Turbo-generator Room
194 Power Station
195 No. 2 Boiler Room
196 No. 1 Boiler Room
197 Fan Rooms
198 Water-softening Machinery
199 Tanks
200 Baggage
201 Mail Space
202 General Cargo
203 Double Bottom

Prologue

I had a barrister tell me once that a good story is like putting together a jigsaw puzzle. Each piece builds on another until you have a complete picture and it all makes sense, not only to you, but hopefully to the jury.

I'm not a barrister. I'm head nurse aboard the RMS *Queen Victoria*, a three-stacker luxury passenger liner that primarily plies the North Atlantic between Southampton and New York and back, and I'm very good at what I do, thank you very much.

I took the job a little over three years ago, in 1926, and I enjoy it immensely. The *Victoria* is a beautiful ship to work aboard, and the crew are tight knit. We spend more time with each other at sea than we do with our family at home on what Shakespeare referred to as "this sceptered isle." That's from *Richard II*, I think.

Anyway, back to the barrister. He was one of those old gentleman white powdered horsehair wig sorts, and he liked to drink single malt Scotch whisky. Apparently he'd been drinking a lot of it in New York, Prohibition be damned, and he didn't let up when he boarded the *Victoria* for the trip home. As a consequence he spent a lot of time falling down, and on that particular voyage I spent a lot of time, in fact, an inordinate amount of time, getting him back on his feet again.

"Maeve," Thomas said to me, because after his fifth visit to the ship's hospital in four days we were on a first name basis, "someday you'll tell this story about me. Just be sure to include all the pieces of the jigsaw puzzle. Leave nothing out."

Well, he fell down the gangway when we arrived in Southampton and broke his bloody neck, so I hope I did him justice in the telling.

Still, his words about the 'jigsaw puzzle' stuck with me.

And I promise that in what I'm about to tell you, I haven't left any of the pieces out.

I

The day Doctor Harper first came aboard the *Queen Victoria* was typical for me – I banged my head, broke some glassware and cut my finger, all before we departed Southampton.

The new PMO – that's Principal Medical Officer to you landed types – had scarcely set foot in the ship's surgery before he had to stitch up his head nurse, who, at the ripe old age of 28, should have known better. I had hoped to make a good first impression.

Of course, I didn't.

Doctor Harper pushed open the door from the waiting room to the examining room and gazed down at me in all my sprawled-on-the-floor glory.

I decided to brazen it out, managing a weak smile for my new chief. "Bit of an accident, sir," I said, mentally cringing. Honestly, was that the best I could do?

"I can see that. Nurse Chandler, is it?" I nodded. His warm blue eyes swept across the aluminum tray on the floor, past the broken glass syringes and boxes of gauze wrapping, and then back to me. "Impressive. Usually takes a force eight or better on the Beaufort to knock things around like this, yet you can do it when we're docked and dead still." He ignored my pained look. "How did this happen?"

"I dropped a box of gauze, sir."

His high forehead wrinkled. "A box of gauze caused all of this?"

"That was just the start of it. I knelt down to pick up the box and put it back on the service tray, then stood up, banged my head on the underside of the exam table, dropped the tray and lost my footing, and then came down in the midst of it all."

He shook his head, as if he couldn't quite believe that one person could wreak so much mayhem in so short a time. But, as anyone who knows me can tell you, this sort of thing is a fairly regular occurrence for me. So clumsy I could trip over a piece of string, that's what my mum used to say. I winced, suddenly aware of a shooting pain in a finger. I glanced down and saw blood.

"You're hurt."

"Just a little cut," I said as he knelt on the floor next to me and gently took my hand in his.

He smelled like delicious. Like Vinolia soap. Pricey. On my wages I could barely afford Lifebouy. I bit my lower lip as he examined the wound.

"Not that little," corrected Harper. "I think there's some glass in there."

"I'll wager you never thought your first patient on the *Victoria* would be your head nurse."

"Never crossed my mind." He opened up the box of gauze I'd dropped, then wrapped a length of it tightly around my finger. "Here, hold this," he said, then helped me to my feet and across the room to the examination table.

"Sorry for the bother. I was trying to tidy up a bit before you arrived, sir."

He took off his jacket and rolled up his sleeves then went to the basin and began washing his hands, looking at my reflection in the mirror. "Hurt much?" he asked.

"Oh, no, sir, not much at all." He gave me a quizzical look as he dried his hands. "All right, I'll admit it. It hurts like bloody hell, sir, if you don't mind my saying."

"I don't. Knock yourself out."

I laughed in spite of myself. "How American you sound, sir," I said. "A regular Broadway, you are."

"I spent some time across the pond with our Yankee cousins after the war." He held my hand up and began to slowly unwind the now-stained gauze. "I do beg your pardon, nurse, but we didn't get much of a chance for full introductions. My full name is Leslie Harper. You can dispense with the 'sir.'"

"Thank you, sir. I mean, thank you. Maeve is mine."

"Maeve?" He peeled back the last of the gauze and began a closer examination of the cut. "You don't hear that every day."

"My mother's name was Margaret. My grandmother's name was Eve. Combine them, you get Maeve."

"Maeve it is, then." He gave me a stern look. "This is going to need a stitch."

"Top middle drawer, right hand cabinet," I replied. "Ligature sets and what-not."

"Procaine?" asked Doctor Harper. "That is, if you think you need it."

"Bottom shelf, upper left cabinet." I gave him a half smile. "I don't mind pushing them into other people, but I'm not fond of needles going into me."

"Spoken like a true Florence Nightingale."

"Some people deserve a good poke with a needle," I said. "I've thought about sending that line to that American gossip man, Walter Winchell." I watched him begin to gather supplies. "Syringes are on the next shelf. I'm afraid the ones on the floor are ruined."

He took a syringe from the box. Unlike me, he didn't have to push up on his toes to do so. A tall man, lean but broad-shouldered, I thought to myself, taking advantage of the chance to look him over while his back was turned.

"Winchell," he said. "He's the chap who writes about Broadway and New York's night life, isn't he?"

"Yes." I was a bit amazed at his knowledge of such proletarian matters. "He's only been writing in the *New York Daily Mirror* since June. I mean, I don't read it all the time, you know." I shrugged. "It's all trash, of course. I could do without it if I had to."

Harper cast a glance to the stack of *New York Daily Mirror* papers on the leather couch, then looked back at me. I blushed.

"Yes, I'm sure you could," he said, "but as you say, only if you had to. Any siblings?"

"I had an older brother. He went down with the *Britannic* when she hit that mine in 1916."

"I'm sorry to hear that."

"He was part of the engineering staff. Always fascinated by the big ships. I guess some of that rubbed off on me. Chief Engineer Duncan jokes that I know enough about *Victoria* to have worked at the John Brown and Company shipyard. They built the *Victoria*, you know."

"Sounds like you enjoy being here." He dipped a pair of tweezers in alcohol solution, fitted a fresh needle to the glass syringe and filled it with a small amount of Procaine, then turned back to me. "Not allergic to this, are you?"

"What?" I said, now trying to decide if I did like being here. My career was stuck in neutral but I had to admit to myself I enjoyed the sea. "Oh, the Procaine. Find out, I guess." I put on my best devil-may-care attitude. "Give it your best shot."

"Now who sounds American?" He swabbed my finger with alcohol, then slowly injected the anesthetic. A nice touch he had. Very nice indeed.

"It's a lot of our trade, Americans," I said, closing my eyes as the drug was administered. "Rich Americans. The way they act, you'd think they won the war alone."

"Money talks," said Doctor Harper. "And if our Yankee brethren hadn't shown up when they did after Russia collapsed and the Germans moved a million men to the Western Front, the war might well have turned out differently." He set the syringe down. "Let that take hold and I'll get that piece of glass out of there and tidy it up."

He picked up the tweezers, took my hand in his left hand and carefully touched the cut with the instrument. "Feel anything?"

I did, but I wasn't about to let him know it. "Not a thing. Go ahead."

Doctor Harper worked quickly. The glass fragment came out and he broke open the suture set, took two small stitches and then finished by wrapping the finger in gauze. I said nothing, but watched him the entire time. He knew what he was about, that was certain. When he was done, I let out a sigh.

"Thank you."

"My pleasure. Try to keep it dry, etcetera, etcetera." He began to clean up. "Where is the rest of the staff?"

"Alice Johnson – she's the secondary nurse – won't be on this trip. Her mother took ill late last night and there's no time to get a replacement. So you'll have to make do with me, I'm afraid."

"I'll try and suffer through," he said with a wink.

"I'm sure you'll do fine, sir." I held up my hand and looked at the neatly wrapped finger. "Doctor Bratton, he's the ship's surgeon. He's probably up in second class, going through the sailing medical reports." I frowned. "Doctor Bratton can be a bit of a wet blanket. I don't think he's very happy." I looked around the room, nodding at another door. "The dispensers and the physical therapist will be along before we sail."

"Quite a staff."

"Sometimes you might think it's not enough. We have to take care of the *Victoria's* complement of 700 or so crew plus nearly 2,000 passengers – the equivalent of a small town. Plus deal with the occasional call for help from another ship." I sighed. "Working a passenger liner can be difficult at times."

"Try working aboard one of His Majesty's battleships when the entire German fleet is trying to sink you," Harper countered. "This will be heaven compared to the time I put into the Navy."

"I imagine so." I eased myself down off the exam table and reached up to my hair. My fingers touched nothing. Terrific. "I lost my cap."

"It was off when I found you." Harper glanced around, located it underneath a chair, and handed it to me. "Here we go."

"Thanks. You must think me a regular music hall comedienne, without the orchestra pit. Just as well, I'd have probably fallen in that, too." I gingerly felt of the top of my head. "Bit of a lump on my thick skull."

"Let me see." Harper deftly pushed aside the blonde mass of hair. "Just a small knot. You didn't break the skin but I think you might do away with the cap for the rest of the day." He gave me a wry smile. "Aspirin wouldn't hurt either."

"Thanks. Where are you from, Doctor, if you don't mind my asking?"

"I retired from the Navy in 1925. Took a Harley Street office, but after a few years found myself bored. A friend rang me up and said this situation was vacant. I made application and here I am. I took it so quickly that I never got the chance to meet anyone. The *Victoria* arrived in Southampton from New York day before yesterday and I arrived today." He looked down at the shards of glass on the floor. "I'll call someone and get this cleaned up."

"No need," I said, opening the broom cupboard. "I've been cleaning up after myself since 1919."

"1919?"

"That's when my husband died. He was a lieutenant in the army."

"Influenza?" Harper asked. I nodded, busy with my sweeping.

"Just one more casualty of the big epidemic, one of the millions, but after the War who was counting the dead anymore?" I emptied the glass into the dustbin before putting the broom and tray away. Doctor Harper's face was still as he listened to me. "I'd always thought I'd like to be the person who would discover the cure for my sister's condition, or a way to prevent the illness that took my husband and so many others. So when he died, I took the plunge. I actually got a degree in chemistry, but no one wanted to hire." I slammed the cupboard door shut. "Did you know that it was only nine years ago that the Chemical Society decided to admit women?"

"I remember," said Harper.

"Well, after being snubbed enough I went into nursing. That's where women are supposed to be, isn't it? I mean, a girl has to earn a living." I exhaled slowly. "Sorry, sir. My parents were educators and it rankles me. What about you?"

"What about me? I'm a doctor. My job is to heal the sick, but I agree with you. I've known a lot of men who shouldn't be doctors, and a lot of nurses who should." I smiled at that. "And I don't like talking to large gatherings or eating broccoli." He took off his gold wire rimmed glasses, the round lenses glittering, and his eyes were even more blue. He held the glasses up in his hand. "Up close work only." He dropped them in his jacket pocket and smiled at me "And at any rate, I don't need my glasses to make an accurate prognosis of the patient."

"And what's your prognosis of the patient, Doctor Harper?"

"Very promising, actually. I think Nurse Chandler needs to take it easy for the rest of the day, and show Doctor Harper the ship."

Sunday, October 27, 1929

II

When I was a girl, I loved parades. My brother and I would always line up early for them, and point and giggle and laugh at the marchers. Not very polite, of course, but entertainment for children was at a premium in the small university town I grew up in. Maybe that's why one of the things I love about working on board the *Queen Victoria* is watching the passengers embark. The *Victoria* is a true luxury ship, like the old *Mauretania* or *Olympic* – and so far much luckier than *Olympic's* sisters, *Titanic* and *Britannic*, God bless my brother, ever were. Of course, I was just a girl when the *Titanic* went down in 1912 – I barely remember it. How time flies.

The *Queen Victoria* was known more for service than speed. Passengers enjoyed pampering, and if it took us 20 hours more to reach New York than it did some of the other North Atlantic liners, no one really seemed to mind. This voyage was due to depart this afternoon, Sunday, and arrive at the Manhattan piers around ten on Saturday morning.

One by-product of our style was that we were very attractive to the rich and famous who were looking for a vacation as much as passage to and from America and the United Kingdom. Film stars, politicians, giants of industry – you name them, we carried them.

And this particular trip was no different.

Doctor Harper and I were standing to the side near the entrance to the First-Class promenade when I saw him come aboard. I gave Doctor Harper a nudge.

"Take a look, Doctor," I said. "Important person coming up the First-Class boarding gangway."

"Who?" he asked.

"Harvey Wilson," I replied, pointing to a stout man in his early 60's trundling up the gangway with an imperious walk.

"Should I know him?" asked Harper.

"He's that wealthy American bloke," I said. "Rich as Croesus, so they say. Spending a fortune putting up monuments to the American war dead in France. He's always in all the newspapers, made his money in munitions. The more people that got killed in the war, the richer he became. He even held a patent license on a primer used in some German munitions."

"What?" Harper was genuinely startled.

I nodded. "It's true. All of this came out about two months ago. After the war there was a private accounting for what he was owed, and it just now made the papers. I guess the lawyers ran out of roadblocks or some reporter got really enterprising. I read that he got about a dollar American for every five marks the Kaiser's armories spent utilizing his primer patent. A lot of people are very unhappy with his making that deal with the devil in the first place." I shook my head. "But he owns and runs the Wilson Company, so he has no board of directors and no stockholders to answer to."

Harper was dumbfounded. "So Imperial Germany paid him for the right to kill American soldiers?"

"American, British, French." I shuddered. "It's indecent. No wonder he's so bent on placing all of those memorials to ease his conscience."

Wilson reached the top of the canvas-sided gangway, presented his papers to the deck officer in charge and was reverentially shown through the open doors.

"And even with all of that he gets preferential treatment." Harper was amazed.

"One thing I've learned, Doctor, is the golden rule. Those that have the gold, make the rules."

"I'm sure there will be a final judgment some day," said Harper.

"One can only hope."

The low-voiced 'hoom' of the *Victoria's* horns reverberated through the air. Doctor Harper looked up. "I thought the horns would be louder than that," he said.

"That was just the warning shot. You'll know it when they really blow." I smiled at him. "Come along, Doctor."

Beneath us the baggage handlers were still busy loading tons of passenger luggage and trunks through several open cargo doors. A small steam crane chuffed away on the fore deck, lifting netted commercial crates off the pier and gently depositing them down into the yawning caverns of one of the two forward holds, a steady cloud of white vapor escaping from the valves as it worked, while above the ship gulls wheeled and turned in the salty morning breeze. Harper followed me through a set of entry doors and remarked about the transformation that had come over the ship since he'd boarded barely an hour earlier. He was right.

Stewards and pursers and maids and attendants and pages and a small legion of waiters had materialized out of nowhere. All were immaculately clad in whites and navy blues, the official colors of the Stoddard Lines, the blue matching the paint around the top of the *Victoria's* three funnels. Activity was everywhere; the forward bank of elevators just outside of the main dining salon doors was constantly in motion, and the ornate stairs were always crowded – and not just with the arriving passengers. As with any great liner, inebriated well-wishers more often than not accompanied the passengers on board. The tradition of continuing the raucous parties that had begun on shore, many of them the night before in London that had then spilled over onto the boat train heading for the docks, was old and established. I can't tell you how many of our First-Class passengers endured a day of holy hell as they fought to get their sea legs while at the same time fighting a huge hangover. To top it all off, giant baskets of fruit and arrangements of flowers competed for space with luggage in the hallways, along with the pursers and stewards who were already taking orders for the coming voyage from the more experienced and savvy passengers. The air was scented with heavily polished wood, mildly antiseptic cleaning solutions, flowers and salt air, all mingled with a faint tinge of bunker C fuel exhaust smoke that I always felt surrounded the ship like a warm and comforting blanket. The sound of the horn was heard again, warning visitors it was nigh on time to leave.

I stopped and waited on Doctor Harper, standing alongside doors leading to a flight of stairs. "We'll go back out and up on deck now. You'll be able to watch them cast off." I pushed the doors open and hurried up the steps, Harper following at a more sedate pace. When I reached the top, there was another set of double doors and again I stopped, waiting on him to catch up. I smiled. "Out of shape, Doctor?"

"It's been a while since I tramped up and down through a ship this size," Harper replied. I laughed.

"We'll take the elevators back down to the hospital. Come on."

Harper followed me across the teak boards of the Boat Deck. The wind had picked up and was quite invigorating, as we were now standing some forty feet above the pier. Beneath us, the swirling maelstrom on the pier was gradually coming to a close. The gangways connecting ship to shore were beginning to be retracted. Four were already gone, and a fifth was slowly winding its way back into the ship. Beefy, able-bodied seamen were casting off ropes and hawsers, while another group was securing hatch covers. Even more stewards were making a final sweep of the upper decks, ensuring that those left on board now were supposed to be on board. Harper watched them for a moment, then turned to me.

"Ever have stowaways?" he asked.

"Stowaways?" I nodded. "Sure. It's happened a few times. A ship this size, there are lots of places to hide. But not for long. Once the daily routine sets in, there's very little they can do. The deck officers constantly peel the covers back and check the lifeboats, so there's no hiding there – and the stewards can quickly spot someone who seems out of place. And even if they do get to the other side without being noticed, doesn't matter if it's New York or Southampton, it's practically impossible to get off the ship without being caught, though I suppose one could if one really tried and didn't mind getting wet." I watched the crew going through their paces like some vast, synchronized burly ballet. "And once they're caught, well, if they're lucky, they get taken to Mister Armstrong, the Master-at-Arms, and he confines them."

"If they're lucky?"

"Mister Armstrong's a big, jovial Father Christmas type fellow," I explained. "Or maybe more like Falstaff, once you've seen him in the ship's company pub. If they're not lucky, they get taken to Chief Steward Harvey. And he's likely to put them to work in the sculleries to earn their passage. This ship goes through more pots, pans and plates in a day than you can conceive." I took a deep breath of the sharp salt air, my tunic ruffling in the breeze.

"And where are they confined if Mister Armstrong gets them instead of the Chief Steward?" asked Harper. "The brig?"

I laughed. "Oh, Doctor Harper. You've never really served on board a passenger liner, have you? We don't really have a brig, per se. Chief Purser Collins's office has a safe, and I suppose you could use a small holding area in the specie room on E Deck, but it's very tiny and I don't think it's ever been used for locking people up. Besides, people would get upset about being handcuffed and locked inside the specie room, though I suppose the Captain wouldn't care one way or another. No, the average stowaway gets confined with us."

"Us?"

"Us," I nodded. "We shove them into the quarantine wards. Mister Armstrong puts a guard outside the door and that's where they sit until we make port and they're handed over to the proper authorities."

"Doctor and jailer," mused Harper. "No one said anything about that to me when I took this job." The horns went off again, and this time they were deafening. Harper winced. "My God, I've never heard anything so loud, not even on a warship."

"They say the *Victoria* can be heard for ten miles in clear weather." I pointed up. "That's the bridge there, just forward of the number one funnel off the Sports Deck. You can see Captain Webster through the windows – the man with the beard."

Harper followed my finger. The bridge was 25 feet above us, set squarely between two flying wings to port and starboard with partially open observation cupolas on either end. Through the large plate glass boxing in the sides of the bridge itself we could see the officers hard at work. "We've already taken on the harbour pilot, then," said Harper.

"Oh, yes," I said. "Look." I gestured over the side of the ship. The last of the gangways had disappeared, and men were slipping the final hawsers off at the pier. "We're about to move away from the pier. Fingers in ears," I advised Harper, then quickly covered my own ears.

Harper followed my lead. Without warning, the whistles blew three times in succession, a shrill of steam shrieking coupled with the deep-throated roar of the Flying Scotsman blasting past at top speed. I lowered my hands. "Three times," I said. "We're going to back away now." I placed my hands on the white metal railing. "Feel that?" Harper followed my lead. "The vibration? It's very slight, but it's there. The turbines have been engaged."

Harper nodded, then looked at me in surprise. "We're already moving!"

I grinned. The *Queen Victoria* was, indeed, ponderously moving away from the pier, engines reversed full slow, assisted by tugs to guide her path. "Next stop, New York."

"How long?" asked Harper.

"Depends on the weather. Usually about five days and the better part of a sixth. We're not out to grab the *Blue Riband*. We ought to make Manhattan by Saturday morning." I glanced up. "Oh, my heavens."

"What is it?"

"Look, quick." Harper lifted his gaze. Captain Webster was looking down at us. He gestured with his hand that we should come up, then turned back to watch the pilot taking the *Victoria* away from the wharf. I turned to

Harper. "Well, that's a first," I exclaimed excitedly. "You are certainly going to get the tour."

"Maybe he means we're in trouble."

"Don't be silly," I said. "You saw the Captain. He was clearly looking at us." I took hold of the handrails and began climbing. "And believe me, you don't turn down an invitation from Captain Webster."

"If you say so."

We reached the top of the stairs, turned a corner, and went through a door labeled 'Crew Only.' We climbed another set of stairs, white enameled walls on either side that led onto a long linoleum tiled hall. I walked it briskly, my crepe-soled shoes making no noise; Harper's heels clicked loudly. I stopped before a heavy door marked 'Bridge.'

"Ready?" I asked. Harper nodded. I rapped sharply on the door, then stepped to one side. It opened instantly. Doctor Harper smiled, face to face with an earnest young crewman.

"Permission to come on the bridge?" Harper asked. The young man gave Harper a careful look, then he looked at me. I nodded.

"New PMO," I said. "Doctor Harper." The rating stiffened.

"Yes, nurse. Sir, yes sir, welcome aboard, sir."

"Thank you," I said, perhaps a bit haughtily. I followed Harper onto the bridge as the officer closed the door behind us.

Fourteen windows of heavy plate glass afforded a spectacular view of the receding pier. Directly ahead, at what seemed quite a distance, was the pointed bow of the ship with the waterline far beneath. Doctor Harper and I stood silently at the back of the bridge. "Have you ever seen the like?" I whispered.

"Nothing this big," he admitted.

The bridge of the *Queen Victoria* was about the size and shape of half of a tennis court, stretching, as it were, from net to service line, and just as wide. Gleaming brass, shining white paint, glowing mahogany, banks of telephones, engine telegraphs, brightly button-lighted control boards outlining the ship and its watertight doors and bulkheads – it was at once reassuring and dizzying. Besides the pilot, there were at least a half dozen officers and ratings in attendance, each one quietly busy with some task, and keeping a close eye over all of them stood Captain Webster who looked more like he belonged in a boardroom than on the bridge of one of the world's most luxurious ocean liners.

The Captain was in his early 60's, stood about five and a half feet tall, and his salt and pepper beard was closely trimmed. He had been at sea since he was a boy in the age of sail. His hands were clasped behind his back as he stood next to the pilot, both of them standing next to the quartermaster before the wheel. We watched in fascination as the quartermaster, with seeming effortlessness, tended the highly polished wheel like a yachtsman on holiday in the Mediterranean under the careful instruction of the harbour pilot.

Webster turned his head and looked at Harper, acknowledging him with a curt nod, lifting one quizzical black eyebrow in my direction before returning his attention to the pilot and the quartermaster. I tugged on Harper's uniform sleeve.

"I don't think I'm supposed to be here," I whispered. "I think maybe he just meant you to come."

"Nonsense," said Harper. "You're the chief nurse. We were both standing there."

"I hope so," I said. I had finally made up my mind to the question Harper had asked me earlier. "I like this berth. I'd hate to be told to take my kit and go."

"Not as long as I'm the Principal Medical Officer," said Harper, giving me a smile which I returned weakly.

Telephone bells jangled and a senior officer picked up a receiver, spoke briefly and hung up, resuming his position at one of the front windows gazing steadily out toward the bow. Southampton harbour and all its myriad traffic of liners and freighters was beginning to open up as the *Victoria* moved clear of the docks and headed for the open sea.

"Doctor Harper," said Captain Webster, his voice a low growl, his attention still fixed on the pilot and the wheel. "My apologies for failing to personally welcome you aboard this morning. As you can imagine, sailing day is always rather busy for me."

"Thank you, sir, I quite understand," said Harper. "I'm pleased to be here."

"You're a naval man, I understand." Webster gently touched the pilot on the shoulder and made a slight gesture forward.

"Sixteen years in His Majesty's Navy, for my sins."

Captain Webster watched the pilot delicately give some slight instructions to the quartermaster, who turned the wheel in response. Another officer picked up a phone. "You served in the Great War, then. See any action?"

"Jutland, sir."

Captain Webster nodded, almost absentmindedly. "I lost some friends there. Bloody awful row. We'll have to talk about it some time. You can make dinner at my table tonight?"

Harper nodded. "It will be my pleasure," he said.

"Good," said Captain Webster. He continued to stand, hands clasped behind his back, alternately glancing through the window before him, to the pilot, to the engine room telegraphs, to the wheel, and back again. "I'll expect you then. Thank you."

"Thank you, sir." We turned to leave.

"Oh, and Doctor Harper," said Webster, still not turning around.

"Yes, sir?"

"Bring your little shadow with you. It's one less space at table that I have to endure a passenger." Webster raised his binoculars to his eyes. "I'm sorry you've hurt your finger, nurse. I trust the doctor took care of it to your satisfaction."

Harper looked down at me. My eyes must have looked like saucers. "Yes, sir," he said grinning at me, "I did, and dinner tonight will be our pleasure." He opened the door and we stepped off the bridge. When the door had closed I looked up at Harper.

"Dinner? At the Captain's table?" I was close to being overwrought. "Do you know I could have gone my whole life and never had that? And how did he know I cut my finger?"

Harper grinned. "I've found that captains know everything. And you said you wanted to live the exciting life. Maybe Mr Winchell will put you in his column, after all."

The whistles blasted their shrill roar again as the *Victoria* slowly glided to a stop to let the harbour pilot off to the ferry ship. Once they were clear, the great liner's propellers thrashed the water and she began her trans-Atlantic crossing.

Ever seen a couple of dogs sizing each other up for the first time? That wary look, the circling around, a little bristling, a little growling, the getting close enough to sniff each other's – well, you know. That's kind of the way it was when the new PMO met the current – and now outranked – ship's doctor. Minus a bit of growling and the – well, you know.

Doctor Thomas Bratton stood stiffly in the hospital waiting room, his cap tucked beneath his arm, the unmistakable image of a proper naval officer. "Doctor Bratton, I presume?" asked Harper cheerfully, stepping forward and extending a hand. I hung back, waiting for the storm.

Bratton shook it, but without any apparent warmth. "Doctor Harper," he said in a slightly nasal tone. "Pleased to finally meet you." I thought there was just a hint of accent on the word 'finally', but Harper chose not to address it and let it go, shooting up another notch or two in my estimation. Bratton rocked back on his heels and looked up at Harper. Our new PMO was at least, I estimated, six foot two inches tall. Bratton was short – not in my league short, but still short. "I understand Nurse Chandler has been showing you the ship."

"Yes, she's been very accommodating," said Harper. I tried to make myself invisible.

"Have you had a chance to examine all of the medical operations of the *Queen Victoria* yet?"

"Not yet. It was something of a rush getting me on board. Your last PMO ending his duty so quickly." Harper frowned. "I never did find out – "

"Rather," said Bratton dryly. "The line was fortunate to find you available."

"It was a unique opportunity," said Harper.

I watched the two men sizing each other up like a pair of competing costermongers in Covent Garden. I was just relieved there were no over-ripe tomatoes at hand.

"I understand you had a practice in London."

"On Harley Street, yes. Before that in the Royal Navy." Doctor Harper looked over at the brightly colored Stoddard Line travel posters on the wall. "I trust there won't be much need for amputating a man's leg above the knee due to shellfire while working for the Stoddard Line."

"If there is, we do have a fully equipped surgical theatre on board," said Bratton. "I'm sure you've seen it."

"Had a glance this morning," Harper replied. "Nurse Chandler tells me the worst we'll usually see are broken limbs." Harper sat down in one of the chairs, stretching his long legs out over the linoleum floor.

"I'm sure Nurse Chandler filled you in on plenty of items. As to the broken limbs, in rough weather, yes, we get our share," agreed Bratton. "As I'm sure you know, the North Atlantic run can produce some very nasty weather. And of course, the usual sea-sickness. Occasional emergency surgery, appendectomy and the like." Bratton nodded. "Well, then, I'll get back to my duties." He started for the door, then stopped. "I had hoped to dine with you tonight but I understand you have other dinner plans. Another time?"

"Yes, thank you."

He gave Harper a brief salute, glared at me, then turned on his heel. The door clicked in place behind him. Harper exhaled slowly and looked at me. I was biting my lip.

Harper ran a hand to his tight collar, adjusting it. The hospital was situated just above the waterline on D Deck, almost directly above the fan rooms in the machinery and engineering spaces. While this ensured a certain amount of stability for the surgery, it also meant that warmth from the massive boiler rooms below us radiated upwards. Earlier, with only two of her boiler rooms fired to provide power as the *Victoria* began preparing for embarkation, that warmth had certainly been welcome. But now, with all five boiler rooms going and the *Victoria* making headway, the only relief from the heat came from the cold fresh sea air blown down the topside ventilators.

"You were right about Doctor Bratton being — what did you say? - a wet blanket?"

"I think he wanted your job. I know he put in for it." I sighed. "He's always been prickly, but now, being passed over for PMO — I'm sorry."

"Not your fault." Doctor Harper smiled at me. "I think you and I will get along just fine."

I felt my cheeks flush. "It's getting warm in here," I said to him. "And look at the time. I've got things to do, and I'm sure you do, too." I headed for the door.

"Don't forget dinner," said Doctor Harper.

God, I thought. Like I could ever forget that. What the bloody hell was I going to wear to the Captain's Table?

The First-Class dining salon was on C Deck, two decks down from Doctor Harper's stateroom and First-Class consulting room on A, and one up from mine near the hospital. When I reached it I was dressed in a dolled-up blue silk chemise with a daring décolleté. I must have dressed and undressed five times before finally giving in to the chemise. It was the best thing I owned, and anyway, my shore leave clothing selection was by necessity limited in the small stateroom. Besides, it was, after all, 1929 – time for a woman to be a woman, I thought. Several male passengers had given me admiring looks as they entered the First-Class dining salon, not so their wives. I didn't care. I was dining at the Captain's Table, not them.

When I saw Doctor Harper approaching I put on my most winning smile. He was resplendent in his officer's dress uniform. He gave me a polite nod. "Nurse Chandler."

"Doctor Harper." Suddenly I couldn't help myself and tried to stifle a laugh. He looked at me.

"Something strikes you as amusing?"

"Just this. Me, the head nurse, and you, the PMO, and it's your first day on the ship and I've been serving aboard for three years and it's my first time to eat in the First-Class restaurant and - it just seems rather silly."

Harper glanced at his wristwatch. "It won't be if we're late to table." He headed for the tall bronze doors to the salon, but I took his arm, stopping him.

"Look there," I said. A neatly dressed boy of about six was standing alone near the bottom of the carpeted stairs that led upward to First-Class, obviously frightened, being ignored by the press of passengers hurrying about their business. I went to him, Harper behind me. When the boy saw the doctor his brown eyes went wide.

"Captain," he said as he fought back the tears, "I can't find my room."

Harper went down on one knee, bringing himself to the child's height. "I'm not the Captain," he said gently.

"I'm a doctor. But maybe I can help you. Lost, are you?" The boy nodded. Harper smiled and tousled his head. "That's all right, it's a big ship. I get lost, too."

"Really?" snuffled the boy.

"Really," said Harper with a friendly nod. "What's your name, son?"

"Bradley Alston," the boy spoke resolutely

"Well, Bradley Alston, do you remember which deck your stateroom is on?"

"No, sir."

Harper looked up at me. "Purser's station," I suggested. "They'll have a list of all passengers and berthing assignments."

Harper turned back to the boy. "Let's get you up to the purser's station. They'll be able to find out where you belong. Is that all right?" The boy nodded, wiping his eyes and rubbing his hands across the serge of his knickers.

"Down this corridor, around the corner," I said.

"Lead on, nurse." Harper took the boy by the hand and they followed me, the boy scuffing his shoes over the thick carpet. Bemused passengers gave us a curious glance.

"A bit late in the evening for you to be out and about, isn't it?" Harper asked the boy as we walked.

"Mum and Dad were fighting," said Bradley, a serious expression on his otherwise cherubic face.

Doctor Harper and I exchanged glances. "I see," he said, "and you just thought you'd take a little walk, is that it?"

"Yes, sir."

I looked down at the boy. "Without telling them where you were going? Or that you were even going at all?"

"I don't like it when they fight," said the boy.

"I dare say," I replied.

"He hits her," the boy said. Harper and I both stopped dead.

"What?" said Doctor Harper.

"He hits her. He's not my real dad." Harper gave me a worried glance.

"That's a pretty hard thing to say, young man," he began, but the boy bolted away from him toward a modestly dressed and very pregnant woman talking to a purser's attendant some fifteen feet away. The boy threw his arms around her waist, burying his face against her. The purser gave us a nod and resumed his work.

"Bradley!" she said in startled relief. She reached down and pulled him away from her, looking him over for damage with the scrutiny that only a mother separated from a lost child is capable of attaining. "Are you all right? Where have you been? You've had me worried to death, you know."

"I was lost," said the boy, "but the Captain found me."

"Captain?" The woman looked up from her son as we approached.

"Principal Medical Officer Leslie Harper, Mrs Alston. My head nurse, Maeve Chandler." She appeared startled.

"How do you know my name?"

"Sorry," smiled Harper. "The boy told us."

"We found him outside the First-Class salon," I added. "He was just lost. It's a big ship."

"Thank you," said the woman, giving us a wan smile. She put out her right hand for me to shake. I spied a blush of purple above her wrist. "Clara Alston. I don't know what possessed him to wander off like that."

I glanced at Doctor Harper, wondering if he was thinking what I was thinking, recalling what the boy had told us, but instead he simply said, "He's a boy."

"Boys are like that," agreed Mrs Alston. She winced suddenly and clutched at Harper's forearm.

"Mrs Alston, are you feeling well?" I asked with concern. The woman's face contorted briefly.

"Fine, thank you," she said, her voice quietly strained. I took her by the left wrist to check her pulse.

"I'm astounded someone as far along as you would attempt a sea voyage," said Doctor Harper.

"My husband," she explained. "He's an American and is absolutely firm that the baby be born in New York."

"New York is still a good distance away," Harper replied. "And if we encounter bad weather, the North Atlantic and not your husband may have the say in the matter of where and when this baby is born."

"No, it's America or nothing," she said. "He sometimes feels that by marrying a Briton he's demeaned himself."

"Well, of all the - " I began, but Harper cut me off.

"I'm sorry to hear that." Harper looked up at the ornate clock above the entryway to the dining salon. "It's dinnertime. Are you going in?"

"Not for Third-Class," she said quietly. Harper tacked about quickly to cover her embarrassment and without knowing it blundered into another pitfall. My heart bled for the man.

"Is Mr. Alston off looking for the boy?"

A tinge of rose colored her high cheek bones and she lowered her eyes. "Mr Alston is engaged at the moment," she said quietly.

I winced inwardly and jumped in to cover Harper. "I'll check on you in the morning, if you don't mind."

"Thank you, Nurse." Clara looked down at Bradley. "Ready?" She smiled at us. "Thank you for your help."

"Certainly." Harper pointed a mockingly stern finger at the boy. "Mind yourself, young man."

"Yes, sir. Thank you, Captain and Mrs Captain." Mother and son walked away, engaged in animated conversation.

"Troubling," said Harper, looking after them.

"More than troubling. There was a fresh bruise on her right wrist. She tried to cover it with makeup, but her sleeve rode up and gave it away." I watched them turn the corner and disappear. "And that guff about her husband being engaged at the moment. I bloody well wonder what he's engaged with. More like who."

"I should report it to the Master at Arms," Harper said, looking thoughtfully after them.

"You can't. Not unless you see it happen." I shook my head. "Rule number one of working a liner, Doctor. Don't get involved with the passengers."

IV

The feeling I got upon entering the palatial First-Class dining salon of the *Queen Victoria* was something akin to the reverence I might have felt upon stepping inside of a great cathedral, if I was so inclined to feel reverence in that way. It was all so grand.

The intricately decorated ceiling soared fifteen feet above the second floor mezzanine dining area, which itself stood nearly twenty feet above the main floor. Fabulously cut and polished hardwoods and paneling covered the walls, and over that hung ornate and thick drapes. Lush potted plants – some taller than a man – sprouted in various corners and intersections of the room. In one alcove a small tuxedoed orchestra played a string of subdued melodies – the American jazz would come out later, after dinner.

White-jacketed waiters flowed like a starched river between the linen covered tables, carrying trays and platters of the choicest foods that the *Victoria's* kitchens could prepare, the equal of any five-star hotel and elegant restaurant in Europe. The room was populated by women in daring backless evening dresses, sumptuous gowns – some quite low cut, so I didn't feel so self-conscious about my choice - and glittering jewels; the men in an almost equal mix of glistening wool evening wear and Brooks Brothers and Savile Row suits – and now, us. An imperious maître' de approached with an obviously reproachful expression on his face. Great, I thought. Monsieur DuMont.

"Good evening, sir. I don't believe we've met?" he said with supercilious unction. God, that man was irritating.

"Dr. Leslie Harper. I'm the new Principal Medical Officer."

"Ah, yes," said the maître' de, with his sad-eyed Frenchman look – rather like a basset hound, I thought. "I am Monsieur DuMont." He gave me an appraising look, his eyes lingering a bit on my breasts, making me feel undressed. "And Nurse Chandler. I don't believe we've had the pleasure of your company before."

"I don't believe you have," I replied coolly. He gave me a smirk and glanced at his watch.

"And yet, on such an occasion, you are late." DuMont gestured up at a table on the second level of the salon. "I think, perhaps, the empty chairs are for you?" Harper followed the man's gaze. Captain Webster, two officers, and two First-Class couples – despite the Captain's stated abhorrence of socializing with passengers – were already dining. "The soup course is done, M'sieur Doctor and Mademoiselle Nurse," said DuMont, "but I think we can still salvage you for the fish."

"Very kind." Harper smoothed his uniform jacket and, following DuMont, we mounted the wide and gently curving staircase to the upper level. The waiters were clearing away the soup plates when we arrived. Captain Webster looked up at us. I immediately began wondering if this was such a good idea.

"Doctor Harper and Nurse Chandler," said DuMont briskly, by way of introduction.

"Glad you could join us," Captain Webster said evenly. "You missed a very nice consommé, Doctor."

"I apologize," said Harper. He stepped to one side as waiters drew our chairs out and seated us. DuMont clapped his hands and more waiters appeared to attend to the opening of our napkins. DuMont looked at me, pursed his lips, thought of saying something, thought better of it, and excused himself. I made myself a promise that if I ever got the opportunity to give him an injection it was going to hurt like bloody hell.

"No need to apologize, Doctor." The Captain nodded at me. "Nurse Chandler's arrival at table outweighs any lateness on your part." I smiled weakly. Captain Webster politely cleared his throat and addressed the table. "Please let me introduce Doctor Leslie Harper, the *Queen Victoria's* new Principal Medical Officer. And Nurse Maeve Chandler, the *Victoria's* head nurse." There was a small chorus of hellos. "To your immediate left, Doctor and Nurse, are Mr and Mrs Stanford Burnett, of Hartford, Connecticut. On Mr Burnett's left, our first officer, Mister Jackson."

"Pleased to meet you, Doctor. And always a pleasure to see you, Miss Chandler."

"On Mister Jackson's left, Mr and Mrs Hampton Steele, of London."

"Some sort of medical emergency detaining you this evening?" asked Mr Steele, an index finger resting on the rim of his glasses. "I see Nurse Chandler has a bandage on her finger."

"I dropped some glassware," I said. "Nothing serious. Doctor Harper patched me up."

"And on Mr Steele's left, and my right, is our Quartermaster, Mister Carter." Mister Carter smiled at me. I was always struck by how he and Mister Jackson had almost identical builds; each stood six feet tall, at least. From the back you couldn't tell them apart.

"The Captain tells us that you're a Navy man," said Carter.

"Was. His Majesty and I came to an amicable parting of the ways a few years ago."

"When did you leave the service?" Jackson took a sip of his water.

"1925." Harper shifted in his seat to allow a waiter to serve the fish.

"And then a land-based practice?" asked Carter.

"Yes. Until the opportunity presented itself to join the *Victoria*. I couldn't turn it down."

"With the nurses you have, I can see why," said Mr Burnett, clearly the cad. I gave him a slight nod in acknowledgement.

"You are very kind," I said.

"He's got a roving eye," said Mrs Burnett. "But don't worry, my dear, it never goes beyond that. Tell me, how did you get such an unusual first name?"

I inwardly sighed, cursing my parents, and began the story. Mrs Burnett sat attentively for a moment, then suddenly set her fork down and glanced across the table. "Mrs Steele, are you quite all right?"

"Yes," said Mrs Steele quietly. She was gazing with some concern across the table. "But I don't think he is." She tilted her head to the floor below as the murmur of voices and music began sliding to a strained halt. A man sitting with two women and another man had half-risen from his chair, clutching at his throat. His three dinner companions stared in shocked but momentary silence, then one of the women screamed as the man gave a violent upheaval from his mouth. Harper threw down his napkin and bolted out of his chair with me a close second. The Captain and officers were still rising as we were running for the stairs. I took about four steps, then reached down and tore my heels off so I could keep up with Harper. By the time we reached the table the man had toppled out of his chair and was lying still on the floor on his side, the saliva froth on his lips mixed with blood, his eyes fixed and staring. The woman was still screaming.

Harper rolled the man onto his back. The mouth was fixed in a snarling rictus of agony. Harper loosened his collar and felt his carotid for a pulse. A moment later I instinctively reached a hand out toward the dead man's mouth, and Harper clamped his hand hard around my wrist.

"Ow," I said. "Doctor Harper - "

"Don't touch his face, Maeve," he said quietly.

"But - " I began.

"There's nothing you can do," Harper said urgently. He glanced around, then spoke quietly in my ear. "Or me either, for that matter. Don't touch him," he repeated again, then stood. By now a knot of people had gathered around us, and everyone else in the salon was standing at their tables, craning their necks to see. The vast room was eerily silent save for whispered voices. The woman had stopped screaming, and was instead quietly sobbing in the arms of the other woman.

"What happened?" Doctor Harper asked.

"He took a drink, and then just had a fit," said the second woman.

The man nodded. "He had complained that his stomach was paining him, ever since we came in to eat. It just kept getting worse. He said he was going back to his cabin, just before he – he – "

"How long had his stomach hurt?" I interrupted. Harper glanced at me.

The man looked at the two women. "We'd had a drink in the First-Class observation-lounge about a half hour, 45 minutes ago. Maybe an hour." He looked distant. "Time passes so quickly onboard."

"What did he drink?" I was standing now.

"I don't know," the man said. "A gin and tonic? I think he ordered one thing and got another. But he drank it anyway. You know you can't get a drink in America with Prohibition."

"Damned silly rule," said Harper. He glanced down at the table. "What about dinner?"

"He drank some of the wine," one of the women said, nodding at the man's glass. She swallowed back tears. "He's dead, isn't he?"

"I'm afraid so." Harper looked up at the others who had been at the table. "Anyone else drink the wine?" The man and one of the women nodded. Harper gave me a curt nod. I gently led them back to their chairs, keeping myself and the table between them and the dead man and sat them down, talking with them quietly but keeping one ear cocked to the proceedings. Captain Webster had joined the table by now.

"Well?" he asked, not taking his eyes off the dead man on the floor.

"Dead," I heard Harper say.

"I can see that, Doctor." Webster was unruffled. "How and why is he dead, that's what I want to know."

I came back to Doctor Harper. "No symptoms," I said. "Fright, and I can certainly understand why."

Harper beckoned two waiters. "Get a stretcher, and get him down to the hospital. Get Doctor Bratton. And don't touch his face or any of the mess he made. Lift him by his clothes. Your life may depend on it. Tell Doctor Bratton the same thing."

Monsieur DuMont had shouldered his way through the passengers, accompanied by a solidly built man with salt and pepper hair and an air of agitation. Both men looked down at the body on the floor. DuMont snapped his fingers at a waiter. "Get a tablecloth to cover him." The waiter began to move but Harper put a hand on his shoulder.

"Give me the tablecloth. I don't want you to touch him. Understand?" The waiter nodded and hurried away.

The other man looked at Harper, then at me, raising his eyebrows. "Doctor Harper," I said, "this is Mister Harvey, our Chief Steward. In charge of dining facilities, bars – "

"And every other bloody thing that has to do with keeping the paying customers happy, it seems," said Harvey. He put out his hand.

"Principal Medical Officer Leslie Harper." They shook hands. Harper frowned down at the dead man. "Sorry to be meeting under such circumstances."

"C'est la vie," said Harvey. "Poor bugger."

Harper spoke quietly to the Captain. "Let's get these people back on even keel, if we can. There's nothing more we can do here now."

"I agree, Doctor," said Webster. He turned to Jackson and Carter. "Get the orchestra going again, and get these people resituated."

"What do you want us to tell them?" asked Carter, looking first at the Captain and then to Harper and myself.

"A stroke?" I suggested. Harper shrugged.

"Good as anything else."

"Stroke?" Carter asked doubtfully, looking down at the man. "But his face - " Captain Webster gave a deep sigh.

"Stroke, Mister Carter." He looked at us. "I'm going up to the bridge. Let me know what you find out, medical people. Don't worry about it being after hours." Webster gave a last glance down at the dead man. "I imagine I'll be up rather late tonight. I'll countersign the death certificate, of course."

"Yes, sir." Harper gave the Captain a salute, and I nodded. Webster, Jackson and Carter made their way to the large doors, being stopped every few steps by nervous passengers anxious for reassurance.

I crossed my arms. "No one else at the table is suffering any sort of symptom at all," I repeated. "And for my two pence, I don't think there's a thing wrong with what was served to them tonight, either the food or the wine."

"Wine?" asked Harvey, suddenly nervous. He looked at DuMont. "Something wrong with the wine? With my wine?" He and DuMont reached for the bottle on the table.

"Mister Harvey, no!" I said, stopping him in mid-motion. Harper pulled a handkerchief out of his jacket and gingerly picked up the bottle.

"Don't sample it," he said.

"And why not?" Harvey was indignant. "Nurse Chandler just said there wasn't anything wrong with it."

"I said I didn't think there was anything wrong with it. But if the wine is by some chance bad," I said to Mister Harvey, "do you really want to go out like he did?" DuMont licked suddenly dry lips and backed away. Harper held the bottle up.

"The other three drank from the same bottle, so I agree with Maeve — I don't really believe the wine is bad."

"Or was bad when their glasses were filled," I said. DuMont's eyes went wide.

"Are you saying someone tampered with the bottle, Nurse Chandler? In my dining salon? Impossible!" Harper turned to me.

"You seem to have a gift for saying just the right thing, Nurse."

"You don't know the half of it, Doctor Harper," said Harvey. "I've worked with her for years."

"Funny," I said. "A regular music hall riot, you are. Go ahead and have a drink if you're so certain, Mister Harvey."

He shrugged. The two waiters arrived with the stretcher at the same time as the waiter with the fresh tablecloth. Harper took the cloth from the man, unfolded it and reverentially covered the corpse. The waiters then gently placed him on the stretcher and carried him away. I touched Harper's hand.

"Look over there," I said, gesturing with my head. "I think," I said, with a touch of barely disguised malice, "that his nibs has no stomach for this sort of thing."

Harper turned to look. Harvey Wilson was lolling back in his chair, one of the women at his table daubing at his temples with a napkin she kept dipping into a water glass. "Go and see to it," said Harper.

"Gee, thanks, Boss," I replied without feeling.

"Boss?"

"It's my gift," I said. "You told me so." Harvey observed Wilson and shook his head ruefully.

"That damned rich old blood money American," said Harvey with spite. "Making money off our dead soldiers. Casey will have a field day with this," he said. Harper looked at him.

"What? Who?"

"Nothing," said Harvey. "I'm sure you'll meet our roving press representative in due time." The music had struck up again. Waiters were moving back through the crowded salon, assisting passengers who were returning to their seats amid a now heavy buzz of conversation. Harper looked back at the table at which the dead man had been dining and picked up the man's overturned wine glass.

"I'll hang onto the bottle and glass for a while, if you don't mind," he said. Harvey shrugged.

"Suit yourself. Less that I've got to take care of." He snapped an imperious finger at a passing waiter. "Get rid of this place setting and take away that empty chair." Harvey turned and gazed down at the three tablemates of the dead man, sitting with shocked expressions on their faces. He smiled like the Cheshire cat. "Fresh bottle of complimentary wine?" he asked graciously. They looked stunned.

"Now who's got the gift?" I asked the Chief Steward.

"Speaks the woman with no shoes," Harvey replied.

Harper shook his head and turned away.

Sunday, October 27, 1929

V

In my experience, nothing puts the damper on having a good time quite like someone dropping dead at dinner. When we left the dining salon the mood was subdued, to say the least. I could feel judging eyes upon us from the passengers, as if it was our fault the man had died and their evening was spoilt. I don't know what they had to be upset about – I was the one who had to give up dinner at the Captain's table.

Harper, Bratton, Harvey and I stood around the examining table in the ship's surgery, looking down at the sheeted body in front of us. The leading edge had been pulled back, revealing a darkly handsome face still distorted in death, with jet-black hair swept back and pomaded. Doctors Harper and Bratton had donned surgical gloves and closed the man's mouth and wiped him dry. Mister Harvey consulted the paper in his hand.

"Name's Thomas Morten. 37 years old. English. Home is in Hackney. He's a - " Harvey checked himself. "He was a wine salesman by trade. Boarded at Southampton, came in on the morning boat train from London with a load of other passengers." He looked at Harper. "Traveling alone."

"He's not married," I said. Bratton gave me one of his exasperated looks.

"Because he's not wearing a ring? I saw that too. Doesn't mean a thing. A lot of men have been known to slip a wedding band off their finger before making an ocean voyage," said Bratton with more than a touch of sarcasm.

I frowned at him. "Not this one, Doctor. See how tan he is? Wouldn't you think if he'd removed a ring before boarding, there'd be a white band on his finger where the sun was blocked out?" I looked at Harper. "Or if he'd recently been divorced, maybe?"

"Perhaps," admitted Bratton irritably. "I've never done it, so I don't know."

"Never been married or never removed a ring?" I asked.

"As you well know, never been married, Nurse Chandler," Bratton said tartly. Harper smiled at me.

"Observant, aren't you?" he asked.

"When you've been a widowed single woman as long as I have, you notice things." I turned to the Chief Steward. "What about his baggage, Mister Harvey?"

"I called Chief Purser Collins. It's in his stateroom, under lock and key. There's an additional trunk in the hold. No one will touch it before we arrive in New York."

"Good." Harper nodded.

"Well, if that's it," Harvey said with a sigh. "I've got to go and deal with that bloody press agent. I'm sure Casey's tearing down my office door by now." He looked down at the dead man again. "Poor fellow." Harvey pursed his lips. "Stroke still the official word?" he asked in a doubting tone.

"Stroke," said Harper. Bratton shot him a quizzical look, but said nothing. Harvey nodded.

"Ah. And so young. Well, I'm off. Good night, Doctors, Nurse Chandler."

"Good night, Mister Harvey." I saw the Chief Steward out as Bratton turned to Harper.

"Stroke?" Bratton was incredulous. "Doctor Harper, you know as well as I do that this man didn't die of any stroke."

"I know that," said Harper. "And so does Mister Harvey and Nurse Chandler. But for now, that's the story."

"What about Captain Webster?"

"He has his suspicions."

"Then that's five of us that know it wasn't a stroke including the ship's master." Bratton arched his eyebrows. "How long do you think it'll stay a secret?"

"As long as we need it to stay a secret," I said, surprising myself. Harper and Bratton both looked at me with curiousity. I shook my head, plunging forward. "Honestly, Doctor Bratton, you, Doctor Harper and myself aren't going to talk, the Captain doesn't want the passengers to know anything's amiss, and Mister Harvey has restaurants and a very large staff to keep under control."

"Nicely covered, Nurse Chandler. And the death certificate?" Bratton folded his arms across his chest and looked at me. "Which, if I might remind you, is a legal document."

"I think we're all perfectly aware of the niceties involved, Doctor Bratton. I'm sure you and Doctor Harper signed plenty of them during the war."

"We're all agreed it wasn't a stroke," said Harper, cutting off the sniping. "What was it, then?"

Bratton bent down to examine the late Thomas Morten a bit closer. "Without an autopsy, of course, I'm not certain, but based on what you told me happened I think it was some kind of systemic poison. How and why he got it is beyond me right now."

"Why not do one?" I asked.

"Do one what?" Harper said.

"An autopsy. You know, Scotland Yard and that sort of thing."

Bratton shook his head. "You should know better than that, Nurse. It's out of the question." He looked at me and began ticking off his fingers. "First, we don't have the facilities to conduct an adequate one here; second, we'd need to get next of kin permission - "

"And we'd need a coroner's order," said Harper.

"Did you need one to sign off on cause of death on a battleship?" I asked.

"Almost without fail, cause of death in the Navy was due to enemy action," Harper said. "It was relatively simple to pronounce a man dead from a shell fragment ripping off his shoulder; I knew exactly what had happened. This…" Harper let the words trail off. Bratton was giving the dead man a closer examination. Both men ignored me. I stood and fumed quietly, tapping my heel. Doctor Harper and I were still in our evening wear.

"I think we can rule out cyanide." Bratton pointed to the man's mouth. "Look. No burn marks."

"I agree," said Harper. "He took far too long to die, and it looked far too agonizing." Harper shook his head. "If it had been prussic acid or any close relative of it he'd have been dead before he hit the floor, much less standing up at his chair." Harper sighed and straightened. "Which really narrows it down."

Bratton nodded. "If it wasn't that, then maybe we can operate on the assumption that it was an accident? Maybe salmonella – though it would have been the most virulent I've ever heard of. You said he complained of an upset stomach. But then, no one else has gotten sick, so we can forget about that." Bratton paused and considered his next statement, aware of its possible impact. "Ruling out the occasional accident, I've never heard of anyone being poisoned except on purpose."

"That's a reassuring thought," said Harper. "Though I wouldn't care to take up the issue of food poisoning with Mister Harvey right now. He was positively tweaked over the chance that the wine might be bad." Harper looked at Bratton. "And according to Morten's tablemates, his stomach complaint began before dinner, after they'd knocked back a drink in the First-Class lounge." Harper puffed out his cheeks. "Forgetting autopsies for the moment, I don't suppose you've got even a wee bit of toxicology work under your belt?"

Bratton shook his head. "Only enough to carry on a conversation in a pub. I'm proud to say my career has been spent primarily on the living and keeping them that way."

"Mine, too," said Harper. "Bloody hell." I politely cleared my throat. Even though they appeared to be at least professionally bonding, this had gone on long enough.

"Excuse me, doctors," I said. Harper and Bratton looked at me. I raised my eyebrows. "It's his first day, so I didn't expect Doctor Harper to think about it, but you should have remembered, Doctor Bratton. We do have a dispensing chemist on board. He might be able to give you some help in regard to what may have killed Mr Morten." I looked at Harper. "I don't think my chemistry degree would be of much help here. Mister Reedy has a masters from Oxford."

Bratton rubbed a hand across his chin. "Not withstanding degree levels, Nurse Chandler, a dispensing chemist is not the same thing as a toxicologist."

"We're in the North Atlantic, Doctor. Beggars, as they say, can't be choosers."

"If he's all we have, he's all we have. Can you get him here, Maeve?" Harper asked.

"Yes, Boss," I said with a smile, picking up the telephone.

"What about the wine glass and bottle you brought down?" said Bratton.

Harper sighed. "The wine bottle isn't going to tell us much except that it's a very nice French Beaujolais from 1927. Everyone else at the table drank out of it without ill effect, so that eliminates it as a source. Everyone else at the table ate the same meal." Harper paused. "In fact, a great many people on this ship ate a lot of the same thing tonight. However - Mr Morten's wineglass could be another story."

"Mister Reedy is on his way," I announced, ringing off. "What were you saying about the wine glass?"

"Someone put something inside of it?" asked Bratton.

"I don't know. We'll let Reedy examine it. Morten gagged into the glass and fortunately he didn't drop it. Setting it down on the table was his last coherent act. I put a napkin over it to keep it safe for the time being." Harper went to the sink, stripped off his gloves and began to wash his hands. "Maeve, is there any way of finding the glass from his previous drink in the lounge?"

"Not a chance," I said. "I'm certain Mister Harvey can find the steward who served Mr Morten, but that glass has long ago been washed and put back into service. It may have gone through three use and wash cycles by now."

"She's right," Bratton concurred.

Harper nodded. "Fine. In the meantime, as Doctor Bratton and the Captain pointed out, I need to fill out a death certificate. And this body has to go somewhere."

"There are transit caskets in one of the store areas on E Deck," said Bratton.

Harper looked taken aback. "You're having me on."

I shook my head. "Remember what I told you about a passenger liner being like a small city? We've had deaths occur before."

"Fatal heart attack two voyages ago," said Doctor Bratton. "Older gentleman." Bratton smiled – for him – weakly. "No foul play."

"He died in his stateroom," I added. "So there really wasn't any fuss, except for the young brunette that was with him. We took the covered casket up on a cart and rolled him out in the middle of the night. Less chance of passengers seeing," I explained.

"I'm very glad to hear that," Doctor Harper managed. I inwardly grinned. He coughed politely and looked down at the late Mr Morten. "That's nice for keeping him out of the way so the passengers don't stumble over him, but New York's still a ways off and we certainly can't embalm him."

"Refrigerators," I said. Harper looked at me.

"You've thought this through."

"Nowhere else to put him," agreed Doctor Bratton.

Harper shrugged as if to accept defeat. "We just slid them over the side in the Navy," he began, but the door to the surgery swung open and a gaunt man in his early thirties joined us.

"Terry Reedy," I whispered up to Harper. Harper peered at Reedy. His dark hair appeared to be permanently tousled and cow licked and he had prominent purplish circles under his eyes.

"Reedy, this is Doctor Leslie Harper," said Bratton. "He's taken Doctor Caldwell's place."

"Sorry to call you so late," said Harper.

"Not at all," Reedy replied in a voice which I had always thought perfectly matched his name. "I was up. I don't sleep very well, sir." He looked at Bratton. "Sirs," he corrected. He looked at me, a bit too closely for my regards. I regretted not having changed out of my dress. "And Nurse Chandler." I shivered. Whatever kept Reedy from sleeping well would give me nightmares. I had always thought he resembled a corpse in the daylight, and at night the resemblance was even more pronounced.

"Well, Reedy, take a look at this, will you?" Bratton stepped to one side and Reedy moved forward to the table and delicately lifted the sheet. There was no sign of shock or any other emotion across his thin features as he studied the man's face for a moment.

"Passenger," he said. Harper nodded. "When?"

"About forty minutes ago. In the First-Class restaurant, at dinner."

"Choke on something?"

"In a manner of speaking."

"Hmm." Reedy reached into his pocket and pulled out a pair of the most discolored white cotton gloves I'd ever seen and put them on, then opened the man's mouth and peered inside. He looked up at us after a moment. "You don't need me to tell you this. This man didn't choke. A stroke maybe. Or a heart attack." He closed Morten's mouth. "Again, in either case, you don't need me for that diagnosis."

"Look at this," I said, gingerly handing him the wine glass covered in its linen napkin. Reedy carefully unwrapped it and held the glass up to the light in his gloved fingers, turning the stem to examine the diminutive contents of the bowl.

"That's not wine in here," he said almost immediately.

"The man frothed at the mouth and vomited," said Harper. "Whatever's in that glass, he expunged – or was already in the glass when he drank from it."

"Would you take a look at it please, Mister Reedy?" I asked.

Reedy nodded, his mind already at work on the problem. "Right-o. I'll go turn on the burners and see if we can find out what it is." He carefully covered the glass, keeping it upright. "With a bit of luck, who knows?" He shrugged. "Want to help, Nurse? We may be up all night."

"No, thank you."

"Reedy," said Harper as the chemist went to the door, "keep this to yourself for now."

"Certainly, Doctor." After a last lingering glance at me, Reedy shuffled out of the surgery. I went to a cabinet, pulled out a bottle of disinfectant and scrubbed the door knob he'd touched with his dirty gloved hand, though I felt more like scrubbing myself. I put the bottle back, washed my hands and returned to the table where both men were standing looking down on the mortal remains of Mr Morten.

"Well, Doctor," said Bratton. "You said Captain Webster wanted an answer. What are we going to tell him?"

Harper wearily rubbed his forehead. "I wish I knew. We'll know better when we get the report back from Mister Reedy." He looked at me. "You appear ill at ease, Maeve."

I nodded. Call it my Gaelic heritage, women's intuition, or whatever you want. I definitely felt uneasy looking at the corpse, and I bloody well didn't feel the need to wait for Reedy to get me a report.

"Tell me," Harper said quietly, those blue eyes peering into my soul. Bratton looked on with keen interest.

I swallowed. "With all due respect to your initial diagnosis, doctors, don't you think we should stop dancing around the maypole?"

"I beg your pardon?" said Harper.

"Look. You've both all but agreed it was a poisoning of some kind. Even Reedy realized it wasn't natural causes." I looked at both of them. "If you don't want to say it, I will and not because I read too many mysteries. I believe this man was murdered."

Monday, October 28, 1929

I

omeday, when I'm rich, I'm going to sleep in every morning and ring for the servants to bring me tea, cakes and the *New York Daily Mirror* in bed to start my luxurious day. (How the *Mirror* would arrive in England same day as printing in New York was a trick I hadn't quite worked out yet.) Awakening well in advance of my wind up alarm, I lay in my bunk with my eyes open, stretching beneath the blankets and the colorful quilt a writer friend in the States had made for me several years ago. Normally I shared the stateroom with the other nurse, Alice Johnson, so this crossing was a bit of a luxury to have the entire very small space to myself. One minute passed. It was obvious the staff once again had the day off. I sighed and swung my bare feet out to the chilled linoleum floor to begin the day.

Getting up earlier than usual meant much less of a wait at the crew lavatory to which I was assigned. I finished my toilet – a hot salt water shower followed by purified water – then returned to my stateroom to complete hair and makeup. I picked up a cup of tea – milk and sugar, thank you! – at the crew dining hall, then made my way to the hospital, stopping short when I turned the corner and found Terry Reedy standing in the corridor. It was a very disheveled looking Terry Reedy, even for him, but in his defense the hour was unconscionably early. Thank God I was in my rather sexless nursing uniform rather than the low cut number from last night.

"Good morning, Nurse Chandler," said Reedy in his monotone voice.

"Good morning." I held the door open and ushered him into the waiting room. "You don't look like you've had a wink."

"Not one," said Reedy. "Up all night." He slumped into a chair. "Very interesting, Doctor Harper's wine glass."

I sat down across from him, balancing my cup of tea on my lap and giving the spare pharmacist all my attention. "How interesting?"

"How did you say your patient died?"

"We didn't."

"No?" Reedy was apparently feeling very self-satisfied. "I think I can tell you: it began with panic, upset stomach and a choking sensation, followed quickly by paralysis of lungs, coughing up blood, muscle spasms and death."

"That's right." The gruesome events of last night's dinner would always remain vivid in my mind.

Reedy nodded. "A death like that is almost indicative of cyanide. Almost, but not quite. That would have acted much, much, much faster. Blink of an eye." He stifled a yawn. "Except his mouth wasn't burned, something I noticed in my examination and I'm certain the doctors did, too. Some discoloration, but nothing like a good dose of prussic acid would wreak on him."

"So you think he was poisoned?" I asked, feeling a shiver of apprehension run up my spine.

Reedy leaned forward as if the two of us were sitting together in the midst of passengers in the First-Class lounge and he didn't want to be overheard. I fought to keep from flinching backward. "Don't you mean to say,

'So you think he was poisoned, too?"' Reedy scratched his nose. "I'm not telling you anything you don't already suspect, Nurse," he said with a hint of disdain. "Why else would you have asked me to look at that wine glass?" I watched in disgust as he rubbed his eyes with a chemically discolored fingertip, oblivious to whatever was on it, then sucked at his teeth. I squirmed uncomfortably. He went on. "From an analysis of his saliva and vomitus in and on that glass I reached only one conclusion, and I don't believe you or the doctors – much less the Captain – are going to like it."

"Try me," I said. Reedy shrugged.

"All right. It was an old poison, but a good one. Been known to man a thousand years or more. Who knows how many people have met an untimely end from it, too. Aconitine."

I pathetically tried to remember my nursing pharmacology. "Aconitine? I thought that had gone the way of hemlock." I was puzzled. "Rather arcane, isn't it?"

Reedy shrugged. "Arcane or not, it does the trick, as the shade of Mr Morten would certainly attest to if he was here." He looked about the examining room. "By the way, where is he?"

"Who?" My mind was still on the subject of aconitine.

"Mr Morten. Where did he go?"

"Oh." I came back to reality. "We put him in cold storage."

"Of course," said Reedy, as if this happened every day. "Couldn't really leave him sitting around out here in the waiting room, could you?" He laughed to himself, making my flesh creep. "Where was I? Oh yes. Aconitine. It's not one of the more glamorous systemics, but it's readily available, if you know what you're looking for. It even obliges poisoners by growing wild in some parts of

England. You've just got to know how to process the plant, that's all."

"Aconitine," I repeated. "You're sure of that?"

Reedy nodded his head. "In as concentrated a form as this was, it didn't take much. Your chap never knew what hit him until it was too late. Probably just thought it was something he ate, or sea-sickness, and it would pass."

"But how did it get into the wine?"

Reedy smiled, showing his poor teeth. "Ah. There's the rub, as they say. That's not my problem, Nurse. You wanted an analysis of the glass, you have one." He stood. "But I don't think it was in the wine. I don't even think it was in his glass. No one else at the table got poisoned from that bottle, did they? I'd bet my last pound that the wine in that bottle is clean. My money says he got the aconitine in another location, served up with a very healthy dose of gin or vodka to mask any possible taste. But again, I'm sure you've already figured that out." Reedy went to the door. "I think I'll try and get some breakfast now. Always a pleasure." He gave me a leer and left the hospital. I sat pensively for a moment more, then headed out the door to inform Doctor Harper.

The other officers were already gathered in Captain Webster's sitting room when Doctor Harper perfunctorily knocked and we entered. The Captain looked at us. "Ah, Doctor Harper. And Nurse Chandler. So good of you to join us for the briefing." He glanced at his watch. "And only five minutes late."

"Apologies, Captain. It won't happen again." Harper slid into a chair next to First Officer Jackson. I'm sure his mind was still reeling over what Mister Reedy had discovered. We had decided it best not to bring it up in the general officer's meeting, though I knew Harper would have to tell the Captain sooner rather than later. I remained standing beside the door, trying to blend in with the woodwork. My stomach was beginning to grumble. I wished I'd taken the time for toast and jam with my tea.

"Yes," said Webster. "That remains to be seen." He cleared his throat. "Though you two did arrive at an opportune moment. I was just telling those who weren't there last night about the incident and that you were looking into it. Perhaps you'd like to fill them in?"

"Certainly, sir." Harper looked at me, then at the expectant faces around him. "For those I haven't met, I'm Leslie Harper, the new Principal Medical Officer. I joined the ship yesterday morning."

"Good timing," said Mister Harvey. The Captain glared at him and Harvey began studying the ceiling.

"Yes, well," said Harper, flustered. "This incident last night - " He paused, gathering his thoughts. "Last night a First-Class passenger died of - " He looked at me. I took a deep breath. "Died of a stroke in the First-Class dining salon," he continued. "His name was Thomas Morten, he was English, from the London Metropolitan area, 37 years old, a wine salesman and traveling alone. His stateroom has been sealed, and the deceased has been laid into a casket and put in cold storage."

Mister Harvey jolted out of his ceiling reverie with a start, ran a hand through his hair, screwed his eyes shut, and then opened them. "Bloody hell, I don't want to know where, do I?" he asked.

"No, Mister Harvey," I said, eliciting a chuckle from the others. Captain Webster gave me a sharp glance and I resumed my bond with the woodwork.

"Anyway, that's what we know," Harper said. He looked exhausted.

"Ah, Doctor Harper," said an officer with a shock of sandy blonde hair and a pronounced Scottish accent. Chief Engineer Robie Duncan. I'm a Liverpool girl, but his accent always touched me in just the right way.

"Yes, Chief?"

Duncan stood. "Thank you, Doctor. I'm Robie Duncan, *Victoria's* Chief Engineer. Welcome aboard. Mister Jackson and Mister Carter told me what happened, and I have to say it dinna sound like any stroke I've ever ken of." He sat back down and crossed his legs expectantly. Leave it to an engineer to make a statement like that. I glared at him. He ignored me.

Harper coughed delicately. "Well, Chief – there's really not much I'm able to do here without an autopsy, and we're not equipped to do that. Plus we'd need next of kin authorization, among other things. And we don't yet know who the next of kin is, or if he even had any." Harper glanced at the Captain, who was watching him carefully. "We're trying to find out of course, if he had relatives to notify. No, in my opinion it was a stroke. Doctor Bratton concurs."

Captain Webster nodded at Harper and myself, then addressed his officer. "I just wanted you all to know the situation as it stands. Chief, if you'll give us the engineering report, please."

"Sir." Duncan got back to his feet and began speaking a volume of technicalities all without benefit of any supporting notes to jog his memory. The man was a steam propulsion encyclopaedia. Somewhere around Boiler Room Two and a peculiarity with the primary fuel feed flow line causing an overnight shutdown in boiler five that wasn't expected to be too much of an annoyance – the *Victoria* had over 24 boilers – I lost the thread of the report.

When the meeting broke up fifteen minutes later, the Captain gestured for Doctor Harper, Mister Harvey, and myself to stay. When the door had closed, he faced us. "Well?"

Doctor Harper took a deep breath, then plunged off the ramp. "The man was poisoned, sir." Harvey gave me a sharp look, and I nodded. Harper continued. "Forgive my not telling everyone. I thought it best to keep the information to as few people as possible for the time being."

Captain Webster nodded. "Agreed, Doctor. Though in future, please take me into your confidence as soon as you have information."

"Yes, sir."

The Captain pursed his lips. "Any chance it was accidental?"

"No, sir, not a chance," said Harper. "He ingested aconitine. It's a deadly poisonous alkaloid derived from various members of the aconite plant family, such as wolfsbane, monkshood, or Devil's Helmet. Mister Reedy confirmed it for me this morning. It was deliberate."

"Suicide?" asked Captain Webster.

"You saw how he died, sir." Harper took a deep breath. "I believe that if someone wanted to kill themselves, they'd choose a much faster acting and much less painful poison."

"And you couldn't save him?"

Harper shook his head. "Only if he'd come to me an hour earlier. And only if I'd known what to look for. I'd have made him swallow plenty of hot salt water and then hope he didn't tear his esophagus apart while he was vomiting his insides out. He'd have been exhausted afterward and maybe wished he was dead, but he'd have been alive. It's a moot point now."

"True," said Webster. "So, he was murdered." He looked at us. "Does anyone have any thoughts as to why this happened?"

"I don't know, sir," I said. "Mister Harvey took a look at his stateroom."

Mister Harvey nodded. "The man was traveling alone, as Doctor Harper said. Chief Purser Collins and I went through his stateroom last night. It all appears untouched. Except for what he was wearing, his jewelry is there, along with a wad of English bank notes," said Harvey. "I don't think anyone stole anything from him. And his room key was on his person."

"Plus, his dinner companions were all people he'd met just yesterday," Doctor Harper added.

"A very affable young man, it would seem," said Webster.

"Begging the Captain's pardon, but he was a wine salesman," said Harvey. "Believe me, by nature they're very hail fellow well met all around. I've dealt with enough of them."

"Ever dealt with this one?"

"Not him personally, sir. The Stoddard Lines have done business with his firm in England."

"Have you notified them?"

Harvey nodded. "I sent a wireless this morning."

"A wine salesman," mused Captain Webster. "Going to America during prohibition. Seems odd."

"He wasn't carrying any samples," said Harvey. "He has a small trunk in the hold but it's far too light weight to be holding bottles." The Chief Steward shrugged. "I think it's nothing more mysterious than a man going on holiday."

Captain Webster sighed. "Very well. Maybe his firm can shed some light on his familial connections and tell us how to deal with the body once we reach New York." Webster mused for a moment. "Traveling alone, you say. Not married?"

"I don't believe so, sir," I said.

"You don't believe so, Nurse? And why is that?" Webster gave me a steady gaze.

I fidgeted. "He wasn't wearing a ring. And if he'd taken one off his finger there was no tan line."

"Nurse Chandler is very observant," said Harper. I blushed.

Webster ignored the remark. "So we have a dead passenger, apparently done in deliberately, with no apparent motive and no suspect."

"That's about the way of it, yes, sir," said Harper. The Captain thoughtfully rubbed a hand over his trim beard, pondering the situation.

"Not a very satisfactory state of affairs," he finally said. "Not satisfactory at all." He gazed out the window at the undulating gray horizon. "Barring any unforeseen incidents – and I see none - we'll be in New York before ten hundred hours Saturday." He turned back to us. "At which point, whoever killed Mr Morten will walk off this ship, unless we have him first."

"Yes, sir, but how do we go about finding him?" I asked, then immediately wished I hadn't.

"I am the master of this vessel, Nurse Chandler," said Webster. "Not Sherlock Holmes. I have a bloody great big ship to run, and by the last count nearly three thousand souls to take care of."

"2,136 paying passengers, plus 700 crew" said Harvey. "Not counting yourself, sir." He paused for a moment. "Or Thomas Morten."

"Thank you, Mister Harvey, for the updated status." Webster's voice was cold. He looked back at me. "As I am so resolutely informed by the Chief Steward, 2,136 souls to take care of aboard ship." Webster indicated the three of us. "And from what you three are telling me, one of that number is apparently a murderer."

"It would seem that way, sir," Harper said quietly. He looked for all the world like a truant student up in front of the headmaster.

The Captain reached for his cap. "Very well. I let the Stoddard Lines know about the death last night, but God knows what I'm going to tell them now that it appears to be a murder." He shook his head. "Given what we know now, if one of you could make time in your busy schedule to apprise the Master-at-Arms, I would be much obliged. But keep it very low profile. Thank you, gentlemen and nurse. If there are any other unusual facts you feel you should keep from me, my door is always open."

"Yes, sir," said Doctor Harper. We three took our cue and left his stateroom, walking in silence along the open Sports Deck for a few moments before reaching the relative shelter of the port flying wing to the side of the bridge. The cupola was empty. We stepped inside out of the biting wind. I gazed through the window at the bow of the ship stretching out beneath us, the brass-capped anchor chain capstans glinting in the occasional burst of sunlight through the tearing gray clouds. The American flag fluttered high above on the forward mast, symbol of the *Victoria's* destination. Some distance beneath it I could glimpse the half-hidden movements of the two lookouts stationed in the open crow's nest, eyes and binoculars constantly scanning the dreary ocean and low-scudding clouds.

"We usually run a tighter ship than this, Doctor Harper," said Harvey. "Please forgive us." Harper exhaled sharply.

"I honestly thought a passenger liner would be an easy practice."

I was leaning against the grab rail, my arms crossed over it, still looking out the window. "Fooled you, huh, Boss?" I said.

Harper turned to Harvey. "Why would anyone want to kill Morten?"

Harvey shrugged. "I haven't the faintest. I read detective novels, but I can never solve them. I don't think the writers give all the right clues. Or they give wrong ones, just to throw you off the scent."

"Ha. I read them and always solve the mystery. We just have to figure out what we have, Mister Harvey," I said.

"By all means, Nurse." Harvey crossed his arms. Harper looked at me.

"Fine." I turned to face them. "Morten is single. He's traveling alone, on holiday. He appears to be a completely likable fellow. He's dining with three people he's never met before, enjoying each other's company. And then he's dead, apparent victim of aconitine poisoning."

"And stored in one of my cold rooms, for Christ's sake," reminded Harvey. Harper gave him a half-smile.

"Sorry about that. If it's any consolation, Doctor Bratton and I stashed him at the back of the ales and stouts."

"Near the Guinness," I added.

Harvey winced. "Galling, for a wine salesman."

Harper leaned up against the cupola wall. "Go on, Maeve."

"I've been giving it some thought," I said. "Why kill him on the *Victoria*, when the murderer can't possibly leave the ship? Why on the first night? Why not early on the last morning? And why in such a public venue? Why not entice him to an upper deck late at night and just heave him over the railings?"

"So who is he, our murderer?" asked Harvey.

"How do you know it's a he?" I crossed my arms. "Poison, you know, that's what I think a woman would use. A Lucrezia Borgia."

"All good points," Harper sighed. "And if I remember anything it's that aconitine takes a while to act. Maybe Morten was poisoned up in the First-Class observation-lounge before he came down to dinner."

"Which then begs the question, who would have been able to put the aconitine in his glass?" I replied.

"The better question might be, who wouldn't have been able to?" said Harvey. "Do either of you have any idea how crowded that bar is on the first night out?"

"Then it could have been anyone." Harper shook his head dejectedly. "And we're right back to where we started."

I shook my head. "I'm going to take a walk, if you don't mind. See you at the hospital, Doctor. Mister Harvey." Both men nodded. I stepped out of the cupola and made my way back toward the tennis courts, then found the steps down to the Sun Deck and from there to the Promenade Deck. At least here I could walk in some shelter, out of the wind. At this time of day, other walkers were also making the rounds of the deck, some striding quickly, others just ambling along.

Deep in thought, my mind jumping from Doctor Harper and his blue eyes, to the late ill-fated Mr Morten, to the fact we had a murderer loose on board the ship, I didn't even notice the lady who had fallen in step next to me.

"Terrible thing, wasn't it?" she said. I looked at her. She had a pleasant face, dark hair, dark eyebrows and was dressed nicely. She looked to be in her mid to late 30's and about five or six inches taller than me. Hard to tell with the wide brimmed floppy hat she was wearing, but as I've said before, just about everyone is taller than me.

"What?"

"That poor man last night." She sighed. "I saw it happen, you know. I was only two tables away. I couldn't have avoided seeing you and the officers gathered around him if I had wanted to." We continued to walk in pace with each other.

"Yes," I said. "Stroke, that's what the Principal Medical Officer says."

"Really?" She seemed almost amused. "I worked in the Voluntary Aid Detachment during the War. You know, helping the doctors and all that sort of thing. I eventually became a dispenser's assistant and took a certain shine to toxins and their use."

"That's certainly an odd interest, if you don't mind my saying."

She smiled. "Well, I'd have to agree with you on that, but it's certainly been helpful to me at times along the way." I blinked and she laughed. "Don't worry, my dear, I don't do anything untoward with the knowledge. Getting back to that poor man last night, it certainly didn't look like any stroke to me."

"Have you ever seen anything like that before?"

"Only in my mind's eye." She smiled. "Were you in the War, Nurse — I'm sorry, but what is your name?"

"Chandler. Maeve Chandler."

"Maeve? What an unusual name."

"So I've been told." I related the story.

"How interesting," she said.

"Thanks. And to answer your question, no, I wasn't in the War. My husband died shortly afterward, and that's when I went into nursing."

"I'm sorry for your loss. I divorced mine last year." I opened my mouth to commiserate, but she cut me off. "Don't be sorry. Best thing that ever happened to me. Do you know that I met a young man?" She looked carefully from side to side. "He's about 14 years younger than me. Scandalous, isn't it?"

"Not as long as you're happy, I suppose." I nodded to a steward who went past us, carrying a tea tray with hot bouillon in mugs on it.

"Good for you, Nurse Chandler." She nodded. "And I am happy. Certainly happier than that poor fellow who died last night." She looked about conspiratorially. "I don't know what your doctor is thinking, but that looked like poisoning to me, and I don't think you believe it was a stroke, either."

I swallowed. This woman was unnerving. "Well, to tell you the truth – " I paused. She smiled.

"I'm Mrs Templeton, Mrs MD Templeton." She nodded to me. "Go on, please."

"Well, Mrs Templeton, no. We don't believe it was a stroke."

"I knew I was right," she said firmly. "It was poisoning if I've ever seen it."

I stopped and looked at her. "Based on your experience as a dispenser during the War?"

"That, and other things."

I looked around. No one was near. "Mrs Templeton, I'm taking a great risk here bringing you into my confidence, you being a passenger and all, and you've got to swear to keep this secret – but I think the man was murdered."

"And your companions?"

"They think so, too." I set my jaw. "But I was the first one to suggest it. And I'm going to figure out who did it, too."

We began walking again. Mrs Templeton spoke quietly. "And how did you arrive at your conclusion?"

I told her about Mister Reedy's discovery, and the examination made by the doctors. When I was finished she appeared thoughtful.

"Aconitine. Dreadful stuff."

"You learned about it during your war service? I asked.

She nodded. "As I said, I picked up a thing or two."

"Are you still involved with apothecaries?"

"Good heavens, no. I wouldn't be traveling First-Class if I was. The pay, as the Americans like to say, was lousy."

"If you don't mind my asking, how have you been supporting yourself since your divorce?"

"The same way I supported myself during my marriage. I'm a writer." She took a moment to smile at another passenger going in the opposite direction, then looked at me. "And I'm taking you into my confidence now, Maeve. My first book earned me 25 pounds and the pay has increased with each book published, I'm happy to say. At any rate, therein lies my interest in what happened to that man at dinner."

"You want to write about it?" I frowned. "Sounds rather ghoulish to me."

"Oh, no. You misunderstand me. I've plenty of other projects going on. That's why I'm going to New York. I'm meeting with my American publisher, Dodd, Mead and Company. What happened here last night just piqued my professional curiousity."

I was at a loss. "What kind of books do you write?"

"Mysteries, mainly."

"Really?" I said, truly interested. "I love reading a good mystery. Maybe I've read one of yours."

"Maybe you have." She stopped and put out her hand to me. "My real name is Agatha Christie."

I ignominiously stumbled over a deck chair. Mrs Templeton – Agatha – knelt and helped me to my feet. I stared at her.

"Not *that* Agatha Christie?" I said.

"Yes, that one." She straightened my nurse's cap for me. "This is a working trip for me, and I prefer to be incognito. That's why I'm traveling under an assumed name. I've no desire to sit at the Captain's table."

I blushed. "I'm afraid I was sitting there last night."

"Yes, I saw you with that handsome doctor." She gave me a wink. "Is there anything to it?"

I felt the blush grow deeper. "I – we just met yesterday. Doctor Harper is very nice." I felt the need to divert the conversation in another direction. "What are you doing here?" I asked, then immediately realized how silly that question must have sounded.

Agatha was bemused. "Doing here? I really am going to New York to meet with my American publishers, and I'm also working on a new book. If that man hadn't died last night, I would probably have gone the entire voyage very quietly."

"But you were in the First-Class salon last night," I said, confused. "Didn't you think you'd be recognized?"

"Not really," she said. "And what if I am? The ship's passenger list says there is a Mrs MD Templeton traveling First-Class. Regular people are mistaken for famous people from time to time. I would just say 'thank you, I wish I was Agatha Christie and you're not the first who has pointed out the resemblance,' and go merrily on my way." Agatha smiled at me. "Sometimes you just have to brazen it out, Maeve."

I stared at her. "Wait – wasn't there a Mrs Templeton in one of your books?"

"Oh, yes," said Agatha. She was a character in *The Big Four*, which coincidentally was my fourth Hercule Poirot mystery."

"That's right. I remember her now. Her son accused her of trying to poison his father."

"And then the son turned out to be a very bad seed." She laughed pleasantly. "Maybe I'm subconsciously trying to redeem her by taking her name for this trip. Just don't give me away," she said. "I know you won't."

"Of course, Mrs Templeton." We walked in silence for a few moments. "What do you tell people you do if they ask?"

"What I do? I tell them the truth, in a roundabout sort of way. I'm divorced, have my own money, and I work for a publisher and read manuscripts."

I gazed at her in wonder. "You really do brazen it out."

"Sometimes it's the best tool a woman can have."

"I would have to agree with you there." Now or never, I thought. "Will you help me?"

She rewarded me with a big smile. "Of course. To tell the truth, I was beginning to be bored with the shipboard routine."

"Thank you." I could scarcely believe my good fortune.

"It will be fun. I've never worked with a female sleuth completely on her own before. Besides, you and I both love a mystery, don't we?"

II

Have you ever wanted to tell someone something so badly you thought you would burst before you got it out? Not something like 'I know what you're getting for your birthday' or 'I know what Father Christmas is bringing you' but something really, really, big? I knew I couldn't say anything but that's the way I felt while waiting for Doctor Harper to come back to the hospital after my encounter with Agatha Christie.

When he finally stopped back in at the surgery in the early afternoon he looked absolutely beaten down. I put my newspaper down on the desk and greeted him with a smile.

"Tough day?"

He slumped down into a chair opposite me. "I dealt with hypochondriacs and malingerers in the Navy, but nothing like this. A couple of First-Class passengers, both wealthy widows, it turns out, who were each sure they were having heart palpitations."

"Do tell." I leaned forward, my head resting on my hands, elbows on the desk.

"They came by my consulting rooms at different times, thank God."

"And there was nothing wrong with either one of them?"

Harper blinked. "No." His brow furrowed. "How did you know that?"

"Oh, Doctor Harper." I leaned back in the chair. "Seriously?"

"I haven't the faintest idea what you are talking about." I smiled inwardly.

Harper went on. "I also attended to one of Mister Harvey's staff who burned his fingers on a roasting pan."

"You can always count on the crew for something unique. I don't think they'd have enjoyed having Doctor Bratton as their sawbones."

"I was surprised to find that the crew fell under my supervision as well as First-Class."

"Got to make sure you have enough to do, Boss. Doctor Bratton has his hands full with Second and Third-Class." I steepled my fingers. "This is going to come as a surprise to you, but we're not the only ones who think Mr Morten was poisoned."

Concern clouded Harper's face. "Who else? I thought we agreed to keep it to our little group."

"We did. This person figured it out on her own."

"How? When?"

"She was a trained apothecary assistant during the War. Knows what poisoning looks like. As to the when, she figured it out last night, probably before you had Mr Morten carted out of the dining room."

"Before I had - " Harper stopped short. "You're telling me that she saw it happen? We have no female waiters. Are you saying this woman is a passenger?"

I nodded. "Yes, Boss. Don't look so aggrieved."

"But from a passenger? Can we trust her? Who is she?"

"The answer is yes, and her name is Mrs MD Templeton."

Harper blinked again. It was charming, in a way. "And what does Mrs MD Templeton have to say?"

"She began talking with me earlier today when I was walking on the Promenade Deck, trying to clear my head." I related part of the conversation to him.

"What does this woman do that makes her interested in our case?"

"She works for a publisher and reads a lot of manuscripts, she said."

Harper frowned. "What kind of manuscripts?"

I grinned at Harper. "I don't know. It's a mystery."

"Stop," he said. I laughed.

"Sorry. Anyway, there you have it. Help is at hand, if we want it."

"Frankly, I don't know." He drummed his fingers on the desk top. "What's the Captain going to say?"

"You heard him, Boss. He wants this person found. I don't really believe he cares how or who does it."

Doctor Harper frowned. "I'm really not used to ignoring the chain of command."

I placed my hands on the desk and leaned in toward him. "Doctor, you've never served under Captain Webster before. I have, for three years. So has Mister Harvey. When the Captain wants something done that's not germane to life on the bridge, he doesn't want to necessarily know how it gets done. He just wants it done."

"I still don't know, Maeve."

I sighed. "Doctor Harper. We have a dead man. We have a murderer. And you know as well as I do that we have very limited resources. Mrs Templeton is interested in the case, and I say we use her. No one is going anywhere for the next few days, anyway." I straightened. "Cheer up, Boss. It's not like I'm going to be the one who gets in the soup. You're my superior officer," I said with a grin.

Harper grunted. "What happened to the *Victoria's* last PMO?" he asked.

"He got hit by a cab in New York City our last trip over."

"Lucky man," said Harper with what I thought was a hint of wistfulness.

"That's the spirit, sir." I turned and banged my shin on the heavy desk leg. "Bloody hell, that hurt," I said, clenching my fists until the first shock of pain had passed.

"You're a walking disaster."

I nodded. "I fell over a deck chair when I was with Mrs Templeton." Harper shook his head slowly.

"I'm sure that instills a great degree of faith in our medical department." The poor man seemed somehow deflated. I limped around to the side of the desk and leaned against it.

"Anyway, Mrs Templeton isn't the only one who's been thinking. So have I."

The doctor grimaced. "I'm beginning to agree with Mister Harvey. He says when you think bad things happen. Go ahead. What were you thinking about?"

"Do you think it's wise to keep our murder diagnosis from the first officer and the rest?" I asked him.

"You mean your murder diagnosis. And Mrs Templeton's."

I folded my arms. "I mean our murder diagnosis."

Harper waved a hand. "As you like." He sighed. "I crossed paths with the first officer today. He expounded on Mr Morten's death. Mister Jackson was adamant that Morten died as a direct result of what he termed a 'corrosive lifestyle' that robbed widows and orphans of their daily bread." Harper shook his head. "He gave quite a damning statement, truth be told."

"Everyone's entitled to their personal opinion, I suppose." I pursed my lips. "But speaking ill of a deceased passenger is certainly unusual."

Harper shrugged. "Maybe he was just having a bad day. I don't know. In any case, to answer your question, yes, I think the murder diagnosis should be kept as silent as possible, the odd passenger apparently not withstanding."

I remained adamant about Mrs Templeton. "I believe she'll be a great help."

Harper drew a hand across his forehead. "Yes." He sighed. "Come up with an answer?" he asked hopefully.

"No."

"Me, either. So much for our careers as detectives." He rubbed his eyes, then indicated the paper in my hands. "You were going to show me something?"

I held up the newspaper. "Maybe we'd do better as reporters. Mister Casey has certainly gotten what Winchell calls "the scoop" on that American millionaire, Harvey Wilson. This is the ship's newspaper, the *Victory*."

"Catchy name." He put his hands behind his head and leaned back.

I gave Harper a sour look. "I didn't name it." I cleared my throat and read aloud. "'Millionaire Harvey Wilson Gives His Views on Today's Finance, exclusive to the *Victory* by John Casey.'"

"I can't wait," said Harper. "Finance has never been my strong suit."

"Doctor, please." I resumed the story. "'This reporter enjoyed an exclusive interview with American millionaire Harvey Wilson on Sunday evening. Mr Wilson is returning to the United States after another extensive trip through France, where he has been funding and erecting monuments to the American war dead. Editor's note: Mr Wilson agreed to this story on condition that his philanthropies and the reasons behind them were off bounds. Herewith, then, are Mr Wilson's views on the American stock market."' I looked up from the paper with disgust. "'Off bounds' and Casey folded on it. Winchell would have chewed right through this."

"The man has a right to his privacy," said Harper. "I'm surprised he agreed to do an interview at all, given the current state of his affairs."

"I'll spare you what I think of his current state of affairs."

"I think I got a good idea yesterday when he came on board." Harper settled himself and I found my place in the article.

"'I asked Mr Wilson if he had been keeping up with the reports posted outside our Purser's office by radio. Many of our First-Class passengers are, of course, heavily invested in the American market, and no doubt a great many of our other classes as well. Did he have any advice for them?'"

"I'll hazard that he did," said Harper, idly toying with a pencil.

"Doctor, please." I resumed reading out loud. "'Two words,' said Mr Wilson. 'Don't panic. Last Thursday was a good example of what happens when people panic. Over 12,000,000 shares changed hands. I understand the ticker tape machines couldn't even begin to keep up with the orders.'

'Were you buying or selling?' I asked him.

'On Thursday, neither. I waited until Friday, then instructed my brokers to buy some bargains. Folks got caught up trying to dump their margins.'

'Please explain," I asked him.

'Stocks are bought on margin, or credit. For instance, let's say you want to buy two hundred shares of Ajax, and those two hundred shares are currently worth 2,000 dollars. So you would pay up front ten percent, or two hundred dollars. The other 1,800 of the purchase price is what's called the margin. And that's where it gets interesting.'

'Please tell our readers how,' I asked.

'Well, you've got to pay off that 1,800, don't you? So your broker lets you pay it in easy monthly payments. Now, if you are buying a Duesenberg or a Rolls Royce, this works out fine. The value of the car tends to change. In fact, it begins to go down from the moment you buy it, but you perceive that it's worth your cost of 20,000 bucks, so you pay it off."'

Harper whistled. "20,000 dollars for an automobile. Can you imagine?"

"Yes," I said, then resumed reading. "'But with a stock it's different,' said Wilson.

'How?' asked your reporter.'

'Because everyone else bought the stock, too. And that drives up its value and price, something that doesn't happen with your automobile. Before too long, that 20,000 dollars is now worth 40 thousand. And for all practical purposes, you are paying off your margin by the increase in the value of your stock. Which, by the way, is also your collateral securing your credit to purchase it on margin in the first place.'

'Which means?'

'Which means a financial empire built on credit issued as collateral on stocks that are subject to the vagaries of the market isn't going to last forever. Sooner or later the bill is going to come due for this party, and when it does, I think it's going to be a whopper. To let your readers know, I've instructed my broker to begin selling off some of my investments and converting them into cash. Remember, no matter what happens, a hundred dollar bill is still a hundred dollars backed by our gold standard. In Britain a hundred pounds is still a hundred pounds backed by your own gold standard. But a hundred dollar share of stock may devalue down to one buck, or worse.'

'What about the London Stock Exchange crash last month?'

'Well, that certainly did inject a cautionary note into American investments overseas. You'll remember that in the days leading up to the London debacle, there had also been periods of high volume trading and selling, then ever-briefer moments of recovery along with rising stock prices. But, and this is important, the London episode was set off by the arrest of Clarence Hatry for fraud and forgery. When England's top investor is taken down like that, of course there is going to be market instability.'

'And on that note, our interview ended as Mr Wilson excused himself and went in to dinner."'

I put the paper down. "Despite my dislike for the man, he seems to know his stuff."

"When did that come out?" asked Harper.

"This afternoon."

Harper stopped playing with the pencil. "Well, that's all very interesting, as you say, but is there no mention of Mr Morten?"

I nodded. "Oh, yes. Inside front page. A brief piece detailing his untimely death from a stroke, according to ship's Principal Medical Officer Doctor Leslie Harper."

"I don't recall giving him an interview. In fact, I still haven't met him."

"He came by this morning. You were already off on your patient tour." Harper frowned. "I'm sorry. I didn't think you'd mind. He had to be told something."

"No, you're right. And you're right about Mrs Templeton, too. We can use all the help we can get. Harper drummed a finger against the armrest for a minute, then finally looked at me. "Maeve, do you have, uh, dinner plans? I hear the orchestra is going to treat us to some songs from Cole Porter's *Paris* tonight."

"Why, Doctor Harper, you amaze me," I said. "I would never have imagined you as listening to Cole Porter. Waltzes, maybe." I gave him my best malicious grin. "But to answer your question about dinner plans, no, not yet." I thought my tone was sufficiently coquettish and I was trying hard to hide a smile.

He gave me a steady look that threatened to unhinge me. "Do you want dinner plans?"

My heart was beating. "That depends."

"On?"

"On whom is asking, of course. Are you playing Cyrano de Bergerac for some Christian de Neuvillette and I'm an unknowing Roxane?" Harper rolled his eyes.

"No. Just being polite."

I smiled. "In that case, Doctor, I accept your invitation to dinner."

"Very good," said Harper. "Shall I call for you at your quarters?"

"That would be unseemly, Doctor," I said. "I'll meet you in the restaurant foyer again."

"I'll be there with bells on."

"Your uniform will be quite sufficient, Doctor."

"Eight, then?"

"Of course. Thank you."

Harper smiled at me and left the surgery. I sagged back in my chair, again cursing the fact my cabin mate was out on this voyage.

I could use her extra wardrobe.

There are moments in a young girl's life when she imagines herself a princess, the veritable belle of the ball. I don't know about you, but these moments were few and far between in my life. My wedding day, the day I graduated from university, the day I got my first job. Dining in the First-Class salon two nights running was right up there, and I was still lost in my reverie of what to wear when there was a timorous knock at the surgery door. I touched my hands to my cap and set the newspaper to the side.

"Come in."

Clara Alston came through the door. She smiled softly.

"Are you still open, Nurse?"

"Certainly, Mrs Alston. My apologies to you. I said I would check on you this morning and I didn't."

"I'm sure you were busy with the death of that poor man. I read it in the ship's paper today."

"Yes," I said. "It was very sad. How's the boy?" I asked, anxious to change the conversation.

"Bradley hasn't gotten lost again," said Clara. "But he does know his way around – what do the Americans call it? The soda fountain."

"It was put in for our American travelers to feel more at home, but every nationality seems to enjoy it," I agreed. I smiled and stood up. "Come in to the examining room and have a seat." I followed her and went to the sink to wash my hands. "Is everything better now between you and your husband?" I began to dry my hands. "I'm sorry, I don't mean to pry."

"No, that's fine," she said. "I think we'll reach New York before the baby comes."

"And if we don't?"

Clara shrugged. "Then you'll get a chance to deliver a child at sea. I'm sure it won't be the first birth at sea, and I doubt it will be the last." She held out her arm as I reached for her wrist to take her pulse. The bruises I'd seen yesterday evening were still visible, only slightly reduced. I finished counting and gently laid her arm down in her lap.

"Any pains?" I asked.

"No, none." She smiled. "And believe me, I know what it feels like."

"I'm certain you do." I continued the examination. "Bradley's birth was normal? No complications?"

"I was in labor sixteen hours," Clara said. "But any woman will tell you that any amount of time spent in labor is too long."

"I've never had a child, but I can believe that." I stepped back and crossed my arms. "At just a cursory look, you appear to be doing fine. Nothing to do but wait."

"Thank you."

I debated a moment, remembering what I had told Harper about getting involved with the passengers, then thought the hell with it. She was a lovely woman, and if I could help her - "Those – ah – bruises, Mrs Alston. Is there anything - "

"Anything you'd like me to tell you?" The young woman's outright frankness took me aback. "My husband can be very demanding."

"Mrs Alston," I began, but she shook her head and took me by the hand. Her eyes were tearing.

"No, Nurse, I need to tell someone. If something were to happen to me, or the baby. Or Bradley. Bradley's not his son. He's mine by my first marriage."

"I see."

"My first husband was killed in an auto racing accident. Frank had been his lead mechanic. Our first couple of years together were pleasant enough, but Frank had an argument with the team owner and got cashiered."

"I'm sorry."

Clara held up a hand. "It gets worse. He also hit the man with a spanner. After three months in chokey Frank was blacklisted and virtually unemployable, so he started drinking. You can imagine how well that went over, so he decided to return to his American roots, and that meant uprooting all of us. He sold our cottage to pay for this trip. His uncle owns the Chevrolet house in Buffalo. Frank has grandiose ideas about hooking up with someone like Eddie Rickenbacker, as if someone like Mr Rickenbacker would associate with someone like Frank. He has ideas of making a fortune, but he never will."

I put a hand on her shoulder. "If there's anything I can do – "

"You just need to know that to my husband's way of thinking, Bradley has always been a kind of second-rate citizen. I'm sure this baby will get everything." She sat straight in the chair and looked me in the eye. "I'm telling you this, you understand, because I trust you."

I nodded. "Patient confidentiality is something I would never breach. But Mrs Alston, please – don't let yourself come to harm."

"I promise you, I won't." She raised a silk sleeve and looked at the mottled yellow bruises on her forearm. "He did this a week ago. I told him afterward that if he dared touch me again, I'd leave him."

"And?"

"And he hasn't. He stays to himself. He spends as little time in our cabin as possible." She set her jaw. "I've decided to divorce him when we reach New York."

"That's a big step," I said. "But I think it's the right step."

She nodded, then touched her belly. "First, I have to think about this little one."

I extended a hand to help her up out of the chair. "If you need me, have someone send for me, if you can't get here yourself."

"I will." Clara moved slowly to the door and opened it. "Thank you for your time."

"Anytime, Mrs Alston. It's what I'm here for." She gave me a soft smile and went out, gently closing the door behind her.

I met Harper at the great doors to the First-Class dining salon shortly after eight. As Principal Medical Officer it was, of course, Harper's privilege to dine there, and not just when he was invited to sit at the Captain's table. Naturally, it was Monsieur DuMont who took us to a small table in an alcove off the main floor.

"A terrible thing last night, Doctor," he said. "Terrible. A stroke, you say?" he asked, hoping for reassurance from the doctor.

"Yes, I'm afraid so," replied Harper. DuMont clicked his tongue.

"*C'est dommage*, I suppose." He pulled out a chair for me. "Mademoiselle," he said, gallantly seating me, a trace of slyness on his fox face. I was wearing a simple black dress that fell just below the knee, and a ruffled-front jacket and was, I had to admit, very fetching. "Doctor Harper." He nodded to us. "Please enjoy your meal." He gave Harper a wink. "And your evening."

When he had gone I frowned. "Don't think I didn't see what that old Gallic busybody did," I said. "This ship may burn oil but it thrives on gossip and DuMont is one of the chief purveyors." I glanced in the maître d's direction. DuMont leered back at me. I sighed and turned back to Harper. "We are going to be big talk before this is over." Of course, I thought, not that I would mind. I looked across the cavernous, yet intimate, room. "This is how I'm supposed to live," I said. "And someday, I shall."

Harper smiled at me. "I have no doubt that you will get your wish. Your name in Winchell's column and everything that goes with it, but hopefully only for good." Harper waited while a waiter filled our water glasses. He tilted his glass toward me. "Your health."

"And yours." We watched each other for a moment, waiting to see who would drink first. "Oh, this is ridiculous," I finally said and took a sip. "Lightning doesn't strike twice, right?"

"Right." He swallowed some of the water and set the glass down.

I felt giddy. "This is terribly exciting, isn't it?"

"I'm glad you're enjoying yourself. To me, it just looks like we have a murderer that's going to get away with it come Saturday morning."

"We won't let that happen." I reached across the table and put my hand on top of his. His fingers didn't move. The moment lasted a second before I withdrew my hand, reaching up to touch my long hair now piled up on top of my head. "I'm sure Mrs Templeton will be able to help," I said. Doctor Harper nodded absent-mindedly. I realized that any frilly thoughts I might have entertained about our dinner together had taken flight. I sat back in my chair and cast an eye around the dining salon.

It was the usual mix of swells and high hats, though I thought I detected a shade less exuberance in them than there was last night before Mr Morten died. Perhaps some were thinking of that, but I thought it more likely that many were thinking of the interview done by Mr Wilson in the paper. My wandering gaze finally went to the huge entry doors, where I saw Agatha Christie at the maître d's stand.

"Mrs Templeton just came in," I said to Doctor Harper. "Shall we invite her to join us?"

"Certainly, of course."

I flagged down a passing waiter and gave him instructions. In a couple of minutes, an extra place setting was going down and Mrs Templeton had been escorted to our table. Doctor Harper and I both stood.

"A pleasure to meet you, madam. Nurse Chandler has told me of your much appreciated offer to help us. I hope you don't mind the sudden invitation for dinner?" asked Harper. She smiled.

"No, not at all. And helping will be my pleasure." She watched as our waiter performed his office. "Thank you," she said to him as he filled her water glass.

"I'll give you a few moments to look over the menu," said the waiter, bowing. He disappeared into thin air.

Agatha settled back in her chair and took in the view. "I could get used to this, I think."

"Couldn't we all, Mrs Templeton," I replied.

She smiled and gave Harper a gentle look. "And, Doctor, I would trust that I'm not yet at the 'madam' stage. I'm only 39."

Harper bowed his head. "Of course. Thank you."

Agatha smoothed out the napkin in her lap. "Now, in case you're wondering, Maeve, I haven't solved the murder yet."

I laughed. "Neither have we. In fact, we were talking earlier about what poor detectives we must be."

"Nothing like Sherlock Holmes," added Harper.

"Well, let's be honest, Doctor. No one is like Sherlock Holmes," said Mrs Templeton. The waiter returned and for a few moments we busied ourselves with the menu. Clear turtle soup, roasted squab with pearl onions, glazed roast duckling and green peas and a gooseberry tart accompanied by Stilton cheeses for dessert rounded out our evening's dining. When he had gone, I shook my head in awe.

"So many choices. I really wanted the caviar."

"Which one?" asked Agatha. "I saw at least three listed."

"Beluga," said Harper. "You can't go wrong."

"Speaking of going wrong, Maeve, how are you faring after your cropper on the Promenade Deck today?" Agatha asked me.

I must have looked quite sheepish. "I recovered, if only long enough to bang my shin into a desk in the hospital."

"And your finger?" asked Agatha.

I held up the still-bandaged digit. "I did this yesterday morning. Doctor Harper stitched me up."

"Useful to have friends with needle and thread," said Mrs Templeton.

"When you're as accident prone as I am, it certainly is."

"In all honesty, I'm a bit concerned about turning her loose on the paying customers." Harper smiled at me. "I'm sorry, ladies, I forgot to ask – would you like some wine with dinner? Maeve? Mrs Templeton?"

"No, thank you," said Agatha. "I neither drink nor smoke. But please, have a glass without me."

"Nurse Chandler and myself are also non-smokers," said Harper. "Tobacco is very bad for one's health. But after the day I've had - "

Agatha held up a hand. "I quite understand."

Harper caught the eye of an attendant and ordered a gin and tonic. He looked over at me. I nodded. "Make it two," he said, before turning back to the table. "Have you given any thought to our problem, Mrs Templeton?" he asked her.

"Yes." She lifted her water glass and took a sip. "When you read as many manuscripts as I do you see so many styles of doing away with people. Guns, knives, swords — but poison is always a hands-down favorite. Since it seems there were no Samurai or American gangsters at the dead man's table, and that no one else at the table became ill, and that all drank from the same bottle, it therefore follows there could not have been anything in the wine. So, something was placed in the glass prior to the wine being added."

"But how could anyone know where someone would sit? The place settings were already out before the diners came in last night, just as they are every night," I said.

Agatha sat back as the soup course arrived, along with our drinks. Doctor Harper raised his glass. "Cheers, all."

Our glasses clinked. Agatha took another sip of water and picked up her soup spoon. "In one manuscript poison was also used, but the real killers then incriminated an innocent man to try and get away with it." She nodded in approval. "This is quite an excellent soup."

"So the detective was having to follow two trails?" I asked before savoring a spoonful of soup. I thought that if

I was to continue eating in First-Class I'd soon have to let out my wardrobe.

"Exactly so," said Agatha. "Are we to think a seemingly innocuous wine glass set out in an entire room of hundreds of wine glasses picks one man at random?"

"That's true." I raised a hand and began to tick the points off on my fingers. "We really have no motive. Nothing was taken. No one on board knew Mr Morten. He's traveling alone. There has been no follow-up to the crime; Mister Harvey – he's our Chief Steward – says no one has gone near his stateroom or down into the hold to get into his trunk. Random is exactly the word for it."

"Then," said Agatha, delicately spooning her soup, "I would posit this to you: Mr Morten was murdered, as you say, but by accident."

"What?" Harper set down his spoon. "Mrs Templeton, how do you accidentally murder someone?"

Agatha gave a delicate shrug. "I can think of half a dozen ways. Perhaps you are going to shoot someone at a distance with a rifle. Just as you take aim on your subject and begin to squeeze the trigger, someone else walks between you and your intended victim, but it's too late, your shot is off."

"And someone other than your chosen victim is accidentally murdered," I said.

"Exactly." Agatha finished her soup and delicately blotted her lips with her napkin.

"An accident?" Harper took a swallow of his gin. "No one accidentally poisons someone with aconitine." He considered. "Well, maybe they do. I don't know. I must have missed this class in medical college."

"And if he wasn't the victim, then that means we can reasonably expect our murderer to try again?" I asked.

Harper looked at me with fresh interest. "Have you always been this devious?"

I looked at Agatha. "So if Mr Morten wasn't the right man – or possibly woman -- who is? And of course, we still have the murderer, or murderess, to deal with. Our Chief Steward pointed out this morning that there are 2,100 plus passengers aboard, and 700 crew. That's a lot of suspects."

"You're already becoming quite the detective, Maeve," said Agatha as our soup course was cleared.

I know I must have blushed. "Thank you, Mrs. Templeton. I've always had a naturally inquisitive mind. My father said it would get me in trouble."

"And has it?" She smiled coyly.

I laughed. "Once or twice, maybe." We watched as the main event was laid out before us on the table.

"I must say the service on this ship is impeccable," said Agatha.

"I'm told it's what we pride ourselves on." Harper picked up knife and fork.

"You're told?" asked Agatha.

"I only joined the crew yesterday morning," said Harper. "Maeve here is the expert."

"Please," I said. I swallowed a bite of the glazed squab. "Mrs Templeton, did you happen to read the interview with Mr Harvey Wilson in today's ship's paper?"

"I did. After what happened in London a few weeks ago, I find the recent gyrations of the American market troubling." She took a forkful of duck. "Fortunately – or unfortunately, I suppose – I'm not quite at the stratospheric financial level I suspect most of the passengers in this room inhabit."

"That goes double for me," I said. "But I heard a lot of people talking about the American stock market today and

Chief Purser Collins and the bank exchange were absolutely buried when I went past after luncheon. It certainly didn't look like a lot of people were taking Harvey Wilson's advice."

"Maybe they didn't read the paper," said Harper.

"I heard more than one man say he would be wiped out if last Thursday happened again." I sighed, letting my eyes wander across the beautifully dressed passengers intent on enjoying their evening. "It would be a shame if all of this came to an end."

"What would it matter to you?" asked Harper. "You're not a part of their class. Neither am I."

"How very proletarian of you, Doctor," said Agatha. Harper shook his head.

"Not really. You should hear our First Officer go on if you want someone proletarian." He took another bite. "But I digress."

"But it's something I aspire to," I said. "I've told you, Doctor. I'm not a part of it yet, but I have my dreams."

"I concur," said Agatha. "Be strong and go after what you believe in. More women should do the same."

Harper gave me a steady gaze. "I didn't know you felt so strongly about it."

"I feel strongly about a lot of things," I said. "Such as that." I inclined my head. "Look over there. It's Harvey Wilson again. Looks like he's got a new crop of table mates."

Agatha and Harper turned their heads to look. "He keeps company with a lot of pretty women," said Agatha. "I remember seeing him last night."

"It's all about the money," I remarked drily. "Women like that are just looking for their next sugar daddy."

Agatha stifled a smirk. "My, but you do have some strong opinions on things."

"Not a nice thing to say," Harper admonished me gently. "You've got to quit reading Winchell's column."

"I don't care." I felt petulant. "I've told you, I've worked hard all my life to get to where I am today." I turned my attention back to my dinner. "And if any of the women at that table ever really worked for a living, except for, well, you know, I'd be very surprised."

"I'd have to agree with you, Maeve," said Agatha. "I've seen the kind before, and I don't like it."

Doctor Harper tried to calm the waters. "Maybe he had a big day trying to keep up with the stock market and is just enjoying a relaxing evening of conversation".

"Maybe," I said unconvincingly. "But I doubt it. I don't think conversation is a big part of their attraction."

Harper gave me a scornful look and took a sip of gin, then lifted his napkin from his lap. "Perhaps I should go and see if everything is all right?"

"Doctor," I said, looking at him and raising a restraining fork, "you've had a long day. Sit and enjoy your supper. That's my prescription."

"I heartily agree, Maeve. Nothing to be gained there," added Agatha.

"Right." Harper smiled and cut another piece of duck.

IV

Let me tell you a little about where I live most of the year, except for when she's laid up for annual maintenance in dry dock. The *Queen Victoria* is a rather large ship. She's a shade over 1,000 feet long, and about 175 feet tall from the keel to the top of any of her three funnels, and has in total 12 decks. These 12 decks rise up from the very bottom of the ship known as the Tank Top. That area is mainly filled with space for water ballast, whether pure or not, and the like. There's also a small cargo area – designers like to make the most of a ship. But fuel stowage took the bulk of space because the *Victoria* burns a lot of oil for her boilers to make the steam that drives her propellers. I'm told by our Chief Engineer that she moves forward about 11 feet for every imperial gallon burned. Yes, you read that correctly.

As I said, the Sports Deck is the highest deck on the ship with the bridge at the bow and open air tennis courts and quoits areas wedged between the funnel bases heading aft. Popular during the day, it was almost always deserted in the evening. Temperate weather - a relative term on the North Atlantic run – would bring players out in the day if the sun was shining, but no one was abroad tonight. The wind was already bitingly cold without the added impetus of the *Victoria*'s cutting ahead through seas that were beginning to build into long swells.

Every once in a while a quick flash of light indicated a door opening from the bridge forward of the first funnel, and an officer would scurry along, wrapped up tight in his uniform greatcoat. Though it was only 21:45 and the bars and restaurants were still in full swing, other than sparse crew we didn't encounter a single soul as we neared the stern of the ship, walking from pool of light to pool of light. The scent of salt air mingled with the smell of burnt fuel oil and steam rising from the funnels. I'm telling you all of this because, even on a ship this size, there are odd moments when you can feel all alone, without anyone else in sight. For myself, I couldn't have picked a more romantic spot.

But I could have picked a more romantic partner.

Agatha had excused herself after dinner and gone back to her stateroom to read a manuscript. She gave me a knowing smile as Doctor Harper and I bade her good night outside of the salon, and I smiled back. How could I not?

I had managed to coax Doctor Harper into a stroll around the Sports Deck after supper, and hoped to turn the conversation in a direction I was feeling interested in, but it was not to be. We hadn't made two steps onto the teak decking before he shoved his hands in his jacket pockets. "It's cold. I think I need my heavy coat."

I hugged my wrap tighter around my neck. "It's not that cold. And I'm in a dress."

"Yes, and it looks quite ravishing on you," I heard him say in my mind, instead of "And I can't believe you aren't freezing," which came out of his mouth. Another gambit shot down. He nodded his head in the direction of the doors behind us.

"If you don't mind accompanying me to my stateroom, I'll dodge inside and get my coat."

His stateroom? I began to think the evening might be salvageable. "Going to show me your collection of medical degrees?" I asked coyly.

"Completely above board, I assure you," countered Harper.

Derailed again, I thought – but I laughed lightly, not knowing what else to do. I tagged along behind him as we made the trek to his stateroom and examination room, and I had just about formulated one more last ditch effort at turning the evening around when we turned into the corridor outside Harper's stateroom and office and my heart fell.

"I think you've got company."

Harper looked down the corridor. Clara Alston was standing near his office door. She saw us and gave a tentative wave. Harper waved back, then turned sotto voce to me. "Our pregnant passenger again."

Even Captain Smith of the *Titanic* finally reached a point that fateful evening where he had to throw in the towel, and so had I. I gave up. "So I see. At least she's not one of your hypochondriac doctor-chasing widows," I said, hoping I'd put enough bite on the words.

"Shush," said Harper as we approached. He smiled. "Good evening, Mrs Alston. It's rather late, isn't it? Is there something we can do for you? Are you feeling well?"

She nodded. "I'm fine, thanks for asking. Nurse Chandler saw me this afternoon."

Harper looked at me. "You never mentioned it."

"You never asked." I smiled gently at Mrs Alston, as if to say 'your secret is safe with me.' "How may we assist you?" I asked.

"I was just wondering – you were so much help yesterday - "

"Looking for Bradley again?" said Harper.

"Yes." Clara's face was drawn. "He disappeared from our cabin around eight this evening." She looked at me with a mixture of - was it envy? - and curiosity. "I'm sorry, I didn't mean to intrude."

"Intrude?" Harper was momentarily flustered. "No, no. Nothing to interrupt. We were just taking a walk, taking the air." I didn't know whether to laugh or slap him.

Relieved, Clara drew her shawl tighter around her shoulders. "So you haven't seen him?"

"We haven't seen Bradley, Mrs Alston," I said. "I doubt he would have gone up on deck. It's very dark, it's becoming very cold and the seas are running a bit faster."

"You don't know my son, Nurse Chandler." She looked at us again, taking in my dress. "I'm terribly sorry if I upset anything, Doctor."

"Nothing at all. We were simply having dinner." I gave Doctor Harper a scathing look that he blithely ignored. He touched his officer's cap. "Now, let us see if we can find young Master Bradley. Shall we go, Nurse Chandler?"

"Yes," I said coldly. "Let's." I looked at Clara. "I think it best you stay here. There's too much chance of a slip and fall topside. I believe there's a comfortable chair to sit on inside of Doctor Harper's consulting room."

"Thank you," she said.

"Unless you would feel better in your own stateroom," Harper offered. "Maybe Bradley is there already."

"I doubt that. He won't stay there alone with Frank." She shuddered. "I don't like to stay there alone with Frank." Harper looked at me pleadingly. Damn him.

"Let me talk with the Chief Steward and Purser," I said to Clara. "Perhaps we can arrange a second stateroom for the duration of the voyage."

She looked so grateful I could have cried. "That would be very nice, Nurse Chandler. But I can't pay for it. We can barely afford the one we've got."

"Let me worry about that, Mrs Alston," I said. "I'm sure that Doctor Harper would help me, wouldn't you?" My tone of voice gave no doubt that he would help, and gladly.

"Of course, of course," he said, finally tumbling to my meaning. "I'll just let you into my office here, then Nurse Chandler and I will be on our way."

Our search first took us through the open rooms along the promenade, but it was fruitless. Bradley Alston was nowhere to be found. We made our way back from the children's playroom with its brightly painted walls and silent toys, then took the stairs up to the Boat Deck. That too, was quiet, save for a few romantic – not that I had any feelings on the subject one way or the other - couples braving the cold weather in the shelter of the funnel bases.

"I can't imagine where he's gotten off to," said Doctor Harper finally.

"Like I said before, it's a large ship, Doctor." We trudged in silence up the stairs to the Sports Deck.

"You're angry with me," he finally said.

"What makes you say that?"

"Telling Mrs Alston that she wasn't intruding on us."

"Was she?"

Harper stopped walking and turned to me. "Yes, she was." He cleared his throat. "I've only known you for a couple of days, but – well - "

I suppressed a grin. Maybe I wouldn't slap him after all. "Doctor Harper," I said with mock severity. "Are you trying to tell me something?"

He put his hands on my shoulders. Despite the wind, despite the cold, I felt intensely warm. "What I'm trying to say, Nurse - "

"Maeve," I corrected him. He smiled, the corners of his eyes crinkling up.

"What I'm trying to say, Maeve - " He stopped suddenly, cocking his head. "Do you hear that?"

"What?"

"Crying?" He stepped away from me. "I hear crying."

Bloody hell. The moment was gone. I listened, trying to filter out the wind, then I heard it too. A snuffling and weeping sound, coming from behind one of the great ventilator hoods that supplied fresh air to the bowels of the ship. "There," I said, peering into the almost complete darkness at the base of the hood.

Bradley was squeezed into the tiny space behind the hood, his back to a bulwark. The nearest electric light did nothing toward penetrating the deep shadows. He had his arms wrapped around his knees and his head down, sobbing. We hurried across the deck and knelt at his side. Doctor Harper reached to touch him, but the boy shuddered and withdrew even further into the corner. "Let me," I said. "Bradley?"

He looked up at the sound of my voice. Tears stained his cheeks. His cherubic face suddenly contorted and his lower lip quivered, then he burst into loud wails. I gently took him by the arm and brought him out of his hiding place. Doctor Harper slipped off his coat and wrapped him in it, then tried to pick him up. More tears and wails. "I don't think he wants to be carried," I said. I knelt beside him again. "You're not hurt, are you, Bradley?"

"No, Mrs Captain," he sobbed.

"Then what is it?" I asked.

Bradley just shook his head. "I – I want to go to bed." I took him by the hand and we both stood.

"Then that's what we'll do, Bradley. We'll take you to bed." I began to walk with Bradley toward the nearest stairs down from the Sports Deck. He clung to me tightly.

"Don't go near the side," he implored me, looking toward the white metal railings gleaming faintly in the near darkness.

"We won't," I assured him. "We're just going to go down to the Boat Deck, and then inside. Doctor Harper stood on his other side, then reached down for his hand. Bradley jerked and pulled away from him. I looked at Doctor Harper. "He doesn't want you near him," I said.

"So I see."

"Why don't you walk behind us." I squeezed Bradley's hand. "Are you ready to go see your mum?" He snuffled an acknowledgement. I stepped carefully away and he stuck to me like treacle. Doctor Harper followed at a discreet distance behind. We retraced our steps down, finally re-entering the *Victoria* and making our way to Harper's examining room. I noticed that Bradley relaxed appreciably once we were back indoors, out of the wind and open spaces. By the time we got to our destination he had stopped sniffling entirely.

I pushed open the door to the examining room and walked inside. Clara stood up with a start as Bradley broke away from me and ran to her, casting the doctor's coat on the floor. "We found him on the Sports Deck," I said. "He was hiding behind a ventilator shaft hood."

"Bradley, are you all right?" asked his worried mother.

"He seems to be," said Harper. "I'll just give him a brief examination to make sure." He reached his long arms toward the boy, who immediately backed away. "Or not," said Harper.

"I'll do it," I said. "If you two don't mind for a moment." Clara looked up at Harper, concern on her face. He nodded and ushered her back out into the corridor, closing the door behind them.

Ten minutes later I pronounced Bradley to have a clean bill of health. There was a stain of grease along one sleeve of his coat and on his hand, but boys will be boys and other than that he appeared to be fine. He yawned mightily as his mother took him by the hand.

"You're welcome to sleep here tonight, if you'd like, Mrs Alston," said Harper. "I can find other quarters." She shook her head.

"You've done more than enough, Doctor Harper. And you, Nurse." She gently touched the boy's head. "We'll go back to our own cabin. It's past midnight. Frank won't be in for hours yet. Goodnight."

"Goodnight, Mrs Alston." We watched them disappear down the corridor. I turned to Harper.

"I guess this is goodnight, then." I smiled, but ached inwardly.

"Goodnight, Nurse Chandler." He nodded and closed his stateroom door. I stood alone in the corridor, feeling rather like a fool, and not even close to being sleepy.

High atop the funnels the great-throated horns boomed out as the *Victoria* continued her inexorable course toward New York.

V

The crew of the *Victoria* served her passengers well and faithfully, and as a rule the Stoddard Lines were generous in return – pay, not so much, but in other amenities. One of those amenities was the crew pub. The 'Boar's Head' didn't measure up to the panache of any of the passenger pubs on the *Queen Victoria* but we didn't really care. It had its own special charm. For starters, it doubled as extra storage space on C Deck about as far aft as you could go – well beyond any passenger facilities on that deck –and there were exposed pipes and electrical carries running up and down the walls. I had either run into or backed into most of those on numerous occasions. The floor wasn't tiled or inlaid with expensive woods; rather, stained and sometimes pock-marked cement was underfoot. The bar itself was a scarred affair that looked like it had been knocked together out of a variety of shipping pallets, wooden boxes and cast-off items from the passenger lounges, which indeed it had, and the ventilation system was lacking, causing a constant pall of smoke to hang in the air. However, there was an ancient piano being pounded with gusto and an amiable buzz of conversation pervaded the pub, making it as friendly as any land-based establishment in Southampton. And right now, friendly was what I needed. I was annoyed and disturbed. Well, more annoyed than anything else. And I still wasn't ready to call it a night.

Senior Steward Bertie Evans was throwing darts and drinking beer when he saw me come in. "Oi, mate," he said jovially. "Haven't seen you in a while, but you are certainly a sight for sore eyes." He gave my clothes a once over. "Are we going to the theatre, your Grace?" I smiled weakly.

"I had dinner with our new PMO, then we had to search for a lost little boy. It was a long day." I stepped up, immediately banged my knee into the bar, cursed and ordered a sherry from the bartender. I then leaned against the bar massaging my knee as it was poured. Bertie threw his last dart and came over.

"Dinner with the sawbones two nights running?" He gave me a wink.

"Shut it, Bertie."

"As you say." He took a sip of beer. "Long day? Aye, that's for sure. An' it started for you with that poor bloke keeling over last night at dinner, eh?"

"I'd rather not talk about that, if it's all the same to you, Bertie."

"Suit yourself." The barman set the sherry out. "This one's on me," said Evans.

"Thanks." I took a delicate sip. I'd really felt like ordering something with a bit more heft to it, but it was late. I nodded toward the dart board. "You in?"

A broad smile crossed Bertie's face. "I think I can manage you all right." He picked up the darts. "You know what gets me, Nurse? All of these Americans worryin' about their stock market. All of the lords and ladies in old London town got a good pasting last month from the same thing, and I say best thing to ever happen to them, not that they've ever worked a day in their bloomin' lives. Livin' off the sweat of others, they are, and these Yanks, too. The way they carry on you'd think the whole world was comin' to an end."

"For some of them, it might well be," I said. Bertie laughed.

"More money than the Rothschilds, that's what they have. And I tell you how they got it – swindlin' the fine, hard workin' man and woman, just like they did to us back at home." He handed me my darts. "I've got no pity and no use for their lot. Let 'em try eatin' dollars when they can't buy food. Throw for first? Two out of three?"

"Fine." I set my glass down and took aim, then let fly quickly, one after another. The darts thudded home with devilish accuracy. Apparently I was more agitated than I realized, and Bertie's diatribe didn't help matters, either. Bertie added up the numbers and whistled.

"I won't even try to beat that. Go ahead."

"Thanks." I walked to the board and retrieved the darts.

"So, did that chap really die of a stroke like the paper says? Got what's comin' to him?"

"Christ, Bertie." I shook my head. "For your information, he was just a poor working stiff like you and me, on holiday. Probably took him a couple of years to save money for a First-Class passage. It would have been a once in a lifetime trip for him, poor man." Bertie momentarily looked abashed. I cast a glance around to see if anyone was listening. "All right, the truth is, he died of the plague. But don't tell anyone."

"Cor'," said Bertie, his eyes wide. I laughed.

"I'm fooling you. He really died of a stroke." Honestly, men were so gullible. I threw a dart. "Did you think otherwise?"

Bertie took a swallow of his beer. "I don't know. I was in there last night. And even on the other side of the room, it looked more like he was caught in a Hun gas attack at Wipers than anythin' else."

"You mean Ypres," I said, giving it the correct pronunciation.

"Ypres, sure, but Wipers is how we said it. I was in the trenches. I saw those gas attacks happen." He shivered. "Poor blighters, 'orrible way to die. And for what? To make the rich richer."

I threw my last dart. Hard. It smacked into the board and quivered.

Bertie spat his beer. "Nice grouping."

"I was thinking of someone." I drained my glass and set it down on the table a bit too hard.

"Poor fellow," said Bertie. I glared at him. He held his hands up, palms out. "Sorry, love."

"Grab my darts, will you? I'm going to the bar for another. Want anything?"

Bertie tapped his glass. "I'll have another." He held up his glass. "Harp. Thanks."

I made my way over to the bar and waited in the queue. The barman smiled at me.

"Good evening, Nurse," he said, setting his hands on the scarred bar top. "Hope your knee feels better. You need to mind the gap, as it were. What will you be having?"

"Another sherry, Josh. And I need a Harp for Mister Evans."

"Coming up." He set to work, talking as he went. "You know, I was just thinking how upset Mister Harvey would have been if he'd seen the foul up with that poor bloke who died in the salon last night. Happened in the First-Class lounge yesterday after we cleared the limit and started serving drinks."

My ears pricked up with interest. "What happened?"

He shrugged. "I was behind the bar and he was sitting at a table with two women – the same ones he was with last night at dinner when I was serving, he must have been quite the lady killer. Ha! No pun intended."

"You're horrible. None taken."

"Anyway, you know how people – mainly those poor parched Yanks - stand shoulder to shoulder at the bar once we get underway and out into international water?"

"I've seen them," I said. "They want to get the earliest start on their legal drinking that they can, having to do it illegally at home. Stupidest law I ever heard of."

"Right-o," said Josh. "So it's crowded as bloody hell, orders flyin' this way and that way. Like I said, I see this dapper man across the room seated with two women and he's waving to a steward, holding his drink in his hand. The steward goes over, the man gestures and points at the glass. The steward nods, makes as if to take the drink back, but the man apparently decides against it and sends him off. And then a few hours later, he dies." Josh finished topping off Bertie's beer. "I just thought it was odd, that's all. Poor sod."

"Who was the steward?" I asked. Josh shrugged.

"No idea. His back was to me and there were a lot of people in there."

"Thanks." I dropped some coins on the bar. "See you later."

When I came back to the table, Bertie was fiddling with the tailfeathers on one of his darts. "It's not going to fly any more true with you mucking about with it like that," I told him.

"I know, Nurse. But it makes me feel like I'm accomplishin' somethin'." He threw the dart and missed the board entirely. Bertie sighed. "How about a trick?" he asked me, taking out his handkerchief and a half crown.

"Watch this." He pushed the coin up into the handkerchief and waved his hand over it, then with a flourish removed the handkerchief and shook it out. The coin was gone.

"Bravo," I said. "Learning a new trade for after your retirement?"

Bertie laughed. "Not hardly. I do have some family in America, out in California. My oldest sister and her husband moved there after the War. I've got two nephews. Maybe someday I'll get to see the little lords." He pocketed the handkerchief and picked up the darts again. I suddenly thought that I really didn't need a second sherry.

"Bertie, do you mind if we call it a night?" I asked.

He gave a look to the clock on the wall. "Lord love a duck. Is that the time? An' me with early shift." He drained his mug. "Might as well give it up. I'm never going to beat you, Nurse."

"I throw syringes into people," I said. "It's a natural skill. Darts are nothing." I picked up my glass and took a last swallow.

"Right ho, your worship." Bertie gave me a wink and headed back to the bar as I knew he would, early shift or not, while I slipped out through the doors and headed for the crew lifts.

I had plenty of thinking to do, and it was shaping up to be a sleepless night.

I

t seems to me that sometimes, no matter how good a start a day gets off to, there is always something or someone standing in the wings ready to hurl a spanner into the works. (Or a monkey wrench into the gears, for you Yanks.) You get started bright and cozy, and the next thing you know, bang, that spanner comes flying out of nowhere and the world starts to come apart at the seams. That's the way it was on this Tuesday, October 29, 1929.

Despite increasingly rough seas, the morning began routinely enough as the *Queen Victoria* met the sunrise and started her second full day at sea. Massive breakfasts were served to the passengers, and let me tell you that the *Victoria's* breakfast menu is legendary, featuring everything from California figs in syrup to baked apples to Wiltshire and Virginia ham. (Honestly, there are nearly 75 items to choose from, none of which are kind to your waistline.) Programmes of today's entertainment (printed in the *Victoria's* print shop overnight) were distributed, and some of the hardier souls ventured up onto the Boat and Sports Decks to take their strolls in the cold salt air. Just another normal day at sea, the kind I've seen and enjoyed so many times throughout my career.

And then the bottom dropped out of the overcast gray sky.

The wireless room began passing urgent messages on to the well-heeled passengers, and soon afterward rumours began to float around the First and Second-Class smoking lounges. By lunch the rumours became a groundswell. By 13:00 hours the groundswell became a tidal wave. And by 14:00 hours Captain Webster had restricted access to the *Victoria's* wireless room and required the operators to post New York bulletins at Purser Collins's bank every quarter hour.

The wireless officers and their staff felt like they were under siege. It would have been an understatement to say that yesterday's worries had turned into today's troubles - a full blown panic was afflicting the First-Class passengers, and the cold grasping tentacles of fear were spreading throughout the ship to those less well-off but still acutely worried about losing what little they had. Not only were those unfortunates showing much less interest in the gaiety of shipboard life than they had previously, (the death of Thomas Morten was just one of those things, a sad incident already mostly forgotten) but so were the domestic staff traveling with most of them. Few, if any, of the maids, governesses and valets hoped to actually have a job once they and their apparently suddenly financially bereft employers landed at the Manhattan piers Saturday.

I had to agree with Doctor Harper here. I too am not a financial genius, but it appeared to me that an economic disaster of Biblical proportions was taking place on the stock exchange in New York. The *Victoria's* powerful Marconi radio set up suddenly took on a hitherto unknown importance. Requests to relay messages began arriving from other ships, asking that the *Victoria* please send along frantic sell orders from their passengers to Manhattan. A ship with a more powerful wireless transmitter is generally happy to provide a forwarding service, but today the wireless room made no promises; requests were taken but with the caveat of "when our passengers are done" coming first; bona-fide distress calls, of which fortunately there were none, automatically going to the top of the queue.

As the afternoon wore on, the crisis changed to panic, and the panic changed to pandemonium. Nervous passengers, many holding damp disintegrating radiograms in their sweaty hands, repeatedly asked the deck officers if the *Victoria* could go faster; yes, they were told, she could, but only in a life and death emergency; this, in the Captain's view, did not constitute one. Was Saturday still the earliest the *Victoria* was scheduled to dock in New York; yes, it was, maybe a bit earlier than scheduled, and yes, the officers agreed, the news was bad; yes, the wireless room was doing all it could to keep up with the increasing volume of traffic. No doubt some of the more astute passengers were wistfully recalling the flight almost a year earlier of the *Graf Zeppelin* from Europe to America in just over 111 hours, or Lindbergh's epoch-making flight in 1927 in just over 33 hours and wondering if air travel might indeed someday be faster than plowing through unforgiving waves in a ship, even a ship as grand as the *Queen Victoria*.

It was, all in all, a tumult never before seen or experienced by even the most seasoned officers.

And somewhere in the midst of all of this hue-and-cry, Harvey Wilson went missing.

It was the bellboys who noticed it first. They had been hand-delivering sheaves of radiograms to the luxurious suite on A Deck, but there was no answer to their knocks at the door. Disappointed – no answer meant no tip, and with an American millionaire inside, who knew what they might expect – they just slid the urgent messages under the door and went back for the next set.

Doctor Harper, Doctor Bratton and myself were being run ragged by upset First and Second-Class passengers. It was one call after another, without a break in between. Nothing life threatening, but plenty of anxiety and hyperventilating to go around, and that included the crew.

I paid a call on Chief Purser Collins shortly after 15:00. At the best of times, Collins was a man who laughed nervously and was very focused on his job, sometimes to the detriment of his own health. I was afraid today's events and demands were going to push him over the edge. He rubbed a hand across his fevered brow and tried to make order out of the chaos that was his desk while I tried to take his pulse and blood pressure.

"Mister Collins, please. Sit still."

"This is insane," said Collins. "Never, not once in all my years at sea, has there been a day like today. Passengers going crazy. Radio traffic at an all-time high. Constant posts and updates from New York." Collins reached for the cup of tea that had been delivered to him and took a sip, then brushed against a stack of notes on the edge of his desk, sending them toppling to the floor. Collins cursed, set down the cup and bent to pick them up, noticing among them a single *Queen Victoria* stationary envelope simply addressed to "Chief Purser, David Collins" in a simple type face. "What the bloody hell is this?" he said. I gave up trying to get his pulse. I'd have better luck seeking out Agatha and working on the Morten case.

"Why don't you open it and find out?"

Collins rocked back in his chair for a moment, then very precisely tore the end off the envelope and extracted the letter inside. He scanned it. "Bugger all," he said, handing it to me while he rang the bridge. In twenty seconds we were out of his office, heading topside.

Fifteen minutes later a grim group assembled in the Captain's conference room. Captain Webster and First Officer Jackson were joined by Quartermaster Carter, Mister Harvey, Mister Collins and Master-at-Arms Armstrong. Doctor Harper and I stood to one side. Webster was holding the letter in his hand.

"Genuine?" he asked Collins. The purser shrugged.

"I don't know, sir. I can't imagine that anyone would do this as a prank."

"I'd agree," said the Captain. "A suicide note from an American millionaire – my God, what's next?" The Captain folded the note and put it back in the envelope. "Has anyone actually seen Wilson today?" he asked. "I would think that of all of our passengers, he'd be in the forefront of the press at your bank, Mister Collins."

Collins shook his head. "Of course, there have been messages for him today. The boys have been delivering them to his stateroom non-stop."

"No response?" rumbled the Master-At-Arms, his normally jovial moon-like face intense.

"None that I've seen." Collins dabbed at the perspiration on his forehead.

"And you haven't gone and checked for yourself?" asked the Captain. "Either you or Mister Harvey?"

Harvey and Collins exchanged nervous glances. "No, sir," said Harvey. Captain Webster bristled, one of the most fearsome sights I've ever seen. The man could stare down a shark.

"Mister Collins, Mister Harvey – I realize we are having an unusual day here, but I really believe someone should go and check on Mr Wilson's stateroom."

"I'll do it," said Collins.

The Captain gave Collins a curt nod. "Then go. And leave this note out of any conversation you may have, for now."

"Yes, sir." Collins shot through the door, glad to be out. I couldn't blame him. The Captain turned back to the rest of us, his face a mixture of cold fury and indignation that this was happening on his ship.

"Fine. Not a word. Mister Jackson, Mister Carter, Mister Armstrong - quietly – and I mean quietly – search the ship. Back here in three hours." He looked at myself, Harper and Harvey. "You three stay a moment. That's all, gentlemen." Mister Jackson gave us a curious glance as he left the room, but said nothing. When the door had closed Captain Webster crossed his arms. "First Thomas Morten and now this." He looked at Harper. "Nothing new to report there?"

"I'm afraid not, sir," said Harper. I politely cleared my throat. The Captain looked at me.

"Yes, Nurse Chandler?"

I bit my lip. "I'm sorry, Captain, Doctor Harper. There is something new." A wave of anxiety rolled over me. "I completely forgot to tell you in all the tumult this morning. I was speaking with the bartender in the ship's pub late last night after Doctor Harper and I searched out the Alston boy - "

"A search last night? For a boy?" The Captain looked at Mister Harvey. "Did you know about this?"

"No, sir," Mister Harvey said with a frown directed at me.

"He had just become separated from his mother," said Doctor Harper. "We found him without difficulty."

"He wandered away on Sunday evening, too," I offered. Harper closed his eyes. The Captain grunted.

"Perhaps his mother should invest in a good quality British leash. Get on with your story, Nurse."

"Yes, sir. Josh, the bartender, told me that Morten apparently had some sort of issue with a drink served him in the Observation-Lounge before dinner."

"What kind of issue?" asked Harvey.

"Josh didn't know, he was busy pouring and mixing. He just said he noticed Mr Morten seated with two women, and he was talking to another steward like it was about his drink. The steward tried to take the drink back, but Mr Morten apparently decided to keep the drink after all. He and the women kept talking and drinking. Of course, an hour or so later Mr Morten died. Josh didn't know who the steward was, he only saw him from the back across the room."

"Mister Harvey?" said the Captain.

"Josh can be a bit thick sometimes, but he's still one of my best. I'll check it out." The Chief Steward left the stateroom. The Captain turned back to us.

"Anything else, Nurse?

"Just one tiny thing."

"Let me be the judge of that. What is it?" the Captain said.

If I didn't actually appear to be squirming on the outside, I certainly was on the inside. "Well, there's a passenger."

"Passenger? What passenger?"

I glanced over at Harper. "She's given us some insight into the death of Mr Morten."

"Murder of Mr Morten," corrected Harper.

The Captain's face was carved from granite. "And how did a passenger come to gain knowledge of this incident?"

"She was interested and she talked to me," I said.

"I see," said the Captain. "And is she an officer of the Crown? I'm going to suppose she is because of this preferential treatment." He eyed me. "And you're going to tell me she's not, aren't you?"

"Yes, sir."

"Well?"

"She's one of the First-Class passengers. Mrs MD Templeton."

The Captain's face was blank. "And this should mean something to me?"

"Well, no, sir," I said. "You just wanted to be kept apprised of the situation, and Mrs Templeton has offered her help. She was an apothecary assistant during the War."

The Captain's jaw tightened. "I suppose that makes her as qualified as anyone else." He stroked his beard. "If this was two centuries ago, I'd be sorely tempted to make the pair of you walk the plank. However, you say she sought you out, and is giving you help in your investigation." He clasped his hands behind his back. "In spite of my better judgement, I'm inclined to allow you to continue. But keep this quiet." He gave us both a cold eye. "I mean it."

"Sir," said Harper.

"Yes, sir," I replied.

"Very well, then." He handed the envelope containing the suicide note to Harper. "You might as well take charge of it as anyone else."

"Thank you, sir."

"Don't thank me, Doctor. You and Nurse Chandler seem to have become the de facto repository for the occasional dead man. Might as well add the missing to the list."

"Begging your pardon, Captain," I said. "But shouldn't that go to Mister Armstrong instead?"

What passed for a smile crossed the Captain's face. "Our Master-at-Arms is very good for the occasional professional gambler or inebriated passenger. I'm afraid suicides of American millionaires may be out of his depth."

"Yes, sir." I swallowed. "And murder?" Harper gave me a sharp look.

Captain Webster gestured at the porthole. "Look out there, Nurse. What do you see?"

"Ocean."

"Exactly. Big, empty ocean. Not where I would like to have a panic because someone is poisoning passengers and millionaires are apparently committing suicide. Doctor, I'm charging you and your merry crew with cleaning it up. Do I make myself clear?"

"Yes, sir," said Harper. "Quite."

II

'I've never had the dubious pleasure of being aboard a sinking ship or one that has struck an iceberg or been torpedoed but the way I was feeling right now must have been running a close second. One man apparently murdered, another man apparently missing and we were only about two days out of Southampton. I looked again at the suicide note as Doctor Harper and I walked away from the Captain's quarters.

"It's all so neatly typed out," I said. "Maybe that's how Americans do their farewell messages."

"Who knows how Americans think?" said Harper.

I held the note up to the light. "Miserly chap, too, using our ship's stationary. You'd think he'd have brought his own."

"Who knows what was going through his mind when he wrote it?" Harper took the paper from me and read aloud. "'It is with deep regret that I now understand how impossible it is to make up for the crimes I helped to perpetrate. My only desire is that the Wilson Foundation maintain honors to the Allied war dead through perpetuity. I am atoning for my sins in the only way I know.'" Harper folded the letter and put it back in the envelope. "Maybe he grew a conscience about his blood money after all."

"Maybe," I said. I opened a door marked 'Crew Only' and we passed down a staircase, then through another door to arrive in First-Class where the linoleum floor that was in crew quarters magically changed to a plush carpeting.

Harper shook his head. "I still find it hard to believe, though. A cheap suicide note from a millionaire who has everything."

"Perhaps you should say 'had everything,'" I replied. "Maybe he lost it all in the panic that's going on in New York right now." I paused, thinking. "Then, again," I began.

"What?"

"We're just working with the assumption that Mister Collins got the note today and it happened today. What if it was delivered yesterday?"

"What if it was?"

"What if it was, and he killed himself yesterday? A day before all those fortunes began disappearing on the New York Stock Exchange?" I pursed my lips. "Something to think about."

Harper shook his head. "And what if it was delivered yesterday and he did it today, and the New York events just spurred him?"

I cringed. "Well, there's that, Boss." I looked at him. "Sorry. Thought I was on to something." Another thought occurred to me. "Maybe he's hiding somewhere. Sometimes they feign it, you know, for attention."

"And sometimes they don't. In my practice I've seen notes that basically said nothing more than 'toodle-oo, dearie' and the next thing you know they're hanging from an attic joist."

"Charming." I bumped a knee into a poorly placed bench and cursed. Harper looked amused.

"You know, it's a wonder you can walk at all."

"Thanks, Boss." I rubbed my knee. "I apologize for not having the chance to tell you about what Josh told me regarding the drink incident Mr Morten was involved with in the First-Class Observation-Lounge."

"No apology needed. It's been a hectic day." We resumed walking, or limping, in my case. "But now that you've brought it up, what do you think?"

"I spent a lot of time on it last night after I found out," I told him. Too much, actually. I'm a girl who loves her sleep.

"And?"

"And one thing suggested itself to me – oh, blimey." I put out a hand and touched Harper's jacket sleeve. "Take a gander. Just what we don't need."

"What?" asked Harper.

"You're about to finally meet Mister Casey, purveyor of sometimes facts and all times gossip with the ship's newspaper."

Casey was only two inches taller than myself, but I felt both a physical and moral superiority over him. I gave him a brittle smile as he approached.

"Glad tidings and top of the day to you, Nurse." He looked at Harper. "You must be the new sawbones, heh heh."

"Doctor Leslie Harper, Principal Medical Officer," corrected Harper icily. Casey's face twitched and he doffed his fedora. Unlike the rest of the crew, he dressed in civvies – said it made it easier for people to talk with him. For the crew, the battered brown fedora made him easier to spot and avoid. Harper remained cold. "I understand Nurse Chandler gave you a statement from me regarding the unfortunate death of Thomas Morten."

"She did, she did, and a great help it was, too."

"In future, you will please take statements attributed to me only from me. Not from my nurse." I involuntarily raised an eyebrow. This was the former naval officer coming through in him. I knew he wasn't mad at me, but I assumed the look of the chided and downcast inferior anyway.

"Sure, sure," Casey grinned, showing tobacco stained teeth. "Morten's death was a terrible thing. But it happens, heh heh." He lit a cigarette. "I don't suppose either of you have seen our resident American millionaire today? I did an interview with Harvey Wilson yesterday – maybe you read it? - and I was hoping to follow up on it today, what with the wheels coming off in New York and all." He flicked ash on the carpet, a habit for which Mister Harvey had more than once threatened to bodily toss him overboard.

"I haven't had the pleasure of meeting him yet," said Harper. "Though Nurse Chandler did read me the interview you mentioned. Quite a - " he looked at me " – what do the Americans call it? A bulletin?"

"A scoop," I corrected him. Casey beamed.

"A scoop," he repeated. "Yes, I rather think it was." He took a deep drag. "And with what I hear is going on in New York today, I thought a follow up 'scoop' would just fit the bill, heh heh."

"Well, we haven't seen him," I said truthfully. Casey shrugged, dropping ash again.

"I know this ship better than anyone," he boasted. "He can't elude me forever."

"And why would he want to?" I added.

"Right-o. A tenner says I run him to ground before first dinner seating this afternoon." He touched the brim of his hat. "Nice to meet you, Doctor. Nurse, always a pleasure." He crushed out his cigarette on the wainscoting, let it fall to the carpet and turned away, then turned back again. "Say, I've got another question."

"Lucky us," I said.

Casey raised his eyebrows. "None of your ginger there, Nurse." He rubbed his chin. "No, I heard someone say they thought there was some famous author on board the *Victoria*." He looked at us. "Know anything?"

I shrugged. Harper appeared perplexed.

"What kind of author?" he asked.

"I don't know," said Casey. "An author. You know, someone who writes books."

"Like the books in the children's playroom?" I said. "That would be more your type. I think an interview with an intellectual author might put an undue strain on you, Mister Casey."

"That's right," Harper added. "Between the stress of covering what's going on in New York and talking with a children's book author, I might have to recommend you for medical leave."

"Funny." He glared at us for a moment, but I've been glared at by the best and it didn't faze me at all. "All right," he finally said. "You don't want to help, that's fine. I'll find this children's author and interview him myself."

"Can't wait to read it," I said. Casey turned and stumped away. "Sod off," I said under my breath. Doctor Harper pulled out a handkerchief and very delicately picked the cigarette off the carpet.

"Well, he was everything you said and less." He dropped the cigarette into a nearby ash stand.

"Much less, I'm afraid. May I?" I indicated the envelope still in Harper's hand. He turned it over without a word. "Thanks. I'm going to go see Mrs Templeton. We've got a while before the search party comes back. I'll join you on the bridge later."

From time to time, as we travel along our paths, something will happen that affects us in ways we never imagined. Obviously, the War and my husband's death were such mile markers, but there was another that reached out to me. It had to do with Agatha, and believe what you will, when it was over and done with I came out feeling she was, in truth, a very strong woman.

It was in December of 1926. Agatha Christie simply vanished from her home in Berkshire and remained missing for ten days before being found at a hotel in Harrogate. It turned out she and her soon to be ex-husband had quarreled, he'd gone off to his mistress and she'd just left. When she was discovered, she had registered under her husband's mistresses' surname – a move that impressed me to no end. The episode was national news, even reaching the United States, and over 1,000 police officers scoured the English countryside for her.

I didn't expect her to bring it up with me, and I certainly wasn't going to ask. She was getting married again, seemed very happy and I saw no need to pry into her past life. I have to admit that part of me was curious to hear her version of events, but I knew it was going to stay unanswered, like the apparently eternal questions of did Richard III murder the princes in the Tower and the identity of Jack the Ripper.

When she let me into her stateroom, I declined an offer of tea and got right to the point.

"Really?" asked Agatha. Her face betrayed no emotion. "Gone missing?"

"Sometime overnight or this morning, I guess," I said, looking around. Her stateroom was not as large as the suite that had been occupied by Wilson, but it was still lavishly decorated and turned out. The woman occupying it suited the furnishings, I thought. Civil, polite, charming – everything you would expect from a lady. I found later that she had come from a wealthy, upper-middle class upbringing.

Agatha moved her writing materials to the side of the table. "What do you think?"

"I think it rather odd that an American millionaire disappears just as the financial world is coming apart in New York."

"Perhaps not that odd. A purser told me today that the *Leviathan* reported two passengers overboard during last Thursday's battle on Wall Street." She reached for her tea cup. "He says they weren't recovered."

"I wonder if they just did it on a whim, or left a note?" I produced the envelope. "Ours left a note."

"Did he?" She put her cup down. "Let's have a look." I handed the envelope to her. She extracted the brief missive, then read it twice before replacing it in the envelope and handing it back to me.

"What do you think?" I asked her. She gave a slight lift to her shoulders.

"The ribbon on the typewriter was fresh. But the keys need cleaning. Look here where the 'o' is partially obscured with ink at the bottom, each time it's used. And the lowercase 'w' jumps just a bit higher in the line of type.

Putting that aside, the language seems – stilted. Do you know what this Wilson Foundation is?"

"A non-profit, I believe they call it. Continually self-funding through investments, interest payments and the like. Like the note says, it exists to honor the Allied war dead in France through time immemorial."

Agatha took a sip of tea. "I wonder who runs it?"

"I think he ran it himself."

"Quite the ego." Agatha mused for a moment. "I take it that Mr Wilson's disappearance is not yet public knowledge?"

"No. Just you and I, the Captain and senior officers, the doctor, Chief Purser and Chief Steward." I frowned. "It sounds like a lot, but everyone except you is crew and we're under strict silence orders from the Captain."

"I assume there's a search going on now for him?"

"Yes, of course," I said. "Stem to stern, as they say."

"And this pithy remark about atoning for his sins," said Agatha. "I wonder if that's supposed to be related to the recent, less palatable news about him and his deal with the Kaiser."

"I'm sure that's what we're meant to believe," I said.

"A wealthy American helped kill all of those fine young men," Agatha shook her head. "It was a hard story to read in the papers these past few weeks. I still have difficulty with it."

"'Politics makes strange bedfellows,'" I said. "Or something along those lines."

"No, you have it right, Maeve." Agatha sighed. "Charles Dudley Warner. He was, fittingly enough, an American writer from some forty years ago." She resumed her tea. "Was he travelling alone?"

I gave her a grim smile. "You saw what I saw at dinner. I'm sure he was about as alone as a widowed American millionaire could ever hope to be."

"Hmmm," said Agatha, enumerating as she wrote on a fresh sheet of paper. "Widower. Traveling alone. Outrageous fortune paid for in blood by American – and British and French as well – soldier's lives. Typed suicide note with the lower case 'w' out of registration and the lower case 'o' partially blacked, and very archaic word use. Very liberally endowed memorial foundation that is designed to live on after him."

"And he disappears before the stock market begins its fall today in New York," I added. She gave me a sharp look.

"How do you know that?"

I felt superior. "Just deduction. Mister Collins – he's the Chief Purser – said that the bell boys had been delivering radiograms to Mr Wilson's suite all morning, with no reply."

"Has his suite been checked today?" She gazed at me with a level view. "That seems a very elementary thing to look into, don't you think?"

"It's being checked into right now." I felt a blush coming over my cheeks. Maybe my deduction wasn't that great. "Everyone just assumed the worst right from the start, that he'd jumped ship as his fortunes ebbed away on the market." Agatha reached across and patted my hand.

"Never assume," Agatha smiled at me. "There's always a reason behind everything. Where else would I get my motives? How else would Monsieur Poiroit solve his mysteries?"

I nodded. "I guess there's nothing to do but wait until the search is over and we hear about his suite."

"Unfortunately, yes. Remember what Sherlock Holmes said – 'It is a capital mistake to theorize before one has data.'" She settled back in her chair. "You know, part of *The Man in the Brown Suit* takes place on board a ship." Agatha looked around her stateroom. "Not as big and fine as this ship, of course."

"May I?" I indicated the chair opposite her.

"Of course."

I sat down. "This ship may be big, but there is one area where it lacks in the fine department. Our shipboard newspaperman, Mister Casey. He's somehow got the scent that there is a famous author on board."

"Oh, dear." Agatha leaned forward.

"Yes, he questioned Doctor Harper and myself about it just a little while ago. I'm still not quite sure how I did it, but this should make you feel better. By the time Mister Casey walked away I had him certain beyond the shadow of a doubt that he was on the trail of a famous author of children's books." I smiled at Agatha. "Who also happens to be male."

She laughed. "The only truly famous children's author I know of any note is AA Milne, but I haven't seen him aboard. Nor Pooh, Piglet, Eeyore or Christopher Robin."

I bit my lip. "And one more thing. The Captain knows passenger Mrs MD Templeton is assisting us. He gave it his blessing."

"Hmm." She thought a moment. "I can't see any harm coming of it and I suppose one needs the Captain's blessing." Agatha gave me a wink. "As long as it's you sitting at his table and not me."

"Nothing to worry about from that quarter," I said. "The Captain gets his table duties out of the way first night out. He detests sitting with passengers, though he always makes a good show of it. Most of the time he takes his meals on the bridge or in his quarters."

"A pragmatic man," said Agatha.

"Very," I said. "I will take a cup of tea if you don't mind, Mrs Christie."

"Something else on your mind?" She poured and handed me a cup.

I nodded. "You're a successful woman in an unusual field."

"Mystery writing? Oh, there are others in my field. Mary Roberts Rinehart, for one. She's American. And then there's Dorothy Sayers, with her Lord Peter Wimsey character. Very popular." She laughed lightly. "I've often wondered what would happen should Wimsey and Poirot ever meet."

"It would be quite entertaining, I imagine." I sipped my tea. "I want to be a doctor. But there are times that goal seems in another universe."

Agatha smiled. "Don't give up. The world is changing. My advice to you is to keep after your dreams. Did you know that my first book got the boot by six publishers and languished for five years before finally being printed?"

I smirked. "I'll bet I know six publishers who are kicking themselves right about now."

"One can hope," said Agatha with a laugh. "Do you have children, Maeve?"

"No. My husband died before we could start a family." Agatha reached over and put her hand over mine.

"I'm so sorry. I was just thinking what a great mum you'd make."

"Thank you." I pushed some memories out of the way. "Do you have children?"

"Yes. I have a daughter, Rosalind. She's about ten years old. Smart as a whip. I don't have a photograph of her with me, but I assure you, she's darling."

I took a sip of tea. "Does she read your books?"

"Oh, good heavens, no," said Agatha. "I'm afraid they are a bit over her reach right now. She enjoys Winnie-the-Pooh. However, rest assured that when I write *Hercule Poirot and the Case of the Pilfered Jam Jar,* she'll be first in line to purchase."

I laughed. "With a title like that, so will I." I put down my cup. "I just bought *The Mystery of the Blue Train* when were in Southampton, before we left," I said. "Cost me seven and six. I can't wait to get into it."

"Thank you," said Agatha. "Truthfully, I'm not quite certain I like the way the book turned out, but Monsieur Poirot will take you for what I hope is a lovely ride." She picked up her pen and poised it above the paper again. "Now, what else can you tell me about this Mr Wilson?" she asked. "And let's not forget poor Mr Morten, either."

So I told her everything you already know, leaving nothing out.

I had never seen Mister Jackson or Mister Carter looking so glum in the time I'd served with them; in point of fact they resembled Anne Boleyn and Catherine Howard awaiting a gentle discussion about their future job security with Henry VIII – otherwise known as Captain Webster, who was in fine fettle. The fact they were both clad in wet rain slickers did nothing for their appearance either.

"Are you absolutely certain?" asked the Captain. Carter nodded. We were standing at the back of the bridge, and the few officers on duty now as opposed to when we got underway paid us no heed. The Stoddard Lines expects its employees to keep their minds on their work. Unless the Captain barked at us, we existed for nothing more.

"We've been fore to aft and port to starboard and G Deck to Sports Deck and back again. Not a sign of Harvey Wilson. All we found was this caught in a railing on the Boat Deck at the Lifeboat Ten station. It was snagged just inside the aft davit for the boat and down low. We almost missed it." Carter held out a piece of dark wool fabric, maybe one inch by three inches. The Captain took it in his hand.

"Feels like maybe it's part of a man's overcoat," he said. He handed it to Harper, who then handed it to me. I rubbed the nap between my thumb and forefinger.

"Definitely an overcoat. Expensive fabric, sir."

"We thought so too, Nurse," said Jackson. "Anyway, there you have it. Mister Armstrong has a few final places he's checking now, but it's our belief that Harvey Wilson is no longer aboard the *Queen Victoria*."

"Bloody hell," murmured Harper. Collins looked like he was going to faint.

"If that man was on this ship, we'd have certainly found him," said Jackson. "We looked in all the usual stowaway places, even the ones he'd have been too large to fit inside."

Captain Webster gazed through the fog-streaked bridge windows, past the foremast to the very bow of the ship as it ploughed ahead through the Atlantic. Large cold drops of rain were thumping into the thick glass. "Well, search it again."

"Yes, sir." The Quartermaster and First Officer turned away and left the bridge. If they had any qualms about plodding the length of the *Victoria* again in a heavy driving rain, they kept their thoughts to themselves.

"What about his suite, Mister Collins?" asked the Captain.

"Nothing out of the ordinary, sir. It appears perfectly normal. Of course, I can't tell if anything is really amiss, having no idea of what was there to begin with." He cleared his throat. "Captain, if I may be dismissed, I'm sure the traffic still hasn't let up at my office." He looked at the clocks on the wall. "It's nearly time for the market to be closing in New York, thank God."

"Go."

"Thank you, sir." Collins disappeared as if he'd been turned into a wraith. The Captain turned to Harvey.

"And what did you discover about the incident with Mr Morten at the First-Class observation-lounge?"

"Not much more than Nurse Chandler told us earlier, I'm afraid," Harvey said.

"Not very satisfactory, Mister Harvey."

"Sir."

Captain Webster rubbed a weary hand across his eyes. He frowned. "What a day. I hesitate to ask how much worse it can possibly get." The rain was now increasing in strength and intensity. The wipers had been switched on, raking across the glass with a monotonous regularity, pushing the cold water across the windows. The clearview screens were spinning at maximum rpm to provide a completely rain free circle to look through as well. "Throw in some nice October rain, too," said the Captain. "It just doesn't get any better than this." He looked at Harvey. "I'll be taking my evening meal here on the bridge, Mister Harvey. Doctor, if you'd like, you may anchor my table tonight. I'm sure the passengers sitting with you will be thrilled." He cast a glance in my direction. "Probably more thrilled if Nurse Chandler joins you again."

"Thank you, sir," I said demurely, but not without reservation. Sweet fanny adams, but my meagre wardrobe was taking a beating from all of these evening invitations.

An hour later I was in the ship's hospital, finishing a run through our medical supplies. The seas had picked up even more, and topside the rain was coming down in lashings. Doctor Harper was doing what the Americans would call a land office business in sea sick remedies, which, truth be told, was more a placebo than anything else. In my experience, either one got *mal de mer* or one didn't, and if one was handed something they believed would cure – and were given some useful knowledge like avoiding spicy foods and not trying to do needlepoint – they'd usually pull through with no ill effects.

"Expecting a rough night?" Doctor Bratton put down the copy of the *Lancet* he'd been idly flipping through.

"I hope not. Sunday night was about as rough as any and I'd just as soon not repeat it."

"I'm sure our passengers would agree with you."

Even the ones who are missing, I thought. Doctor Bratton, like almost everyone else on the ship, was blithely unaware of the disappearance of Harvey Wilson. "I'm sure they would, Doctor." I sighed. "I hope no one breaks anything. I'd have to do reports. I hate doing reports."

"They do tend to cut into your private time," said Bratton.

I bristled at that. "And what is that supposed to mean? That I'm not allowed private time?"

"Oh, no, far from it." Bratton's lean face was expressionless. "It's just been remarked you seem to be spending a lot of time with Doctor Harper."

"Been remarked by whom? DuMont?"

"And others."

"DuMont is a weasel. I tell you, Harvey needs to give him more to do, like polishing all the tea pots or something. Twice a day and three times on Sunday." I crossed my arms. "I'm the chief nurse. He's the PMO." I gave an indignant sniff. "I think that being seen together from time to time would only be natural."

"Even dinner? Rather, dinners?" Bratton said, correcting himself with what passed for a smile from him.

I drew myself up to my full height, which again wasn't saying much. "How I choose to spend my off hours is strictly up to me." I thought a moment. "Who said something besides DuMont?"

"The Chief," said Bratton. My eyes widened.

"Chief Duncan? I thought all he had eyes for were his engines and boilers."

"Apparently not."

"Really?" My interest was piqued. "And he said something to you?"

"Oh, not directly - more in the Chief's offhand way, you know." Bratton cleared his throat, stood and assumed the Chief's lanky droop. "Burning the fuel oil is cleaner, to be sure, and there's not a soul misses the old black gangs shoveling the fire, but you know there's times I prefer the heft of a lump of Newcastle coal in my hand, and how's Nurse Chandler getting on with the new doctor?" he said in a fair imitation of the Chief Engineer's Scottish burr.

"Me, the black gangs and a lump of coal in the same sentence," I said. For those who have never spent time deep below decks in the very bowels of a ship, the black gangs were the stokers who, before the advent of the oil-fired furnaces, used to shovel coal into the voracious maws of the furnaces that heated the boilers every single minute of every day and night we were at sea. The coal dust turned them darker than midnight, and the brutally searing heat and working conditions made them tougher and meaner than Lucifer himself. "Coming from an engineer, I suppose I should be flattered." I looked at Bratton. "You've a gift for mimicry, Doctor. Sometimes I think you're really human under there somewhere."

"I honestly hope not," said Bratton, picking up the magazine again. The telephone rang and I picked it up.

"Surgery," I said.

"Quartermaster Carter here. With the Captain's compliments, would you please report to his conference room? Thank you." He rang off, leaving me holding the receiver.

"More sea sick First-Class passengers?" Bratton peered at me over the magazine.

"Yes," I said. "That's exactly what it is." I gave Bratton a smile. "Impressionist and a psychic. You should get onto the music hall." I left him there and hurried off.

While I normally enjoyed getting outside on deck as much as I could for the sun and wind, I was thankful today for the inside staircase entrance to the officer's quarters, bridge and chartrooms. Looking like a drowned rat and not knowing what I was going to wear to dinner was a combination I just wasn't very interested in trying. I rapped on the door and was admitted to the sanctum.

"Thank you, nurse," said the Captain. I glanced up at Harper. He was intent on the Captain, who was holding up a piece of paper.

"This is a radiogram we received fifteen minutes ago from the *Adriatic*. She is about ten hours behind us, following our track."

"Are they in trouble? Do they need our help?" Jackson asked.

"No, Mister Jackson. They haven't arrived at the leading edge of the storm and won't for some hours. It's still calm for them. And anyway, our met tells me that it's breaking up, so that's one less problem we'll have to deal with after a while." He shook his head. "No, this is something else." The Captain sighed. "Mister Carter, Mister Jackson, Mister Armstrong – thank you for your efforts in searching the ship. As you surmised, Harvey Wilson was not on board." We all exchanged glances. The Captain paused a moment, then continued. "In point of fact, he has not been on board the *Queen Victoria* for at least the past ten hours."

"I beg your pardon, sir?" said Mister Armstrong.

"He has not been with us, because he – or rather, his body – has been with the *Adriatic*. They fished him out of the sea."

IV

During the late War, I'd seen a lot of people die. While the great majority of them were young men taken too soon, there were also a few who decided that ending their lives on their own terms was preferable to the anonymity of being blown to atoms by German shell fire. To this day I remain undecided on who held the moral or bravery high ground between the two.

"So it was a suicide," Doctor Harper said quietly.

Armstrong shook his head sadly. "Pity the bloke. Drowning's a hard way to go."

Mister Jackson looked at the Captain. "Nothing more to be done, I suppose, sir."

"Are they sure it's him, sir?" I asked, still not believing a man like Harvey Wilson would kill himself.

The Captain nodded. "He was a well-known man on both sides of the Atlantic, nurse. And he was carrying a few of his business cards."

"Anything else?" asked Dr. Harper.

"A few tenners so sodden they couldn't be prised apart. Some loose change. His room key."

"The scrap of overcoat we found?" I said. The Captain pursed his lips.

"He was dressed in evening wear, Nurse. No overcoat. Thank you, gentlemen." Armstrong saluted and left the room. "Mister Carter, if you wouldn't mind checking on the helm, then notifying Mister Harvey and Mister Collins."

"Sir."

"Mister Jackson, stay just a moment, please."

The Captain waited until the door closed, then took off his cap and scratched his head, looking at his First Officer. "Mister Jackson, there's something you need to know and I apologize for telling you now on top of our latest bad news." The Captain looked at us, then back at Jackson. "Thomas Morten didn't die of a stroke. He was murdered, whether accidentally or on purpose, we don't know."

"I see." Mister Jackson's face was impassive. The man was cold as mackerel on ice. I felt it was a dead certainty that someday he'd command a vessel of his own. "Perfectly understandable," he said. "No need to panic the passengers."

"Exactly so." The Captain looked at Harper. "Doctor? Will you please take it from here?"

"Yes, sir." Harper turned to Jackson. "Mr Morten ingested a lethal dose of aconitine. It's an alkaloid with rather unpleasant side effects, as you noticed."

"I noticed," said Jackson. "And you have no suspects?"

"None," said Harper. Jackson nodded.

"Who else knows?"

"Other than the four of us, only Doctor Bratton, Mister Harvey and Reedy, the dispenser. He did the analysis of the dead man's wine glass. And a passenger."

"Passenger, Doctor?"

"Mrs MD Templeton. She approached Maeve and offered to lend her expertise to the case. She was apparently an apothecary's assistant in the War."

Jackson turned to the Captain. "Surely this is rather unusual, sir? Involving a passenger?"

"We've not the resources of Scotland Yard, Mister Jackson. If the nurse and doctor believe she can help, I'm willing to let her try."

Jackson clamped his mouth. "Yes, sir." The Captain looked at us.

"And you managed to keep Casey in the dark about Mr Morten. Impressive, Doctor." I was actually the one who kept Casey in the dark, I thought, but what the hell. "I'm not sure how long we can keep Mr Wilson's death a secret, though."

"Why bother?" Jackson asked. "The *Adriatic* knows. As far as we know, he just committed suicide by jumping in the ocean. We have the suicide note. With what's been going on in New York, I'm sure it won't come as a major surprise to the passengers."

The Captain nodded. "No doubt you're correct, Mister Jackson." The telephone jangled and the Captain picked it up. "Captain Webster. Yes, thank you, Doctor Bratton." He rang off and looked at me. "It seems you're wanted by a passenger – a Clara Alston. She pushed the button for a steward from her stateroom. He says when he got there she seemed in distress and only spoke through the closed door."

"Do you need me to go with you?" asked Harper. I shook my head.

"No, but thank you. Dinner may have to wait." I hurried from the room.

No rest for the wicked, that's my motto. Someday I'll have it inscribed on my headstone, if I live that long.

Muffled voices answered my rap on Clara's stateroom door. I heard the shuffling of feet and then a clang as if two pieces of metal were knocked together, then the door opened a crack and a bloodshot eye peered out at me.

"What do you want?" said a truculent voice.

"I'm Nurse Maeve Chandler. I was called to the stateroom by Mrs Alston."

"Oh, you were, now?" The door opened a bit wider. "There ain't nothing wrong with her." By his accent, an American and not a very pleasant one at that. But I'd been warned. I could see Clara seated on the edge of the bed.

"I'll decide that, sir, if you don't mind." I pushed against the door. "Let me in or I will call the Master-at-Arms."

"All right, don't need no flatfoot." The door swung slowly inward to reveal a thin man with a hard pinched face. His hair was brilliantined and brushed back off of his forehead in the style of the day. A pencil-thin moustache above thin lips helped contribute to the over-all gruesome effect – like something out of a Madame Tussaud's waxworks nightmare. He slid a stubby thumb beneath a suspender. "Name's Frank Alston. Clara's my wife. What do you need?"

"I'm not making this call for what I need, Mr Alston. I'm making it for what Mrs Alston needs." He turned and looked at her. For the first time, I saw Bradley hiding behind her.

"She don't need nothing. She called you without my say so. Waited until I was in the john to do it, too."

I ignored him and walked over to Clara, kneeling on the floor in front of her. "Is it the baby?"

"The ship keeps moving. I vomited until I couldn't anymore, then I tried to lay on the bed, but it didn't help." Her face was pale. I touched a hand to her cold cheek, then looked up at her husband – or what passed for her husband.

"She's dehydrated. She needs fluids. I'm going to take her down to the surgery." He shrugged, finally conceding the point.

"As long as she quits her moaning, I don't care." He gestured at Bradley. "You might as well take the brat, too. I'm going out tonight to do some big business and I don't know what time I'll be back to the cabin."

"I hadn't planned on leaving him here, thank you very much," I said with as much coldness as I could muster. What a conceited shite. "Clara – Mrs Alston – can you walk all right or do I need to ring for a chair?"

"I'll walk. Just please take me out of here." She turned to her son. "Bradley, get your jacket. We are going to go for a little turn."

"Don't make it on deck," said Prince Charming. "I hear the kid yowls like a cat in heat."

"Really, Mr Alston," I said. I put out a hand for Bradley. "Come along with me, Master Bradley." I opened the front door, then put out my free arm to help balance Clara. "I'll send a steward back for her necessaries."

"The only necessary she's going to need is me," said Alston. "If tonight goes the way I expect it to, we'll be in the money."

"Gambling is frowned upon on this ship, Mr Alston," I said.

"I didn't say anything about gambling, sister." He looked at Bradley with disdain. "Maybe I'll even buy the whelp his first real suit. Get him out of those sissy limey shorts." I guided Clara and Bradley through the open stateroom door. "I'm telling you, my ship is coming in. We'll be rich before we ever reach New York, and you'll be sorry for leaving me, you little British - "

With great satisfaction I slammed the door in his face.

"Rat bastard he was, too," I said to Harper. "Sorry about the language, sir, but that's the only way to describe him." Harper and I were sitting at a table in the Boar's Head against the back wall. The battered piano was in full swing and the bar was standing room only; once the novelty of having one of the ship's officers partaking of the festivities had worn off, no one had really given us a second glance.

"I could tell you had something that needed saying all the way through dinner," said Harper. I gave him a smile.

"Did I forget to tell you that rule? Don't speak ill of a passenger in front of other passengers?" I took a sip of my sherry. "Anyway, Doctor Bratton started her on fluids and put her to bed. Young Master Bradley was occupied with some storybooks and toys I had sent down from the First-Class children's playroom." I looked around the bar. "Do you really believe Harvey Wilson killed himself by jumping overboard? I let Mrs Templeton know about his body being recovered. She didn't seem surprised."

"And what did she think about the rest of it? The suicide note, for instance?"

"She pointed out that the keys for the lower case 'o' and 'w' had some oddities. I guess we could search for that machine on board, but if Mr Wilson was murdered, I think that typewriter is at the bottom of the Atlantic now." I frowned. "I should have asked Mister Collins if there was one in his stateroom. I'll have to do that in the morning." I blew out my cheeks. "If we just had a witness to confirm that Harvey Wilson went over the side of his own accord."

Harper shrugged. "Suicides being by and large a purely personal statement, there are rarely witnesses. Do you believe it's a suicide?"

"No. He had to be missing before the market came apart today. He could certainly never have jumped from the ship in broad daylight without being seen. It had to have been last night. And why would he kill himself last night? He had no knowledge of what today would bring." I drummed my fingers on the table. "Plus that article he did for Casey. It wasn't exactly doom and gloom. It was measured and precise – the way I would think someone with his money would react."

Harper swirled his gin and tonic. "You're absolutely right. I've been doing some investigating on my own. I took the opportunity to have a little communication with the *Adriatic's* doctor before dinner tonight. Our chief Marconi operator – what's his name?"

"Cameron."

"Mister Cameron moved us to a more discreet frequency so we didn't have half of the Atlantic Ocean listening in." Harper took a swallow of his drink. "Bloody good thing, too."

I leaned forward intently. "What?"

Harper set his drink down. "First," he said, enumerating with a finger, "there was practically a complete absence of sea water in Wilson's lungs. You know what that means?"

"He was already dead before he went into the water." I bit my lip. "Which means he struck something as he fell, or possibly tripped and was struck by something before he fell." My eyes widened. "Or was struck by something held by someone before he fell."

Harper nodded. "You're correct on all counts, unfortunately. The *Adriatic's* PMO says there is a visible bruise at the base of his neck. He didn't offer any thoughts on how it got there. Wilson could have certainly slipped and fallen backward, breaking his neck. Plenty of things out on deck to trip on, especially at night." He frowned. "But that wouldn't solve the problem of how he went overboard. He should have been found dead on the deck if he tripped, not overboard."

I brightened. "That piece of fabric Mister Carter found torn off in the railing. Since Mr Wilson wasn't wearing a coat, maybe it came from the killer's overcoat," I said. "So that would mean we would only have to - "

"Examine every single overcoat on board for a tear that matches. And supposing it hasn't already been thrown overboard, and even if we could do that, do you seriously think anyone is going to say 'Yes, that's mine, and I tore it tossing a man over the rails?'" Harper frowned. "It's just like Morten. No witness to how it happened, but it happened."

"His neck was broken before he hit the water," I said. "That's the key. But as you said, how was it broken?" I took a sip of my drink. "We can't just assume foul play when he left that note behind. Maybe he changed his mind at the last minute but had leaned out past the point of no return and fell anyway. There's just no telling."

"Walking on an unfamiliar deck at night is dangerous," agreed Harper. "The railing on the Boat Deck is high enough to prevent anyone falling over by accident –he'd have to lean out over it and let go." He thought a moment. "So we have three scenarios. He either jumped and broke his neck on the way down, he leaned out too far, lost his nerve but slipped over and broke his neck on the way down – pretty much the same as the first scenario - or someone else broke his neck for him and then heaved him over the rails."

"If we're following the murder route, then I think that's a reasonable assumption," I said. "Having him appear to commit suicide by jumping overboard makes perfect sense. Except by pure chance the body's found, examined by a competent doctor, and determined to have been dead before going into the water."

Harper finished his drink. "The evidence certainly appears to point toward a murder and not a suicide, but I just can't believe it. Maybe he hit something like the rudder after he was in the water? That would certainly account for his broken neck."

"That lifeboat station is too far forward for him to have reached the rudder. And if he had drifted back, the rudder wouldn't have been what killed him. That far astern he'd have gone directly into the path of the propellers, been sucked under, and there wouldn't have been anything to find. Or not much of anything, at any rate. I saw that happen once several years ago. It was ghastly." I screwed my eyes shut at the thought. "And we haven't even considered this: if he was alive when he went over the side, he would have certainly made some sort of cry on the way down, suicide or not. It would have been instinctive, I think – not that he would have been heard over the wind on the Boat Deck."

"Which means – again, maybe – that he was killed before he was pitched over." Harper rubbed his forehead. "If we just had a witness."

"Doctor Harper, as you well know from our brief sojourn last night, after dark the Boat Deck and the Sports Deck are the most inhospitable places on the ship. It's cold and it's windy. Who would go out there?" Except couples who might want some privacy for a romantic stroll, I thought bitterly. "It would take some sort of inducement, I should imagine."

"And so it did," said Harper. "For once I get to drop the bombshell. Those ten pound notes the *Adriatic's* doctor found on the body? They turned out to be folded over a small slip of paper that looked like it had been snipped from a telegraph form. He didn't see it until they'd dried enough to tease them open. The words 'Boat Deck, nine tonight, come alone' were printed on it in pencil."

"Lord love a duck!" I exclaimed. "So someone wanted him topside last night, and he went. I wonder who?"

"That's the question, I guess." Harper slumped back in his chair. "The *Adriatic* is hauling him on to New York for us. Captain Webster said we weren't turning around to go pick up a body, even if it was one of our First-Class passengers."

"For which I'm certain Mister Harvey will be eternally grateful to you. He only has so much refrigerated storage to go around." I pondered a moment. "I need to tell all of this to Mrs Templeton."

"You're putting a lot of work onto that poor woman," said Harper.

"She says she's turning the facts over in her mind. I have faith in her," I said, thinking that Harper would too if he knew who she was. A sudden thought occurred to me. "What about Mister Casey? He doesn't know all of the details, does he?"

Harper rolled his eyes. "Hardly. As far as he's concerned, Harvey Wilson slipped and fell overboard. We're leaving it at that. No need to go into the apparent suicide coverup." He smiled. "Maybe I'm finally getting one step ahead of you."

"Don't flatter yourself, Doctor. I'm a woman, you know."

"And very fetching you look tonight, if I haven't already said."

I felt a slow blush creep over me. "Why, thank you, Doctor. That's the first non-murderous thing you've said to me."

Harper laughed, crinkling up the corners of his eyes. "The table talk tonight was pretty dull, wasn't it? All about the stock market. Everyone seems to have forgotten Mr Morten." He took a drink. "I'm sure it will be more lively tomorrow after Casey's paper comes out."

"I'm sure it will be," I said.

Harper laughed again, a warm and pleasant sound. "It's amusing, isn't it? A week ago I was a landlocked doctor, and now I'm having a night cap with a beautiful nurse and wondering why we have two dead bodies on our hands."

"Only one," I corrected him. "Mr Wilson is aboard the *Adriatic*." I smiled. "But thank you for the compliment."

I

You'd think that with everything going on my nerves would be enough on edge that I'd find it impossible to fall asleep. *Au contraire*, as Mister DuMont would say. When my head hit the pillow I was down for the count. Not even my missing cabin mate, who was notoriously noisy when coming home for the night, could have wakened me. It's no surprise that I opted for hot black American coffee the next morning instead of tea; I even considered giving myself an intravenous drip of the stuff. I was beat.

After Harper and I had called it a night – and once again, to my chagrin, that's all it ended up being – I placed a call to Agatha's room. It should be noted here that the *Victoria* is very modern in that First-Class passengers have telephones in their staterooms and suites, a very innovative feature for the time. Agatha didn't seem to mind that I had awakened her, and when I passed on the news about the note that had been found on Wilson's body by the *Adriatic's* PMO she fired off several questions, none of which I could answer. I also filled her in on what Harper and I had conjectured about the fact Wilson already had a broken neck before he ended up in the ocean, concluding by saying that Doctor Harper and myself would be meeting at the hospital around eight in the morning, and she was welcome to join us.

I got to the hospital at 7:30 to check on Mrs Alston. Doctor Bratton had her in one of the beds, still getting a slow drip of fluids. He and I exchanged notes, then he was away to get breakfast, taking Bradley with him. Mrs Alston was in much better spirits than the night before; her vital signs were good and she was resting comfortably. I ordered something light for her to eat from the kitchens, then went back to the waiting room to drink my coffee and listen to Harper talk with Mister Harvey, though talk wasn't the right word. It appeared to be more a monologue on the Doctor's part, like he was trying to explain something very simple to a child who refused to understand. For the fourth time, Mister Harvey nodded his head blankly. I watched with detached interest for a few moments before reading the newspaper article on the tragic accidental death of Harvey Wilson.

'Tragedy at Sea. The crew and passengers aboard the *Queen Victoria* were saddened to learn of the death of American arms magnate Harvey Wilson. Mr Wilson apparently accidentally plunged overboard to his death sometime late Monday night.' Well, at least Casey didn't get the part about the broken neck and suicide note, I thought. The story went on with a few brief details.

'Mr Wilson's wife was among those who perished on the *Lusitania* when the ship was torpedoed by a German U-boat in 1915. His only son was killed in action in France in 1918 while serving with the United States Expeditionary Force. Mr Wilson, who was heavily invested in munitions, had spent much of this decade setting up and funding memorials to the Allied war dead in France through his Wilson Foundation. It only recently came to light that much of his fortune was derived from a patent licence shared with a large German arms maker prior to the war, but one in which books were kept and a final payment made to Wilson Industries by the German Weimar Republic for their use several months ago. When that became known, it was widely expected that Mr Wilson would be called in front of a U.S. Senate investigative committee to answer questions.'

I pursed my lips. Maybe Casey actually could redeem himself. With Wilson gone he seemed to have had no qualms about publishing information about the munitions patent story. I folded the paper and dropped it into the rubbish bin. Mister Harvey and Doctor Harper were still at it.

"So we just told the *Adriatic* to keep silent over what appears to be a non-accidental death," said Mister Harvey.

"We told the *Adriatic* to keep silent about the conditions of his death," Harper corrected. "As far as anyone other than their doctor and presumably the *Adriatic's* master knows, Mr Wilson was just an unfortunate victim of an accident, falling into the sea."

"No mention of the suicide note?" asked Harvey.

"We thought it best not to muddy the Wall Street waters any more than necessary," said Harper.

Harvey rubbed his cheek. "Just so I'm straight, we know Wilson went up to the Boat Deck to meet someone. And that someone is presumably still on board and knows as well as we do that Harvey Wilson didn't commit suicide. That note left with Mister Collins is a fake, I would bet you London Bridge on it. Only he – " Harvey looked at me. "Or she, doesn't know that we know what they know." Harvey ran a hand over his eyes. "I'm glad you're clear on all this, Doctor."

"I'm just following the links in the chain." He looked at me. "Maeve helped weld them together."

"Helpful little thing, aren't you?" asked Harvey. I smiled up at him.

"I try," I said, getting up to answer a knock at the door.

"Right," said Harvey. "Then let's just wind your chain back up a bit on the windlass, shall we? This man Morten on Sunday night – apparently done in by – what did you say?"

"Aconitine poisoning," said Harper.

"Aconitine poisoning." Harvey nodded. "From what I saw, something I hope to never come in contact with again."

"Don't we all," said Mrs Templeton. Harvey spun around.

"I'm sorry?" He looked questioningly at Doctor Harper.

"This is Mrs MD Templeton. Mrs Templeton, this is our Chief Steward, Mister Harvey."

She put out her hand. "A pleasure, Mister Harvey."

He doffed his cap and shook her hand. "Delighted, I'm sure." He again looked at Harper. "Confused, I most certainly am."

"Mrs Templeton was in the salon when Mr Morten died. She was seated just a few tables away," said Harper.

Harvey nodded to her. "I'm sorry that you saw that, Mrs Templeton."

"Nonsense," said Agatha. "If I hadn't seen it, I wouldn't be here. I sought out Nurse Chandler the next day and offered my assistance. I handled drugs during the War and I immediately recognized that poor man's death as the result of a poison, not a stroke as your newspaper erroneously reported the next day." Mister Harvey goggled at her.

"We've taken Mrs Templeton into our full confidence, Mister Harvey," I said. "She knows everything we do about Mr Morten and Mr Wilson."

"I see." Harvey was obviously nonplused.

Agatha took the floor. "Maeve and I were chatting," she said. "Doctor, your information from the *Adriatic* that Mr Wilson's neck was broken before he went over the side certainly makes it a murder in my book."

I nodded. "We're all agreed on that."

"What about this note instructing Mr Wilson to come up to the Boat Deck?" asked Agatha. "What exactly did it say again?"

Harper shrugged. "Simply the words 'Boat Deck, nine tonight, come alone'. It was written in pencil on a small slip of paper. The paper was cut off the bottom of a telegraph form, which could have been one of ours. The problem is, they're all standardized, so it could have come from anywhere. The note was written in pencil."

"How was it written?" asked Agatha. "Printed? Cursive? Upper case? Lower case?"

"I'm sorry, I don't know." Harper looked ill at ease. "I can radio the *Adriatic* and ask, if you'd like."

"Please do, Doctor. One never knows on how small a detail a case may turn. I find it interesting that while the man left behind a typewritten suicide note it was a note in pencil that lured him to the Boat Deck." Agatha looked at me. "Was there a typewriter in Mr Wilson's cabin?"

"No," said Harvey. "After Mister Collins – he's our Chief Purser, Mrs Templeton – walked through yesterday afternoon, I went in and had a look around. Nice suits, travel implements, a book or two to read. An open file on the table with notes on the current state of memorials from that foundation of his, all very mundane and above board. No typewriter. For a wealthy man, he travelled very light."

Agatha addressed us all. "So this is apparently what it all boils down to. We have one man already dead and certainly not accidentally, and now a second man dead, with a strong probability of not accidentally."

Harvey looked over at me. "Wait. We?"

I nodded. "I told you. Mrs Templeton is helping us. The Captain gave it his approval."

"Well, then," said Mister Harvey, still not entirely convinced but realizing he was outflanked. "Welcome to our club, Mrs Templeton."

"Thank you, Mister Harvey."

He looked at Harper. "Does Casey know about her?"

"No," I said. "And we'd prefer he didn't find out, either."

"We talked to him briefly yesterday afternoon," said Harper.

"Unctuous little blister," said Harvey. "Someday he'll set fire to one of my carpets with his cigarette ash and I really will throw him over the side."

"What did I tell you?" I said to Harper. "Go on, Mister Harvey."

Harvey gave me a crooked look. "Thank you. As I was about to say, what did he want?"

Harper shrugged. "He wanted to know if we'd seen Mr Wilson. He wanted to do another interview with him. We said we hadn't seen him."

"He did a little piece on Wilson apparently jumping ship sometime yesterday. It's in the rubbish there if you want to read it." I drank more coffee. "I wouldn't worry about Casey too much," I said. "With Mr Wilson gone, he's now off on the trail of a famous author aboard the ship."

"There is no famous author aboard the ship," said Harvey. "I've seen the First-Class passenger list."

"He seems to think it's a children's author," said Agatha, giving me a glance. "Like Mr Milne."

"Crikey," said Harvey. "If AA Milne is aboard this ship, you can call me Eeyore. A pox on Casey and his blasted newspaper. It's a wonder he puts anything out at all. His office is so full of old papers and magazines that it's a fire hazard. Chief Duncan has threatened to lock him out of it."

"Eeyore?" I asked.

"My niece reads the stuff," said Harvey defensively. "Not me."

"Eeyore," I said again, looking at Agatha. "That's cute."

"Darling," said Mrs Templeton.

"I mean to say, it's a bit thick, now, isn't it?" Harvey was on his soapbox. "Between people dropping dead in my restaurant and American millionaires going bonkers and leaping the rails and Lady Peter Wimsey here following all the clues - " He rolled his eyes at me. That was too much. I punched him in the arm.

"Don't you roll your eyes at me. Just because I'm a woman – "

"And she is more of a detective than Lord Wimsey ever hopes to be," said Agatha. She frowned and rolled her eyes. "Forgive me, Dorothy."

Harper put a steadying hand on my shoulder. "We've been through a lot in the past two days," he said. "Everyone's emotions are on edge." I jerked my shoulder away from him.

"Why couldn't it have been that lovely Mrs Alston's husband who went overboard instead? If anyone deserves a trip to Davey Jones' locker, it's him."

"What?" Harvey was confused. "Who is Mrs Alston?"

"Yes," said Agatha. "Who is Mrs Alston?"

"I'll tell you both later," I said. "She's a pregnant passenger with some marital issues going on." I sighed. "I'm sorry I hit you."

Harvey rubbed his arm in indignation. "Apology accepted."

"What's the line from Shakespeare?" I said to no one in particular. "'The play's the thing wherein we'll catch the conscience of the king?'" I looked at Agatha. "I think someone used Mr Wilson's guilty conscience to lure him to the Boat Deck last night. And Mrs Templeton has suggested that perhaps Mr Morten was the unintended victim of murder – that the poison he got was meant for someone else." I took a sip of my coffee. "We all have to agree there seems to be zero motive for anyone to kill Morten. So where does that leave us?"

Harper shook his head. "It leaves us with the fact that Morten's dead – and now we've got Harvey's death to add to it."

"And I think Mr Morten's death is linked to Mr Wilson in some way," I said stubbornly.

"I agree," said Agatha.

Harvey shook his head. "You have really been reading too much Agatha Christie, Nurse Chandler."

I glanced at Mrs Templeton. "On the contrary, I don't believe I've been reading enough." She smiled.

"There's got to be an answer," said Harper.

"Of course there is," said Agatha. "We simply don't have enough information to find it yet."

"And we will find it," I said. "I don't know about you, Mister Harvey, but I'm not interested in waiting to see who turns up dead next. The *Victoria* is a big ship." I set my coffee mug down and folded my arms, leaning against the desk. "Who's to say our murderous friend won't start in on the crew for round three?"

Harvey looked at Harper. "You know, I hate it when she makes sense."

||

'm sure that at some point or other in your life, you've encountered someone so grateful that you almost felt embarrassed for even the slightest bit of good you could do them. A simple word of encouragement, a hug, even standing them tea when they were down and needed a friend – I firmly believe it's these acts of human kindness that make us better people.

And so it was with Mrs Clara Alston.

Doctor Bratton released Mrs Alston at ten in the morning, and Mister Harvey personally escorted her and her son directly to their new stateroom in First-Class. Mister Harvey and Mister Collins had gathered enough funds from the crew – once they had heard the story of abuse – to get the transfer made. Mister Harvey told me that several crewmen had expressed a desire to thrash her husband to within an inch of his life if warranted; Harvey said he would let them know.

Mister Harvey also rounded up a pair of stewards to collect their belongings from the old stateroom and carry them up. In the meantime Mrs Alston and Bradley were, of course, welcome to dine in the First-Class salon. Clara looked at me with tears in her eyes.

"I can't believe this, Nurse. I can never thank you enough."

"It's nothing, Mrs Alston. The crew of the *Victoria* is generous to a fault."

"Too generous." She looked about the stateroom. "I'll never be able to pay this back." I smiled.

"I don't think that's something you have to worry about, Mrs Alston." I looked past her shoulder. Bradley was quietly sitting on the floor playing with a toy aeroplane. "I see that all of your belongings made the trip up."

"Yes – but – " Clara pursed her lips and pulled the stateroom door to behind her. We stood in the hallway. "It's Bradley. When he saw the stewards at the door with our baggage, he just had a fit. The poor men were absolutely flustered, I tell you. I was never so embarrassed."

"What does he have to be upset about in that regard? Did your husband – "

"No, not Frank. Not this time. I really don't know. We were here in the new cabin when the stewards knocked at the door. I let them in and they had just begun moving our baggage inside when Bradley came out of the loo and caught sight of them. He uttered such a cry and ran back into the bathroom, and slammed the door." Clara slowly shook her head. "The stewards had stopped and were looking at each other, then at me. I had no idea what to say or do. When they left, I found that Bradley had locked the bathroom door. I finally got him to open up and found he'd been crying – but he absolutely refused to tell me about it. He's been very on edge. I would have thought that spending the night in the hospital with me would have worn him out, but he still won't sleep." She fretted. "He won't talk about it with me – and he won't talk about it with you, either, if that's what you're thinking. He just clams up." Clara's face was sad. "I know he feels badly about Frank and I going our separate ways, even though

Frank was never kind to him. He's such a sweet boy. I don't know what to make of it."

"How odd," I said. "And the stewards didn't say or do anything out of the ordinary?"

"Not a thing. They finished unloading the cart, thanked me, and left. I tipped them what I could afford, though I'm afraid it wasn't very much. Then can you believe, they wouldn't accept it?"

I made a mental note to praise Mister Harvey about the quality of his stewards. "Everyone is just happy to see you doing well, Clara," I said. I glanced down at my wrist watch. "Do you think you could come down to the hospital around five? I know Doctor Bratton cleared you this morning, but I'd like to give you a once over, too, if you don't mind."

"Of course. Thank you."

"Won't take but a moment," I said. "In the meantime, they're still serving luncheon. I suggest you and Bradley go in and enjoy your first meal in the First-Class salon. Don't worry, Mister Collins and Mister Harvey are helping pick up the tab." I grasped her hands. "And I shouldn't worry too much about Bradley. Once he's gotten used to his new surroundings, he'll be back to his normal self."

"I hope so," said Clara, but it was clear by her expression that she was doubtful.

Leaving them behind, I made my way down to B Deck to seek out our Chief Stewardess. I found Miss Kelly behind the desk in her cramped office, wedged in near the male and female hairdresser's stations and on the same side as Doctor Bratton's consulting room and the male and female isolation and quarantine wards. It was apparent at a glance that she was perturbed about something, and when she was perturbed the stewardesses serving under her knew better than to exacerbate the situation in any fashion. Kelly, of Italian-Irish descent, had a withering gaze and acid tongue that when unsheathed, her staff swore, could cut through a steel water-tight door. Accordingly, those beneath her cut a wide swath when she was in ill-humour, and it was widely thought that even Chief Steward Harvey went out of his way to stay out of her path at such times – and Wednesday morning appeared to be one of those times. I stood quietly while she did her imitation of Mount Vesuvius.

"Do these people make this much of a mess at home as they do in their staterooms here?" Kelly shook out her shoulder-length red hair, her green eyes flared and her normally pale cheeks reddened, the high cheek bones adding a hint of imperiousness to her pretty face. "I swear, Americans are the worst. Towels and sheets everywhere and the single gents don't seem to mind if a stewardess walks in and catches them with their nethers out." I nodded gently.

"Well, yes, Miss Kelly, I agree." Sometimes you just had to let her vent. "It's deplorable behavior. I trust His Majesty's subjects are better behaved when traveling."

She looked at me, clicking the pencil against the desk. "What can I do for you, Nurse?"

"Would it be possible to get a little extra attention paid to Mrs Alston and her boy in their new stateroom in First-Class?"

Roxanne put down her pencil. "Mister Harvey told me the story," she said. "I'll have the stewardesses do extra checks on their stateroom."

"Thank you," I said. "I appreciate it."

"And what about Mr Alston?" she enquired. "I take it that he's staying in the original stateroom in Second-Class?"

I nodded. "Truthfully, he doesn't deserve a bloody thing," I said. "If no one checked on him or serviced his stateroom until we arrive in New York I'd be happy."

Miss Kelly smiled grimly. "Yes, that's the feeling of my girls, too." She casually broke her pencil, picked up a second and broke it, too. "And to be honest, myself as well. I have no patience for a man like that."

"He probably wouldn't notice," I said. "Mrs Alston says he spends all of his time in the bars." I pursed my lips. "If I had my way, he'd be spending time behind bars."

"Life isn't fair," she said coldly. "If I had my way, he'd be keel-hauled." She turned her attention back to the reports on her desk. "Don't hesitate to let me know if there's anything else I can do for you, Nurse." I heard a desk drawer slam as I closed the door. "How come I can never find a pencil in here?" she exclaimed as the door clicked shut.

Doctor Harper was on duty in the hospital front room, engrossed in a two month old copy of *Colliers*. He looked up as I came in. "Where have you been? You missed all the excitement."

"Excitement?" I closed the door. He nodded.

"I set a broken arm."

"That's hardly exciting," I said. "I've done it dozens of times." Harper smiled.

"It wasn't just any arm. This arm belongs to your Clara Alston's husband."

Suddenly I found myself interested. "Do tell," I said, dropping into a chair.

Harper continued, enjoying his moment. "He said he slipped stepping out of the bath this morning but the break looked like it had occurred some hours ago. I don't know how he stood the pain. Drink, probably. Anyway, it didn't look like any fall break I'd ever seen. Usually that's a wrist as someone tries to catch themselves. This was the middle of his left forearm, like he'd raised it to fend off a blow. I saw it in the Navy when two mates would go after each other and one had an iron rod or something. Lot of bruising. And the way he carried on down here while I was setting his arm, my Lord! Such a foul-mouthed little rat of a man. I tell you, I was glad to be shed of him."

"Where did he go?"

"He went back to his stateroom to lie down – though he's probably safely wedged into a bar seat by now." He eyed me speculatively. "What's new with you?"

"Nothing new, I'm afraid. I got Clara and her son settled into their new stateroom, but it seems that the stewards frightened him. He bolted into the loo and locked the door behind him. Took a while for Clara to talk him out."

"Stewards too?" Harper asked. "I thought it was only us medical type doctors that he had fits around."

"He's a boy," I said. "And from what I've seen very pampered by his mother, so who knows what's behind it. I also looked in on Chief Stewardess Kelly to ask her girls to do extra welfare checks on them."

"I don't believe I've met Kelly yet."

"She's an Irish-Italian redhead. Believe me, you'll know when you've met her."

"Thanks. Can't wait." He gave me a careful appraisal. "You look worn down. Why don't you go take a nap for a bit."

"That sounds good, thanks." I consulted the clock. "I'm meeting Mrs Templeton at tea time, on the Promenade Deck. She wanted to walk over the Boat Deck where the overcoat fragment was found."

"Enjoy your visit," he said. I headed for the door, then stopped and looked back at him with a smile.

"Don't despair, Boss. What more could possibly happen?"

Harper frowned. "On this ship, what couldn't?"

I left the loudspeaker turned on in my stateroom just so I wouldn't be caught asleep when the ship's bugler called for tea time, and the tinny sound of his trumpet jolted me off the bed with a start. I looked in a mirror. It didn't crack so I tried to to reset my face and hair, then smoothed out my uniform and promptly fell over the only chair in the whole bloody stateroom.

Obviously, I was going to need more than just a nap at a later point in my life. Maybe somewhere around 1957. I sleep-walked into the corridor and headed for the Promenade Deck.

I found Agatha looking bright and refreshed, lounging in a deck chair with her big floppy hat on and a tea service on a tray sitting next to her on the deck. She looked up at me over the book she was reading – *The Unpleasantness at the Bellona Club* by Dorothy Sayers.

"Last year's Lord Peter Wimsey book," she said. "After that remark by Mister Harvey this morning, I felt I ought to catch up. Found it in the ship's library." She thought a moment. "I haven't decided if I'm going to tell Dorothy what I said about you being more of a detective than Lord Wimsey." Agatha smiled. "I believe you're showing a natural flair for the work."

I frowned. "I feel like I'm always just one step away from one of Alice's rabbit holes."

"You are. That's the fun of detective work." She closed the book and sat up. "So. We're going to go visit the scene of the crime, as it were?"

"As it were." I felt in a pocket and pulled out the square of fabric. "This is what the deck officers found on their search for Mr Wilson." I handed her the fragment.

Agatha turned it over in her hands, then held it up to the sun that was beginning to wane. "It's definitely torn. You can see the ragged edges. If it had been clipped it would be much neater. Where do you think it came from?"

"A man's expensive overcoat," I said.

"Or a woman's. I have something with a very similar fabric." She handed it back to me and we began walking.

"I don't think it's a woman's," I said. "Do you believe a woman could have broken Mr Wilson's neck and then heaved him over the rails?"

Agatha nodded. "You're thinking. Good. To my recollection of seeing him at dinner, Mr Wilson was a large man."

"Well, I thought he was large," I said. "I guess he was pretty fair sized. Running to corpulence, certainly. I think a man with Doctor Bratton's build would have strained to get him over the railing."

"Doctor Bratton?" asked Agatha.

"Oh – you haven't met him, have you? He tends to stay mostly in the surgery. On the other hand, Mister Harvey or Doctor Harper could certainly have done it alone. A woman, no. Not any I've seen aboard. And certainly not any of the party girls he was always surrounded with at dinner."

"Those party girls," Agatha remarked. "They seem to have disappeared, didn't they?"

I let out a snort of contempt. "Of course they have. The chance to land the big fat fish is gone. They're off to other prospects."

"You're very jaded," said Agatha. "Not that there's anything wrong with it," she added quickly.

"I've just had to work for every single thing I've ever gotten. My husband died before he and I could build anything together. And I'm tired of having doors closed in my face because I'm an intelligent woman." I fumed for a moment. "It just makes me angry, so I try to keep it in because no one likes an angry woman."

"I understand," said Agatha. "But you need to let it out every once in a while. Focus it on something positive."

"Like finding our killer?"

"That will certainly do for a start. Tell me about this passenger of yours, the one who is pregnant."

I exhaled slowly. "Clara Alston. There's an interesting story." Agatha listened intently as we leisurely walked the length of the Promenade Deck and then climbed up the stairs to the Boat Deck. "And then," I said in conclusion, "he takes one look at the stewards who moved their baggage and runs for the bathroom and locks the door behind him." We mounted a flight of stairs.

"Poor woman." Agatha frowned. "My heart goes out to her, and not just because my mother's name was also Clara. What a horrible man her husband is. And that scamp of a boy inconveniently disappearing. She must have been sick with worry, not to mention his odd antics today, and her about ready to be confined." Agatha opened her purse and took out a tenner. "Please send this in her direction. I'm fairly certain that her husband's claims of getting rich by the time we reach New York are just so many castles in the air. Or in his case, dungeons."

"You're very generous." I tucked the bank note into my pocket. "I'm sure Mrs Alston will appreciate it, but she'll also try to give it back."

"Don't you dare accept it."

"I'll do my best." I stopped at the top of the stairs. "Here we are." The Boat Deck had little foot traffic. It was just someplace that people walked through to climb the stairs to the Sports Deck above. Perhaps it was the reminder that a ship like the *Victoria* even carried life boats that people didn't want to acknowledge. Ever since the *Titanic* disaster, ships were required to carry enough boats for everyone on board. The *Titanic's* sister, *Olympic* – one of our competitors on the North Atlantic run – had been one of the first to undergo the refit.

The *Victoria* carries 24 boats – two 30-footers and 22 36-footers. The smaller boats were mounted up at the bow, near the bridge. The remaining boats were laid out, 11 to each side, down the length of the Boat Deck. All were equipped with diesel engines, full life saving gear and were covered by tightly fitting tarps when not in use.

Each of the big boats had its own set of launch davits, two to a boat. The boat hung poised between these tall outward curved bands of steel that extended up from the deck, ready to be let down into the water at a moment's notice with a full complement of human cargo. As you might imagine, with all of this running the length of the ship on both sides, much of the Boat Deck was in shadow at any given moment. At night it was even worse. I mentioned that to Agatha and she agreed.

"I suppose if you were going to pick a spot, this would be the most convenient and most likely to be quiet in the evening," she said, looking up to a catwalk overhead. "What's that walkway for?"

"It gives access to the davit lift machinery. Only crew are allowed up there. As you can see, it runs the length of the boats here, and also on the other side."

"Even more cover at night," said Agatha.

"Right. Here we are. Lifeboat station ten." I pointed out the sights. "Looking straight ahead to the bow down the row of boats, the back of the bridge is about 150 feet away from us. Lifeboat stations eight, six and four are between us and the bridge. Lifeboat two is actually mounted near the bridge."

Agatha gazed ahead. "And the curve of the ship effectively blocks off any view from that quarter."

"Yes." The wind against my face felt soothing. "This place was well-chosen."

"It certainly was. This was carefully planned. It wasn't just a spur of the moment thing." Agatha put her hand on the railing next to us and peered over. The ocean rushed past the hull in an endless swirl far below. Agatha tested the rail gate. "Hmm. Locked, but it would only open to the inside."

I nodded. "Safety feature to keep passengers from accidentally doing something they'd regret for the rest of their very short lives," I said.

"Passengers," echoed Agatha. "I honestly don't believe a passenger would think of this location. At night, it would be remote and cold on a ship full of people." She tapped the railing with her hand. "Maeve, we're looking for a crew member. Not a passenger."

"That certainly narrows down the suspects. Kind of. There's over 700 crew on board."

"I remember you telling me that." Agatha peered out over the railing again. "And no one saw him fall overboard here. That is, if we're accepting the bit of evidence found here as proof that this is where it happened. Anyone else could have torn an overcoat on that davit at any other time."

I sighed. "Why must everything be so suspect?"

"Maeve, if it was all laid out in black and white, it wouldn't be a mystery, would it? Hercule Poirot can put together a jigsaw puzzle out of the box as easily as you or I. But figuring out which pieces are missing from an overturned puzzle and then reconstructing them – that's what makes him a detective." She tapped me on the shoulder. "Here comes your handsome doctor and another officer."

"Don't call him my handsome doctor," I said. "The man appears to be a total wash in the romance department."

"Maybe he just needs some inducement," Agatha whispered to me. She put out her hand. "Doctor Harper. How lovely to see you again."

Harper touched his hat and took her hand. "And you, Mrs Templeton." He nodded at Mister Jackson. "I'd like to introduce our First Officer, Mister Jackson."

"Mrs Templeton," said Jackson. "I've been instructed by the Captain to assist your investigation by providing whatever you might need." He looked over at me. Nurse Chandler, good to see you."

Harper folded his hands behind his back. "So this is where it happened, is it?"

"We were just discussing that," I said. "Mrs Templeton thinks that just because the overcoat fragment was found here doesn't necessarily mean it happened here."

"Really?" said Mister Jackson. He approached the rail and looked over. "It seems as likely a spot as any." He knelt down beside the inner rail of one of the davits.

"Right here is where we found the fabric. It was stuck onto this little projection of steel."

"Have you made any progress?" asked Harper.

Mrs Templeton nodded. "I think we can safely say that our suspect is not a passenger. This location was chosen because it's out of sight lines, even more so at night. Someone with a working knowledge of the ship made this decision, and that points to crew, at this time."

"I see," Harper nodded. "Oh, I've also put in a radiogram to the *Adriatic*, asking their doctor to more fully describe the note found on Mr Wilson's person."

"Note?" asked Mister Jackson.

"Yes," said Harper. "A penciled note asking him to meet someone up here on the Boat Deck the night he disappeared. It was in an inside pocket of his jacket."

"Thank you, Doctor." Agatha handed me her purse and did a careful walk of inspection around the lifeboat davits.

"What are you looking for?" I asked.

"The same thing Poirot would be looking for. Where Mr Wilson broke his neck."

"I'm sorry?" said Jackson. "Did you say 'broke his neck?'" Agatha looked at him.

"Yes, Mr Wilson broke his neck before he went over the side. Interesting, isn't it? Doctor Harper got that from the *Adriatic's* doctor who examined the body."

Jackson looked at Harper. "Then that makes it murder," he said.

"Yes, I'm afraid it does."

The First Officer turned to Agatha and myself. "Not a word of this to anyone."

"Oh, dear, no," said Agatha.

"Of course not," I said.

"Is this related to Mr Morten? Have you told the Captain?" I had never seen Mister Jackson so serious looking. "The last we were all gathered it was a suicide."

Harper shook his head. "We don't know if it's related to Mr Morten or not. And no. I didn't get the proof that Wilson was murdered until last night. I was planning on telling him later."

Jackson went to the rail, then ran a hand along the davit. "Maybe we're jumping to conclusions. I don't doubt what the *Adriatic's* doctor says, but maybe he fell, broke his neck and went overboard all on his own."

"Was he climbing on the davit or the catwalk up above like a little boy?" Agatha asked sarcastically. Jackson ignored her.

"He was lured up here, Mister Jackson," I said. "And once he arrived, he was despatched."

"Who knows about this?" asked Jackson.

Harper counted us off on his fingers. "You, myself, Nurse Chandler, Mister Harvey, Mrs Templeton, Wireless Officer Cameron, and of course the doctor on the *Adriatic* and presumably the ship's master, too." Harper thought a moment. "And our Captain, as well, once he's told." He looked at Jackson. "Do you want to do the honors? He's already got one dead from me and I'm the new employee. I'm not interested in wearing out my welcome."

"He's not going to be happy," said Jackson, thoroughly morose.

"Neither was Mr Morten," I said.

"Or Mr Wilson," Agatha added.

Mister Jackson clenched his jaw and looked at the doctor. "He's going to want to talk with you."

"Of course," said Harper. He turned to us and sighed. "I might as well get this over with, ladies. I'm sure I'll see you both later, if the Captain doesn't strip me of rank and confine me to quarters. Lead the way, Mister Jackson."

"The bridge is dead ahead, sir." The two of them walked forward. Agatha turned to me.

"I hope Doctor Harper doesn't get in trouble," she said. "If he only found out about the report from the *Adriatic's* doctor last night – "

"The Captain likes his reports fresh. Something on the order of before the incident in question even happened." I looked after them as they rounded the curve and disappeared from sight, then back to Agatha. "I don't think there's anything more to be gleaned here," I said.

She shook her head. "No. The storm we had the other night would have washed anything away." She looked up. "But I would like to take a peek at what's above us."

"Certainly. There are stairs up to the Sports Deck at the next lifeboat station." We walked leisurely forward to the number eight lifeboat station and climbed the stairs. Agatha looked at a large enclosure opposite us as we arrived on the Sports Deck.

"What is in there?" she asked.

"That's one of the lift motor houses. There's another one on the other side, opposite of us." Even over the wind playing across the Sports Deck we could hear the continuous whine of the electric motors housed inside. "It's always a bit noisy," I said.

"And conveniently close to lifeboat station ten," Agatha remarked. "The noise would certainly have drowned out any sounds of a struggle that the wind hadn't already carried away." She looked thoughtful. "Yes, our killer chose his spot with care."

Directly in front of the lift motor house was the deck tennis area, taking up the empty space between the massive back of the base of funnel number one and the equally massive front of the base of funnel number two. To either side of the base of funnel one were officer quarters, and then directly in front of them the bridge with its unobstructed view of the bow. Directly behind us and just forward of the base of funnel two were the dog kennels set in behind the lift house and just opposite the lifeboat station ten position on the Boat Deck, and a small balcony accessible for tennis spectators. Every so often the landscape was broken up by one of the enormous ventilators, taller than a man, that scooped in air and forced it down into the depths of the ship.

To my surprise, the Sports Deck was still popular at four in the afternoon. It wasn't an afternoon at Brighton Beach but at least it was no longer raining and passengers didn't feel they needed to wrap themselves head to toe to survive out of doors. Agatha and I walked behind the courts and along the front of the funnel two base.

People were trying to forget their cares and what awaited them in New York by indulging in tennis and shuffleboard, while bellboys walked passenger's dogs along a prescribed route from the kennels. The wind and the tang scents of the ocean mixed with the exhaust from the funnels was refreshing; the muted roar of the *Victoria* cutting ahead through the sea a benediction. Agatha leaned against the railing closest to the steps up from the Boat Deck and took in the scene.

I looked around the base of the funnel. "If only the ship could talk we might get some headway on the others."

Agatha nodded. An errant tennis ball bounced past us and caromed off the leg of a cast iron bench before sprinting through the gaps between the rails, sailing to ricochet off of the taut tarp over lifeboat eight and thence out into space over the side of the ship. We watched its descent into the churning foam far below. I shook my head.

"I just wonder how many gross of those we go through during a sailing."

"Oh, Sister," a woman cried out from behind us.

I glanced at Agatha. "Do I look like a nun from the back?" She was barely able to suppress a smile at me being addressed in such a fashion. I turned around.

"I'm Head Nurse Maeve Chandler, Miss," I said stiffly. "How may I be of service to you this afternoon?"

"Well," said the young woman, clearly American. She popped a wad of chewing gum from her mouth. "Didja see a tennis ball come over here, kinda quick-like?"

My face softened slightly. "Yes, Miss."

"Well," asked the young woman, swinging her racquet in her hand, "where did it go?"

"I'm afraid it went over the side, Miss," I replied with a certain amount of pleasure. Agatha coughed and turned away, then coughed again.

"Over the side!" The woman turned and called back to another girl. "Hey, Michele! Match! Mine! Your serve went into the drink!" The other girl shrugged and pulled her sweater tighter around her shoulders. I looked at my athletic tormentor.

"Would you like a fresh ball, perhaps?"

"No, thanks." She rubbed the racquet against her flannel trousered leg. "Starting to get kinda chilly." She looked at me. "Really? A nurse? This ship has a nurse?"

"And a doctor, a surgeon, a dispenser, and others, Miss."

"Well, if that ain't the bee's knees." She gave me a careful appraisal. "Itty bitty thing, aren't you?" She smiled at us. "Well, so long."

"Good afternoon, Miss," I said. The woman sauntered away, making toward the gate that blocked passenger access to the base of the first funnel. "Miss," I said, "that area is restricted for passengers."

"Wadja say?" she stopped, leaning her hands against the latch.

"I said, that gate is restricted. It's crew only."

"Oh," the woman said blankly. She reached a hand up to pull her pink cloche tighter over her auburn hair, then suddenly whipped it off and examined it. "Horsefeathers! Look at this!" she shouted at me.

I rolled my eyes at Agatha. "Back in a moment," I said.

"You shouldn't have to face it alone. I'll go with you."

"Yes, Miss," I said as I walked up to her. She thrust her cap out toward me.

"Look at my cloche! It's ruined!"

"Miss?" I said, pretending hard to care.

She tucked her tennis racquet under her arm and turned the cap in her hands. "Grease! It'll never come out." She handed it to me, then looked down at her white trousers. "My slacks! They're greased, too!" She turned and looked at the gate. "There it is," she said accusingly. "Grease all over this latch!" She wheeled on me. "What are you going to do about this?" she demanded.

I steeled myself, weighed my options, realized that tossing her over the side to join Mr Wilson wasn't one of them, and knew there was only one course of action open to me. I forced a smile. "I'm certain, Miss, that you will find that our retail shops on the Promenade have suitable replacements." I did some quick mental math. "I'll have the Chief Steward extend you a complimentary credit for four pounds in your name."

Her face softened. "Really? Four pounds? How much is that American?"

Agatha thought a moment. "A little over twenty of your dollars." She looked at me. I shrugged.

The American considered this a moment, then stuck out her hand. "Deal."

I swallowed and gingerly took her hand in mine. "Deal," I said, not without discomfort.

"That would be the cat's pajamas! Name's Linda Morash. B-18." She turned to go, then looked back at me. "You won't forget, will you?"

"How could I forget you, Miss?" I said dryly. Agatha stifled a laugh.

"Great!" She skittered off to rejoin her friend.

"The Stoddard Lines is lighter by four pounds, but the customer is happy," said Agatha, watching her go.

"You mean Mister Harvey is lighter by four pounds. And he won't be happy." I frowned. "Remind me to get someone up here to look at that greasy latch before we get nicked by another American." We walked to the court railing and looked down. We were directly above the access catwalk, davits and Number Ten lifeboat on the port side, about fifteen feet beneath us on the Boat Deck. Agatha frowned, wrinkling her brow.

"Trying to figure out what happened Monday night?" I asked her.

Agatha nodded and pointed down to the boat station. "The path that Mr Wilson must have taken when he fell would have carried him directly past the Promenade Deck drawing room windows beneath, then past the staterooms and suites on A Deck and after that there would have been no one to see his body plunge into the ocean in the night."

"And the Promenade Deck drawing room windows would have been draped shut, too," I said. "No help from that quarter."

Agatha looked forward. "The base for the forward funnel and the ventilators above it effectively block out any view from the back of the bridge, and at any rate I would imagine the bridge officers would have been concentrating their view ahead, not behind. Just looking at the sightlines, the bridge itself blocked the view from the crow's nest on the forward mast to this small section of the deck." She nodded to herself. "Clever, very clever."

"You're right. You would have to be standing right about here if you had any hope of seeing what was going on below. And what are the odds of – oh, my God." I stared ahead of me. One of the big ventilators stood jutting out of the deck, just forward of the port side tennis court.

"What is it?" asked Agatha.

I turned to her. "Listen," I said. "Remember what I told you about Doctor Harper and I searching for the boy the other night?"

"You found him behind a ventilator, as I recall."

I vehemently shook my head. "Not behind *a* ventilator. Behind *the* ventilator." I pointed. "That one right there to the side of the officer's quarters. How could I be so dumb?"

"Whatever are you going on about?" said Agatha.

"The boy was cowering behind that ventilator, back in the shadow, as close to the wall as he could wedge himself. And the next day Mr Wilson goes missing. What if the boy saw what happened at lifeboat station ten and hid himself away out of fear it would also happen to him?"

"That's quite a reach, Maeve."

I put my fingers to my temples. "Wait, hear me out. It's obvious that boy was terrified of something, and he won't tell his mum what it is."

Agatha mulled this over. "From what you told me, it's just the stewards he doesn't like. And Doctor Harper. You said he wouldn't let Doctor Harper come near him the night you found him up here. Very curious." She looked at the ventilator, then at me. "On the other hand, you may well be on to something. I'd like to talk to the child, if you think I could."

Sometimes a little distraction can be a good thing. The magician uses it to perform his sleight of hand – now you see it, now you don't – and at one time or another most nurses like myself had used a similar ruse when giving an injection to a young child. Now, I was going to knowingly perform a ruse on Clara Alston to get information from her young son. I didn't know whether to congratulate or hate myself.

I gently rapped on Mrs Alston's stateroom door. After a moment I heard movement inside, and then the door opened just a crack. "Hello, Clara. May I come in?"

"Certainly. I just wanted to make sure it wasn't Frank." She opened the door, then stepped back in surprise on seeing Agatha.

"She's a friend of mine. This is Mrs Templeton. She's also one of your fellow First-Class passengers."

Agatha put forward her hand. "So pleased to meet you, Mrs Alston. Nurse Chandler told me what a delightful woman you are, and I just asked to say hello. I hope you don't mind."

"No, not at all." Clara looked at me with caution in her eyes. I smiled.

"It's not often we get an expecting mother and her child travelling with us," I said. "Mrs Templeton has a young daughter."

"Is she with you?" asked Clara. Agatha laughed lightly.

"No, she's ensconced at home with her Winnie-the-Pooh books." She looked past Clara at Bradley, who was still playing with his toy aeroplane, giving us a curious look. "Does your young man read Mr Milne?"

"His father doesn't approve."

"So sorry to hear that," said Agatha. "The stories are quite amusing."

Clara gave her a gentle smile. "I'm sure they are, Mrs Templeton." She opened the door. "Won't you both come in?"

"Thank you," I said. Clara seated herself in an armchair and Agatha and I went to the couch, and I launched my rocket. "You know, Clara, Mrs Templeton is a bit of a child psychologist."

Agatha shot me a look, her eyebrows raised, then recovered. "Yes, it's a bit of a hobby, learning how children think." She looked at me again. "And sometimes how adults think, as well."

I ignored the barb. "Clara, I was telling Mrs Templeton about Bradley's reaction to the stewards today. I thought she might be able to help."

"If you can get anything out of him, be my guest." She smiled down at Bradley. "Bradley, would you like to chat with Mrs Templeton?"

He looked up. "About what?"

"Oh, I don't know," said Agatha. "Whatever you'd like." She gestured. "That's a nice aeroplane you have."

The boy brightened. "It's the *Spirit of St. Louis*. When I grow up I'm going to be a famous pilot like Mr Lindbergh."

"Yes, 'Lucky Lindy,'" Agatha nodded. "Quite the hero. Maybe people will call you 'Bold Bradley'."

Bradley giggled at that. "Did you hear that, mum? 'Bold Bradley'!"

The relief on Clara's face was discernible. "Yes, I heard." She smiled at him. "Who knows what you may become?"

"Do you like aeroplanes, Mrs Templeton?" Bradley asked her.

"Oh, yes." Agatha leaned forward. "But I'm also partial to the big shiny Zeppelin."

Bradley looked up at Clara. "Mum says the Zeppelins bombed England once."

"That's true, I'm afraid. But it was before you were born. Now the *Graf Zeppelin* is used for good. It travels across the ocean just like we are doing now. Someday you may ride in one."

"I'd like that. Or maybe I'd just fly alongside of it in my own aeroplane."

Agatha indicated the floor. "May I sit with you, Bradley?"

The boy shrugged. "I guess so. Can we talk about aeroplanes?"

"We can talk about whatever you'd like," Agatha said, settling herself carefully on the floor next to the boy, her skirt wrapped around her legs. Clara gave an approving smile, then looked at me.

"I would never have imagined this several hours ago," she said. "Your friend certainly does appear to have a knack for talking with children."

"Yes," I said. "Mrs Templeton has many talents." I watched them huddled together, Bradley occasionally raising the toy aeroplane and talking in animated hushed tones as Agatha listened intently and interjected sparingly.

"It looks like I may make it to New York after all," Clara said, indicating her swollen belly. I nodded.

"I heard your husband had a bit of an accident."

"Yes," she said without emotion. "He went down to the hospital."

"Doctor Harper set his arm," I said. "The doctor says your husband told him he slipped in the bathtub." Clara gave a sharp, short laugh.

"He came in with it broken this morning, just as Bradley and I were leaving, after we'd packed our bags. He was holding it with his good arm and cursing a storm."

"What happened?" I asked.

"I haven't the faintest idea, nor do I care." Her lips compressed into a thin line. "He probably fell off a bar stool and didn't want to admit it to the doctor."

"I hope your personal troubles resolve themselves."

"I'm sure they will." She stopped, a dart of pain creasing her face and a gasp escaping her lips. I reached for her hands.

"Are you all right?"

Clara looked at me, a curious expression on her face. "I think – I think - " she stopped and sucked in air again, then grimaced. "I think what I said about New York a moment ago may have been premature."

"Contraction?"

Clara nodded. "Lower back pain, then contraction. It's the baby." She managed a smile. "I've been through this once before, remember?" She grimaced again. Agatha looked up at us.

"What is it?"

"Labour," I said. I went to the telephone and put through a call to the hospital.

Two rings and Doctor Harper picked up. "Doctor Harper, it's Maeve. I'm with Mrs Alston in her stateroom and we may be about to add another passenger to Mister Harvey's list." Agatha was on her feet, holding Mrs Alston's hand. "Yes, we're coming now. Thanks."

"I'll keep Bradley," said Agatha. "If that's all right with you, Mrs Alston."

"I'd appreciate it," she said. Bradley looked up at her.

"Mum, I want to go with you," he said earnestly.

"No, Bradley, stay here with Mrs Templeton. She can take care of you while I'm gone."

I looked at Clara with a reassuring smile. "I've been aboard the *Victoria* from the beginning and yours will be our first birth," I said. "Nice change from everything else that's gone on during this trip."

"I'm happy to oblige you, Nurse." She clenched her fists. "If it's a girl, I'm naming her Maeve."

I smiled. "I wouldn't wish that on anyone. I'd rather you name her Victoria instead." Agatha and I helped her to stand, then Agatha opened the door as I hobbled her out into the corridor toward the lift.

"Don't worry about us," Agatha said. "Bradley will be fine."

"Thank you, Mrs Templeton," Clara managed to huff out. "You're very kind."

When we got to the hospital, Doctor Bratton took direct charge of Clara and ushered her into the surgery while Doctor Harper and I scrubbed and dressed. "Well," he said, "this is a nice change of pace from the usual mayhem."

"Enjoy it while it lasts." I recounted what had taken place when I visited Clara and since Agatha and I had seen him and Mister Jackson earlier in the afternoon.

"I thought the boy seemed somewhat overwrought. Do you think Mrs Templeton will get anything out of him?"

"She had him relaxed and telling her about his toy before his mum went into labor. What about you and Mister Jackson? How did it go with the Captain?"

Harper tied his mask on. "About as well as you'd imagine. He actually didn't seem all that surprised that Mr Wilson was apparently murdered." Harper gloved up. "Mister Jackson, on the other hand, viewed it as a personal affront."

"Maybe he just doesn't like murder." I snapped one glove on. "I'm sure it affects some people like that."

Harper's eyebrows raised. "You've become a much more cynical person since we met on Sunday."

I shrugged and pushed open the door to the surgery. "Maybe murder affects me like that."

Mister Harvey was waiting for us when we came out of the surgery just past eight that evening. Harper pulled his mask down. "To what do we owe this visit?" he asked pleasantly. "You look healthy enough. By the way you've got one more mouth to feed. Mrs Alston has a baby girl."

"A bright spot in the midst of everything else," said Harvey. "My congratulations to her on behalf of the ship. I'll have flowers and an appropriate gift or two sent around."

"It is a bright spot," I said, picking up the telephone. I connected with Clara's stateroom. "Mrs Templeton? Yes, a girl. Mother and daughter are doing fine. Would you mind bringing Bradley down to the hospital?" I listened for a moment. "That's what he said? All right, yes. Mister Harvey and Doctor Harper are both here. Thanks." I hung up the telephone. "Mrs Templeton is on her way down with Bradley." I looked at Mister Harvey. "She ended up looking after him when Mrs Alston's labor started."

"Kind of her. Always good to have help." He set a manila folder down on the desk. "I've enlisted a little help myself. I didn't care for being burned by the Captain the other day when he asked me about the First-Class Observation-Lounge drinks."

"I remember," said Harper.

"It browned me off pretty badly. I set both Josh and the manager to doing a little bit of digging through the Sunday evening receipts in the Observation-Lounge. They came up with some interesting facts." He opened the folder and drew out a sheet of paper. "These are the table assignments and drink listings – who ordered what, when, etcetera. Here," Harvey pointed a finger, "is Wilson's drink order. And here's Morten's."

Harper glanced down. "Aside from the fact that they're both heavy drinkers, I don't see what you're driving at."

"I'm trying to show you a connection between the two of them," Harvey said testily. "If you don't want to see it – "

"Sorry," said Harper with a smile. "Go ahead."

"Thank you." Harvey shook his shoulders back, much, I thought, like a bird preening. "Now look here. The same steward was in both serving areas."

"And a bad one, at that," I said. "One of Morten's table mates said that Morten had been served the wrong drink in the Observation-Lounge before coming down to dinner, which fits with Josh's recollection." I took the paper from Harvey's hands and looked at it more closely. "What are these numbers here?"

"Table assignments." Harvey came around behind the desk to look over my shoulder. "See, here's Wilson at table six."

"And Morten and his party at table nine." Harper's face grew serious. "Served by the same steward, you said?"

"Yes. Man named Mike Woldert. New to the ship. Came on board this past Saturday. Oddly enough, he's sharing a berth with Bertie Evans."

"Bertie hasn't mentioned a new cabin mate to me," I said. Harvey looked annoyed.

"Are you the social director or what? Do you want to know what happened or not?" I nodded. "All right, then," continued Harvey. "It's pretty easy to figure out."

"Of course it is," said Harper. "This man Woldert just served the wrong drinks to the passengers."

"Or served the right drinks – but got the wrong passengers," I said.

"What do you mean?" asked Harvey.

I pulled a notepad toward me on the desk and picked up a pen, then drew a big "6" on the pad. "What do you see?" I asked Harvey.

"Six."

I reversed the pad. "And now?"

"Nine." Harvey blinked. "What are you suggesting?"

"I'm suggesting that this steward brought a drink intended for Wilson at table six – to Morten at table nine. It's the only time their paths ever crossed before Mr Morten died a few hours later."

Harper looked at me. "That's got to be it – that's got to be the connection between Morten and Wilson. Maeve is right – Morten was accidentally poisoned. He got the drink that was meant for Wilson." Harper scanned the sheet again. "The tables and servers don't cross again in this shift."

"No," said Harvey. "That would mean the passengers left the bar."

"To go to dinner. Where we all saw Thomas Morten succumb from drinking the aconitine which was meant for Harvey Wilson." Harper pointed a finger at me. "You, Nurse Chandler, are a genius."

"Not hardly."

Doctor Bratton came through the surgery door, pulling off his cap and mask. "All indications are that she'll have a normal puerperium," he announced. "Mother and daughter are doing just fine."

"What?" asked Harvey. I gave him a haughty gaze.

"Convalescence after giving birth," I said.

"Oh." Harvey was embarrassed.

"She's tired, but she's asking for her son," said Bratton.

"Mrs Templeton is bringing him down. They're on the way now."

"So I finally get to meet the legendary Mrs Templeton." Bratton pursed his lips. "Perhaps I should go put on my uniform."

"I don't think she'll care one way or the other." I looked at Doctor Bratton. "Very nice delivery, by the way."

"Thanks. I wish they were all that easy." Bratton pulled off his gloves. "Mister Harvey, good to see you again."

"Mister Harvey was just informing us about the likelihood that Mr Morten got the aconitine laced drink meant for Mr Wilson," said Harper. "Who, by the way, was killed before he went over the side. Someone broke his neck on the *Victoria*."

"Good God," said Bratton. "Is this ever going to end?"

"We're in New York in around sixty hours or so," Harvey remarked.

Harper shook his head. "I'm beginning to face the fact that they've got us. Unless someone comes up and knocks on our door and introduces themselves as Mr Murderer, they're going to walk off this ship Saturday morning and through the New York customs shed and disappear into the depths of the United States of America and we're never going to find out what happened."

"Well, something will turn up," I said, glancing at my watch. "Look at it this way – we've gone nearly forty-eight hours without anyone else making an unscheduled departure."

Harper rubbed his eyes. "That's not much consolation, but I'll take it."

I gave him a weak smile. "Best I can do right now, Boss." The door to the hospital opened and Agatha and Bradley came in. I looked down at Bradley. "You remember the doctor, don't you, Bradley?"

Bradley shied back from Harper as he had on the Boat Deck Monday night. Harper gave me a beseeching look and I got down on one knee. "Bradley, you have a new baby sister. Would you like to meet her?

"Yes, please."

"Doctor Bratton here will take you in," I said.

"Doctor Bratton?" said Agatha. She extended a hand. "I'm Mrs Templeton. I've heard so much about you."

"The same." He shook her hand. Agatha looked down at Bradley.

"Will you go with Doctor Bratton?" she asked. "He's a very nice man. I'll be here when you get out and you can tell me all about it." The boy nodded silently.

"She's right through there," said Bratton. "Come on, old sport." He led the way and Bradley followed at a discrete distance, still clutching his toy aeroplane.

Agatha waited until the doors had closed behind them, then exhaled. "What a story I've got to tell," she said.

"And us, Mrs Templeton," said Harvey. "We've got a link between Mr Morten and Mr Wilson." He explained the apparent drink mix up to Agatha.

"My goodness," she said. "It's basic detective work, but it's good." She looked at Harper. "And how did your visit with the Captain go?"

"It was very refreshing, Mrs Templeton," said Harper.

"I'll just bet it was." Agatha looked at us. "Well, I had an interesting talk with young master Bradley. Did you know, Mister Harvey, that he has a distinct aversion to stewards?" She gazed at Harper. "And to doctors too, it would seem, except for Doctor Bratton. Interesting."

"Stewards? What do you mean, stewards? My stewards?" said Harvey.

"Well, the two that you sent around to move the Alston's baggage from their old stateroom to their new stateroom, anyway," I said.

Mister Harvey frowned. "Evans and Woldert?" He ground his teeth. "If I find there's been any monkey-shines, I'll - "

I held up a hand. "It was all above board, Mister Harvey. The boy was just frightened." I looked at Agatha. What did you find out, Mrs Templeton?"

"Well," said Agatha, "the night you two found him behind the ventilator on the Sports Deck, he'd gone missing because his parents were fighting. He slipped out of the cabin and made his way up to the Promenade Deck, then climbed the stairs to the Boat Deck."

"Good Lord," said Harvey. "Didn't he realize how dangerous it is to walk around that deck after dark?"

Mrs Templeton smiled. "Weren't you a boy once, Mister Harvey?" She looked at him. "I'll warrant you gave your mother no end of trouble, didn't you?"

Harvey coughed. "That's neither here nor there, Mrs Templeton." A faint trace of a smile played across his face. "But yes, I was a boy once."

"Eeyore," I said to him.

Harper held up a hand. "Enough, children. Get on, Mrs Templeton, please."

"Thank you, Doctor. To resume, he went to the Boat Deck."

"How did he know he was on the Boat Deck?" I asked. Agatha gave me the kind of look usually reserved for the class dunce.

"Because he told me there were little boats on it. Really, Maeve." She took a breath. "He was on the Boat Deck when he heard voices up ahead. He stopped and listened. The voices grew louder, then there was a thudding noise and they stopped all together. He risked a peek around the corner of his hiding place and saw something large fall over the railing. Another figure stood and watched it tumble down."

"Bloody hell," said Harvey.

"Did he see a face?" I asked. Agatha shook her head.

"Nothing. It was too dark."

"What did he do?" asked Harper.

"He did what any boy would have done. He headed for higher ground. He says he climbed a flight of stairs almost directly in front of him - "

"That means he was probably at Lifeboat Station Six," I said. "There are stairs up to the Sports Deck at Station Eight." I looked at Mister Harvey. "And the next station is ten, where the scrap of fabric was found."

"Exactly so," said Agatha. "The boy clambered up the steps, trying to be quiet, but the gate to the Sports Deck clanged shut behind him in the wind. Bradley says he ran past the tennis courts and slipped through the gate to the base of the first funnel and took refuge behind the ventilator, where you found him later."

"Slipped through the gate," I said. The image of the tennis player came back to me. "The gate is over-greased. A passenger was complaining about it to me this afternoon. That must be where Bradley got the stain on his jacket that I saw Monday night after Doctor Harper and I found him. It matches."

"Poor boy," said Harper. "No wonder he was so terrified."

"What are we going to do now?" asked Harvey.

Agatha's face was set. "Keep this information among us — and keep an extra-sharp eye on that young man in there with his mother."

"We'll watch him," I said. Agatha looked at me.

"You need to do more than watch him. Hasn't it occurred to you that if he was able to see our mystery man, then our mystery man may have been able to see him?"

My eyes widened. "And he can't have any witnesses."

"Exactly so," said Agatha again.

The telephone jangled and I picked it up. "Hospital. Yes, he's here. Of course, right away. Thank you." I rang off and looked at Harper.

"Our night's not over yet, Boss" I said. "There's been an accident in one of the stern lifts."

"Accident? What kind of accident?" Harper looked positively distraught.

I looked at the faces riveted on mine. "Someone fell down an open shaft."

"Oh, my God," said Harvey.

"Where did it happen?" asked Harper.

"It started on A Deck. I'm afraid it ended on F Deck."

"Without a stop in between, I assume?" said Agatha. I nodded.

Harper reached out for his medical bag. "Then let's be on our way." I slowly shook my head.

"You won't be needing that, Doctor. And you've got plenty of time to get out of your surgical gown." Harper stopped in mid-reach, finally comprehending.

"Bloody hell," said Harvey. "Another murder?" He looked at Harper, whose face was set.

"I hope," Harper said fervently, "that this time it really was an accident."

"Me, too," I said. "I'll catch Doctor Bratton up and tell him not to allow Bradley to leave the hospital, then Mrs Templeton and I will join you." I waved Mister Harvey and Doctor Harper off. "F Deck stern port passenger lift station."

IV

Ever since Galileo Galilei performed his famous ball drop experiments from the leaning tower of Pisa, humans have been interested in learning how quickly something will fall. (Plenty of pilots during the War found out the hard way.) Galileo wanted to prove that all objects fall at the same rate, no matter their mass weight. He was interested in the downward flight of the object, giving little thought to the landing. However, as any of the aforementioned pilots could tell him, it's not the fall that should concern you. It's the sudden stop.

The broken body at the bottom of the lift shaft had mercifully been covered by a blanket – now blood soaked – before Agatha and I arrived. Captain Webster and First Officer Jackson were in attendance at the open lift doors along with Doctor Harper and Mister Harvey. The Captain tilted his head toward the figure beneath the blanket.

"He's a passenger, Nurse Chandler – rather, was a passenger, but he's got no identification on him. However, Doctor Harper says he made a positive identification, and that you can verify it for us." He looked down at the grisly scene at the base of the shaft. "If you please. Mrs Templeton, I really don't believe - "

"Thank you for your consideration, but I was in the War, Captain."

The Captain nodded, then gestured to Harper who bent and lifted an edge of the blanket. Agatha and I peered over his shoulder. The man had come down directly on top of the stops at the base of the shaft. One of them had clearly broken his back, which was arched at an unusual angle. A forearm encased in a now-cracked plaster cast was jutting out at an odd angle. The unpleasant face of Frank Alston was frozen in a terrified grimace. Harper dropped the blanket back down.

"Don't leave us all in suspense," said Harvey. I looked at Mister Harvey and the Captain.

"It's the father of our new baby girl," I said.

"Him?" said Agatha. "That's the Mr Alston I've heard about?"

I nodded. "The very same." I looked at the Captain. "His wife just had a baby girl in the hospital."

"Yes, Doctor Harper told me about the delivery." He rubbed his beard. "Mother and daughter doing well, then?"

"Yes, sir." I looked down at the body. "And if I may be so bold, they'll be doing much better without him."

"So I've been told," said the Captain.

I looked at Harper. "What are we going to tell Clara?"

"I'm sure you'll think of something both sanguine and Christian," said the Captain.

"Who found him?" I asked.

Mister Jackson shook his head. "God help us, a passenger. An inebriated gentleman trying to get back topside to his rooms, ended up lost, then forced the doors to the lift and found this inside." Jackson exhaled, looking down at the sheeted body. "I should imagine it sobered him up tremendously. I had a crewman escort him to his stateroom. I doubt we'll see much of him before New York."

"I should think so," said the Captain. "And before you ask – Mrs Templeton, Nurse – this was no accident. Chief Duncan and the ship's master electrician have both checked the lift. The gate on A Deck had been forced. Unless this man wanted to commit suicide by leaping down an elevator shaft, someone jammed open the gate and helped him."

"Where was the lift attendant?" I asked.

"The lift was temporarily out of service and had a sign posted," said Harvey

"Have you discovered anything new since last we met, Mrs Templeton?" asked Jackson.

"Oh, no. Well, perhaps one or two little things. It's been a quiet evening up until now."

"I see," said Captain Webster. "I'm sure I don't need to remind you that the gangways go down in just under sixty hours." He looked again at the still form in the base of the lift shaft. "sixty hours, my steadfast paladins. Take care of this poor sod and keep me informed. I'd like to hear from you at 06:30."

"Yes, sir," said Harper. Webster and Jackson strode purposefully away. Harvey looked at Harper, then down at the body.

"Poor bastard," he said. "Well, on to the practical side. Another body to take care of. I'm correct in assuming that this goes down as a fearful accident should anyone ask?"

"I think so," said Harper.

"Without question," said Agatha.

Harvey sighed. "I suppose you'll be wanting to use my cold storage again, won't you?"

Harper consulted his watch. "Only for the next sixty hours."

Mister Harvey shook his head, then picked up the service phone beside the lift. He spoke quietly into the receiver for a moment, then rang off.

"Excuse me, Boss," I said. "No love lost for his departure, but what exactly are you going to tell Clara?"

"That's both sanguine and Christian?" added Harvey.

"Tell her?" Harper pursed his lips. "Tell her nothing right now. She's exhausted, and she's got the baby and Bradley in there with her. It can wait."

"She's going to have to know before we get to New York," said Agatha.

"I'm aware of that, Mrs Templeton," Harper replied.

We became respectfully quiet as two seamen arrived with a stretcher. One of the crewmen lifted the blanket. "I'll be blowed," he said, gazing down at the broken body. The other crewman gave a low whistle.

"Sorry," said Harper. "I should have warned you. He fell down the open shaft. Accident."

"Thanks, Doc." The men hoisted Frank Alston's body up and out of the lift well, setting him down on the stretcher. The blanket was quickly put back over him and the men lifted him up, but Frank's right arm slipped off the stretcher and hit the floor. His fist opened up and a small circular object rolled out and toward the open shaft. Agatha moved with surprising speed and stamped a shoe down on it, then picked it up. "Apologies," said the crewman, lifting the arm back up.

"Where do we take him?" asked the first crewman. Harper gave Harvey a beseeching look. The Chief Steward screwed his eyes shut, then opened them.

"The New York Department of Public Health is going to close this ship down when they do their inspection, you know," he said to Harper and Maeve. He turned to the waiting crewmen. "Take him to the carpenter's stores. I think we might still have an empty coffin or two. When you're done packing him away stick him in the ales refrigerator next to the other casket."

"Trying to put us off drinking, Mister Harvey?" asked the second crewman. Harvey glared at him.

"Just do it," he said. "And if anyone asks, like Doctor Harper says, it was an accident. Don't offer information otherwise."

"Right away, Mister Harvey." The two headed down the corridor. Agatha beckoned us over.

"Look at this." She held out the object between her thumb and forefinger, partially obscuring it.

"It's a button," said Harvey. "Maybe he snagged his jacket."

"Look closer," urged Agatha. She dropped it into my open palm where we could see it in its full brass glory. Harper's eyes widened and I gasped.

Harvey nodded. "It's a button, all right. It's a button off of a *Queen Victoria* steward's jacket."

Not even a late meal in the *Victoria's* magnificent dining salon served to lift our mood over the discovery of Frank Alston and the button clutched in his dead hand. The only good news, as far as Doctor Harper, myself and Mrs Templeton could ascertain, was the birth of Clara's daughter and the information Agatha had gotten out of Bradley.

"The way you handled the boy was marvelous, Mrs Templeton," I said. "And I'm sorry I threw you into it like that, with the whole child psychology routine. It's all I could think of on the spur of the moment."

"Thanks," said Agatha dryly. "That makes it even worse."

"But you did perform quite well, Mrs Templeton," said Harper. He raised his wine glass to her.

"Well, thank you, Doctor." Agatha sighed. "He's a sweet little boy. I hate that he's been so ill-treated. Please tell him hello for me when you get back tonight. His step-father, on the other hand," she took a sip of water. "What was it you were telling me about his belief that his ship had come in and he was going to be rich? Though I daresay for a man like he was, having twenty pounds in his pocket would qualify him as wealthy."

"Yes, that was yesterday," I said.

"And then last night he tells his wife he's out, and doesn't come back until early this morning, and sporting a broken arm in the bargain." Agatha looked about the nearly empty salon. A few passengers lingered at their tables, having an after-dinner brandy or other libation. "And then tonight someone helps him down a lift shaft." She pursed her lips. "I think that Bradley may not have been the only witness to Mr Wilson's demise."

"Frank Alston?" Harper was incredulous. "Mrs Templeton, that makes no sense."

"No," I said, following her reasoning. "It makes perfect sense."

"Go on, then," said Agatha.

"Well, Mr Alston brags Tuesday about how he's going to be rich before we reach New York. This is after Mr Wilson has been murdered Monday night. Mr Alston goes out on Tuesday night, and returns early this morning, with a broken arm. Given what we know about his character, it's possible he also saw the murder, and more to the point, saw the murderer's face. He went out last night to blackmail the murderer, somehow got his arm broken, probably in a fight with the murderer. Remember your remark about his arm, Doctor? Tonight he's back out again, on A Deck – a place he wouldn't normally go given his passenger status – and he's escorted to a conveniently rigged lift shaft by whomever he met."

"And," added Agatha, "the fact that the shaft was already set as a trap lends credence to the fact that the murderer knew Mr Alston would be coming back for a second visit and probably suggested it as a meeting place."

"But he was clutching a button from a steward's jacket," said Harper. "No steward makes the kind of money that someone like Alston would blackmail for."

"Maybe it was a higher-ranking person wearing the jacket?" I suggested. Agatha shrugged.

"That is something we won't know until we reach the end of this skein of yarn." She put her napkin down and stood. "Have you decided how you are going to break the news to Mrs Alston about her husband?"

Harper pushed his chair in to the table and straightened his tie. "No. But after hearing Maeve make you over into a child psychologist, I'm sure she'll come up with something before we reach the hospital."

I gave Harper a look. "Thanks, Boss. Mrs Templeton, you'll check in with us in the morning?"

"Of course." She smiled. "Thank you both for an interesting afternoon and evening."

Casey was parked in the hospital waiting room smoking the inevitable cigarette when we opened the door. I glared at him.

"Don't you ever sleep?" I asked. "It's the midnight side of 11."

"Shh." Casey put a finger to his lips. "Doctor Bratton and your patient and her children are asleep in the next room."

"You spied on them?" I asked. "Even for you, that's pretty low."

Casey looked annoyed, but then, with Casey it was always hard to tell. "I thought I'd get a plus for not waking them," he replied. "Tell me about our newest passenger. Boy? Girl?"

"Girl," said Harper. "Delivered about 20:00 hours this evening."

"Well, I just wanted to make sure that I got the scoop and didn't miss anything, heh, heh." Oh, brother, I thought. If you only knew. Casey whipped out his notepad. "Name?"

"Doctor Leslie Harper."

Casey gave Harper an exasperated look. "Not yours, Doc. The baby."

"Oh. Victoria, I think." He looked at me. "Wasn't that it?"

I nodded. "Victoria."

"Victoria," repeated Casey. "Why, that's fine! Named after the ship?"

"No, after Admiral Nelson's victory column in Trafalgar Square," I said. Casey gave me a squint.

"Funny."

"I believe so, yes."

He licked the point of his pencil and poised it above the pad. "Mother's name?" he asked.

"Clara Alston," I said.

"Father's name?"

I looked at Harper. Harper looked at me. I shrugged. "Frank Alston."

"Good, good." Casey dutifully wrote it down. "Where can I find the happy father?"

"I'm afraid he's not with us," said Harper.

"Wasn't able to make the trip, eh?" The pencil scratched again.

"Something like that," said Harper. I gave him an admiring glance. Casey read back from his pad.

"The *Queen Victoria* welcomed a new passenger aboard last night around 20:00. Victoria Alston was born to passenger Clara Alston, wife of Frank Alston. Both mother and daughter are doing well." He stuck his pencil back behind his ear and shook out a cigarette. "That's fine. Fine stuff." His lighter clicked out and he took a puff, blowing acrid smoke toward me. I waved it away with my hand.

"Have you had any luck running down your children's author?" asked Doctor Harper, giving me a sidelong glance.

Casey expelled smoke through his nostrils and pushed his fedora back. "Not yet. But I'll find him before we reach New York, you can bet your life on it." He jammed his pad back into his coat pocket and gave us a knowing look. "Nothing gets past Casey. You'd do well to remember that, Nurse."

"Bugger off, Casey."

"I'm going. But don't think you and the Doctor here haven't been seen with your deckside dalliances."

Harper lunged forward and I grabbed him around the waist. "Doctor, no!" Casey stepped back.

"Struck a nerve, eh?"

"If you don't get out of this hospital right now I'll strike something other than a nerve," growled Harper.

"I'm going, I'm going." Casey backpedaled through the doors, leaving a cloud of foul-smelling cigarette smoke in the air behind him. I released my grip on Harper.

"I'm beginning to understand Mister Harvey's aversion to that man," he said.

"Maybe you two can flip a shilling to see who gets to toss him overboard." I tried to smooth out my nursing smock. "Anyway, that was, as the Yanks like to say, mighty quick thinking on your part when he asked about the father."

"First thing that popped into the old lemon." Harper took off his cap and scratched his head. "I think I've been around you too long. Those little lies come too easy to me."

"You know it's not going to take him long to come up with the fact that there is actually a Frank Alston booked as a passenger and then start looking for an interview."

"Let him look all he wants. Frank Alston's not giving interviews." Harper yawned. "I can't think about it anymore right now. I've got to get some sleep."

The door from the surgery opened and Bradley came through with Doctor Bratton.

"I've got a little sister, Captain!" said Bradley. For the moment at least his exuberance overrode his fear of men.

"So I've heard," Harper replied. "How is she?"

"She's all red and wrinkly and she cries a lot." I stifled a laugh.

"Well, she'll straighten out in no time, I'm sure," said Harper with a smile. He looked at Bratton. "How are our patients?"

"Fine as can be expected, with all this noise out here." He yawned. "Was that Casey I heard?"

"Yes," I said. "We talked to him and gave him the birth information for his paper."

"Better you than me." Bratton stretched. "I just didn't want to leave her and the baby alone. Bradley fell asleep in my lap. Nice kid, but I'll never get these kinks out." He looked at Harper. "Nurse Chandler told me where you were going. Lift accident?" He glanced about the area. "I'm going to take it that our services were not needed?"

"You would take it correctly," said Harper. He glanced at Bradley, who was sketching an aeroplane on a prescription pad on the desk. "I'll tell you about it later."

Bratton went to the desk. "May I borrow this pad for just a moment, Master Bradley?" Bratton tore off the page the boy had been scribbling on and handed it to him along with a pencil, then pulled a pen from his coat and went to work on a fresh sheet of scrip. He tore off the note and handed it to me. "Do you mind getting this?" he asked.

I read the prescription. "Just enough for Mrs Alston? Don't you think we could all use a helping?"

"'Physician, heal thyself,'" said Bratton. "I don't know about you, but I'm going to have no difficulty in sleeping tonight." He reached down and tousled the boy's hair. "I think it's time for you to go back to bed, young man."

"I don't want to be by myself." The boy's mood changed like lightning. I looked at Harper, then to Bradley.

"It's fine, Bradley," I said. "You can bunk with me for the rest of the night. It's not as fancy as what you're used to, but it will be good for you to see how the other half lives." I handed the scrip back to Bratton. "Normally I'd be happy to do this, but would you be all right filling it for yourself just this once? Doctor Harper and I need to talk with Bradley's mum for a moment. Perhaps Bradley would like to go with you to see the dispensing station? Then you can bring him back here and we'll be off."

"Oh, yes. Certainly." Bratton gave me a quizzical look.

"I'll explain later." I nodded my head to Harper. "We'll explain later."

"Fine. I've given up sleeping again, anyway. Come on, Bradley. We get to go roust Mister Reedy out of his comfortable bunk. Won't that be fun?" He took the boy's hand and they went out the door.

"I've about given up sleeping again, too," I said to Harper.

"No rest for the wicked?" he said with a sad smile.

"Something like that." I sighed. "Come on. Let's get this over with."

Clara was propped up in bed holding little Victoria. She smiled at us. "Thank you again for everything. Isn't she beautiful?"

"Yes," I said. "Very lovely."

"Just like her mother," said Harper.

"You're both very kind." Clara looked around. "Where is Bradley?"

"He's with Doctor Bratton. They went to get a prescription filled for you," I said.

"Do you know Doctor Bratton has been in here for hours and hours." She cooed at Victoria. "He said he wouldn't leave us alone, in case Bradley had another of his spells or if Frank came down here. And Bradley talked very nicely about your Mrs Templeton. He said they had a nice chat, but he wouldn't tell me what about."

"Yes, well – she is very nice. I'll find out what they talked about and let you know," I said. "May I sit down?"

"Of course." I gently settled on the edge of the bed.

"The fact of the matter is, Mrs Alston, we have something to tell you," said Harper.

Clara nodded. "It's about Frank, isn't it?"

"I'm afraid so." I put a hand over hers. "He's dead."

Her expression never changed. "How?"

"Someone helped him down one of the lift shafts without benefit of the car." Harper stopped, and then went on. "The fall killed him."

"Someone helped him?" Clara's brows knit. "Do you mean he was pushed down an open shaft?"

"He was clutching a button from a steward's jacket in his hand when his body was found," I said.

"Why would a steward want to kill Frank?" Clara looked confused. "I can think of a lot of people who would have liked to have seen him dead, but a steward on board a ship in the middle of the Atlantic Ocean?"

"We're going to find out," said Harper. "Don't worry."

"Oh, I'm not worried about that, Doctor." Clara's eyes were focused on something in the middle distance. "Whoever it was has certainly done me a service. When did it happen?"

"About two hours ago," I said quietly. "We're sorry to be the ones telling you."

Clara held Victoria closer and gently stroked her head. The baby was fast asleep. "Someone was going to tell me sooner or later," said Clara. "It may as well have been you as anyone else."

"We have the body in cold storage," said Harper. "I'll do the paperwork when we get to New York to get him released to his family."

Clara's face hardened. "You can push him over the side for all I care. I'm glad he's gone." She cooed to Victoria. "Glad he's gone."

"Bradley doesn't know," I said.

"Thank you. I'm sure he won't miss him either." She was silent for a moment. "Does anyone know what he was doing before?"

"Not yet." Harper looked at me. "We'll find out."

"Drinking, I'll warrant." She looked at Harper. "Did he tell you how he broke his arm today?"

"He said he slipped in the bathtub."

"Bathtub?" She gave a brittle laugh and shook her head. "No. I suspect he probably fell off a bar stool."

"Had he been having any arguments with anyone on board?" I asked. "Any sort of set-to?"

"If he had it wouldn't have surprised me. All he was ever good for was gambling, drinking, whoring and penny extortion, and he wasn't very good at the gambling and extortion."

"Penny extortion?" asked Harper. Clara nodded.

"Yes. The kind of two-bit racketeering the Chicago gangsters do that I read about in the papers." Harper and I exchanged glances as she shifted Victoria in her arms. "But believe me, he was never going to be Al Capone."

"Thank you, Clara," I said. "We've taken up enough of your time. Doctor Bratton will be in the outer office the remainder of the night. If you don't mind, I'll keep Bradley in my quarters."

"That's very kind of you." She proffered Victoria. "Would you put her in the bassinet? Thank you." I laid the baby carefully on her back on top of the covers, then pulled the bassinet close up to the bed as Harper answered a gentle knock at the door.

"I'm back," announced Doctor Bratton. Bradley eyed Harper warily for a moment, then went to the other side of his mum's bed. Bratton opened a small bottle and shook out two tablets. "Take these with a sip of water, Mrs Alston. It will help you sleep more soundly and relieve some of the afterpains."

Clara did as she was told, setting her water glass back on the nightstand. She nestled back into the pillows. "Bradley," I said, "why don't you tell your mum and new sister goodnight, then come on out and you and I will go to my quarters."

The boy nodded, and Harper and I bade our goodnights and ushered Doctor Bratton out of the room.

When the door was closed behind us he folded his arms. "So, just what's going on?" he asked.

"That person in the lift accident — that was her husband," I said. Bratton paled.

"Oh, my God. Does she know?"

Harper nodded. "We told her." Bratton blinked.

"I had heard that he was no prize, but still - "

"He was murdered," I said. "Probably by a *Victoria* crew member."

"Oh, my God," he repeated. "And I take it you told her that, too?"

"I'm afraid so." Harper looked around the waiting area. "I'll stay down here with you tonight. If someone was out to get the husband because he saw something, they will probably be out to get the wife and boy, too."

"I'll be sure to bolt my stateroom door," I said.

"And set your alarm. We have a meeting with the Captain at 06:30."

"Terrific. No rest for the weary."

Bradley came out of the room and closed the door behind him. "I'm sleepy," he announced.

"I've no doubt of it," I said, taking his hand. "Come along with me and we'll get you comfortable for the night." Bradley nodded, and with another askance look at Harper, went with me out the hospital door.

I

As I've mentioned before, and contrary to all possible evidence and plausibility, I was a child once. I don't remember a lot of detail about my early childhood, when I was Bradley Alston's age. I suspect it was spent in cadging candy from doting relatives and the like. I also suspect, given my propensity for desiring a good night's sleep, that I looked forward to nappy time with a fervor that probably perplexed my mum. It was no surprise to me, then, that young Bradley slept like the dead. What did surprise me was his complete lack of inhibitions. Bradley was down to his shorts and climbing into my absent cabin mate Alice's berth before I even had my shoes off. By the time I switched off the lamp, a rhythmic soft snoring had been coming from him for over ten minutes.

I got up once to see if I had, indeed, bolted the door, then made my way back to my bunk and climbed in, drawing the sheets up to my neck. I'd only slept that way once before, after reading *Dracula,* and it had worked: no vampire had bitten me in the night. I pulled the sheets closer and hoped they'd work just as well with the murderer, or murderers, we had roaming loose on the *Queen Victoria.*

Not that I was going to be sleeping much anyway. There were just too many odd bits and pieces floating around in my mind, jostling each other for space and generally refusing to be quiet and let me have some much-needed rest. My mind kept churning through what Bradley had told Agatha, compounded now by the death of Frank Alston.

Don't get me wrong. I felt no sadness at his sudden departure, nor, I was little amazed to find, at the way he departed. Clara was going to be better off without him, no doubt of that. But what had he been doing to warrant getting a broken arm? And what fresh hell was going to rise from the dead man to plague Clara and her little family? Part of me was also wondering what Agatha might be thinking, or was she sound asleep, secure in her knowledge of events?

Morten to Wilson to Alston. Or should it be Morten/Wilson to Alston? Or Morten/Wilson/Alston? I finally fell asleep to troubled dreams in which the three murdered men had their arms around each other's shoulders and were performing some kind of macabre high kick routine like a chorus line of dead cross-dressing Ziegfeld Girls.

A rapid banging on my stateroom door awakened me what seemed like 15 minutes later. I rose, wrapped my shift around me, banged a toe into the edge of my bed, resisted waking Bradley up with a particularly juicy curse word, and answered the door. Harper was outside, his face clouded.

"Someone just got into Mrs Templeton's stateroom," he said. I gasped.

"Is she all right?"

Harper nodded. "She 'phoned down to the hospital. Doctor Bratton is still inside with the door locked. Get dressed. You'll need to take Bradley there before we go. I don't want to have to deal with another of his fits. I'll be over at the starboard lift."

"Right." I closed the door.

Twenty minutes later at precisely five in the morning and joined by a disheveled Mister Harvey, we were standing in Agatha's suite. It looked like she'd managed to run a brush through her hair and even apply some rudimentary makeup before dressing in a shirt and slacks. Efficient, I thought. No wonder she could crank out the novels.

"That's correct," said Agatha. "I was asleep when a rattle at the door awakened me. It took a moment for me to realize that someone was trying the knob, and then I heard a key sliding into the lock."

"Pass keys?" I asked Mister Harvey. "Who has them?" His brow furrowed.

"Easier to say who doesn't. Housekeeping. Senior stewards. Officers, myself included."

"But no passengers," I said.

"Only if there were two or more to a room. Which, in this case, there aren't." Harvey frowned. "So that narrows it to crew."

"That's something, I suppose," said Agatha. "When I heard the key in the lock I dared not breathe. The lights outside in the corridor were out; I suppose the visitor had thrown a switch or unscrewed a few of them. I had already turned off the lights in the sitting room when I went to bed. It was completely dark. He wasn't carrying a torch; at least if he was, he didn't use it."

"What happened, Mrs Templeton?" asked Harper.

"I heard a clink of glass; I suppose it was the water pitcher in the sitting room. I didn't wait to find out more. I sat up in bed and yelled out 'Who's there?' and that, I will tell you, got results. There was a thud as the intruder apparently ran into a chair, and then I heard the door to the corridor open and slam shut. That's when I switched on the bedroom light and called you."

"The corridor lights were on when I got here," said Harvey to us. "That means the intruder definitely was a crewman; if the lights had been unscrewed by anyone else, I doubt they would have taken the time on their exit to put them back in place; that means they were switched off by cutting the power. Only a member of the ship's staff would know where to access the circuit breakers for the lighting in the corridor, and even then, only a crewman with a lot of knowledge of the ship."

"Mrs Templeton, you haven't touched the water pitcher there, have you?" asked Harper.

She shook her head. "No. And I won't either."

I looked at Harper. "Take it down to Mister Reedy?"

"Post-haste, I think."

"Mister Reedy?" asked Agatha. "Oh, yes. The dispenser who identified the aconitine in Mr Morten." She gave Harper a steady gaze. "Do you seriously think someone is trying to kill me?"

"I honestly don't know what to think anymore, Mrs Templeton," he replied.

Mister Harvey looked about the suite. "How long will it take you to pack up, Mrs Templeton?"

"Not too long, I suppose. I only have necessaries with me here; the rest of it is in a trunk in the hold."

Harvey nodded at her. "Good. Please pack up, then. I'm moving you to a new location, and I'm also going to have the ship's carpenter change the lock out on the new stateroom and give the key to you. I'll keep the other. Neither will have a duplicate pass key anywhere on board. If anyone wants in, they'll have to break in."

"That's oddly reassuring," said Agatha. "Thank you, Mister Harvey."

I went to the bathroom and picked out a hand towel to drape over the top of the water pitcher, then wrapped another around the pitcher before carefully picking it up. "Mind you don't spill anything," said Harper. "Regardless, wash your hands and any exposed skin carefully, and tell the same to Mister Reedy."

"Oh, Maeve – wait. I have a pair of gloves here somewhere." Agatha went back into her bedroom and after a moment returned with ivory kidskin gloves. "Better than nothing," she said, handing them to me.

"Thanks," I said, slipping them on. "Well, I'll see everyone later, I hope."

"Be careful," Agatha called after me. I just hoped I wouldn't trip up somewhere.

Reedy, as might be expected, was none too happy to be wakened out of a sound sleep for the second time in the space of a few hours, but he bore it well. By 'well' I mean that he didn't throw any lab ware when he unlocked the dispensary door, but his attitude could certainly have used some adjustment. Not that I could blame him. So could mine.

He lit a burner and took down some chemicals and small beakers, then went to work. Nothing but the occasional grunt passed his lips, until finally he turned off the burner, pulled off his gloves and looked at me.

"Well, well, ain't we got fun?" he said to me.

"What?"

"More of your aconitine. Except this time there's enough in that pitcher to kill a horse. You said this was in a passenger's stateroom?"

I nodded. "It looks like someone let themselves in with a pass key and doctored the pitcher."

Mister Reedy gingerly took the pitcher to the drain and poured the contents down, then liberally doused the inside of it with soap and ran hot salt water inside. "Your passenger was quite fortunate they didn't take a sip of water this morning, then. This dosage would have produced a much faster death than what killed Mr Morten a few days ago." He leaned against the lab counter. "That is, of course, if they had gotten it down."

"What do you mean?"

"I mean that aconitine really doesn't like to dissolve into water. If someone dumped this amount into a full pitcher and was thinking it would disappear, they were either very naïve or woefully uninformed on how to use it."

"But Mr Morten – " I began. Reedy cut me off with a wave of his hand.

"As I told you before, Nurse Chandler, it's been my belief that Mr Morten received his dosage in a drink served to him several hours before he expired. Aconitine is soluble in a mixture of alcohol and water if the level of alcohol is high enough – and you know how heavy handed they pour the drinks up in the Observation Deck lounge. All he would have tasted was alcohol while his body absorbed the killing dose of aconitine."

"Thank you, Mister Reedy," I said. "You've been very helpful."

Now the question begging an answer was – who wanted Agatha Christie dead?

Thursday, October 31, 1929

‖

There's something indescribably beautiful about a sunrise at sea. The rosy glow coming up over the horizon, the first rays touching the water, spreading out like a glorious chrysanthemum of fire. It's absolutely breathtaking and something you will never forget. On the other hand, there's absolutely nothing beautiful about the hour before dawn at sea, especially when one is being called to account in the Captain's quarters.

I met Doctor Harper on the bridge at 06:30; Harper looked the way I felt. Captain Webster, meanwhile, looked his usual staid self. I wondered if the man ever got tired or even slept.

"Doctor Harper, Nurse Chandler," said the Captain, looking ahead through the windows at the darkness. There was a very light rain falling, and a glorious sunrise just didn't seem in the cards. "How was the rest of your night?"

"Miserable, sir," answered Harper.

"I thought as much." The Captain nodded.

Harper coughed politely. "No, sir. There's more to it than that. Someone entered Mrs Templeton's stateroom early this morning and poisoned her water pitcher."

The Captain's eyebrows shot up like distress rockets. "I'm sorry, Doctor, I could have sworn you just said someone entered one of our passenger's staterooms with the intent of doing them harm?"

"Yes, sir," I said. Somewhere behind us a bell rang and one of the bridge officers picked up a telephone, speaking quietly. He rang off and gave low instructions to the helmsman, who repeated them back and gave the wheel a gentle touch.

"This person is in custody?" asked the Captain.

"Not yet, sir." Harper was intensely uncomfortable. "We are absolutely certain it was a crew member using a pass key. They also turned off the lights in the corridor outside her stateroom by apparently throwing a breaker – something Mister Harvey pointed out that only a crewman with select knowledge would know how to do."

The Captain's jaw tightened. "Bloody hell. Is there no end to this? How is Mrs Templeton?"

"She's fine," I said. "Mister Harvey is moving her to another stateroom and having the locks changed on the new stateroom door. There will only be two keys – one for Mrs Templeton and the other for Mister Harvey."

"Why?" asked the Captain. I looked at Harper.

"Well, because Mister Harvey thought it safer to move her, and we agreed." The Captain closed and opened his eyes, obviously trying to maintain control.

"No, Nurse Chandler. Why would someone try to get into Mrs Templeton's stateroom."

"Because they wanted to kill her," I said, amazed at how matter-of-fact it sounded.

"Are you serious?" asked the Captain. He looked at Harper. "Is she serious?"

"I'm afraid so, sir." Doctor Harper spoke quietly. "The water pitcher had been laced with a heavy dose of aconitine. Mister Reedy confirmed it just a while ago."

"Aconitine? The same as Mr Morten?" The Captain rubbed his beard. "Again, why?"

"Someone believes she's a threat," I said.

"You'll forgive me," said the Captain. "But I don't see Mrs Templeton as a threat."

"Not a physical threat. But she's asked some pointed questions regarding our investigation. It's possible she was overheard by someone. I don't know who," I concluded.

The Captain looked about the bridge. "Mr Morten murdered with aconitine. You and Mister Jackson tell me yesterday that Mr Wilson was killed before he went over the side. Someone apparently tried to kill Mrs Templeton early this morning, again with aconitine. And then that poor sod who went down the lift shaft last night." He looked at us. "Did you tell his wife?"

"Yes, sir," I said. "She didn't seem too concerned. More relieved that she wouldn't have to put up with him anymore."

"To each his own," said the Captain. "Anything else?"

"After you and Mister Jackson left, while the body was being moved, Mrs Templeton discovered this." I fished out the steward's jacket button from a pocket and handed it to the Captain. "We think Mr Alston pulled it off a jacket as he fell backwards into the shaft."

The Captain rolled the button in his palm. "Another crew member? Or the same one who tried to murder Mrs Templeton?"

"It's unclear, sir," said Harper.

"There's too bloody much on this ship right now that's unclear, Doctor." The Captain handed the button back to me. The bridge door opened and Quartermaster Carter came in with a salute to the Captain, then went to the helmsman's station. The Captain nodded up at the three large regulator clocks on the bulkhead over the front bridge windows. They were labeled 'Southampton,' 'Ship's Time,' and 'New York' respectively. "We're barely fifty-three hours out. It's my belief that we're fast approaching the time when 'unclear' needs to quickly change to 'clear.'"

"Yes, sir," I said.

"I'll take a trip down to the hospital later this morning to check in with your mother and daughter, if that's all right with you," said the Captain.

"That would be good of you, sir," said Harper.

Webster snorted. "There's nothing good about it. Standard Captain's duties." He gave Harper a sidelong glance. "Though I'll wager there was little call for this particular duty in His Majesty's navy."

"No, sir, not for that one." Harper paused. "But there is for another one, I'm afraid." He handed the Captain a filled-in death certificate. The Captain looked it over.

"Cause of death, accidental fall. Hmm." He took a pen from inside his jacket and signed the report, giving it back to Harper. "And you'll be happy to know that you won't find this little accident in today's newspaper. Mister Casey was up here an hour ago. He said he'd already talked with you about the birth of our latest passenger, and after you showed him the door he was up here sniffing around about a possible lift accident."

I looked at Harper. "That didn't take long."

"I exercised a Captain's prerogative for censorship with him. Two deaths at sea are quite enough thrills for the paying passengers. Three is unnecessary largesse. No need to immortalize this one in print." Mister Jackson brushed past us and saluted, taking his station at the bridge a few feet away.

"There is some good news, sir," I said.

"I'm all for good news, Nurse. Pray tell."

"We've found one steward who seems to have a connection to Morten and Wilson. He served both men drinks on Sunday evening before dinner," I said.

And," Harper held up a finger, "a witness has surfaced who may well have seen everything that happened on the Sports Deck Monday night."

Webster turned, his bushy eyebrows raising. "Who is it?"

I steeled myself for the reaction. "A young boy. The stepson of the man who was killed in the elevator shaft."

Captain Webster took off his cap and ran a hand across his forehead. "Is this voyage cursed?" He thought a moment. "Any connection between what the boy may have seen and his stepfather's death?"

"We don't know, sir," said Harper.

"And the boy?" the Captain bit off. "Where is he?"

"Currently in the hospital with his mother," I said. "Doctor Bratton is looking after both of them, and given the current state of things, he's locked the door."

The Captain put his cap back on. "How did all of this come about?" Harper related the story Mrs Templeton and I had told him, from Bradley's nocturnal excursion on Monday night to his fear of stewards to the oil spot on his clothing. Webster listened thoughtfully, interrupting only to ask clarification of one or two points. Finally, he asked Harper: "These two stewards – you know their names, I take it?"

"Yes, sir," said Harper.

Webster looked out at the dark sea. "And now you and Mister Harvey are going to have a chat with them?"

"Yes, sir." Harper nodded. "After we make a stop at the wireless room. Just a point I want to clear up with the doctor on the *Adriatic*."

"Good." The Captain clasped his hands behind his back. "Is there anything else, then?"

"No, sir," I said.

The Captain thought a moment. "Mister Jackson," said the Captain.

"Sir?" Jackson turned around, brushing a few drops of rain from his uniform sleeve.

"You're familiar with Casey? The ship's newspaper?"

An expression of distaste crossed Jackson's face. "Yes, sir, I'm afraid I am."

"Good. I have an errand for you." The Captain turned to us. "These two brought me some disturbing news about an attempt being made on a passenger's life early this morning."

Jackson's eyes widened. "Sir?"

"We don't know who, and it was thankfully unsuccessful. The passenger in question is Mrs Templeton. She's fine."

"Glad to hear it, sir." The Captain steepled his fingers.

"I don't want to see it in the newspaper. Do whatever you have to do."

"Sir, Casey will scream about restricting the press."

Captain Webster scratched at his beard. "I'm sure he will. Please remind him that on board this ship, we are not a democracy. We are a dictatorship. And I am the dictator. Understood?"

"Sir, yes, sir." Jackson saluted and left the bridge. The Captain watched him go with some degree of satisfaction.

"Maybe that will be of some help to you. One less distraction."

"Thank you, Captain," I said. He turned away from us to gaze out the bridge windows.

"Then I'd suggest you get started. It sounds like you two have another busy day ahead of you. *Tempus fugit.*"

"'Curiouser and curiouser!' cried Alice,'" I quoted on the way down to the wireless room on the Sun Deck. Harper gave me a sidelong glance. The rain had stopped for the moment and much to my surprise the day was dawning beautifully, the ocean air clean and brisk. Under any other circumstances it would have been a romantic sight, but I had to finally admit that I'd given up on romance, and beauty was starting to take a back seat.

"Indeed," said Harper. "We've got two dead men stuck in our coolers and another taking passage on the *Adriatic*. I shudder to think what would have happened if Mrs Templeton was a heavy sleeper." He walked carefully down the steel steps, holding the railing. "I'll wager Sherlock Holmes never had these problems."

"Sherlock Holmes has Watson backing him up," I replied. "All you have is me and Mrs Templeton." I thought a moment. "And Mister Harvey, I suppose. Don't worry, Boss, we'll figure it out." I started to add something to that but lost my footing on the slippery steps and fell flat on my bottom. Harper pulled me to my feet.

"Anything hurt?"

"Just my pride." I tried to discretely rub my damp derriere. "I always forget how treacherous the footing gets out here when it's been raining or misting. Think I'd know better by now."

"At least you didn't break anything or fall over the side," said Harper. We walked in silence forward to the wireless room door. Harper looked at me. "Coming in?"

"Why not. Everyone on this ship knows I'm an accident waiting to happen. May as well let the wireless staff broadcast it to the world."

"That's the spirit," smiled Harper. He rapped on the door then opened it.

The wireless room always fascinated me. The *Queen Victoria* had between two and four Marconi operators on duty around the clock, and the tremendous power of the big transceivers absolutely hummed in the background. The room was also very warm, owing to the size and number of the valves – that's vacuum tubes to you Yanks – used inside of the gear. The operators sat along a desk shelf that extended the length of the room, each of them wearing a headset. Every so often a typewriter was poised on a cut out of the long shelf. To complete the picture, a smell of ozone, stale cigarettes, and tea permeated the atmosphere. All in all, a very congenial atmosphere. My rain-dampened bottom fit right in.

"Mister Cameron," said Doctor Harper, putting out his hand. Cameron stood up and pulled his headset off.

"Good morning, Doctor. I have that reply you're looking for from the *Adriatic* – somewhere here." He shuffled through a stack of papers on his portion of the desk, finally pulling out a radiogram form. He handed it to Harper. "Sorry for the delay. I suppose they've been just as busy as we have with that cock up in New York City right now." He looked at me. "Pardon me, Nurse."

"I've heard worse," I said.

"Thanks." Harper took the sheet and read. "'Reply your question re: pencil note: Boat Deck, two words, capitalized, nine tonight, nine as 21:00, come alone, lowercase. Printed, not cursive. Regards, etc. etc.'" Harper looked at me. "I don't see what difference this makes to Mrs Templeton."

"I have to admit I'm stumped there, too." I took the paper from him, looked at it and felt my heart jump. "Wait a minute. Look at the 'w' and the 'o' here. The bottom of the 'o' is filled in, and the 'w' is out of registration with the rest of the letters on the line." I turned to Mister

Cameron. "Which typewriter was used to take this message?"

"Mine, right here," said Cameron.

"Doctor, are you still carrying that suicide note from Mr Wilson?" I asked. Harper nodded, tapping a pocket on his blue jacket.

"Let me see it, please. Mister Cameron, could I use a sheet of paper and your typewriter for a moment?"

"Certainly, Nurse." He rolled a blank radiogram form around the platen of the typewriter as I sat down with the note.

My fingers flew across the keyboard as I typed. 'It is with deep regret that I now understand how impossible it is to make up for the crimes I helped to perpetrate. My only desire is that the Wilson Foundation maintain honors to the Allied war dead through perpetuity. I am atoning for my sins in the only way I know.' I rolled the paper out of the machine and laid it on the shelf, next to the original. "Look."

Harper looked, as did Mister Cameron. "They look the same," said Harper.

"Not just the same. They're identical." I pointed with a finger. "Look at the 'w' here, how it doesn't line up. And the lowercase 'o' that's half filled in. Both of these notes were done on this typewriter."

"Good God," said Harper.

"You're right, Nurse," echoed Cameron.

"It's a dead certainty that if we took the ribbon off that machine and rolled it back, we'd find where the original note had been typed." I looked at Mister Cameron.

"Do passengers ever come in here?"

"Never." Mister Cameron lit a cigarette. "Any passenger messages given to us to send come straight from Mister Collins' office."

"Does anyone other than the wireless officers use these typewriters?" I asked.

Cameron shook his head. "No. Maybe an officer comes in to write out a message for us to send when it's really precise and they don't trust their own handwriting." He laughed. "Some of them could be doctors for how badly they write longhand – no offense, Doctor."

"None taken," said Harper. "Anyone come to mind?" He was still studying both sheets of paper.

Mister Cameron took a puff and shrugged. "Mister Carter. Mister Harvey, he's very precise about the victualing of the ship during turnarounds. Mister Jackson, with direct orders or queries from the Captain." He looked at Harper. "Your predecessor, Doctor. He had horrible handwriting."

"When do the officers come in, Mister Cameron?" I asked.

"Whenever. No set schedule. We're open around the clock, just like the bridge and engineering."

"Thanks Mister Cameron," I said. "You'll keep this conversation to yourself?"

"Of course, Nurse." He stubbed out his cigarette and reached for his headset. "Mum's the word."

"One thing leads to another," said Harper. We were sitting with Agatha in the First-Class library. "It was the answer from the *Adriatic* on your question about the penciled note found on Mr Wilson's body that tipped Maeve off to the wireless room typewriter." He took the original suicide note out of his pocket along with the one I'd typed and handed it to her. She looked at them with interest, then handed them back.

"So it was a typewriter in the wireless room that produced our very precise and very stilted suicide note."

"And here's your reply for how the penciled note was written out," said Harper, handing it to her.

She mused over it. "The writer capitalized Boat Deck," she said. "And used 21:00 to mean nine pm. That's certainly not something I would expect a passenger to write." She looked up as Mister Harvey appeared, delivering a cup of breakfast tea. "Thank you, Mister Harvey."

"My pleasure," he said, pulling out a chair and joining us.

Agatha took a sip of the hot tea. "From what your wireless operator told you, it certainly seems to positively link a high ranking member of the crew to Mr Wilson's murder."

"But," said Harper, resting his hands on the table, "how can we be sure? Maybe one of the officers did type the note, but what if someone else committed the murder?"

"I agree with Doctor Harper," said Mister Harvey. "I don't think we've got enough to go on."

"Very well, gentlemen." Agatha took another sip of tea. "Let's table this for a moment and get to something near and dear to my heart – who tried to kill me early this morning?"

"A crew member," I said. "That's what we all agreed on."

"Yes, dear, but which one?" She put her cup down. "Forgive me, but I'm a bit finicky on that question."

"We don't know, Mrs Templeton," said Harvey.

"Well, I've been giving it some thought." Agatha settled back in her chair. "There's only one reason I can come up with as to why someone would want me out of the way. I'm getting too close to our killer for comfort." She gave me a steady gaze. "And if I'm getting too close for comfort, then that means you're getting too close for comfort, Maeve."

I involuntarily put a hand to my throat. Harper looked at me. "Mrs Templeton is right. I don't think either of you should go anywhere on board alone. Stay in our company or blend in with a larger group of people."

"Blending in with a larger group of people wasn't much help for Mr Morten, was it?" I asked.

"I'll continue seeing to your food and drink," said Harvey. "And I'll add you to the list, Nurse. There won't be any middle man."

Agatha smiled. "That's reassuring, Mister Harvey, thank you." She raised her cup. "And thank you for the new quarters."

"Of course, Mrs Templeton." Harvey stood. "If there's nothing else immediately, I'm off to speak with Miss Kelly. If someone requested a new steward's jacket this morning, or turned one in without a button, she'll know it."

"Good hunting, Mister Harvey," said Agatha. "Although I think our killer is far too smart to do anything like that, despite the odd come hither note to Mr Wilson. Still, worth a try, I suppose."

"Got to do something," said Harvey.

"Mister Harvey," I said.

"Nurse?"

I looked at Harper. "We're forgetting something here. When can we talk with Bertie and that new steward about the incident with Bradley Alston?"

"Ah, of course," said Harvey. "Yes." He consulted his wristwatch. "They're both working the First-Class breakfast. Shall we say ten? I'll ask them to come to my office."

"I look forward to it," said Agatha. She sipped her tea. "Very much so."

I have always found the picture of a mother and newborn to be quite bucolic. There's something so peaceful about it, like a country village at dawn, a fresh morning arriving, untouched by whatever unpleasantries may yet lie ahead – and right now, unpleasantries were all that the *Queen Victoria* was providing for her hard-working head nurse. That being said, I squelched any maternal instincts I might have been feeling and forced myself to concentrate on the job at hand.

Clara was sitting up in bed holding Victoria in her arms when Doctor Harper and I knocked and were allowed entry to the hospital. Doctor Bratton had moved her to one of the patient beds out of the surgery, and had even managed to procure an arrangement of flowers for her bedside table. I had to admit the man had unplumbed depths hidden deep beneath his exterior. I found out later it was Mister Harvey, but I was still willing to give Doctor Bratton the benefit of a doubt.

"Good morning, Nurse Chandler," she said. "And Doctor Harper. Doctor Bratton tells me you had to leave much earlier this morning."

"Yes, that's right. Just a slight emergency."

"I hope it all turned out well," said Clara. "And thank you for looking after Bradley. I hope he wasn't too much of an imposition."

"Oh, no. He was fine," I said. "Thank Doctor Bratton for taking him when Doctor Harper and I had to make our call this morning."

"We're getting along fine," said Bratton. "He's quite the inquisitive lad."

"Are we going to go see the stinky place again?" Bradley asked, looking up at Bratton.

"Stinky place?" Clara was perplexed.

"The dispensary," said Bratton. "No, I don't think so, Bradley. Not this morning. Your mum is doing fine." He looked at us. "Since you two are back, I'll take Bradley for breakfast. I've ordered a tray for Mrs Alston."

"Can I get a scone with blueberry jam?" asked Bradley.

"You can get whatever you want," said Bratton. "I understand that Mister Harvey is paying for it. I might even have a rasher of Virginia bacon. Come along."

I locked the door after them and returned to Clara and Doctor Harper. He was listening to Victoria with a stethoscope, and then he gently turned her and listened to her from the back. After a moment he handed her back to Clara. "Fit as the proverbial fiddle, Mrs Alston. Must be all the sea air."

"That and the fact she's starting out in life without the dead weight of her dead beat excuse for a father." I gave her a silent hurrah. She looked at us. "Well, now that I've gotten that out of my system, have you found the man I should thank for this blessing?"

"I understand how you feel, Clara," I said, "but we are dealing with a murder here, no matter who the victim is."

"Yes, you're right. I'm behaving miserably. I'm sorry." For the first time she gave us a really close examination. "You two look like you've been busy with more than just a little emergency."

I sat on the edge of the bed. "I'm afraid so. Someone tried to poison Mrs Templeton this morning. I didn't want to say anything about it while Bradley was in the room."

Clara looked shocked. "Mrs Templeton? Who on earth would want to kill her?"

"That's what we're trying to find out." Harper rubbed his cheek. "I need a shave," he said to no one in particular.

I ignored him. "Someone got into her stateroom before light and slipped poison into her water pitcher. Fortunately she's a light sleeper and was able to scare them off."

"That's terrifying," said Clara. I nodded.

"What's even more terrifying is that I think it's somehow connected to your late husband's death. He was killed because he posed the same liability as Mrs Templeton."

"Frank? A liability? What do you mean?"

"I mean, he knew too much." I took her hand in mine. "I don't know if you've noticed, but we've begun locking the hospital door and your room door."

"Whatever for?"

Harper took a deep breath and exhaled slowly. "Because, Mrs Alston, Bradley also falls into the same liability category. He knows too much. And Mrs Templeton's uninvited guest this morning may believe you know too much, as well."

"I don't understand. What does Bradley know?"

"Mrs Templeton got it out of him last night, Clara," I said. "He finally told her what was upsetting him. He saw one man push another over the railings on the Boat Deck and into the sea on Monday night. The man that got pushed was Harvey Wilson."

"The American millionaire? I saw a bit on it in the paper – Bradley?" Clara held Victoria tight against her. "Did they see him?"

"I think so. Unfortunately Bradley wasn't able to make out any faces because of the darkness, and in his panic he ran up some nearby stairs to the Sports Deck. He was able to hide behind one of the ventilators."

"That's what we mean by Bradley being a liability," said Harper. "We haven't left him alone since Mrs Templeton told us this story last night."

"And because you're his mother, the murderer has every reason to believe that Bradley may have told you what he saw." I grasped Clara's hand. "We believe you're in great danger, too – hence the reason for keeping you here under lock and key."

"And because Bradley told Mrs Templeton – that's why someone tried to kill her last night?"

"I don't think it was necessarily because of that," I said. "Mrs Templeton has been very curious about what's been happening. As have I."

"Then perhaps you should see to your own health." Clara leaned back against the pillows. "You said Frank is connected to all of this?"

I nodded. "When you told me yesterday afternoon what Frank had said about his ship coming in before we reached New York, I didn't think too much about it. But after he was found at the bottom of the lift shaft clutching a *Queen Victoria* steward's jacket button in his hand, Mrs Templeton and I arrived at the same conclusion. He was trying to blackmail someone and got himself killed for his efforts."

"Blackmail? Who? For what?"

"Bradley wasn't the only person who saw what happened on Monday night, Mrs Alston," said Harper.

"It's very likely that Mr Alston saw it too, and tried to turn it to his advantage. But as you said before, he was no Al Capone when it came to things like that."

"No," Clara said. "He wasn't." She looked down at Victoria. The baby was fast asleep. "How long until we reach New York?"

I looked at my watch. "About fifty hours, give or take," I said.

"Two entire days. And if we get there and this person hasn't been caught yet?"

"He'll walk off the ship a free man and never look back," said Harper. "There would be no reason for him to do anything else but that after getting away with murder."

"Murders," I corrected Harper. He gave me a peeved look.

"That's not very reassuring, Doctor." Clara gently stroked Victoria's forehead. "How can you be certain he won't come back for me or Bradley?"

"I can't." Harper crossed his arms.

"Again, not very reassuring." Clara softly sighed. "It sounds as if there's nothing to do but wait."

"You won't be waiting alone, Mrs Alston," I said. "One of us will always be here with you. Either myself, Doctor Harper, Doctor Bratton or Mister Harvey."

"Thank you, Nurse."

"Well," said Harper. "We've got a little meeting with Mister Harvey soon, Maeve."

"You go ahead. I'll wait here until Doctor Bratton and Bradley get back."

"All right. Lock up behind me." Harper looked at Clara. "I'm sure we'll be talking again, Mrs Alston. The best thing for you right now is rest."

"Thank you, Doctor."

I let Harper out and locked the door after him, then went back to Mrs Alston. She gave me a wan smile. "How much of that do you actually believe?"

"Sad to say, all of it, I'm afraid."

Clara thought for a moment. "This Mrs Templeton, she seems rather astute, doesn't she?"

"You have no idea."

Victoria yawned and began to cry. Clara looked up at me. "I think she's hungry. If you wouldn't mind, Nurse – "

"No, of course not." I went back to the waiting room and dropped into the chair behind the desk, picked up a magazine to read and then froze. Someone was trying the door knob from the corridor. I got up, my heart pounding. The door knob rattled again. "Who's there?" I called out.

"Doctor Bratton. Open the door and let us in."

I felt my body sag with relief. I unlocked the door and Bratton and Bradley came in, Bratton bearing a breakfast tray in his hands. "What's all this, then?" I asked as he set it down on the desk.

"I saw Mister Harvey," explained Bratton. "He told me that he had personally taken charge of you and Mrs Templeton's meals, and felt he should do the same for Mrs Alston just out of caution."

"Very thoughtful of him," I said. Bradley looked up at me.

"I had blueberry jam," he said.

"So I see." I looked at Bratton. "You didn't think to run a wet napkin over his face?"

"His mouth never stopped moving long enough to allow it. The kid's aeroplane crazy and when he wasn't talking about flying he was shoveling in jam and scones to beat the band. I thought I was going to have to put the jam knife into a glass of water to cool it off."

"Some father you'd make." I walked over to the door to Mrs Alston's room and tapped on it gently. "Mrs Alston? Your breakfast is here."

"Please, come in."

I hesitated. "I have Doctor Bratton and Bradley with me," I said.

"As long as you have something for me to eat I don't care if you've got His Majesty the King with you."

"Well, all righty, then." I waved a hand at Bratton. "Off you go." Bratton picked up the tray, and accompanied by Bradley, sallied forth. I sat back down behind the desk. From inside the room I could hear Bradley animatedly talking with his mother as Doctor Bratton appeared to be – at least by his exclamations – changing Victoria's diaper. All at peace, at least for the moment.

The door knob jiggled again. I sat straight up. It rattled once more, harder this time. I gave a glance to Mrs Alston's room, then stealthily, at least for me, meaning I didn't fall over the bloody desk, made my way to the door.

The knob shook a third time, making me about jump out of my skin. I put my mouth close to the door so as not to alarm the others. "Who's there?" I demanded.

Silence greeted my request. "Who's there?" I repeated. This time I was rewarded by the sound of hurried footsteps going back up the corridor, in the direction of the lifts. I waited a few moments then cautiously unlocked the door and peered out.

The coast was clear.

Heart pounding, I closed and locked the door, then made my way back to the desk, sat down and picked up the telephone.

Mister Harvey answered on the first ring. "It's Maeve," I said. "Is Doctor Harper there yet?"

"Not yet. Where are you?"

"In the hospital with Clara, Doctor Bratton and Bradley. Someone just tried the door from the corridor, and when I asked them to identify themselves, they departed rather quickly."

"Good Lord," said Harvey. "Are you well?"

"Yes, everything is fine. It's just that – I don't want to travel to your office by myself. I know it's only one deck up, but could you send someone down to get me?"

"Of course. Mister Evans just walked in. Would that do?"

I nodded. "Yes, thank you. And Mister Harvey – thank you for the tray for Mrs Alston."

"Just doing what I can, Nurse. Mister Evans will be along shortly." He rang off and I replaced the receiver, crossed my arms and leaned back in the chair. I was shaking.

The fifty hours before us to New York loomed ahead like fifty centuries.

IV

I remember seeing some of the older folks in the village I grew up in walking with the aid of a stick or cane. To my young mind, I couldn't quite figure out why one would want to do that – it was just something else to carry. My brother, of course, said if he ever had to use something like that he'd carry a cricket bat just in case a game broke out nearby. It wasn't until I was older that I learned there were things besides a cane one could lean on for support. One of the best was an old friend and I'm afraid I leaned rather heavily on Bertie as he walked me up to Mister Harvey's office on C Deck.

"Are you serious?" he asked. "Someone tried to poison that nice Mrs Templeton?"

"Deadly serious," I replied, "with an emphasis on the 'deadly.'"

"And then you thought someone was trying to get into the hospital a while ago?"

"I didn't think it, Bertie. I saw the knob turn, I heard it rattle, and I heard someone running back up the corridor when I called out."

"Who could they have been after?"

I shook my head. "The only people inside were myself, Doctor Bratton, Mrs Alston and her children."

Bertie gave a low whistle. "This voyage is cursed. First that bloke on Sunday night, then the rich American bird.

Now this with Mrs Templeton. And someone after one of you in the hospital? Blimey."

"Frightening, isn't it?" I thought that at least Mister Harvey's warning to the crewmen who carted away Mr Alston's body to keep his death quiet seemed to be holding. As one of the senior stewards, Bertie was almost as good as Casey at sniffing out a scandal.

"It's very frightening," said Bertie. "And I have just the cure, love. We'll have a bit of fun tonight."

"Fun? On this ship?" I looked at him. "I don't know what you're drinking, Bertie, but I want some of it."

"Today is Hallowe'en," he replied.

"Is it?" I asked. I had completely lost track; the days had blended into one long nightmare with little prospect of waking up.

"Tonight a lot of the Yanks will wear a costume or mask; you know, it's like Guy Fawkes for us, kind of. They'll have some fun, enjoy some japes and will probably drink more than they usually do even for them, which I can already tell you keeps half of Scotland's distilleries open. And after what's been going on with their stock market, a lot of those chappies look like they could use some serious cheering up." He raised a hand to knock on Mister Harvey's office door. "A few of the more lively upper crust I'm lookin' after in my sheds asked if I could find them some costume items." He rubbed his hands together. "Always happy to oblige, if it means a larger tip at the end. Of course, after that market stuff, I guess I'll take what I can get."

"Come in," said Harvey.

Bertie opened the door. "After you."

Mister Harvey was seated behind his desk, Harper in the chair across from him. Agatha was sitting on a small settee in the corner. The Chief Steward looked as if he'd also passed a sleepless night, which in truth he had.

After moving Mrs Templeton to her new stateroom, he'd returned to find that his assistant, Mister Bissell, had already flooded his desk with items needing his immediate attention and sign off on before arrival in New York. Never mind sheets, pillowcases and china. Victualing the *Queen Victoria* is a mammoth task and all of it falls on Mister Harvey.

On a routine round trip from Southampton to New York and back again, we usually went through, among others, 50,000 pounds of potatoes, six tons of fresh fish, 20 tons of meat, five tons of ham and bacon, 60,000 eggs, three tons of butter and five thousand cigars. Now, with New York on the horizon, replenishing supplies in a two day turnaround should have been his main worry – not switching passenger staterooms to keep the paying guests from being killed.

"Welcome back, Mister Evans." Harvey indicated the remains of the breakfast on the tray on his desk and looked at us. "Have either of you had anything to eat this morning? I can have Mister Bissell prepare something."

"Thank you sir. Maybe some tea and toast," answered Bertie in a perfect clipped accent. I had always been amazed at his ability to switch back and forth in his dialects, depending on whom he was talking with at any given time.

"The same for me, Mister Harvey," I said. "Thank you."

"Tea and toast? Suit yourself," said Mister Harvey. "The Eggs Benedict are exceptional this morning. Chef Delacroix can be a temperamental French pill to put up with sometimes, but I can't fault him in the kitchen." Harvey pushed his tray to the side. "Mister Evans, while we wait for Mister Woldert, would you mind asking Mister Bissell for tea and toast for two? He can make it from my office supply."

"Yes, sir. Thank you, sir." Bertie saluted and turned for the door, then stopped. "Mrs Templeton – Nurse Chandler told me about the close call you had this morning. I'm very happy to see you looking well."

"Thank you, Mister Evans," said Agatha.

Bertie nodded. "Back in a flash." He went out, closing the door behind him. Harper, Harvey and Agatha all looked at me.

"It just slipped out," I said. "I'm sorry."

"No harm done, I suppose." Agatha sighed. "Though of course you just laid one of our cards on the table. It would have been interesting to see if anyone wanted to track down my state of well-being."

"To business, then," said Harvey. He looked at Harper. "Being new to the ship, you don't know Mister Evans like we do. Bertie Evans is the most unassuming and likeable chap you're ever likely to meet. And he throws a mean dart." He looked at me. "Not as good as you, of course, Nurse Chandler, but he's certainly nicked me for his fair share of beers."

"I know how alluring a dart game can be, Mister Harvey," said Agatha, "but did you find out anything about our mysterious jacket minus a button?"

Harvey leaned back and crossed his arms. "This is interesting. Mister Evans requisitioned a new jacket for Mister Woldert first thing this morning."

"This morning?" I said. Harper leaned forward in his chair.

"That is indeed interesting." Agatha nodded. "Go on."

"Well," said Mister Harvey, "Evans told Miss Kelly that Mister Woldert had his jacket pinched by persons unknown late last night as he was helping to close down the Observation Bar lounge. Said he had taken his jacket off and tossed it over a chair back, and when it came time to leave the jacket was gone. He told Mister Evans. He was afraid to speak up to anyone else because he's new to the ship."

"What time do they close down the Observation-Lounge, Mister Harvey?" asked Agatha.

Harvey shrugged. "Usually around 23:00 hours."

"And Mr Alston was discovered around eight or so." Agatha pursed her lips. "A three hour difference."

"Plenty of time for whomever killed Mr Alston to realize they needed to replace their torn jacket, and then to find one readily at hand on the back of a chair," I said.

Harper gave me a smile. "I'm certainly glad you know what you're doing, Nurse Chandler."

"I hate to disappoint you, Boss, but I'm making it up as I go. Sorry, Mrs Templeton."

"No, you're right, Maeve," said Agatha. "There's only one path to the truth through this moor, and there are plenty of wrong turns along the way to get bogged down in. Unless we get a pretty big break, then we've got to follow all the side paths, too."

"What's the background on Woldert?" asked Harper.

Mister Harvey opened a folder on his crowded desk. "Mister Woldert is on his first voyage with us. He's previously served on the *Olympic* and *Mauretania*. His Certificate of Discharge book is outstanding. Excellent references. Nothing unusual in his record."

"And yet small boys are afraid of him," I said.

"Without denigrating Mister Evans' character," said Agatha, "you don't know that young Bradley wasn't afraid of Mister Woldert alone."

"Mrs Templeton is right, " Harper said. "There is just no telling what set off the boy. Maybe he doesn't like white jackets and brass buttons."

There was a gentle rap and the door opened. Mister Evans came in, bearing a tray with two cups and toast on a plate. He set the tray down on Harvey's desk. "Mister Woldert isn't here yet?"

"Not yet," said Mister Harvey. "We can start without him. Close the door, would you, Mister Evans?"

"Sir." Bertie did as he was told and stood quietly at attention.

"Take it easy, Bertie, it's not an inquisition. Have your tea and toast. We just have a few questions," said Harvey.

"Thank you, sir."

"You share a stateroom with Mister Woldert, don't you?" asked Harvey.

"Yes, sir. Given Mister Woldert's past work experience, it seems natural. His past postings and his job performance have him heading toward a senior stewardship of his own. I'm happy to be showing him the ropes on the *Victoria*."

"Miss Kelly says you asked her to pull a new jacket for Mister Woldert this morning," I said.

"That's right. Mike – that's Mister Woldert – had his lifted late last night as he was helping clean up the Observation-Lounge." Bertie gave a disapproving look. "Never in all my years aboard the *Victoria* has such a thing happened. It's embarrassing, and especially so to happen to a new man."

"What can you tell us about moving Mrs Alston and her son yesterday?" Harper asked Evans.

"Oh, the baggage part was easy, sir," said Evans. "Mrs Alston and her son had already packed up and left it behind for us – they'd gone to their new stateroom. When we got to the old stateroom to pick it up, the husband was there." Bertie sorrowfully shook his head. "If I never see Mr Alston again on this trip, or ever, it will be too soon. Cursed something like lightning, he did. Directed a lot of it at poor Woldert, gesturing at him with his arm in a cast."

"What did Mister Woldert do?" asked Agatha.

Bertie shrugged. "What could he do, Mrs Templeton? Like I said, he's the new man. You talk back to a passenger, even one like Mr Alston, and you're likely to find yourself without a job at the end of the trip." He looked at Harvey. "Begging your pardon, Mister Harvey."

"There are always going to be extenuating circumstances, Mister Evans," said Harvey. "I've never cashiered anyone without due cause and a complete investigation beforehand."

"Why was Mr Alston singling out Mister Woldert?" I wondered out loud.

Again Bertie shrugged. "It almost sounded like he was blaming Mister Woldert for his broken arm. Of course, Mister Woldert, he works First-Class. He would never have come into contact with someone like Mr Alston in Second."

"What did he say to Mister Woldert?" asked Agatha.

"Things like 'you haven't heard the last from me' and 'I'll get every cent I've got coming, see if I don't'," said Bertie. "The real head scratcher was when he said he'd see Woldert later."

"What did you and Mister Woldert make of it?" asked Harper.

"Well, to be honest, sir, he sounded a bit on the lunatic side, didn't he? And we'd heard of how he treated his poor wife and boy. In fact, Mister Woldert had said within hearing of others that he'd be happy to teach the bastard a lesson in manners. I told him to calm down a bit. A paying passenger is a paying passenger, and all that."

"Rightly so, Mister Evans. I'd heard some wanted to have a bit of a dust up with Mr Alston." Harvey toyed with a pencil on his desk. "What happened when you got the baggage up to Mrs Alston's new stateroom?"

"Well, sir, we knocked on the door, and Mrs Alston opened it up. We started to bring their bags in, but about that time the boy came out of the loo, spotted us, and went diving back in, locking the door behind him." Bertie frowned. "Very strange."

"Very strange," said Agatha. "Why would he have done that?"

"Perhaps he doesn't like stewards?" said Bertie. "I mean, I consider myself a handsome enough chap, but Mister Woldert isn't exactly a matinee idol, now is he? Anyway, Mrs Alston, she tries to smile about it, 'boys will be boys,' she says, then we brought in the baggage and left. That's all there was to it." He thought a moment. "I mean, Mister Woldert may not look like Douglas Fairbanks, but I don't think he looks like Lon Chaney either, you understand. But he does have a face you'd remember."

"Was he wearing an overcoat?" I asked.

"Who, Lon Chaney or Douglas Fairbanks?"

I pursed my lips. "Bertie, please. Mister Woldert. Was he wearing an overcoat when you two did your moving job?"

"Oh." He thought a moment. "No overcoat."

Harvey looked at his watch. "Nearly 10:30. What's keeping Mister Woldert?"

"Would you like me to see if I can find him?" asked Bertie. "It's possible he got lost on his way here, new ship and all."

"I think we've probably sent out enough search parties on this trip as we need to," said Harper.

A brief tap on the office door interrupted him, and then the door opened and a tall (again, for me, given my height) steward stood framed in the doorway. He doffed his cap. "My apologies, sir. Mister Woldert reporting." He coughed politely. "Begging your pardon, but the Steward's office was one below the Promenade Deck on the *Mauretania*, and on the Shelter Deck on the *Olympic*. This is a much larger ship than either of those, but I'm getting my exercise," he said with a smile.

"I'm sure that you are," remarked Mister Harvey dryly. He looked at Bertie. "That will be all, Mister Evans, thank you, you've been most helpful."

"Sir," said Bertie. He gave Woldert a brief nod, picked up a piece of toast and left the office.

"Mister Woldert," said Harvey, "this is Doctor Harper, our new PMO, and head nurse Chandler. Mrs Templeton here is a First-Class passenger."

Woldert's face showed concern. "I trust I haven't done anything wrong or to offend anyone?" he asked.

"No, not at all," said Agatha. "We just have a few queries to make."

"Yes, madam." Woldert smiled and tugged down at the sides of his jacket.

"I just wanted to thank you for taking the time to help Mrs Alston and her son move the other day," I said.

"Oh, that." He seemed relieved. "It was my pleasure, Nurse."

"Anything odd about the incident that you can recall?" asked Agatha.

Woldert's brow furrowed. "Not that I can recall right off, madam. The little boy, he didn't seem happy to see Mister Evans."

"Mister Evans?" I said.

"What was the boy's problem with Mister Evans?" asked Harper. Woldert shrugged.

"I don't guess he likes Mister Evans. He screamed and cried." Woldert again coughed. "The boy, I should say, not Mister Evans."

"Mister Evans said he thought the boy was scared of you," said Harvey.

"Me, sir?" Woldert laughed. "That's funny, now, isn't it? Both of us thinking the lad was scared of the other of us?"

"Funny behaviour for a little boy," said Harper.

"Not really, sir." Woldert smiled. "I screamed and cried a lot when I was a lad, too."

"Mister Evans said that Mr Alston had some words for you yesterday when you were helping to move his wife's luggage out of their original cabin." Agatha gave him an intent look.

Woldert nodded. "He did. I'd never seen the bird before, but I'd heard about him. I would have been glad to break his arm for him, believe me."

"That's enough on that, Mister Woldert," said Harvey.

"Yes, sir. But she was so nice and he's just a real – well, you know what he is, begging your pardon, ladies and Mister Harvey, Doctor." Woldert's face twitched.

"No need to apologize," said Agatha. "According to Mister Evans, Mr Alston said 'you haven't heard the last of me' and 'I'll get every cent I've got coming.'" She peered at him from beneath her broad brimmed hat. "What was that all about?"

"Honestly, madam, I have no idea. Mister Evans and I have discussed it. He thinks Mr Alston is a lunatic, and I'd be just as happy not to cross his path again." He looked directly at me. "But, perhaps you should be asking these questions of him."

"Oh, we will," I said.

"Your *Victoria* jacket fits you well," said Agatha. "Lucky that Miss Kelly had a spare so large in her stocks." Woldert looked down.

"Ah, you heard about that, did you? This one doesn't fit as well as the first one. A bit tight, I'm afraid. The crew's mess on board the *Victoria* is very tempting."

"What happened to the first one?" asked Harvey.

"It went missing yesterday evening late, sir. I got dragooned into doing some 'tall man' chores in the Observation-Lounge bar pantry area as they were closing down. Didn't want to risk getting my jacket dirty, so I took it off and dropped it over a chair in the server's area off the bar. When I came back a half hour later it was gone. I didn't lose it, sir. It was stolen. Mister Evans was able to procure this replacement this morning. Nice chap, Mister Evans."

"Do you own an overcoat, Mister Woldert?" I asked. He looked at me.

"What a strange question, Nurse. Yes, I do. It's packed in my sea trunk in the mail hold – I'm carrying it and some other things to a cousin in New York."

"One last thing," I said. "Mister Evans says you were the waiter for Mr Morten – the man who died in the dining salon – before dinner on Sunday night in the lounge?"

Woldert nodded. "Yes, Nurse. I was absolutely stunned when I read the next day he'd died of a stroke at dinner. He seemed a nice enough chap, though he was a bit put off at first that his drink order came up wrong." He smiled. "But you know these thirsty Americans. He up and drank it anyway, and left me a nice tip in the bargain."

"Indeed," said Agatha.

Woldert nodded and peered over Harper's shoulder at the clock on the wall. "If you don't mind, Mister Harvey, I've got to return to the floor. Preparations for the first luncheon seating."

"Certainly, Mister Woldert." Harvey waved him off. Woldert gave a final glance toward Agatha and myself, then left the room. When the door closed Agatha shuddered.

"The gunman," she said.

"What?" I asked. Harvey and Harper looked at her with concern.

"The gunman. It's a nightmare I have. I'm at a tea party, or somewhere else where I'm supposed to be relaxed, and then I get an uneasy feeling. A man with blue eyes is watching me, and his intentions are not friendly." She sat uneasily. "Mister Woldert has blue eyes."

"I don't think we can accuse a man based on the color of his eyes, Mrs Templeton," said Harvey.

"No, of course not." Agatha frowned. "I'm sure it's just me."

"Look," I said, "I think we're going at this all wrong. Let's break it down. Would you all agree that Mr Morten received a poisoned drink meant for someone else?"

Harper nodded. "Meant for Mr Wilson? Yes, I'll go with you on that one."

"Yes, it's entirely plausible," Agatha said.

"All righty, then," I said. "And we're all agreed that Harvey Wilson was murdered. Why, we don't know yet. But he didn't commit suicide."

"Fair enough," said Mister Harvey.

"Well," I continued, "that leaves us with Mr Alston's trip down the lift shaft last night. Judging by the evidence of the button at the very least, that was no accident, either." I looked at Agatha. "And then we have the attempt on Mrs Templeton this morning early, and someone was interested in getting into the hospital not too long ago."

"It has been a rough morning." Agatha adjusted her hat.

"'Rough' is not the word I would use," I said. "Now, what are the reasons someone commits a murder?"

"Love?" said Harper.

"Who could love Frank Alston?" I said.

"Jealousy, perhaps." Harvey rubbed his chin.

"Who in their right mind would be jealous of Frank Alston?" I shook my head. "And then trying to kill Mrs Templeton and do God knows what in the hospital if they'd gained the door this morning."

"What are you thinking, Maeve?" asked Agatha.

I crossed my arms. "How about this: murder to cover up murder." I looked at Agatha. "We know Bradley saw something. He may have told his mother. And it's apparent that someone thinks Mrs Templeton knows too much. And I fall into that category, too."

"What about us?" asked Harvey, indicating Harper.

"What about you?" I said. "You haven't raised a profile high enough to get into our murderer's sights."

"Yet." Agatha gave the men a smile. "But we've still time to New York."

"That makes me feel better," Harvey said to Harper. "How about you?"

"Much better," Harper replied. "And then there's Mr Alston, who we believe witnessed Mr Wilson's murder along with his stepson, both unknown to the other."

"Whoa," said Harvey. "What?" I briefly explained our theory to him.

"That's fine, Nurse," he said, "but shouldn't a witness be able to, well, give witness? You may have noticed that Mr Alston is no longer talking."

"Yes, he is," I said. "That button he was clutching in his fist."

"Which goes to a jacket we haven't yet seen," said Harper.

"But has gone missing – presumably to the same place the torn overcoat went missing," said Agatha. "Over the side of the ship." She shook her head. "It's frustrating. We've plenty of evidence, but nothing to directly link to a suspect, and no motive, if we could. A mixed-up drink ticket, a jacket button, a scrap of overcoat, a note for Mr Wilson that lured him to his death, and a bogus suicide note typed out on one of your wireless office's machines. Plus my water pitcher, and the word of a little boy. Hardly the kind of thing one could go to the assizes with and accuse someone, I think." She bit her lip. "And three dead men and a killer who's looking for myself, Maeve and the lad."

Sometimes my Irish kicked in without any urging from me, and right now was one of those times. I had finally had enough. "As the saying goes, 'Desperate times call for desperate measures,'" I said. "I'm tired of having the fight brought to us."

"What are you thinking?" asked Harper.

"I'm thinking it's time to bring the fight to our opponent." Agatha looked at me with interest.

"And how do you plan to do that?" asked Harvey.

"First of all, by not taking anyone at their word anymore. Someone on the *Victoria's* crew isn't telling the truth, and I agree with Mrs Templeton's feeling of uneasiness about Mister Woldert."

"Have a care, Maeve," said Agatha. "You can't just confront him straight out."

"I have no intention of doing anything of the sort." I stood up and set my nursing cap. "I'm going to sneak around. I'm not daft." I looked at Harper. "Coming, Doctor?"

"Whatever for?" Harper looked perplexed.

"I want to go look in Mister Woldert's sea chest, and I need someone to hold the torch."

Thursday, October 31, 1929

V

You've probably never been down inside a ship's cargo hold. Let me tell you, you aren't missing anything. The *Queen Victoria* has four holds, three larger and one small. The small hold – and "small" is a relative term – is reserved for mail. That's a big part of the money the *Victoria* makes for the Stoddard Lines, carrying the mails. It's also where the ship gets her prefix of "RMS" for Royal Mail Ship.

When there is room, Stoddard Line employees are allowed to pay a small fee to stow limited baggage in the mail hold on E Deck; however, unlike the paying passengers, once it is in the hold it is there for the duration of the voyage. No one comes down to check on it, and why would they? The mail hold is a dark, dank, dungeon, with the pungent smell of leather cases, canvas bags and cold steel, mixed with the always enticing aroma of bunker fuel made even stronger being trapped with no air circulation, and for the unwary or terminally clumsy – like me – a hundred places where you could turn or break an ankle in the Stygian gloom. Add to that the groan of the ship's hull plating as the ocean rushes past the ship – the cargo holds are well below the waterline – and the whine from the huge steam-driven turbines, and you can see that no one in their right mind would descend into these depths on purpose while we were underway at sea.

Which, of course, is why we were there.

"I don't like this," said Harper. The beam of his torch passed across a riveted bulkhead, damp and shiny with condensation. "This is where the torpedoes always struck home."

"The war's long over, Doctor," I replied. "I doubt there are any rogue U-boats in these waters."

"Small consolation. The *Titanic* didn't need a torpedo and I'm painfully aware of how thin the hull plating is. Tell me again why Mister Harvey didn't join us?"

"Mister Harvey suffers from mild claustrophobia." I shone my light and picked out a railing I had almost walked into. "And I think down here it would have blossomed into full grown claustrophobia."

Harper shook his head. "It amazes me that we got here by walking through a regular door off the First-Class lounge that says 'Crew Only,' and then that spidery spiral staircase down. Who would have guessed?"

"It's amazing how much of the ship is hidden in plain sight, Boss."

"Like our murderer, apparently."

"Apparently," I agreed. I stopped and shone my torch. "We're here."

"Where, exactly, is here? It all looks the same to me."

"Mail is rarely shipped inside of sea trunks, Doctor." My torch illuminated a stack of sea chests secured into a heavy steel rack. "Only a standard sized flat top is allowed, no domed trunks," I said. "Makes it easier to stack. The owner's name is stenciled on the end of the chest." My torch played over the rack. "We're in luck. Not too many crew taking advantage of Commodore Stoddard's overwhelming generosity this voyage."

Harper stepped forward and handed me his torch. "Here's Woldert," he said, grasping the leather handle and pulling the trunk out. He grunted as he set it on the deck.

"You know, a thought comes to me just now. Woldert only came aboard ship on Saturday, yet he has a sea chest that will fit into the racks and he knows that he can consign it as cargo. Don't you find that a bit odd?"

I nodded. "I'd been on crew for eight months before I found out." I knelt by the sea chest, careful to avoid getting my uniform any more soiled, and pulled a kirby grip (bobby pin for you American women) out that had been helping to hold my nursing cap on. "Shine your torch down here, Boss."

"Are you picking that lock?" Harper was incredulous.

"I am," I said.

"How - "

"A childhood misspent, Doctor. I told you my parents were educators. While I liked learning, it wasn't all play. My brother and I had to make our own fun. There wasn't anything in the house – or a relative's house – safe from me. I always knew what Father Christmas was bringing well before the big event. The trick was in looking surprised. Keep that light steady." I concentrated, imagining the end of the kirby grip moving around the recess of the lock mechanism. One final deft twist and the lock snapped open. I put the kirby grip back. Harper shook his head.

"Remind me to never get on your bad side."

"Yes, Boss. Ready?"

"Open it."

I swung the lid up. The top tray held neatly folded "civilian" shirts, sweaters, undergarments and various sundries. "Not much here," I said. "Can you lift the tray out?"

Harper did as I asked and set the tray carefully on the deck. The lower portion of the trunk was divided into two sections by a thin board that ran crosswise front to back.

One side was taken up with what appeared to be bundles of letters and a scrapbook, along with some well-thumbed periodicals. I picked one up, looked at it with some distaste, and handed it to Harper. "Speaking as an army widow, I find this a bit offensive."

Harper read the title out loud. *"Workers' Life."*

"It's a Communist Party newspaper," I said, riffling through the other material. "All of this is Communist Party and anarchist material. Commodore Stoddard would have him walk the plank if he knew. So would the Captain."

Harper flipped through the paper. "I would have never guessed Mister Woldert for a Communist."

"I wonder if Mister Jackson is," I said quietly.

"Come again?" Harper's voice was sharp.

"Mister Jackson." I held up a photograph that showed Woldert and Jackson side by side. Both men were wearing bathing suits, were smiling, and behind them I could see a background that reminded me of Brighton. I turned the picture over. 'Michael and Thomas, August, 1929" was written on it. I handed the picture to Harper. "Served with him several years, never knew his first name was Thomas," I said of Mister Jackson.

"What in the world is a first officer doing standing with a steward?"

"There's a poser, isn't it? And recently," I remarked.

"Are they on holiday together?" asked Harper.

"To paraphrase your question, Doctor, why would a first officer go on holiday with a steward?"

"Maybe they're cousins?" offered Harper. I unearthed another picture that showed them both together and gasped.

"I hope they're not cousins. This is damning enough."

Harper took the photo and was taken aback. "Good Lord. That's illegal."

"And neither one of them is close to being Oscar Wilde."

Harper shook his head and handed the photos back. "Have you always been this derisive?"

"No. It's gotten worse on this particular voyage." I carefully put the photos back in place. "Let's see what else is packed away. Shine your torch over here." I turned my attention to the other side of the trunk. Protective paper was laid over what appeared to be a bulky object – which in turn was revealed to be an overcoat. A large, black, wool overcoat, folded neatly with obvious care.

"Will you look at that," said Harper.

I nodded. "Moment of truth," I said, running my hand carefully around and over the coat, not wanting to disturb the folds, then slumped back in defeat. "Bloody hell. It's intact. No tears, no patches that I could feel."

"Are you certain?" Harper knelt beside me and put his hand under the overcoat. It seemed to me he lingered a moment over my hand, then looked at me. "There's something else under here." He carefully lifted the overcoat out.

Revealed to us in the yellow light of Harper's torch was a well-thumbed copy of *Text-Book of Pharmacology and Therapeutics* edited by W. Hale White, M.D., F.R.C.P. I lifted it and handed it to Harper.

"Haven't seen a copy of this in a while," he said, handing me the torch. "Published in 1901. Very good text for its time." He opened the book to a place holder. "Oh, my," he said.

"What is it?"

"Page 37. Aconitine. Plenty of scribble marks here in the margins." He handed it to me and took back the torch, shining it on the page. "Look."

"Crikey." I scanned the page. "Practically an aconitine recipe, this is. Refining, dosages – it's all here."

"I think this is the connection Mrs Templeton is looking for," said Harper.

"It would seem pretty damning at first blush." I carefully set the book back inside the trunk. "Communist Party propaganda, an enjoyable day at the sea shore with Mister Jackson, and this book." I looked at Harper. "Pardon my eloquence, Doctor, but what is this bastard up to?"

"Making aconitine, apparently."

"Yes, one would think. And delivering it, too. He would have been able to get a pass key to let himself into Mrs Templeton's stateroom this morning early, before anyone else was moving around. And he admittedly served the deadly drink to Mr Morten. But what about Mr Wilson and Mr Alston?" I pressed my fingertips against my temples. "And now this connection with Mister Jackson?" I carefully placed the overcoat back over the book, then lifted the top tray and put it back in place and closed the lid. Harper handed me the padlock and I snapped it back into place.

"What now?" asked Harper.

"Now?" I looked down at the trunk. "Let's put this back where we got it. No need to tip him off if he comes down here before we reach New York."

Harper hefted the chest back to its original position. "I wish Mister Harvey didn't suffer claustrophobia," he said. "This bloody chest is heavy."

"Mister Woldert is a big man, I'm sure he can lift it with ease, Doctor." I shone my torch around. "But let's get out of here before he shows up and we find out for sure."

257

VI

As I've said before, the *Queen Victoria* is well known for her cuisine. The phalanx of Chefs de Cuisine, Sous Chefs, Chefs de Partie, Pantry Chefs, Pastry Chefs, Chefs de Boucher, Chefs de Poissonier, Chef de Saucier – it goes on and on – that it takes to produce the passenger dining experience is staggering. While some dishes are memorized, others require the use of one of the rather large library of cookbooks carried aboard. However, in all of those cookbooks, I'll wager my salary there isn't one with the title of *Text-Book of Pharmacology and Therapeutics*.

Agatha, myself and Doctor Harper were ensconced in her new stateroom and I recounted what we had found in the trunk.

"Lock, stock and smoking barrel," said Harper. "The *Text-Book of Pharmacology and Therapeutics* is a murderer's dream come true."

"I would agree, Doctor. It's a very authoritative text."

"You've seen it before?" I asked. "It sounds very much like a primer on the refinement of aconitine." Agatha nodded.

"During the War, Maeve." She set her tea cup down. "So Mister Woldert's blue eyes did give me something to fear."

"That's not all we found. There was an overcoat, just as he said. No tears in it, I'm afraid," I said.

"Not surprising. The first overcoat and the jacket with the missing button are at the bottom of the Atlantic now," said Agatha. "And probably your wireless office typewriter too if anyone talked about your visit there. Our opponent seems to be singularly well informed."

"I hadn't thought of that," said Harper. He picked up the telephone and asked to be put through to the radio room. "Hello, is this Mister Cameron? Yes, Doctor Harper here. You don't happen to be missing anything this morning?" Harper listened as Agatha and I watched. He nodded his head. "I see. How odd. Thank you, Mister Cameron." Harper hung up the telephone and looked at us. "You're right. A typewriter has gone missing."

"Ha," I said. "Game to you, Mrs Templeton."

Mrs Templeton gave me a wry smile. "Elementary, my dear Maeve."

"But there's more," said Harper.

"Yes." I leaned forward. "Mister Woldert is apparently a Communist sympathizer, and he had a trip to the shore earlier this year with Mister Jackson."

"Mister Jackson? That nice officer?" Agatha wrinkled her brow.

"A picture in Woldert's trunk showed the two of them posing together, just like the best of friends on holiday," said Harper.

"And," I added, "another picture showed them as a lot more than best of friends. A lot more."

"Oh, my," said Agatha.

"According to Mister Woldert, he's new to the *Victoria*," I said, "but it's apparent he's not new to Mister Jackson in any way imaginable."

"I'm new to the *Victoria*, too," said Harper. "I know what would happen to a Communist sympathizer and a —

well, I won't use the word – on board one of His Majesty's warships, but what would happen here?"

"Mister Jackson and Mister Woldert would be cashiered and cast off," I said. "I doubt the Captain would deign to carry them back to Southampton. He'd just leave both of them behind in New York. Unless word got out to the rest of the crew and they didn't live to see New York."

"So," said Agatha. She looked at us. "Here are the facts. Political and amorous affiliations aside, we have a suspect in Mister Woldert. He apparently has the expertise to both refine and use a poison. What we don't have is a motive, and if we're to believe the accidentally served drinks theory, a clear victim, though it would appear the drink was meant for Mr Wilson. Mr Morten was simply a casualty of bad luck when he downed that poisoned drink."

"Which leaves Wilson and Alston," I said. "If Mr Alston was killed for having seen the murder of Wilson, then we have motive and victim, but no clear suspect."

"That's right," said Agatha. "And with Mr Wilson, we have victim, but neither motive or suspect. And let's not forget me. An intended victim, but no clear motive – although I suspect it's our investigation – and no suspect, although I certainly have my suspicions about one."

Harper put a hand to his forehead. "You're both making my head spin," he said, standing. "I'm going back to the surgery and check in with Doctor Bratton. I'll fill Mister Harvey in on the latest on the way."

"Don't forget to lock the door behind you at the hospital," said Mrs Templeton. "Remember that the boy and his mother are in someone's sights."

"Thanks for the reminder." Harper put on his cap. "Mind yourselves, ladies," he said, and then stopped at the door. "There is a Hallowe'en theme tonight in the First-Class salon. Could I impose on you two to join me for it? My medical opinion, for what it's worth, is that we could all use some recreation." Agatha and I looked at each other.

"Bertie mentioned that," I said. "Do we have to wear a costume?" Harper shrugged.

"Mister Harvey says they will have masks available, or you can make your own. It seems that any dress up items carried on the ship are already spoken for."

Agatha laughed. "Perhaps I will go as that famous children's author, AA Milne. Give your newspaperman something to think about."

I shook my head. "Oh, no. Mister Casey needs nothing to think about. Whenever he thinks, it usually leads to trouble." Now it was my turn to smile. "Still, the thought of seeing you dressed as Pooh…"

"Let's not get carried away, shall we?" said Agatha. "We accept your invitation, Doctor. It's better than staying behind locked doors and waiting to be murdered."

"And here I thought it was strictly due to my charm." Harper opened the door. "I'll meet you in the salon lobby at eight." The door closed behind him.

"What do you think we should do now?" I asked Agatha.

"'Do?'" she said. "Get hold of Mister Harvey and put someone on Mister Woldert to watch his every move and hope he takes a wrong step."

"What about Mister Jackson? We can't just ignore the fact that he knew Woldert before he signed aboard."

"We won't. We'll go to the Captain with our suspicions about Woldert, and make sure Mister Jackson can hear us," said Agatha.

"What about the picture of the two of them at the shore? Much less the other one?"

Agatha shook her head. "No need to tip our hand on that. What we'll have to say to the Captain should be quite sufficient without it."

I sighed. "This is such a bloody mess. How long do you think it will take before it ends?" I asked.

"Well, my dear, if I was writing this, we'd go through a few more pages of suspense and then have the big denouement. In real life, I can't say." She took a thoughtful sip of tea. "Real life is so much more involved."

I could only imagination how Mister Harvey reacted to Doctor Harper telling him about Mister Woldert – but whatever Mister Harvey's reaction had been it was stoic compared to that of the Captain. Agatha and I stood quietly while the Captain digested – or indigested – the news.

"A Communist?" He spat the word out like a spoiled piece of kidney pie. "Serving on my crew?" The Captain drummed his fingers on the burnished brass side of the engine room telegraph.

"Well, maybe not a full-fledged Communist," I said. "But he certainly had a lot of reading material in his trunk."

"Unfortunately, that's not the worst of it," said Agatha. "There was also a medical textbook in his trunk. Dog eared to pages on aconitine."

The Captain fixed me with his eyes. "And you and Doctor Harper just took it on yourselves to make this investigation?"

"Yes, sir," I said meekly. "Truthfully, I coaxed him into it. It was all my idea."

"I see." He looked at Agatha. "And you appear none the worse for wear for your adventure this morning. Doctor Harper told me about it."

"No, I'm quite fine."

I was suddenly aware that Mister Jackson had sidled up next to us, clipboard in hand. He proffered it and a pen to the Captain. "Excuse me sir. Met report."

The Captain glanced at it, then signed it with a savage sweep of the pen. Mister Jackson nodded and retreated a discreet distance away, watching us carefully.

I straightened my back. "Sir, with our witness to Mr Wilson going overboard – the young Alston boy – and now this book, I think we have our murderer."

The Captain nodded. "Where is the boy now?"

"He's with his mother in the surgery," I said. "Doctor Bratton and Doctor Harper are with her. If he's not there, Miss Kelly keeps him. He's attended to at all times."

"Wouldn't want anyone taking a crack at him," Agatha said.

"Let's get back to Mister Woldert," said the Captain. "We're nearly to New York. Be there Saturday morning. I don't see the need to upset the passengers with an arrest; no matter how quietly we do it, word will get out. Leave him be and we'll just detain him aboard ship."

"But the New York Customs Authority," I began. The Captain shook his head.

"Our ship, our problem, Nurse Chandler." He continued the steady tattoo of his fingers on the engine room telegraph. "And just supposing that you're right, even if Mister Woldert did expedite Mr Alston's exit off this mortal coil, that still leaves us with Mr Morten and Mr

Wilson." The Captain looked expectantly at Mrs Templeton and myself.

"Well," began Agatha. "It's Nurse William's belief that Mister Woldert is probably responsible for Mr Morten's death as well."

"That's right," I said. "He served the drink to Mr Morten."

The Captain thoughtfully stroked his beard. "And that leaves Mr Wilson. Any ideas there?"

"Not definitively," I said with chagrin.

The Captain nodded. "You know if he gets a good barrister, he'll get everything dropped. It's all too — what's the word?"

"Circumstantial," said Mrs Templeton.

"Thank you, Mrs Templeton. Too circumstantial." The Captain crossed his arms behind him and gazed out at the ocean in front of us. "Thousands of ships out there, and this is happening to me." He sighed. "If you're not doing it already, I needn't tell you to keep Mister Woldert under observation."

"Yes, sir," I said.

"And Nurse Chandler, if anyone else gets murdered, I don't want to know about it until we get to New York. That's all, ladies."

Outside the bridge Agatha turned to me. "He really didn't mean that last part, did he?" she asked.

"Oh, no," I said. "That was just his attempt at humour. Like Mister Harvey saying he's running low on caskets to store bodies in." I puffed my cheeks out. "Mister Jackson couldn't help but get an earful up there. I hope it turns out like you want it to."

"I'm sure it will," said Mrs Templeton.

The door to the surgery was locked when I arrived. I rapped sharply, and then heard Harvey's voice.

"Yes?"

"It's me, Mister Harvey. Please open the door."

The locks turned and the door cracked open. Harvey peered out at me, then nodded and let me in, locking the door after.

"Any visitors?" I asked.

"None. Not so much as a peep." He consulted his watch. "I've been here about ten minutes. Doctor Harper was here when I arrived."

I glanced about. Bradley was sitting quietly in a chair in the waiting room, legs dangling, reading a story book, the demolished remains of a kitchen tray nearby. I wondered if all boys his age ate like draft horses. Doctor Bratton, I supposed, had already begun his pre-debarkation rounds of the passengers to make sure we didn't inadvertently send a passenger with an infectious disease into the United States.

Mister Harvey accompanied me to the back where we found Doctor Harper attending to Mrs Alston and Victoria. "How are you doing Mrs Alston? And Victoria?" I asked brightly.

"I could not be in better hands or care," she said. "And you can see for yourself how Victoria is doing." The baby was sound asleep in her mother's arms.

"I'm glad to hear it. And I see Mister Harvey has brought you a few things?" A large wicker basket was nearby, crammed with toiletries and sundries.

"Yes, thank you. It's from the ship's passengers and crew."

"And we also booked you passage back to Southampton, leaving New York Sunday night. Courtesy of the Stoddard Lines," concluded Mister Harvey. Harper nodded.

"It's the right thing to do."

I looked at Harvey. "I hate to bring it up, but what about Mr Alston?"

Mister Harvey airily waved a hand. "Regretfully, Mr Alston will not be making the return trip with us. He will be leaving the ship when we get to New York. Mrs Alston helped put us in touch with a relative who will claim the body."

Clara looked at me and shook her head. "Fell down a lift shaft. I've been thinking about that. A fitting end for him, to plunge all the way to the bottom." She sighed. "I won't have to leave the ship in New York to deal with this, will I?"

"No, Mrs Alston," said Doctor Harper. "Mister Harvey and I will bring you the necessary forms to sign to release the body."

"And I don't want to see anyone from his family come on board to talk with me, either."

"We certainly understand that, Mrs Alston. After all, you're a British citizen – and so is Victoria, since she was born aboard a British registered vessel. This ship is technically as much British soil as is Piccadilly Circus." I looked at little Victoria, beginning to stretch and wake up. "All we're concerned about is getting you and your baby back to Southampton." I stroked Victoria's soft cheek for a moment. "We touched on this briefly, Clara, but I'm still curious. What exactly did your husband mean by he would be rich soon? Have you thought about it anymore?"

Clara sniffed. "The less I think of him the better." She closed her eyes for a moment. "All I remember him saying is that he'd seen something, and he was going to take advantage of it."

"I'm sorry, Mrs Alston, my memory has slipped. When was that?"

"Tuesday morning. Before you came to the cabin."

I nodded. "Yes, that's right. I do remember him saying something about being rich as we left."

Clara held Victoria tight up against her. "Well, as usual, he's not rich, but at least he's dead, which is an improvement." She tugged at the sheet. "Could I have a little private time with Victoria? She's acting hungry."

"Oh – certainly!" Harvey sounded embarrassed.

"Call if you need anything," said Harper. "Either Nurse Chandler or myself will stay outside."

She nodded. "Thank you. I'm very grateful." The three of us made our goodbyes.

Back in the waiting room, Bradley had finished his book and was now stretched out on one of the couches, sound asleep. I gently covered him with a blanket, then convened a meeting with Doctor Harper and Mister Harvey on the other side of the room.

"If that doesn't put paid to the theory that Mr Alston saw something he shouldn't have and meant to cash in on it, I don't know what does," I said. "I think we can take it as a fact that he was murdered because he knew too much. And that boy over there is in the same boat, as well as his mother."

"It won't be Mister Woldert, if there's trouble," said Harvey. "Doctor Harper filled me in on your little sojourn to the hold. I instructed Mister Evans to stick to Woldert like treacle."

"Good." I looked at Harper. "Mrs Templeton and I had a chat with the Captain after you left. He knows everything, too – except about the photograph of Woldert and Jackson. We held that back for now."

"Mister Jackson." Harvey ran a hand through his thick hair. "You think you know a man."

"I know, Mister Harvey. I feel the same way." I sighed. "Perhaps the Hallowe'en party tonight will make us all feel better for a moment."

"Yes, Harper told me you and Mrs Templeton would be attending. Do you need party hat or costume materials?"

"If you could get me a cigar, that would be nice," I said. "And if I can borrow one of your civilian coat jackets, Doctor Harper?"

"Of course," said Harper.

"A cigar?" Harvey was perplexed.

"And black shoe polish." I smiled at him. Harvey looked at Harper.

"I'm glad she's your problem, not mine."

VII

When I was a child I always loved the last week of October and first week of November – Hallowe'en followed five scant days later by Guy Fawkes night. My parents, ever the educators, always referred to Hallowe'en as All Hallows Eve. Of course, for my brother and I it was always the warm-up to Guy Fawkes night and fireworks on November 5th. How well I remember the two of us making up an effigy of the hated traitor Guy Fawkes from old hand-me-down clothes, stuffing him with straw and dragging him bump, bump, bump down to the local bonfire to join the jolly old funeral pyre along with the creations of the other children. Looking back on it, it's little wonder that I grew into the odd adult I am today.

Now, seeing myself in the mirror in my stateroom, I had to admit that any roving band of children in my old neighbourhood would consider they'd hit the jackpot by capturing me and consigning my spirit to the flames.

Gone was my blonde hair; instead, a black curly mop was perched on top of my head courtesy of L'Oreal hair color from my absent cabin mate, who kept her hair Theda Bara jet black, and a healthy underpinning of kirby grips to hold it all in place. Black shoe polish eyebrows and a broad shoe polish moustache decorated my face, and I'd removed the lenses from a discarded pair of glasses (also belonging to my absent cabin mate) and had the frames perched jauntily on my nose. As a finishing touch I held up the cigar Mister Harvey had provided.

I'd seen the talkie film comedy *The Cocoanuts* in New York a month ago, and the antics of the man named Groucho Marx had nearly caused me to burst a seam laughing. I smirked at my reflection. Not bad at all. And Doctor Harper's dark civilian coat jacket hung off of me like a badly balanced drape, completing the look. It wasn't often I was invited to a costume ball – especially one at work – and I intended to make the best of it, or die trying.

Well, maybe not die trying.

"What on earth are you made up as?" asked Agatha when I met her in the salon lobby.

"Groucho Marx."

"Who? Who is Groucho Marx?"

"He's a film and stage comedian along with his brothers. I saw their talkie in New York in August." Agatha looked aghast.

"Someone who looks like that is in the cinema?" She sadly shook her head. "Whatever became of stars like Rudolph Valentino?"

"He died three years ago."

Agatha nodded. "That's right. I was rather preoccupied at the time."

I rolled my eyes. "We were at sea when we got the news. Half of the women on board had to go under a suicide watch." I waggled the cigar and tried to imitate Mr Marx' accent. "We had to show *The Son of the Sheik* nonstop. The projection man kept asking how he was dune." I flexed my eyebrows. "Get it? How he was "dune?"

"Stop," said Agatha. "Just stop." She looked past me. "Ah, Doctor Harper. I see you decided to make the most of things and appear tonight as a sea-going physician."

"Thank you, Mrs Templeton." Harper shot his cuffs. "It's my full dress uniform." He gave me a concerned look. "And – you are – an escaped lunatic?"

"I'm Groucho Marx. Gee, you people need to get out and see a moving picture every once in a while."

"I'll take your word for it," said Harper. "Mrs Templeton, may I?" He proffered his arm. "You look lovely tonight. Blue has always been one of my favorite colours."

"Thank you, Doctor Harper." The pair of them strode forward and I followed behind, rather, I thought, like a trained monkey.

The seating was full, the liquor was flowing and the Hallowe'en spirit – pardon the pun – was evident everywhere one looked. Mister Harvey and his crew had decorated the room with orange and black streamers and crepe, and instead of the usual lavish floral decorations on the tables, chrysanthemums, dahlias, bittersweet, black feathers and small pumpkins and other gourds were the order of the evening.

Some passengers were in full formal with masks like Zorro, and others wore more elaborate items that might have been more at home in a Parisian masquerade ball. Still others wore no masks at all, but were not having much luck in hiding the bemused expressions on their faces. Agatha and Doctor Harper fell into this last lot.

Monsieur DuMont seated us, and I suppose because of the daggers I was shooting him from my eyes he refrained from making anything other than the most trivial comments.

We hadn't been at table more than two minutes before my companions noted someone coming up behind me.

"Doctor, Mrs Templeton," I heard Harvey say. I turned around in my chair and looked up at him, eyebrows arched. "Gahhh!" said Harvey.

"Oh, please. It's not that bad."

"It's not that good, either." His brow wrinkled. "What are you – "

"Someone named Marx, Mister Harvey," said Agatha.

Harvey gave me closer inspection. "You do not even faintly resemble Karl Marx," he pronounced.

"Says the man with a Communist sympathizer on his wait staff," I replied.

Harvey waved his hands. "Not so loud." He pulled at the sides of his white jacket. "I'll personally be taking care of you three tonight." He gave Agatha a smile. "No repeats of this morning."

"I appreciate that, Mister Harvey," she said.

"Has Mister Woldert spent an uneventful afternoon?" asked Harper. Harvey nodded.

"As far as I know. I spoke to Mister Evans not twenty minutes ago. He said it was all quiet."

"Is Mister Woldert on the dinner service tonight, Mister Harvey?" Agatha asked.

"Yes," said Harvey.

"Do you think it's safe?" I asked him.

"Mister Evans is watching him like the proverbial hawk." Harvey tilted his head. "They're both on the other side of the room, working the same area."

"And Miss Kelly is watching Bradley in the children's play room," said Harper. "They needed an extra person tonight with so many parents here for the party."

"Well, I'm sure he's having a grand time," I said.

"Indeed," said Harvey. He took out a waiter's pad. "May I suggest starting with the Terrine de Foie Gras, followed by the Plymouth Turbot Poché Hollandaise or the Cassolette de Volaille Rothschild accompanied by the Globe Artichokes in Butter Sauce and finish with a Soufflé Pouding au Citron? I will, of course, select and pour the appropriate wines myself." He smiled beatifically at us, his pencil poised.

I wondered if Groucho Marx ever had dinners like this.

Three hours later, having ascertained that Mister Harvey's dinner selection was truly brilliant, I was ready to call for a tumbril to come and wheel me back to my stateroom. Well, maybe not a tumbril. My thoughts seemed to have taken a dark turn recently; I couldn't imagine why. Agatha seemed to sense it.

"You look troubled." It was the first effort by any of us to breach the silence about the murders during dinner, our conversation instead revolving around Doctor Harper's tales of being a ship's doctor in the Royal Navy and Mrs Templeton talking about her "job" reading manuscripts, which I actually found amusing. My contribution had been the occasional wise crack about someone's costume, which deep down bothered me. I knew I was a better conversationalist than that.

"I am troubled. Here we've been gabbing away like there's nothing wrong, and we'll be in New York the day after tomorrow. And unless Mister Woldert does something really stupid, which I doubt, he's going to walk free because we have nothing really hard we can use to pin him down." I morosely downed the last of the wine in my glass. "I hate being a detective."

"You should try being a ship's captain, then," said a voice behind me. I straightened in my chair as Harper got to his feet.

"Sir," said Harper.

"I trust you three are having a nice evening. God knows you deserve a bit of time off, especially since our casualty list hasn't increased lately," said the Captain. "But I still expect results before we reach New York Saturday morning." He eyed me carefully. Was that a hint of a smile on his face? "I was partial to Harpo, myself, Nurse," he said. "Carry on." The Captain trundled off.

"Harpo?" asked Harper.

"One of Groucho's brothers," I explained. Agatha nodded.

"Of course, with a name like that why wouldn't he be?" She set her napkin down on the table. "Well, as your captain says, it's time to carry on."

I stood. "Where?"

"I'd like to take another stroll along the Boat Deck, if you don't mind," said Agatha.

"Alone?" Harper sounded concerned.

"Of course not alone." She nodded at me. "I'll have Groucho with me."

"That should certainly scare any one away," said Harper.

"You know, I'm standing right here," I said to him. "We'll be fine. Go relieve Doctor Bratton."

"All right. Come by the hospital before you turn in. Goodnight, ladies."

"Goodnight, Doctor," said Agatha. We watched him cross the room, and then she turned to me. "Let us push on, Groucho."

It didn't take long to get to the Boat Deck from the restaurant. It was close after ten pm and the breeze had a biting sting to it. I looked at Agatha. "I hope you're not planning on staying out here very long."

"Only as long as it takes. Would you mind showing me the spot where Mr Wilson went overboard again?"

"Not at all. Lifeboat station ten is close by." We walked in silence beneath the overhanging davits of the lifeboats. "What are you thinking?" I finally asked her.

"As Hercule said in *The Mysterious Affair At Styles*, we are not using our little gray cells." She tapped her head. "At least I'm not."

"What do you mean?"

"I mean I'm not thinking. As soon as I think I've secured one thread, another one slips out of place."

"I understand what you mean." I stopped walking. "We're here."

"Looks even worse in the dark." Agatha walked to the railing and looked over the side at the black sea. She turned around. "Bradley said he saw one figure push another over the railing, but it was too dark to see features or identifying clothing." Agatha turned back to look into the blackness below. "And what did you say? Mr Wilson was a large man. It would have taken someone with a build like Harper or Harvey to push him over the side."

"That's right."

Agatha faced me. "Then Bradley isn't afraid of a steward. He's afraid of a tall man."

A light went on in my mind. "Of course," I said. "It's obvious once you think about it. Bradley was afraid of Doctor Harper. And when he and his mum were moved, he wasn't afraid of two stewards – just the tall one. Mister Woldert." I shook my head. "You're amazing."

"You forgot to mention your First Officer, Mister Jackson. He's also tall." Agatha tapped her head. "And he and Mister Woldert are apparently very close companions.

How do you think Mister Woldert got the inside track on being able to store a trunk in the ship's mail hold when this is his first berthing here? How do you think someone was able to turn off the lights in my passenger corridor this morning early to slip in and try to poison me? Mister Harvey said it would take particular knowledge of the ship to find the electrical panels, didn't he? You wouldn't expect someone on their first assignment here to know that, but you'd certainly expect it to be in the knowledge base of the First Officer, wouldn't you?" She stepped away from the railing. "And while I only met the erstwhile Mr Alston after he'd become a crumpet at the bottom of the lift shaft, I should certainly say that a larger man could have broken his arm for him if, as you surmised, Mr Alston's "negotiations" for a blackmail settlement had gone awry with his intended victim."

"And Mister Woldert did say that Alston all but accused him of breaking his arm," I said.

Agatha nodded. "Again, which means as we surmised, that Mr Alston saw the killer's face when Wilson went over the side. The murderer. The tall man that Bradley is afraid of, but that he can't identify." She frowned. "So who was it?"

"All of the evidence, such as it is, seems to indict Mister Woldert."

"It would certainly seem that way. And yet, I'm not entirely satisfied. And as it's been pointed out numerous times, it's all circumstantial." Agatha tapped her fingers against the ship's rail. "Does Mister Jackson own an overcoat?" she asked.

"All of the officers have them," I said. "You don't think – "

"Just a thought," said Agatha. "Let's go back inside." I led the way back to the stairs and down to the Promenade

Deck. A few hardy couples were still out strolling, some of them in masks or costumes. We got some looks as we walked along until finally Mrs Templeton couldn't stand it any longer.

"My boyfriend," explained Agatha to one enquiring couple, who took one look at me and hurried along. My eyes must have popped. Groucho would have been proud.

"You're incorrigible," I said.

"Thank you, dear."

Friday, November 1, 1929

I

Someday, when I'm retired, I'm going to get a butler (tall and handsome, of course!) whose only duty will be to answer the door and tell visitors that "Madam is not receiving company" or "Madam is not in at present" primarily because Madam would like to spend five uninterrupted minutes alone from time to time. I hadn't been back in my stateroom more than five minutes before someone was urgently knocking at the door. I looked at the clock – it was past 23:00. Shrugging out of Doctor Harper's suit jacket, I answered the door. My visitor stared at me.

"Jesus," said Miss Kelly. "What happened to you?"

"I had a Hallowe'en evening dressed up as Groucho Marx. I'm not going to try to explain it to you. What are you doing here in the almost middle of the night?"

"I lost the boy."

I yanked her into the stateroom and closed the door. "You what?"

"I lost him." I'd never thought Miss Kelly could ever look distraught. "One minute he was there with the other children, and the next – "

"When?"

"About twenty minutes ago. Some of the parents were coming by to pick up their children, and there was a masked pantomime clown doing little magic tricks, dressed up as a Pierrot, and you wouldn't believe the

281

incredible amount of sugar those children had consumed – ”

"Get to the point."

Miss Kelly spread her hands. "It was bedlam. Honestly. And I looked up, and Bradley was gone. And so was the clown. I went out into the corridor, but there was nothing to see. I searched about, and then came down here."

"Have you told anyone else?"

She shook her head. "Not yet. I feel awful. You entrusted him to me."

"Don't make yourself sick. He has an annoying habit of wandering off." But never with pantomime clowns, I thought. "Just as an aside, was this clown tall or short?"

"Medium. Maybe six inches taller than you."

Make that never wandered off with a tall pantomime clown, I thought. "Too bad he wasn't tall," I said out loud.

"What?"

"Never mind. It would take too long to explain." I picked up Harper's jacket and put it back on. "Let's go."

"Like that?" Miss Kelly asked, looking at me.

"It's Hallowe'en," I said. "And believe me, there's much worse things afoot on this ship than me." I closed and locked the stateroom door. "Go find Mister Harvey. I'll meet you on the forward Promenade Deck."

"Where are you going?"

"Checking in on Doctor Bratton and Mrs Alston. Go on, I'll catch up." Miss Kelly nodded and headed toward the lifts. I went in the opposite direction to the hospital.

"Who's there?" said Bratton in response to my knock.

"It's me. Maeve. Open up."

The door knob rattled and then he opened the door a crack. "Good Lord," he said.

"Stop it and let me in." He swung wide the door and ushered me inside.

"She and the baby are asleep," said Bratton. "It's been a quiet evening. No mysterious business at the door."

"Glad to hear it, but we've got other problems. Bradley is missing – again."

Bratton's eyebrows arched. "Lord, but that lad does get around, doesn't he? When?"

I shrugged. "Probably about forty minutes ago. Miss Kelly told me. She'd had him in the children's playroom with the other kids, and lost him, along with an unnamed clown who'd been entertaining the children."

"I never trusted clowns," said Bratton firmly. "Not even as a child. Though that's neither here nor there. Have you started the search?"

"Miss Kelly is on her way to roust Mister Harvey. I just wanted to let you know in case Clara asks for the boy. Hopefully we'll have him in tow before she wakes up in the morning. I'm going to go and get Doctor Harper."

"Why don't you 'phone him?" said Bratton, indicating the desk. "Save yourself some time. I'll keep Mrs Alston out of bounds until morning."

"Thanks." I picked up the receiver and we both froze. The doorknob jiggled, lightly at first, and then with more force. Bratton's eyes fixed on mine.

"Your visitor again?" he asked quietly. I swallowed hard. The sound of a key being fitted to the lock could be heard. Bratton strode to the door. "I have a gun and I'll use it," he said. "Identify yourself or I'll shoot through this door." The scratching stopped, followed by the sound of footfalls receding up the corridor. Bratton turned back to me. "Bloody hell," he said softly. "What kind of a mess have you all managed to dig up?"

"I don't know," I said. "Do you have a gun?"

"Don't be daft, I'd just injure myself."

"Terrific." I went into the surgery and came back with a scalpel. "One never knows. It might come in handy."

"Don't cut yourself."

"It's got the blade guard on." I slipped it into one of my jacket pockets. "Probably wouldn't do you any harm to have one, either."

Doctor Bratton shook his head. "Marginally less dangerous than a gun in my hands." He nodded toward the surgery. "I'll make up a syringe of pentobarbital, stick it in his neck and get out of the way before he hits the floor."

"To each his own," I replied. I slowly cracked the door and peered into the corridor. It was empty, our visitor vanished without a trace. "I'm off, then."

"Take care." Bratton closed the door and turned the lock. I felt again for the reassuring touch of the scalpel, then made my way to the lifts.

Agatha answered her door on the first knock. "Who is it?"

"Maeve. Let me in." I entered and she shut and locked the door.

"Goodness, you still haven't taken that rig off?" she asked me.

"Haven't had the chance, and it looks like the way things are going I'll be wearing it all the way to New York. The boy is missing again."

The news didn't seem to faze her. "Give me a moment to get dressed. When did it happen?"

I recounted Miss Kelly's story to her. Agatha slipped into her shoes. "A shorter man, according to Miss Kelly. So Bradley wasn't afraid of him."

"That's the conclusion I came to. The question is, who is he and why and where did he take the boy?"

Agatha shook her head. "The answer to part of it is obvious. Our tall man has a shorter accomplice who is also apparently interested in keeping the boy silent."

"In the same way they kept Mr Alston silent?"

"Your guess is as good as mine," said Agatha. "Perhaps they just want to hide him away long enough to get off the ship in New York and disappear into America."

"I hate to be callous, but Mr Alston was no great loss to society. Killing a child, though, that would be a different thing entirely."

"Then we'd best be about finding him." Agatha opened her door. "Where are we going?"

"Meeting Doctor Harper and Mister Harvey on the forward Promenade deck," I said.

"The four of us can't possibly search this ship. You're going to have to get the Captain involved, you know," said Agatha.

"Don't I know it," I replied. "Don't I just know it."

"With a clown, you say?" Captain Webster stared at me. We were gathered in his day room. Due to the lateness of the hour the Captain was missing his tie, but that was all. His mood remained as imperious as ever. "So you're telling me in addition to a homicidal maniac, I'm also carrying a clown on board?"

"A masked clown," I said. "A Pierrot. A stock character from the old Italian commedia dell'arte." I turned to the Chief Steward. "Mister Harvey, is that one of the costume fittings and pieces we carry for passengers to rent for occasion?

"Probably. It hasn't been inventoried for a couple of years." He gave a slight chuckle. "Did you know Doctor

Bratton hates clowns? Get him to tell you about the time he – "

The Captain held up a hand. "Mister Harvey. Please."

"Sorry, sir."

"All right, then, there's nothing to do but find him." The Captain opened the door from his day room that connected to the bridge. "Mister Jackson."

"Sir?"

"Organize a search party."

"Sir? At this hour?" Jackson walked over to the Captain.

"You heard me. We're looking for the little Alston boy, Bradley." The Captain indicated the four of us. "They can give you a description." He rubbed his forehead. "At least it's after hours, there shouldn't be too many passengers wandering about."

"A little boy?" asked Jackson. "Begging your pardon, Sir, do you know how many places a little boy could hide on this ship?"

"Do you know how many ships in the Stoddard Line would accept a third officer who used to be a first officer on the Commodore's flagship vessel?" Jackson swallowed. "Yes, I'm aware of the difficulties involved," said the Captain, putting a hand on Jackson's shoulder. "But if anyone can find him, you can." He turned back to us. "Looks like a long night ahead for all of you. Bundle up, it's cold outside. Mrs Templeton, there's no reason for you to be involved in this."

"I've grown fond of the boy, Captain. I'll stick it out, if you don't mind."

"As you wish. Given what someone tried to do to you yesterday morning, I'll ask that you stay close to Mister Harvey for safety's sake." He looked at me. "You and Doctor Harper work as a team. If you find him before three in the morning, I'll give you a cigar from my own box, Groucho."

"Groucho?" Jackson was looking at me. I waggled my eyebrows. He looked uncomfortable.

"Are you going to be warm enough without a topcoat, Mister Jackson?" I asked.

"I'm fine, thank you."

"It is getting colder outside," said Agatha.

"I'll manage. Thank you for your concern."

"Mister Jackson, get the men you need and Mister Armstrong." The Captain nodded. "Off you go. Good luck."

Agatha and I exchanged glances as we filed out of the room and went our separate ways.

Doctor Harper and I elected to start at the top and work our way down. Consequently, it didn't take long for me to begin shivering in the cold night air. Harper slipped off his woolen greatcoat and wrapped it around me. It dragged the deck but I didn't care, it was warm.

"Aren't you cold?" I asked him as we trudged along, poking in and around possible hiding places and checking that doors and hatchways that should be locked were locked.

"Cold?" Harper turned up the collar of his uniform jacket. "It's not too bad. I've stood many watches in worse than this."

"Well, thank you again for the coat." I pulled it tighter. "I must look an absolute fright."

Harper glanced over at me as we walked. "Certainly a different look from when I came aboard a few days ago. Speaking of, those stitches should be about ready to come out now."

"I'll have Doctor Bratton remove them, thanks." I tested a door handle. "Doctor Harper, do you mind if I ask you a question?"

"Go ahead."

"Were you ever married? I mean, Doctor Bratton is a confirmed bachelor, and I just thought – "

"I'm in the same boat with Doctor Bratton. Never found time for it. Always at sea, anyway. And truthfully told, a lot of the women friends tried to foist off on me were, at best, completely vacuous in their conversations."

I grinned. "And I'll wager that none of them ever dressed like Groucho Marx."

He nodded. "You are a definite first."

"Mother always said I was a trendsetter." I looked up. "I seem to remember us taking another walk topside a few nights ago. There were a million stars in the sky. And then we got pulled into a search for Bradley." I frowned. "So much has happened since then and I wish we could go back to where we were before Mr Morten died and New York upended. The world made sense, then. No searches for a killer, or killers. No dead men. No murder attempt on Mrs Templeton."

"Mrs Templeton seems quite capable of taking care of herself."

I smirked. "You don't know the half of it," I said. "If it wasn't for her help we wouldn't have even the slim chance we have now of solving this before we get to New York on Saturday."

"It seems to me you've done a fair amount of sleuthing, yourself."

I stopped and looked up at him. "Not enough. For instance, I'm only now just finding out you've never married."

Harper gazed at me. "I never thought it was that important," he said, reaching a hand out to gently touch my cheek.

"Just like a man," I said, closing my eyes, parting my lips and leaning my head back. For a fleeting moment the world stood still – and then it came crashing down.

"Excuse me, but with the Captain's compliments – he'd like you both to report to Chief Engineer Duncan in the forward engine room, F Deck." The able bodied seaman stood about five feet away, arms crossed behind his back. My head sagged forward, chin dropping down.

"Is there an accident?" asked Harper.

"In a manner of speaking, sir." He looked at me with some curiousity, but whatever his thoughts were, he was keeping them to himself. "You won't need your kit." Harper and I exchanged worried glances.

"I'm afraid I don't know my way down to Engineering," said Harper.

"I'll guide you there, sir." He cocked his head toward a flight of stairs. "This way, sir."

"Lead on, McDuff," said Harper. He strode forward and I scurried behind, trying not to trip on the overcoat's hem. Life, I thought bitterly, was having a right go at me lately.

Engineering on F Deck is one deck above where the boilers are anchored on G Deck and the boilers themselves – each one is about 30 feet tall –extend up through the engineering stations and spaces on F Deck to access hatches on E Deck. Long before we'd gotten there I'd handed the overcoat back to Doctor Harper, who carried it on his arm. His tie was loosened and jacket open; the deeper we went, the warmer the temperature.

It was also markedly noisier.

The *Victoria* is a triple screw ship; that is, looking at the back, or aft end of the ship, there was one propeller on the right, or starboard, another propeller on the left, or port, and one in the middle, the latter rotating in an open space between the ship's hull and the massive rudder. Each of these propellers, some 22 feet in diameter and weighing 30 tons each, were driven by their own drive shaft located on G Deck and powered by giant turbines that in turn were powered by the steam produced by the massive boilers. I was told once by Chief Engineer Duncan that the propellers were so delicately balanced that they could be turned by hand when the ship was on blocks in dry dock. The cacophony made by all of this equipment working in unison along with what seemed to me about a million other pieces of engineering jigsaw puzzle had to be heard to be believed.

Our guide dropped us off at the base of the stairs leading up to the main engine room controls in the forward engine room, a steel wall crammed with dials, gauges, switches, status lights, duplicates of the bridge speed controls, and, incongruously, a large chalkboard with scribbled notations on it. Chief Engineer Duncan beckoned us up the steps.

"Thank ye for comin'," he said, "though I was expectin' the Captain."

"He's on the bridge," said Harper. "Mister Carter and Mister Jackson are both involved in a search party."

"At this time of night? That can't be good."

"It never is, Chief Duncan," I said.

He gave me a closer look. "Nurse Chandler, have ye had an accident?"

"No, I have not," I said coldly.

"Well, then." The Chief wiped his hands on his overalls, his soiled officer's cap the only nod to his rank.

"Someone else has. Come with me, please." Harper looked at me. I shrugged. Together we followed the Chief along a narrow steel grating catwalk with what seemed to me minimal safety railings to keep us from falling into a maze of pipes, large and small, as well as electrical conduit, also large and small, that surrounded us on every side. Men in coveralls were tending to the complicated powerplant that generated over 120,000 horsepower and could move the *Victoria* ahead at a top speed of 28 miles per hour.

As I mentioned to you before, the steam needed to spin the turbines was no longer generated by grimy hard-bitten men shoveling in an endless supply of coal into the blast furnace of the old style boilers; rather, men in clean coveralls – the Chief not withstanding – kept a careful eye on the water and fuel levels. Every single member of the engineering staff was quietly intent on their job and didn't give us a second glance, and no wonder: the engine rooms of the *Queen Victoria* were not a safe place to daydream. Scalding, high-pressure steam and water, fuel oil heated and then sprayed into boilers to fire them, turbines generating 1,300 kilowatts, about a half mile of steam piping and nearly 3,500 miles of electrical and other cable could kill you before you knew what had happened. I didn't even want to think of the consequences if one of the boilers lost its water supply, overheated and exploded.

It was deep inside this man-made version of Dante's *Inferno* that Chief Duncan led us to Boiler Room Two and stopped.

"D' ye ken Doctor a few days ago in the staff meeting when I was talkin' about the problem we were havin' with the primary fuel feed flow line to boiler five in Boiler Room Two?"

"Barely," said Harper. Duncan nodded.

"Well, I know you and the Nurse and Mister Harvey have been busy with passengers droppin' dead," he said perfunctorily but without any malice; it was obvious to us that the engine rooms were his overriding concern. "We've had boiler five shut down these past few days until we could trace the fault and make repairs. We finished up a few hours ago, took a dinner break and then came back to start the process of heatin' it up."

"And?" said Harper.

"And when the boiler got to steam, we started smelling something, and that's when we found this." Mister Duncan pulled a canvas tarp off of a huddled shape at his feet on the catwalk. I involuntarily gasped and stepped back against Doctor Harper.

The man was burned, though his face was still recognizable, and his left arm had been completely crushed. "He was stuck up against the boiler, about halfway down." Mister Duncan looked at the body. "His name's Starling. He was a greaser, one of my best, too. He was small enough to really get into tight areas to put down the oil and grease."

"Any chance it could have been an accident?" I asked. Chief Duncan shook his head.

"None. The sides of the boiler here are smooth. There is nothing that would account for an injury like the one he has. If anything he'd have been wedged in between the boiler and the side supports and had his chest compressed so he couldn't breathe, much less cry for help, but he'd have cooked long before that." He shook his head. "He was nah killed here, I believe."

Harper leaned over the railing and looked down. "There's not much blood to be seen down there," he remarked. "It should be awash with it, owing to the nature of the injury. You're right, Chief. I think he was killed somewhere else and disposed of here."

"Aye, and who would want to kill Starling?" said Duncan. "He's been part of my engineering staff for two years, never a bit of trouble with the poor lad."

"I don't know, Chief," said Harper. "We'll have to get him out of here and into cold storage, though." Harper turned to me. "Remind you of someone?"

"Except he didn't get that arm by falling down a lift shaft. Something closed on him." I looked around. "In here, it could be just about anything."

"I don't know what you're talking about, and I don't want to know. All I can tell you is that no one said anything or saw anything here, Nurse," said the Chief. "All of us that wear the purple are tight knit." His face was grim. "Someone outside of engineering did this."

"You found him when you came back from your evening meal?" I asked. Mister Duncan nodded.

"This area has been closed off for the past few days while we worked. Crew had to go down one deck, cross beneath, then come up from the other side. Bloody nuisance, but we needed the work space. And no, Starling was nah part of the work crew here."

"So how did he end up down there?" said Harper, pointing.

"Look up, Doctor. There's a small access hatch in the ceiling, about ten feet up, just above the ladder there. Open the hatch from the other side, drop the man through, and let the providence of God determine where the poor sod lands, God rest his soul."

"You know I'm new to the ship, Chief," said Harper. "What's immediately above us?"

"Fan rooms and cargo space." said the Chief. "Hatches to the tops of each of the boilers in this boiler room.

Forward of that is the mail room, general storage areas, one of the watertight access doors to the chain locker, and an expansion trunk."

Harper looked at me and nodded. "I'm getting the layout now. We've been to the mail room area." He turned back to the Chief. "Expansion trunk?" he asked.

"Aye. Right over a fuel bunker. Gives headroom for the fuel oil to breathe and expand with temperature changes without risking putting strain on the hull."

"Why don't you stay here and get this man back to the hospital," I said to Doctor Harper. "I'll continue our search — just start working my way back to the top. At some point I'm likely to run into the others. You can check this deck with some help from Chief Duncan's crew, I think."

Harper glanced at his wristwatch. "You're right." He looked down at the body.

"I'm sure it's connected to everything else in some way," I said. "I don't mean to be callous, but Mister Starling will wait. Right now, we've got a child to find before he possibly goes the same way."

II

Now, in the music hall, when the magician makes someone disappear, he has a helper, someone who can steal focus from the audience while the conjurer goes through his machinations. And, I reasoned, for stealing focus nothing could beat another murder. I tried to put myself in Agatha's place as I climbed the stairs to E Deck. Was I doing what she would do right now? Investigate the new murder, or table it and continue the search for the child? I couldn't believe how matter of fact I was thinking. Maybe because it was our fourth murder in almost as many days. Even Poirot probably got jaded after a while.

I arrived on E Deck and swung my torch about. Just as it had been when Doctor Harper and I had visited earlier to take a look at Mister Woldert's trunk, the place was poorly illuminated and noticeably under-populated. As far as I could tell, I was the only one there. Despite the overall dankness, I was sweating. When a drop of perspiration mixed with shoe polish rolled down from one of my painted-on eyebrows and into my eye, my mind was made up. I'd go back to my stateroom, get cleaned up and change clothes, then return with some back up. This was not a place to be going it alone. If a murderer didn't get me — and whomever it was that had killed Mister Starling and dropped him through a hatch on this deck to F Deck below could very well be watching me right now — there was always the possibility I'd trip over something and break my ruddy neck.

It was with some relief that after climbing interminable stairs and bruising my shins beyond belief that I reached the private crew door opening off of the First-Class bar and let myself through. The bar was dark; it was well past closing time. I quietly slipped through without stumbling over anything and made my way to a nearby crew lift.

Twenty minutes later I emerged from my stateroom in a clean uniform with a clean face, though my hair was still jet black and likely would be for some weeks to come. I could see why my cabin mate liked it – L'Oreal didn't kid around with their hair colouring.

To my surprise, Mister Harvey opened the door to the hospital to let me in.

"Thank God," he said. "We didn't know what had happened to you."

"I had to get that war paint off my face and change clothes. Has the boy been found yet?"

Harvey shook his head. "No. And when Doctor Harper showed up a little while ago and said you were going it alone – well, you can imagine what we were thinking."

"Where is he?" I asked.

"Went to tell the Captain the latest news." Harvey shook his head sorrowfully. "He's a braver man than I am." He cocked his head toward the surgery. "Bratton is in there asleep, and so is your guest. She still has no idea her son has gone missing."

"Maeve, dear." Agatha brushed by Harvey and took my hands. "Thank heaven you're safe."

"Mrs Templeton. Doctor Harper and I were diverted thanks to Chief Duncan's gruesome discovery."

"He told us about it," Agatha said. "Though I haven't seen the body yet."

"It went right into cold storage," said Harvey. "I should start charging freight."

"Mister Harvey, really," I said.

"I know, I know. But if I didn't say something like that every once in a while, I'd go bonkers." He adjusted his cap. "I'm going back to the search now."

"Hold a moment, Mister Harvey, and I'll go back with you," said Agatha. She turned to me. "This last murder was brutal. Pushing a man down an open lift shaft is bad enough, but deliberately crushing a man's arm to a pulp — that takes someone with absolutely no regard for pain or suffering. I can't imagine why he was killed, unless, like Frank Alston, he saw something he shouldn't have." She took my hands in hers. "Whomever we're after has only to stay out in front of us another thirty hours or so before we arrive in New York, and they still hold all the cards. Between the two of us, and it hurts me to say it, young Bradley may no longer be on board this ship. Don't endanger yourself in what may end up being a lost cause."

"But we're so close. I feel it."

"Maeve, this is not a book. It's real life, and our adversary is playing for keeps."

"I know," I said. "But when I think of Bradley — "

Agatha nodded. "I feel the same way. All right." She looked at the Chief Steward. "Mister Harvey, a moment more."

"Take your time."

"Actually, I have a question for you," said Agatha.

"Go ahead." Harvey gave her a careful look.

"What would be the best way to keep from being found by a search party on board?"

Harvey shrugged. "That's easy. Be a member of the crew. You already know all the hiding spots."

Agatha nodded. "And what's the best way to keep someone from being found by a search party?"

Mister Harvey rubbed his jaw. "Be a member of the search party looking for them and divert the search."

"Exactly so." Agatha looked at me. "And which crew member might be up to date on everything that's going on?"

I quickly ticked them off. "Doctor Harper, Doctor Bratton, Mister Harvey, Mister Collins, Miss Kelly, Mister Reedy, Chief Duncan, Mister Jackson, Mister Carter, Mister Woldert, Mister Armstrong, and the Captain."

"All right," said Agatha. "I believe we can safely eliminate both doctors, Mister Harvey, Mister Collins – "

"On behalf of Mister Collins, we both thank you," Harvey said dryly.

I nodded at him and picked up where Agatha had left off. "Miss Kelly, Mister Reedy, Chief Duncan, Mister Carter, Mister Armstrong and the Captain." I massaged my temples. "Which leaves Mister Woldert and Mister Jackson."

"And Evans," said Harvey.

"And do you think Mister Woldert has spoken with Mister Evans about what's going on?" Agatha asked him. Harvey shrugged.

I looked at him. "Where is Mister Evans right now?"

"Asleep, I should imagine. Do you want me to turn him out?"

"I think we should." I turned to Agatha. "He may be in danger of his life every second he stays in that stateroom with Mister Woldert."

"What do you think, Mrs Templeton?" asked Harvey.

"Possibly so."

"I'll go get him, then." Harvey turned for the door.

"Wait," I said. "I'll go get him. I want to continue the search for Bradley. Not that I can't take care of myself, but I'd feel better with some company."

Harvey was skeptical. "Not that I'm judging, but I'd feel better if you were in the company of Mister Armstrong."

"Mister Armstrong is otherwise occupied in the search."

Agatha gave me a studied look. "You wouldn't be about doing something you'll regret later?"

"Probably."

"Be careful. It's been my experience that the grandest twists always come at the end of the book."

"That's what I'm afraid of." I opened the door. "If you don't hear from me in a half hour, tell Doctor Harper I picked the search back up on E Deck."

Bertie blinked at me from beneath his rumpled hair as he answered the door to my gentle knock. "What time is it? What do you want?"

"It's about three in the morning," I whispered. "And I want you."

He blinked again. "I thought you were impervious to my charms."

"I am. Sorry to disappoint. I need you for other reasons. Get dressed. Where is Mister Woldert?"

"He's asleep. Why?"

"Don't wake him. You may be in danger from him. Get dressed and get out here, and don't make a sound."

The door closed. I stood quietly, waiting. In a minute it re-opened and Bertie slipped through, closing it softly behind him.

"What's this all about?"

"Three things. The Alston boy is missing. There's been a search going on for him the past couple of hours, but they haven't found him. Second, there's been another murder."

"What? Who?"

"A crewman. One of the greasers in Chief Duncan's engineering department. He was found wedged up against the side of one of the boilers in Boiler Room Two."

"Blimey." Bertie stared at me. "I'm almost afraid to ask what number three is."

"Mrs Templeton and I believe you may be in danger of being knocked off, as the Americans like to say."

His eyes grew wide. "Me? What did I do?"

"It's not what you do, or did. It's the company you keep. Mister Woldert." I began walking up the corridor away from his stateroom at the aft end of D Deck. "Come on."

"What are you talking about?"

"You know Mrs Templeton and I have been following these murders. We believe that Mister Woldert is probably the man we're after. And he probably has an accomplice – Mister Jackson."

"That's nonsense, Maeve."

"Nonsense or no, it's the conclusion we've reached. Except we've got no evidence. We think Mr Alston was killed because he saw something he shouldn't have seen. And now this crewman got the same treatment."

"Because he saw something? Like what?"

"I don't know. But I'm going to bet it has something to do with our missing child. It looks like the dead man fell through an access hatch from E Deck over one of the boilers on F Deck. I want to get a closer look at that hatch, but I need someone watching my back."

"I'm honored. Do you even have a torch?"

I brandished my lamp.

"And what do you plan to do if we meet someone down there? E Deck isn't exactly the safest place on board."

I gave him a smile. "That's your business."

"You know I don't even have any darts on me," he said.

"Not that you could hit anyone with them, anyway."

"That hurts." Bertie kept up with my rapid pace. "I hope we're at least taking the lift down."

"Taking the stairs from the First-Class Lounge. Less possible traffic."

"Wait." Bertie stopped. "There's no need for us to go up three decks just to take the stairs back down again. There's another access stairwell on this deck."

"And I thought I knew where all the short-cuts were."

Bertie shook his head. "You spend almost all of your time down in the hospital and surgery and quarantine wards. I get sent everywhere – sometimes even down to the holds to retrieve an item for a passenger, if I can."

"No wonder you get such great tips for service. Lead the way." Bertie moved out in front of me and walked at a dizzying pace; I almost had to run to keep up with him. We headed continuously forward to the bow past Second and Third-Class accommodations and various ship's departments, storerooms and workrooms until he finally reached a simple white door labeled "Crew Only – Hazardous Space".

"Only one flight down from here," said Bertie, "but you still have to watch your step."

"Don't worry." I stepped onto the platform behind him and let the door close, then switched off the torch and we stood still, waiting for our eyes to adjust to the gloom. "Has Mister Woldert ever said anything to you that might give you an idea of his political leanings? And I don't mean that he's Labour or Conservative."

"Political leanings?"

"And not Labour or Conservative."

"Oh." Realization dawned on Bertie. "Do you suspect him of being something other than the clean cut British lad?"

"I suspect him of being a Communist. And I suspect First Officer Jackson of the same thing."

Bertie turned to look at me. "Those are pretty serious suspicions."

"Not unfounded. Doctor Harper and I searched Mister Woldert's trunk. We found Communist literature and pictures of him and Mister Jackson together." I didn't feel it necessary to go into the more salacious details.

Bertie gave a low whistle. "Lord love a duck. That's the end of Mister Jackson's career, for certain. And you say they're both under suspicion of murder, too?"

"Yes. That's why you're here now. Like I said, you could unwittingly find out something that could cost you your life. After we get done with the search, have Mister Harvey reassign you to new quarters."

"That serious, is it?"

"Bertie, I've known you for years. It's that serious." I flicked the torch back on and shone it down the stairs. "Come on."

Somehow, knowing there had been a murderer running around loose in the hold not too long before, the steps down and the shadows playing on the walls and overhead pipes and conduits seemed even more eerie and discomforting than when Doctor Harper and I had made our descent earlier. The fact that I'd gotten out of the area by myself an hour before without either breaking my shinbone or being frightened to death was a blessing. It was with a sigh of relief that we reached the bottom of the stairs.

"Where to?" asked Bertie, rubbing his hands together in the chill silence, broken only by the creaking metallic groans of the ship's ribs pushing at and being pushed back by the sea.

"Head aft. The access hatches to the boilers are on the other side of the expansion trunk." I played my light around, picking up the shape of the trunk curving away from us. "Around that corner, I guess, is as good as any." I took two steps forward and crashed flat on the concrete flooring. "Christ, it's leaking oil!" I said in a panic. "The floor's wet with it!"

"Here," said Bertie, tossing me some cloth. "Wipe your hands off with that."

I scrambled to my feet and did as he said. To my horror the rag turned red under the beam of my torch. I shone the torch down. The floor was also dark red. I flipped the cloth in my hands and discovered a row of small pom-poms as buttons. A Pierrot costume. I looked at Bertie. He nodded, a small gun now steady in his hand.

"Sorry about the damage to the Pierrot suit. But in all truthfulness, it was wrecked before you used it on your hands." He gestured back over his shoulder. "The crewman the Chief found – he managed to get in the way as I was closing the watertight door."

"Watertight door?"

"To the chain locker. You know how heavy they are. I'm afraid the impact quite killed him. I was dragging him to a hiding space when that bloody hatch opened of its own accord and he fell through. I damn near fell through with him. It was a close thing, let me tell you. Sorry about all the blood here. I was going to come back and clean it all up later."

A sudden wave of cold fear swept over me. "Why were you closing the door to the chain locker?"

"Why does anyone close a door?" said Bertie. "To keep people out."

"Or to keep them in." I took a step forward but his gun moved with me.

"Just keep your distance, Nurse."

"You tell me right now. Is that little boy in the chain locker?"

"Where else was I going to put him?" Bertie easily sidestepped the remains of the Pierrot costume I threw at him. "I have some morals. At least I didn't lock the boy in with a corpse."

"No, only with tons of anchor chain, you bastard."

"Just roll that torch over here, please," said Bertie. I did as I was told. Bertie stooped to pick it up along with the costume, never taking his gun off me. "Here," he said, tossing the costume back to me and shining the torch down. "Go ahead and get the rest of it up."

I knelt and began to push the costume about the floor. "The search party will find him," I said.

"Oh, didn't I tell you? They've already been through this deck. First Officer Jackson led the way. I don't think they missed anything, since Jackson himself searched this area."

"When did you know?"

"You and that woman passenger started nosing around too much after Wilson went over the side. And then when you and Doctor Harper slipped down to the hold, that really got to me. So I followed you down and saw you open Woldert's trunk." Bertie shook his head. "'Cor, but it's hard to get good help these days."

"So you already knew Mister Woldert?"

"Of course I did. Known him several years."

"He's not a real steward?"

"Of course he's a real steward. How else do you think he got a job on board?"

"Bertie, why?"

"He's on board to do a job – rather, oversee a job."

"Job?"

"The British section of the Communist International is lagging in membership. To increase revolutionary membership it was charged with implementing a decision from a higher body. That decision was to make an example of a capitalist who had gotten rich off of the Great War."

"Harvey Wilson," I said.

"A likely candidate," Bertie agreed. "Especially when it came to light that he made money practically every time the Germans fired a shell due to his patent holdings." His face was grim. "I wonder how many of my mates died to fill his coffers."

"Who is Woldert overseeing?" I asked.

"Haven't you figured it out yet?" said Bertie scornfully. "Mister Jackson. And I was overseeing both of them. I've been a member of the Communist Party of Great Britain since 1919, and this is my first major assignment. I'll be a hero when I get to Moscow." He shone the torch down. "That's good enough. Get up. Carefully."

I rose slowly. "What about this?" I asked, holding the costume.

"Keep it. You might want something to drape over your shoulders." He gestured with the gun toward a large watertight door some ten feet away. "The boy's in there. Get over by the door and stand nice and still while I open it."

The blank muzzle of the handgun stared me in the eye. I did as he asked. Bertie set the torch on the floor and then deftly unlocked and pulled the door open. Like almost every heavy door and hatch in the ship, it was delicately balanced so as to open easily — but being caught in the jamb if it was quickly swung closed could kill, just as it had Starling. Bertie picked up the torch again and shone it inside. In the dim pool of light I could see Bradley, hands and feet tied, a gag in his mouth, sitting on top of what looked to be a battered piece of discarded wood paneling. His eyes were wide with fright, tear stains on his cheeks.

I instinctively stepped through the opening toward Bradley. The piece of paneling shifted under my feet and I put out a hand to balance myself, touching cold steel. I looked at Bertie. "Are you insane?"

"No, I don't believe so. Just doing a job, Nurse. He smiled. "*Bon voyage.*"

"Bertie, no, you can't do this - " I began, but the door swung closed with a deeply metallic clang. I heard the outside locks being turned. Bradley and I were left in the black cold. I carefully went to my hands and knees and felt my way over to him, then slipped the gag out of his mouth.

"Don't worry, Bradley. I'm right here." I slipped the scalpel from my pocket, pushed off the blade guard and began cutting the cords binding his hands and feet as he drew in great draughts of air between his sobs.

To tell you the truth, I felt like crying myself. Once I had him freed I drew him close to me, then carefully reached out with one hand past the edge of the flimsy wood we were sitting upon. My searching fingertips again felt cold, damp steel, and I have to admit I thought my heart stopped.

If you've never had the dubious pleasure of being in close quarters with an ocean liner's anchor chains, let me tell you to avoid it if at all possible.

Each link of the chain is about two feet long and weighs around 225 pounds. There is about 900 feet of chain weighing over fifty tons; one end is attached to the ship with what's called – really – the bitter end (so now you know where that term comes from) and the other to an anchor that would do justice to a dreadnought and weighs sixteen tons, give or take an ounce. Double all of this, because there are two anchors. We keep a third anchor out on the open forecastle deck as a spare, but I've never known it to be used.

The anchor chain runs through what's called a hawse pipe as it makes its transit from its home in the chain locker – which was really nothing more than a very tall steel box extending from where we were sitting on top of it on E Deck, down through F and G Deck and finally terminating in the bitter end at the Tank Top at the very bottom of the *Victoria* — up through the ship, across the anchor windlasses, around the capstans, and down into the sea. The noise it makes when doing this is absolutely deafening. Roll a paper tube, drop marbles into it, hold the ends closed and shake it violently, then multiply that by about a million, and you get the idea.

I might add that it's also cold, damp, and the stench is quite nauseating. Makes the bilge pumps of the ship look like the gardens at Notting Hill by comparison. And we were sitting at the very top of this heap of chain that was piled up from three decks below us in what basically amounted to a watertight steel mine shaft, with several links rising from the pile and disappearing into the hawse pipe above our heads.

So much for the technical aspects.

What really bothered me was the physics of what would happen to Bradley and me if anyone decided to drop anchor.

In the house I grew up in there were all sorts of cubbyholes and nooks that were perfect for a child to hide inside of and read. I particularly remember a small passage that went from a cupboard in one room to the cupboard in the next, a cupboard being a closet to you Yanks. I thought it great fun to stretch out in it with my legs in one room and my upper body in the other, and still feel all safe and cosy   not at all like the feeling I was getting now sitting in the chain locker.

I don't know how long we sat there in the dark, listening to the ocean on the other side of the hull. The damp and cold and smell were unbearable, and every time one of us shifted the flimsy board beneath us moved as well, sending me into paroxysms of terror that we were dropping anchor. I kept telling myself over and over that the *Victoria* wouldn't let her anchors go at speed, anchors were designed for anchoring, not stopping, and such a manoeuvre could seriously damage the ship, not to mention us. However, the *Victoria* must eventually stop, and I tried to avoid thinking of what would happen to us when she did.

Bradley had ceased his crying and wailing and was holding fast to me, his head resting on my shoulder as I sat with one leg out behind me and tried to keep us balanced. "Why are we here?" he asked me.

"I don't know, love." Of course I knew, but I wasn't going to tell him. I hugged him. "Don't you worry. We'll get out of here."

"When?"

Well, I had to admit that he had me with that question. Unless someone had seen Bertie and I go through that door one deck up, no one was going to be coming around any time soon; and since Mister Jackson had successfully steered the search party looking for Bradley away from this area, there was little reason to hope a second search party would locate us. Of course, the Captain was the very model of British bulldog tenaciousness.

"Soon," I said to him, stroking his hair. "Someone will be here soon." At any rate, I thought, this was giving me time to puzzle things out. Bertie was overseeing Woldert, and Woldert was overseeing Mister Jackson, who had been assigned by the Communist Party of Great Britain to kill Wilson.

But then there was Frank Alston, and Thomas Morten. My mind raced for an answer, but nothing was forthcoming.

And Bertie. How could I have been so wrong about Bertie? How could one of my trusted shipmates do what he did? Judging by my predicament, Bertie certainly intended that Bradley and I not survive the voyage. Bradley because he was a witness, me because I knew the truth. But that meant Harper, Harvey and Mrs Templeton were also in danger.

Bloody hell. How long had I been in here? I glanced at my wrist, swore softly and made a mental note that the next watch I bought would have a luminous dial. Bradley stirred again.

"I'm thirsty."

"Sorry, love. I don't have anything for you to drink. We'll be out soon."

"Sure." The utter finality in the boy's voice unsettled me. Despite my uneasiness, I felt my head begin to nod.

A sharp bang awakened me with a jerk. I pulled Bradley as tight to me as possible. Were we dropping anchor? I squeezed my eyes shut and put a hand over Bradley's eyes. It will be fast, I told myself. And hopefully not too painful.

"Maeve!" Mister Harvey's booming voice rang out. "Maeve, are you in there?" Again the bang, and this time I knew it was coming from the other side of the door.

"We're here Mister Harvey!" I yelled as loudly as I could. The locking lever turned with a heavy thud and the bolts withdrew. With a heave he pulled the door open.

"Thank God," he said, extending a hand and pulling me to my feet. I gingerly turned and reached out to Bradley.

"Come on, Bradley. It's safe."

"Give him to me, Maeve." Agatha had suddenly materialized next to Harvey; how or why I neither knew nor cared. I helped the boy out and she held him against her. I looked at Harvey. He shrugged.

"Couldn't keep her away," he said, closing the door and swinging the locking lever closed.

"But passengers aren't allowed down here, Mrs Templeton!"

Harvey shook his head. "You'd better be glad she decided to make an exception or we'd never have found you." He shone his torch, picking up the stain on the deck and fragments of the ruined Pierrot suit. "What in the hell is all of this?" he asked. I glanced over at Bradley, sheltering in Agatha's arms.

"Move your light away from it. Now. I'll explain later," I said with a nod to the boy.

"Some of Mister Evans' hijinks?" said Harvey.

"You could say so," I replied as we slowly began to pick our way out of the hold.

"I still thought you might be doing something you shouldn't," said Agatha. "I left the hospital and followed you at a discreet distance and saw you get Mister Evans out," said Agatha. "And when you both went through that door I gave it a few minutes, then slipped through myself."

"Jesus, Joseph, and Mary," I said. "And you came after us?"

"I not only came after you, I heard and saw everything from my vantage point on the stairs. When he locked you in that place, I went for Mister Harvey."

"You know that Mister Harvey is claustrophobic? Hates dark spaces like this?"

"I'm trying not to think of it," Harvey said. "So sod off."

"Mister Harvey. There are children present," said Agatha.

"Are you limping, Mister Harvey?" I asked.

"I've a torn trouser leg and a bloody great cut on my shin, if that's what you're asking."

"Are we going to go see my mother?" asked Bradley.

"Yes, dear." Agatha kept a steady grip on the boy as we climbed.

A thought occurred to me. "Are you sure Bertie went back topside?" I said. "How do we know he's not waiting for us around the next corner? He's got a gun, you know."

"We don't," said Harvey grimly. "But the way I feel right now he'd best make his first shot count, because I'm going to tear him in half before he gets a second one."

A harshly metallic rattling noise suddenly burst in on us. Mister Harvey brought us to a stop. Agatha winced.

"What is that racket?" she yelled in a vain attempt to be heard over the noise.

"Bloody hell," said Harvey. "We've got an anchor dropping!"

My mind pictured the hell that was happening in the chain locker, as tons of anchor chain lifted up and remorselessly banged through the hawse pipes toward the anchor windlasses on the Main Deck. I felt my knees grow weak at the thought of just how close Bradley and I had come to being smeared on the walls of the chain locker. Agatha put out a steadying hand and caught me. Just as suddenly the God-awful din and racket ceased, and the *Victoria* took a slight lurch to her port side as the anchor chain stopped moving. A moment later we could hear a rhythmic thudding as the links were slowly wound back up and dropped into the locker by one of the 292 horsepower electric anchor windlasses. Harvey listened carefully.

"Clever. They dropped just enough chain to allow the anchor to clear the ship and submerge beneath the keel. That way it stopped any side to side movement before the windlass was reversed so it won't bang into the side of the ship."

"That was almost the end of us." I looked at Harvey and Agatha. "If you hadn't followed me – and if you both hadn't come after us – "

Bradley took his hands away from his ears. "What was that noise?" he asked.

I knelt beside him and gave him a hug. "Nothing, dear. Absolutely nothing."

Harvey painfully mounted the stairs. "I think we'll get off on D Deck and go right to the hospital." He consulted his watch. "It's nearly four in the morning. Shouldn't be anyone up and about."

On that cheerful note we trudged upwards in silence until we reached the D Deck entry door. Mister Harvey cracked it and peered through.

"No one there," he said.

Agatha held Bradley against her skirt. "Shall we go?"

"What if we see Bertie?" I asked.

"All the better," said Harvey. "I've changed my mind. I won't tear him in half. I'll tear him into quarters."

"Bit obvious in the corridor, don't you think, Mister Harvey?" said Mrs Templeton.

"I'll make it look like an accident." Mister Harvey, bloodied but unbowed, walked in front while I brought up the rear, sandwiching Mrs Templeton and Bradley between us.

It was with a measured sigh of relief that we reached the safe confines of the surgery. I locked the door behind us as Harper and Bratton took in the sight of our travelling circus.

"Good Lord," said Harper. "Where have you come from?"

"'From going to and fro in the earth, and from walking up and down in it,'" I quoted. Agatha gave me an approving nod.

"The book of Job. Well said."

"I don't understand," said Bratton.

"Bertie locked Bradley and myself in the chain locker. I don't want to think what would have happened to us had not Mrs Templeton and Mister Harvey come along. And speaking of Mister Harvey – " I pointed at his injured leg. Now that I could take a closer look at in good lighting, I could see it was going to require multiple stitches to mend.

"Ouch," said Bratton. "You really came a cropper. Let's go tend it." Harvey grunted and hobbled after Bratton. Harper looked at Agatha and myself.

"You two sit down right now and tell me what happened. Bradley, go see your mother. Doctor Bratton, when you're done with Mister Harvey, would you mind calling Miss Kelly to come down here?"

"Tell her not to tell anyone we found the boy," Agatha cautioned. "Don't tell her Maeve is down here, either."

Harper sat spell-bound while Agatha and I related what had happened. When we'd finished he shook his head. "Bertie Evans killed Mister Starling in cold blood. And he's a Communist, too. He always seemed so pleasant."

"How do you think I feel?" I asked him. "I've known him for years."

"Evans was watching Woldert, and Woldert was watching Mister Jackson," said Harper. "True proletariat committee level assignments, I think."

"Where is Mister Starling?" I asked.

"Where do you think?" came back Harvey's irritated voice from the exam room. "Harvey's economy mortuary, open all hours. You are not going to stick me with that needle, Bratton. Not in the – ow!" His voice mercifully disappeared as Bratton shut the door.

The telephone rang. Doctor Harper picked it up and listened. "Thank you," he said, and replaced the receiver. "The search party has returned. No sign of the little boy."

"Of course not," said Agatha. "And only Bertie and Mister Jackson know where he is."

"And only Bertie knows I'm in there with him. And as far as he knows, that anchor drop made mincemeat of both of us."

"Anchor drop?" said Harper. I nodded.

"Didn't you feel it? One anchor was let go, and then hauled back up not a half hour ago."

Realization dawned on Harper. "We did feel a slight pull to port, but it only lasted a moment."

"Whoever let it go knew we were still in the chain locker," I said to him. Harper paled.

"Good God."

"Let us use this to our advantage. We have two people alive that our adversary believes are quite dead," said Agatha. She gave us a gentle smile. "I think you should ask the Captain to come down. Alone."

Friday, November 1, 1929

One thing I've always been interested in is what is the limit people can reach before they break? My father referred to it as the 'thin line' over which one had dare not cross lest you invite dire consequences. Sometimes, though, it seemed that the 'thin line' was thrust upon us, with ourselves having little, if any, say in the matter. Captain Webster's current mood was indicative of the latter.

"I'm beginning to regret the day you came aboard this ship, Doctor," he growled as he entered the hospital. "I won't even ask if you've any ideas yet about who killed one of the Chief's crew." He sat down heavily. "I wondered when we'd finally get around to having our own people added to the casualty count. And that damnable boy is still missing. Mister Jackson reported the search party came back empty-handed."

"We have a bit of good news on that front, sir," said Harper. "The boy has been found and is presently in with his mother."

The Captain sat straight up. "What? When?"

"Nurse Chandler located him." The Captain turned to stare at me.

"Good Lord, Nurse, you look like you've been through the wars."

I nodded, glancing down at the blood stains on my uniform. "In a manner of speaking, sir, yes."

"Where did you find the boy that our search party didn't? Mister Jackson said they combed the ship."

"Mister Jackson lied," said Agatha. The Captain spun about.

"Mrs Templeton, he is my First Officer. You are a passenger. Be mindful of what you are saying."

"He lied," repeated Agatha again.

"She's right, sir," I said. I indicated the blood stains on my uniform. "This is from Mister Starling. Bertie Evans showed me where he killed him."

The Captain's eyes appeared to be ready to pop out of his head.

"Yes, sir," I repeated. "Bertie Evans killed Mister Starling. And he tried to kill me. And the young boy."

Somewhere deep in his mind, I was certain the Captain was recalling with fondness the carefree days of his youth as a crewman aboard wooden sailing ships. No murders, no nosy passengers, no ship's nurses with blood-stained uniforms. Just acres of white sail filled with wind and the deep blue sea below. His lips had compressed into a thin line.

"Go on," he said quietly, crossing one leg over the other.

"After Doctor Harper and I met with Chief Duncan, I decided to go back up to E Deck and have a look at the hatches above the boilers."

"Why?"

"Chief Duncan surmised, and we agreed, that Starling's body could only have been dumped through one of the hatches from above," said Harper. "The Chief had been doing work on Boiler Two and had that area cordoned off. Starling had lost a lot of blood, but not much of it was around the boiler where we found him. There wasn't any blood indicating a struggle at the boiler, either; he had to have been killed elsewhere."

"Why didn't you tell me this earlier, Doctor?" The Captain was giving him a level gaze.

"Because Mister Jackson was standing right next to you, and I didn't care to divulge any more information than I needed to hand out."

The Captain chewed his lip for a moment. "Mister Jackson again. I suppose you have an explanation for this, too."

"Yes, sir. May I finish with Mister Evans first?"

"Carry on, Nurse." The Captain settled back in his chair.

"Both Mrs Templeton and myself felt that Mister Starling had been killed because he'd seen too much – like Mr Alston. And we were already suspicious of Mister Woldert, what with his Communist propaganda. Bertie rooms with Woldert. We felt it prudent to get him out of there as quickly as possible. I also wanted some back up with me when I took a look at the boiler access hatches on E Deck. I turned Bertie out and we went together."

The Captain looked first at Mrs Templeton, then Doctor Harper. "I had thought you were hired to run a hospital, Doctor. No one told me you'd be overseeing Scotland Yard."

"No one told me, either, sir."

"Apparently." The Captain waved me on.

"The rest was a blur. Bertie admitted to kidnapping the boy and bringing him down to E Deck. I don't know why Mister Starling was there, but he saw Bertie putting the boy into the chain locker and intervened. Bertie crushed his left arm in the door. The man's blood was everywhere." I gestured at my uniform. "Including here."

"Keep going," said the Captain.

"Bertie had a gun and forced me into the chain locker, too. He closed and locked the door. The next thing I knew I was being rescued by Mister Harvey and Mrs Templeton, and not a moment too soon. Someone loosed off one of the anchors. Had we still been inside the chain locker – "

"Mister Jackson," said the Captain in a cold, steely voice. "Mister Jackson said he accidentally hit the port anchor capstan winch override."

"Accidentally, my Aunt Fanny," I said. "Bertie somehow gave him the instructions that we were inside and it was time to eliminate the witnesses."

"Every word is true, Captain," said Mrs Templeton. "I followed Maeve and Mister Evans and saw and heard it all happen. That's when I went back for Mister Harvey."

"And where is Mister Harvey?" asked the Captain.

"Doctor Bratton is tending to him," said Harper. "He bashed his shin when he accompanied Mrs Templeton on their rescue mission."

"Incredible," said the Captain. "And the reason for all of this?"

I looked at Agatha, took a deep breath and plunged into the deep end. "Bertie has been a Communist party member for years, sir. He said this was his first big assignment. He is looking after Mister Woldert, who in turn is overseeing Mister Jackson."

The Captain's eyes widened. "Mister Jackson? My Mister Jackson?"

"Yes, sir. The three of them had been sent a mission to kill Harvey Wilson as an example to those men who became obscenely rich profiteering off the war. They succeeded."

The Captain's eyes now popped so wide I thought I would need a tennis racquet to bat them back in. He stood up forcefully. "A Communist is serving as First Officer on my ship? And he's a murderer as well?" It was always easy to say what order things ranked in with the Captain. Mister Jackson might well serve on as a murderer, but being a Communist meant the end of the line as far as the Captain was concerned. He slammed a fist into the palm of his hand. "By Jove, he'll rue the day he was born when I'm done with him!"

"Captain," said Agatha quietly.

"What, Mrs Templeton?"

"Would you like to have all three at one grab?"

"Of course I would." He turned to Harper. "Why haven't you called Mister Armstrong to pick them all up and clap them in irons?" asked the Captain.

"We had to be sure, sir," I said. "Or at least as reasonably sure as we could be, so no one could wriggle out with a smart barrister," I said. "By trying to kill the boy and myself, and admitting to killing Mister Starling, Bertie provided that certainty."

"Here's our line of thinking, Captain," said Agatha. "First, the murder of Mr Morten was an accident. The poisoned drink was meant for Mr Wilson. The two people involved in the drink itself were Mister Evans, behind the bar, and Mister Woldert, who served the drink – but to the wrong table."

"And when Mr Wilson was killed, probably by Mister Jackson, there were actually two witnesses to his murder," I said. "Bradley, and his stepfather, Mr Alston. "

Agatha nodded. "Both were in different places and didn't see each other. Bradley only saw a tall man in an overcoat from his vantage point. No features."

"But Mr Alston saw the face of the killer, and then made the mistake of trying to blackmail him for his silence," I added.

"The reason we know that is because Mr Alston told his wife that he was going to be rich when he got to New York," I said. "I wasn't sure what he meant at the time, perhaps he was going to fleece some passenger in a card game, but when he was killed the answer became apparent."

Agatha nodded. "I'm certain it was Mister Woldert who disposed of Mr Alston in the lift shaft, losing a button off his jacket in the process. He's more than likely also the one who tried to poison my drinking water."

"And when Mister Woldert killed Mister Alston, he wasn't just getting rid of an eyewitness," I said. "He was also protecting someone."

"Who?" asked the Captain.

"He was protecting Mister Jackson," said Agatha. "They are apparently much more than friends." I'd never seen anyone hit over the head with a poleax before, but the Captain's face certainly mirrored all the symptoms.

"Mister Jackson. And Mister Woldert." The Captain shook his head.

"Nurse Chandler and I found pictures of the two of them together, as if on holiday," said Harper. "And also pictures of the two of them together, if you know what I mean. Those were also in Woldert's trunk. We didn't want to bring it up when we were on the bridge telling you about Woldert's Communist material. Again, Mister Jackson was right there."

"Then the boy disappeared," I said. "Mrs Templeton surmised that a crew member with ship's knowledge could keep one step ahead of the searchers and hide Bradley away – Mister Harvey confirmed that hypothesis and that's exactly what happened."

"In all my days at sea – Agatha Christie couldn't write one like this," said the Captain. I bit my lip. The Captain glanced over at Mister Harvey who had quietly joined us. "Mister Harvey. It seems Nurse Chandler is indebted to you."

"Mrs Templeton did the work. I just rode to the rescue like the U.S. Cavalry."

"Yes, so I'm told. In future, Mister Harvey, please refrain from the Tom Mix films in the cinema." The Captain turned to me. "Nurse Chandler, why didn't you come directly to the bridge after you were freed?"

"Mrs Templeton thought it might be best if Bertie still believed myself and the boy to be dead, after the anchor chain was dropped," I said.

"It will make it easier to catch the three of them unaware," agreed Agatha. "And I have a plan for making it happen."

The Captain glanced at his watch. "We'll be in New York in ten hours. I suppose while I'm down here I should go pay my respects to our new mother and her babe in arms," he said. "If they don't mind such a God-awful early visit." He looked at me. "Do try not to let anything else happen until I get back, will you?"

"Yes, sir," I said. But I really couldn't promise.

IV

Have you ever played chess? My mother taught me the game as a child. At first, I was rather precocious. Well, maybe that's not the right word for it. I would tip the board and pieces would fly all over when I didn't win or was trapped into some stupid move. Of course, the more I played, the better I became. While I'll never be a Grandmaster like Mir Sultan Kahn – if you remember, he won the British chess championship back in August of this year – and although I can hit someone in the nose with a pawn from fifteen paces, at least I don't tip the board anymore when I don't get my way.

Up until now.

Had it not been for a powerful queen – Agatha – and a valiant knight – Mister Harvey – Bertie would have checkmated me for good. It was more than time to return the favour.

I spent the remainder of the day sleeping in the hospital, and night was falling as Doctor Harper, Agatha, Mister Harvey, Mister Armstrong and myself made our preparations. Mister Armstrong was understandably annoyed at how our investigations had proceeded without him, and took particular umbrage at how I let myself get shanghaied into the chain locker – but as the Captain had said, he was much better suited to putting a stop to the occasional shipboard card sharp than he was a quadruple murder investigation.

"It pains me, Nurse, that you almost got yourself killed, along with the wee boy," he rumbled. "And who would the Captain have blamed for that? Me." He looked at Agatha. "And getting a passenger involved?"

I gave him my most charming and hopefully disarming smile. "You're in no way at fault, Mister Armstrong. These are just very unusual circumstances."

"You can bloody well say that again," Mister Harvey chimed in. Clad in a fresh uniform he was now walking with the aid of a cane; whether he needed it or not I didn't want to ask. Men can be so touchy when they're hurt, poor things.

"We must get all three of them at once," said Agatha. "Remember that Mister Evans has a gun, and we certainly don't want him taking a hostage or worse."

"Are you sure we can do it?" asked Harper. "I think we probably need more men."

"The more who are directly involved, the greater the risk for loss of surprise," I said. "Plus we've got passenger safety to think of. Once we secure all three of them at the stern, I'll blow the whistle – " I indicated the whistle hanging around my neck " – and that brings the able seamen that Mister Armstrong has provided out of hiding. Of course, I can't be seen until they are all gathered together. As far as we know, Bertie still thinks I'm decorating the chain locker."

"And how do you plan to get them all together at the same time?" asked Armstrong.

"Simplicity itself," said Agatha. "Doctor Harper goes to the bridge and tells Mister Jackson – quietly – that a steward named Woldert is at the stern and leaning too far over the railing for his liking. He tried to approach him but the man waved him off. At the same time, Mister Harvey tells Mister Evans the same thing. I'll do the same for Mister Woldert, telling him there's a bridge officer named Jackson in a bad way at the stern, asking for him."

"Mister Armstrong and myself will be in the film storage room, just back of the stern," I said. "One of you knock three times on the door when they are all gathered up."

"How will you get Nurse Chandler all the way up to A Deck without her being seen?" asked Mister Harvey.

"I've borrowed a steamer trunk," said Armstrong. "She'll fit. And then I'll put it on a dolly and wheel it up."

I was aghast. I hadn't considered this part of the plan. Mister Armstrong gave me a charming smile. "No worries, Nurse. Can't be as bad as the chain locker, now can it?"

I swallowed. "No. Of course not. Just don't drop me over the side. I haven't made a close study of the late Harry Houdini."

The very stern – or rear, as you prefer – of the *Victoria* is on A Deck. For most passengers, it is what they would actually consider the main deck, since it's where the number one hatch to the holds is located, where the anchor capstans are found at the bow and where the spare anchor sits out in the open. The actual Main Deck, however, is one above A Deck. It's where the number two hatch to the holds is located, and also the steam cranes for depositing cargo into both forward holds. From A Deck to the Main Deck to the Promenade Deck and then to the Boat Deck and finally the Sports Deck where the bridge is located, the ship is tiered like a terrace or wedding cake from either end.

At the stern end of A Deck is a curved railing over which one can look directly down into the sea. If you stand in the middle of that curved railing, you are standing directly over the rudder itself, which is recessed out of your sight lines. The propellers churn the water beneath your gaze, and the Union Jack flies off the pole affixed to the stern. More importantly for us, almost directly to the stern on A Deck is the cinema film storage area, a perfect hiding place with quick access to the open deck through one door. Films taken on board the *Victoria* for projection are not stored near the ship's cinema, which is located on the Sun Deck. As you no doubt know, film is made of nitrate, which is extremely flammable. For the sake of safety, nothing other than the day's programme is left in the cinema projection room, which is a strict non-smoking area. The film storage area on A Deck was fireproof. It was also a tight fit with Mister Armstrong, myself, a steamer trunk and a dolly wedged inside. On the plus side, it wasn't cold and dank like the chain locker, there was an electric light, and the worst that could happen would be a flash fire that would instantly cremate us both.

Mister Armstrong consulted his watch. "I hope someone knocks soon," he said, casting a nervous look at the film cans in racks along the wall.

"What are you worried about, Mister Armstrong? These are First-Class accommodations as far as I'm concerned. You ought to see steerage in the chain locker."

"No, thank you, Nurse."

"All right, but remember, I offered." I bit at my lip. "What about your men?"

"I'm sure none of them would like the chain locker, either."

I punched him in the arm. "No, the ones who are supposed to keep me from getting killed out there."

"Oh, those men." Armstrong smiled. "Distributed discreetly about the area. The Captain is above on the docking bridge."

"He should certainly have a good view from there," I said. The docking bridge is a platform rising off of the Main Deck. The open-air station holds auxiliary controls that communicate to the forward main bridge. It was only used by officers when we were docking or being assisted by tugs. I shivered.

"Are you cold, Nurse?"

"Just nervous." I fingered the whistle about my neck. What if no one came? We'd have to hunt them down separately, and there was still the slight chance they could evade us and slip over the rails once we reached New York.

"Coming up on 23:00, Nurse. The passenger traffic should certainly have died down by now, with us due to arrive in the morning." Armstrong put his hand to the steel door. "And it's getting much colder."

Three sharp raps made me jump out of my skin. Mister Armstrong cracked the door open and peered through. Harper was standing outside.

"They're here," he whispered. "All three of them gathered around the stern rail near the flagpole."

"Where is Mister Harvey?"

"Back behind me, in the shadows. He has Mrs Templeton with him. Couldn't talk her out of coming. She said she wouldn't miss this for the world." Harper stopped speaking and pressed up against the door for a moment, then spoke urgently. "They're giving things a pretty good chin wag. It's now or never, Maeve. We'll stay out of sight until you give the signal."

Mister Armstrong clapped a paw on my shoulder. "Good luck, lass. We won't let anything happen to you."

Doctor Harper slid back out of the way. I swallowed hard, then squeezed past him out onto the open deck. He gave me a silent thumbs up, then melted back into the shadows.

I walked carefully and quietly around the corner from the storage room. A telephone box and the warping winch – used for docking procedures – gave partial cover as I moved forward like a stealthy Indian in one of the American western dramas that Mister Harvey was fond of watching. I was close enough now to hear them speaking in hushed tones about eight yards away from me, and thankful that Mister Armstrong had suggested a black smock to cover my nursing whites.

"Well, that's what she said." It was Woldert speaking. "She said you were here, and in a bad way. What the bloody hell was I supposed to do but come up?"

"Christ," said Bertie. "Old Iron-Bottom told me the same thing." Iron-Bottom? Mister Harvey would surely take offense at that, I thought.

"Doctor Harper was the same." It sounded like Jackson was absolutely biting off his words. "I told you he and Nurse Chandler were going to be trouble after you botched Wilson up."

"Me botched Wilson up?" Bertie sounded indignant. "I was trying to help Woldert, who apparently can't tell a bleeding six from a nine. You put the aconitine in the drink just fine, but then you go and get yourself seen by that bloody kid when you're pushing Wilson over the side."

"He never saw my face."

"But his old man did. So what do you do?" he said, turning to Woldert. "You push him down a lift shaft instead of overboard like I told you to. I swear, the Communist Party of Great Britain doesn't need either of you. I'd have been better handling it all myself. I have no idea of what I'm going to tell the Communist International now."

I slipped off the black smock and stepped forward out of the darkness and into the pools of light. "Why don't you just tell them the truth? You're incompetent."

All three men froze at the sight of me. I must have looked like a ghost.

"Surprised, Bertie, my old friend?" I asked. "I know I'm supposed to be dead but I just couldn't wait to see you again."

"You are dead," he choked out. "Mister Jackson dropped the anchor. You and the boy both. You're dead."

"Really?" I took a step forward. "I don't feel dead. But if you insist – " I blew my whistle. A floodlight flashed on from the docking bridge, brightly illuminating the scene. Jackson and Woldert began to make a break to the right, but were caught up short by several burly crewmen. Bertie's hand flew to his pocket but I heard an ominous click to my left and behind me.

"Nurse, take a step to your right, please." I moved and risked a look. He was standing stock still, a mammoth pistol, even for his large hands, was rock steady in them. "Mister Evans," he said. "This is a Colt .45 Model 1911. I took it from a Yank friend who was killed at Belleau Wood. The bullet weighs 15 grams and leaves the barrel at 830 feet per second. It'll punch you right over the railings behind you and at this range I can't possibly miss."

Bertie slowly withdrew his empty hand from his pocket. Two able seamen stepped forward and disarmed him, but Armstrong kept his handgun at the ready.

"I think you can let the hammer down, Mister Armstrong," said the Captain as he stepped off the stairs coming down from the Main Deck. There was a softer click as Mister Armstrong complied, but the weapon stayed out. I was suddenly aware of Agatha standing by my side.

"Well done, Maeve. Well done."

"I was terrified."

"We all were." She squeezed my hand.

Doctor Harper and Mister Harvey were now standing with Mister Armstrong. The Captain looked at them.

"Gentlemen. Mister Armstrong, will you please place these three men under arrest and confine them in the Specie Room until we reach New York?"

"With pleasure, Captain."

The Captain nodded and turned to the prisoners. "It will be crowded for you in the Specie Room, but I've no doubt you'll have plenty to talk about. Since your crimes were allegedly committed aboard a British vessel sailing in international waters, I suppose the jurisdiction is Great Britain. Of course, two American nationals were among those killed; I'll need to get instruction from the British consulate in New York on maritime law in such an instance. In any case, I'm fairly certain I'm going to have to haul all three of you back to Southampton on our return voyage in two days." He paused for a moment. "Let me make this very clear. As I said a moment ago, I'm handing you into the charge of Mister Armstrong. He is under direct orders to brook no interference, and to mete out whatever punishment he deems appropriate. I would advise you not to antagonize him. That's all."

"No sir, that's not all," said Mister Jackson.

"Yes?" The Captain's absence of using 'Mister' or 'sir' was noted by all.

Jackson tugged himself free from his guards; the Captain put up a hand to signify that it was all right. "Sir, I've served the Stoddard Lines for years, and they've been good to me. But I've also seen a lot of inequity in the way people are treated. I have to say I was happy that the New York stock market had its accident earlier this week. Too many people making too much money off the backs of those who can least afford it."

"I know all about your Communist leanings. Yours too, Woldert."

Woldert sniffed. "Don't forget him," he said, cocking his head toward Bertie. "He's the brains behind it."

Bertie appeared to be thinking of saying something, then thought better of it. Jackson continued.

"For years, no one knew that Harvey Wilson made money off of dead British, French and American soldiers. Germany kept the records, and so did he. You saw it all come out in the papers recently. He got paid for their use of a patent he owned. And then his wretched piety of erecting monuments to the brave war dead. He should have been spending it on all the widows and orphans. God knows the unit I was in left enough of them behind in the mud in France. Believe me, it was a pleasure to perform my duty to my fallen comrades by ending Wilson's gilded life that he'd built on the dead bodies of working men."

"It wasn't your call to act as judge, jury and executioner, Mister Jackson," I said.

"Who else was going to avenge them, Nurse?" Jackson pointed a finger. "You? Captain Webster? Mister Harvey?" Harvey took a step forward but was restrained by Harper. "No, I didn't think so."

"Get on with it," said the Captain brusquely.

Jackson's face was contorted with anger. "I fought in the War like all of these men here, Captain, including you. But do you know that I can't enjoy peacetime? My country won't let me. My country casts a very disapproving eye on me and those like me – the men who fought its war. My country has laws against us enjoying the peace we all bled and died for." He reached across and took Mister Woldert's hand. An audible gasp went up from the assembly. "My country won't let us live in peace, Captain. Maybe the Communists would. I don't know. But what I do know is that they offer a better world than King and Country do. And we, Mister Woldert and I, we tried to do our part to make it a better world for people like us. But now there's no future left at all. Prison or worse for us both. I've lost my career and once this is out my family will never hold their heads up again." He edged closer to Mister Woldert, still tightly gripping his hand.

"That's the choice you made," said the Captain.

"Choice? I heard the way that miserable excuse for a man beat his wife on our ship. What choice did she have in it? Believe me, I was glad Michael broke his arm when he tried to blackmail us. I wish I'd been there when Michael sent him down the lift shaft." He glanced over at Woldert. I caught an almost imperceptible nod between them. "There's nothing here, Captain. But maybe there's something somewhere else, where your rules of society can't follow us." He gave a steady look to Woldert, who had now shrugged off his guard's grip as well. "I love you," he said.

"I love you, too," answered Woldert.

"No!" I screamed, but they were already leaning backwards over the rail behind them, and then they were gone. It happened so quickly there was no time to react. Agatha and I rushed to the rail, even Mister Evans turned around and put his hands on the railing to look, but all that was there was darkness and the steady churn of the ocean by the *Victoria's* propellers. Quartermaster Carter's voice rang out from the docking bridge up above us.

"Shall I order an emergency turn, Captain?"

The Captain looked away, his face tinged with sadness. "No, Mister Carter. There's nothing to go back for."

At seven the next morning I carried a breakfast tray to the isolation ward. With just one prisoner now to look after, the Captain had decreed that Mister Evans be locked up there instead of the Specie Room, for which Mister Collins was grateful. When I arrived Mister Armstrong was sitting in a chair outside the door. He looked up at me.

"Breakfast? Really, Nurse, you shouldn't have."

"This is for Mister Evans. You know I couldn't find a tray large enough to hold your breakfast on." Mister Armstrong smiled at me and stood up.

"Been quiet as a mouse in there all night," he said. "Maybe he's thinking on his crimes."

"Maybe." I waited while he unlocked the door and went in ahead of me; I followed at a respectful distance. Suddenly he stopped short.

"No farther, Nurse."

"Why? What is it?" I tried to peer around his bulk, and, failing that, looked up instead. The tray fell from my hands with a resounding clatter of metal and broken crockery.

A knotted sheet under tension was hanging from one of the overhead steel conduits. I pushed my way around Mister Armstrong.

Bertie Evans was hanging, quite dead, from the other end of the sheet, a chair kicked over on the floor beneath him. We stared at the body.

"I never heard a thing," said Mister Armstrong. I looked down at the chair. A blanket and another sheet were spread around it.

"He muffled the fall of the chair. With the vibration and usual noise of the ship, and the steering gear trunk just outside, of course you wouldn't have heard it."

"Poor sod," said Armstrong. "You know, I don't think I could have shot him last night. He was always so cheerful. Who could have known?" He sighed. "I'll cut him down and lay him on the bed. You'd best go tell Doctor Harper and the Captain."

Twenty minutes later Doctor Harper and I were on the bridge. The Captain gave us a careful once over.

"We'll be in Manhattan in four hours. It's too early for you to be bothering me." He gave Harper a cynical look. "I'm truly getting to the point I hate it when you and Nurse Chandler call. You two have always got a corpse somewhere, it seems."

Harper spoke quietly. "Mister Evans is dead. Hanged himself in the quarantine ward. Nurse Chandler was bringing his breakfast and she and Mister Armstrong found him knotted up with the bed sheet."

The Captain turned and stared out through the glass, finally momentarily at a loss for words. "I'll be damned," he said at last.

The crowds around the *Queen Victoria* when she docked at the Manhattan Piers at eleven were as large as those around her when she had left Southampton. Doctor Harper, Mister Harvey, Agatha and myself were at the rail of the Sports Deck as the *Victoria* steamed majestically past the Statue of Liberty, and were still standing there after the ship docked, watching the passengers stream down the gangways for the customs sheds.

"I'm going to see Mister Jackson and Mister Woldert toppling over the rail into the propellers for the rest of my life," I said glumly.

Agatha nodded. "It's the stuff of nightmares."

"They had no choice," said Mister Harvey. "As Mister Jackson pointed out, what was left for them in our world?"

"I guess Mister Evans felt the same," said Harper.

Agatha shook her head. "Mister Evans at best was looking at a very long stretch at Wandsworth Prison. At worst, he was still facing a hanging for sedition and murder."

"I suppose," I said, looking down at the throngs beneath us. "I bet all of those people will miss the *Victoria's* bars," I said, eager to change the subject.

"Not half as much as Collins will miss their money," said Harvey. "But you know, Collins does actually have a softer side."

"How so?" I asked.

"He's putting Mrs Alston, Bradley and little Victoria into First-Class for the return home. He says he worked out a way to hide the cost." Harvey's face broke into a wide grin. "He's charging it off to Mister Casey's press account."

"Bravo," said Harper.

"Really, Mister Harvey?" asked Agatha. "That's very good of you."

Harvey shrugged. "After everything that poor woman's been through, I think it's proper."

"After everything the boy went through, you mean." I looked at Harper. "But he's young. He'll put it behind him, I hope." I pursed my lips. "At least Clara is rid of that awful husband. But what a way to be rid of him."

"She just has to make a deposition to the authorities, then she's free to go. His family is taking charge of the body," said Harper.

Harvey looked wistful. "I hope someone remembers to return our coffins."

"Mister Harvey!" I didn't know whether to laugh or be shocked.

"Well, we need at least one of them. Got to carry Mister Evans back to Southampton." He looked at Harper. "And not stashed in my ales, for the love of God."

"Duly noted," said Harper.

"Does this sort of thing go on all the time aboard ship?" Agatha asked me.

"Only since Doctor Harper came on board."

"You know, Nurse, you're right about that," added Harvey.

Harper took off his officer's cap and adjusted his spectacles. "That's right. Blame it on the new fellow."

"I wasn't born yesterday, Boss." I gazed back out at the wharf. "This is the part of the trip that's always the saddest for me, Mrs Templeton."

"Why?"

I shrugged. "Just when you get used to this bunch, another brand-new group comes on board. We'll be re-supplied, turned around and out of here Monday."

"That's the nature of the business," Harvey said. "One group off, another group on. The scene stays the same, it's just the actors who come and go."

Agatha smiled. "How poetic you are, Mister Harvey. I believe it's something very much like that, after all." Down below, a fat cab driver was trying to shove a trunk two sizes too big into the back of his car.

"Do you think they all stay in New York?" I asked Harper.

"Probably not. Trains leave here and head on to Chicago and Los Angeles and who knows where. It's a big country. Texas alone is about as big as France."

"Texas," I said. "I'd like to go there someday. See some real cowboys."

"Me, too," said Harvey.

I rested my elbows on the railing, feeling the breeze against my face, then turned and looked at Agatha. "They would have gotten away with it, wouldn't they?" I asked.

Agatha nodded. "They came very close to it."

"And once they were down there," I said, looking at the crowds, "they'd have been gone." I looked back at Harper. "And no one would have ever known who did it."

"Maybe," said Harper. "But it's over now." He rubbed his hands together in the brisk wind. "On more pleasant thoughts, I believe there's time enough to catch a Broadway show tonight, if you'd like. I think we're possibly owed some time off from the ship. Mrs Templeton, if you're free, would you like to join us?"

"Why, thank you, Doctor. I'd like that very much."

Mister Harvey waved his hand. "I'd love to, but I've got to begin overseeing the provisioning for the return trip. I won't sleep for forty-eight hours." He doffed his cap. "A pleasure meeting you, Mrs Templeton. I wish you all the best in your future endeavors."

"Thank you, Mister Harvey. And please convey my greetings to Miss Kelly."

"Right." Harvey nodded at us. "A Broadway show, is it? While I spend all of my free time in the company of Mister Bissell." He shook his head and turned away, then turned around to face us. "Iron Bottom? Maeve, does my staff actually call me Iron Bottom?"

"I honestly don't know, Mister Harvey. I suppose you could ask Mister Casey."

"Casey!" said Harvey. "If he got hold of that I'd have to feed him into a boiler."

I laughed. "He told Doctor Harper and myself that he was going to make us all out to be heroes. Solved the crime of the century, he said."

"Doubtful," said Agatha. "Anyway, I was more or less an innocent bystander."

"And I'm a doctor, not a detective."

"And I'm going to go count carrots," said Harvey. "Ladies, Doctor." He gave us a salute and stalked away. As he rounded the corner we could hear him muttering: "Iron Bottom, my ass."

Laughing, I turned my attention back to the colorful swirl of activity on the dock and at the Customs Sheds – car horns blowing, people yelling, and in the near distance the tall buildings of downtown Manhattan. Mrs Templeton sighed.

"Well, I suppose I ought to disembark, too. My luggage is probably already at the hotel. Speaking of - " She took a scrap of paper from her purse and scribbled on it, handing it over to Doctor Harper. "Here's my information. I'm looking forward to the theatre with you both."

"The same," said Harper. "Mister Harvey, if you'll hold up a second, please." Harper walked away from us. I turned to Agatha.

"Mrs Templeton," I began.

"Yes, Maeve?"

"We had four victims, and each victim had their own killer. One by accident, three on purpose."

"That's how it worked out, yes."

"I was thinking – hypothetically, of course – what if there was only one victim, and four murderers?"

"Oh! Well, that would certainly present some interesting problems. What a novel idea."

I nodded, warming to the subject. "You could set it on a ship, like the *Victoria*."

Agatha laughed. "No, I think I've had quite enough of ships. They're supposed to be places for romance, not solving murders." She thought a moment. "But you're right, setting it someplace where everyone is together and no one can leave is a good idea."

I thought a moment. "How about aboard a train? One of those really fancy ones? And then to keep everyone on board, you could have it get snowed in or stopped by a rockslide or something. What do you think?"

"I think you've a very active imagination." Agatha gave me a hug. "See you tonight," she said, and headed for the steps down to the Sun Deck. Harper and Harvey sidled up next to me. Harvey was working his face into unusual contortions.

"Mister Harvey," I said. "Whatever is wrong?"

"You tell her," said Harvey.

"Tell me what?" I asked.

"Interesting woman," said Harper.

"Very," I agreed.

Harper looked after Agatha as she disappeared from sight. "You know, I've read every single one of her books," he said offhandedly.

I spun on Harper. "What did you say?"

"Agatha Christie. I've read all of her books."

My jaw dropped. "You knew?"

"He knew," said Harvey. "But I didn't. I would have gotten an autographed copy of one of her books for Miss Kelly. She reads the stuff." He scowled at me. "I can't believe you held out on us."

"Not now, Mister Harvey." I looked at Harper. "How did you know?"

"The name 'Templeton' is right out of one of her novels," he said. "*The Big Four* with Hercule Poirot, if I remember correctly. And it's not often, I'm sure, that one meets a woman who is interested in murder almost like it's a sport. It didn't take too long to figure it out, but I respected her wishes to remain incognito. I never let on to her, or anyone else." Harper grinned at me. "You're not the only one who can solve a mystery. Besides, If I gave away all my secrets at once you wouldn't find me interesting anymore."

"I seriously doubt that, Doctor."

One of the *Victoria's* young bell boys approached us, tipping his cap.

"Doctor, Nurse, a package for you. And your newspaper, Nurse." He handed off the goods, gave a touch to his cap for Mister Harvey and smartly stepped away. I examined the label on the package.

"It's from Mrs Temple – " I stopped and frowned at Harper. "Mrs Christie. For us to give to young Bradley."

"Open it," said Harvey. I looked at Harper.

"Do you think we should?"

"She'd probably want it repackaged as a gift," said Harper. "Go ahead."

I tore off the brown wrapper and smiled. It was a copy of *Winnie-the-Pooh*. I opened it. 'For Bradley, from his Aunt Mary Dell Templeton,' was written on the inside front cover. "Isn't that the sweetest thing?" I said.

Harvey peered over my shoulder. "What's that scrawl at the bottom?" he asked.

I squinted my eyes and read aloud. "Best wishes, Bradley. Your friend, AA Milne."

"What?" Harvey pulled the book from my hands for closer inspection. I looked at him.

"Didn't you say that if Milne was aboard this ship, we could call you Eeyore?" I asked with a laugh.

"Eeyore," said Doctor Harper, not trying to conceal a smile.

"Must have been travelling under an assumed name like Agatha," I said. "Won't Casey be surprised?"

"Blast Casey!" Harvey thrust the book into Harper's hands and stalked off, muttering.

I laughed and leaned back against the rail in the pleasant morning breeze, taking the Saturday morning edition of the *New York Daily Mirror* from Harper. When I found Winchell's column I shook the paper back and folded it to make it easier to read. Harper watched me with some amusement.

"Still looking to get your name in lights on Broadway?"

"You bet, Boss." I gave him a sly grin, my eyes lowered to the paper. "It would be nice to lead an exciting life for a change."

Nurse Chandler, Doctor Harper,
Mister Harvey and the *Queen Victoria*
will return in *Queen of Diamonds*.

Read on for a preview of the next book
in the *Voyages of the Queen* series – *Queen of Diamonds.*

Queen of Diamonds

By Scott Finley

Prologue

When I was a young girl my older brother and I would play cards. We knew all the games any kids growing up in England would have known before the War – Snap, Brag, Rummy – even American poker with a couple of variants. (Thanks, Mum!) Don't think I'm a big gambler, though, because I'm not. It's just that our parents provided a very eclectic education.

While my older brother was more inclined to go all in while holding a two, three, five, and seven of different suits with a Knave blithely serving as the face card, I was more inclined to discount the number cards and instead enjoyed the intricate drawings of the face cards. While all of them were pretty, to my eight-year-old eye the hearts, clubs, and spades couldn't hold a candle to the geometric precision of the diamonds. The others were all right, I supposed, in their own boring way, but the diamond – that just said something to me. It wasn't very many years later that it spoke in a more tangible fashion.

My Mum had received a pretty tear drop diamond necklace from my father on the occasion of their wedding anniversary. It sparkled with a fierce tenor from the hollow of her neck where it hung. By this time I had turned twelve, and to my young girl psyche it was something to be coveted. My brother, who had now reached the ripe old age of fourteen, saw it instead as something to be used in a scientific experiment. So, we threw in together and lifted it from Mum's jewelry box.

Our first stop was the garden shed, because my brother wanted to see if a diamond could indeed cut glass. One pane later, we found that it could. His experiment being satisfactorily fulfilled, he handed it off to me and I retreated to my room, where I put it around my neck and preened in front of the mirror for hours as I gracefully met His Majesty and the Prince of Wales and anyone else I could think of worth meeting.

Finally, my fantasies satiated, I went to stealthily return it – only to find my brother frantically waving me off at the bottom of the stairs. He put a finger to his lips, and only then did I hear Mum on the telephone reporting that she had been robbed. Discretion being the better part of valor, as they say, I beat a hasty retreat back upstairs and stashed the gem in the drainpipe outside my window then sat down to wait.

It wasn't too long before the local rozzers showed up at the door to investigate. There were three of them responding to what was apparently the crime wave of the year, if not century, an indication of exactly how dull life in our small university town could be.

Long story short, as the Americans say, the law didn't find anything (they also being as dull as life in said university town) and left the house to pursue further investigation, where, I didn't know and didn't care – though I suspected from the way they talked it would be The Rum and Beagle, a popular town pub. The next day, as if by a miracle, the purloined piece reappeared in my mother's jewelry box. Nothing was ever said about it, and my Mum just "assumed" she had overlooked it in the first place.

My brother, who had covered his tracks by "accidentally" breaking the scratched shed window with a cricket ball, gave me a crooked look because he knew better. But I didn't care.

I had worn it, if only for a while, and was already looking forward to the day when I would be a grown woman and be able to wear as many jewels as I wanted.

But being a twelve-year-old girl, I just wasn't aware of what the cost would be.

Saturday, March 22, 1930

I

ord love a duck, I'll admit it – I truly enjoy going shopping in New York City. Unfortunately, there just isn't that much time for this expensive hobby when the Queen Victoria is doing her turnaround down at Pier 54 in Manhattan, across from West 13th and 14th Streets. Over the two days or less it takes for the Victoria to be provisioned, refueled, and cleaned up for the next round of passengers heading east, crew that can get shore leave take it, if only for a few hours. That's how my cabin mate Alice Johnson and I ended up on Fulton Street in the diamond district.

Like me, Alice is a nurse aboard the Victoria. Well, not entirely like me. I'm Maeve Chandler, head nurse, and I report to Doctors Harper and Bratton. Alice reports to me. And of course, we all report to the Captain, but neither he, Doctor Harper nor Doctor Bratton was with us now – Bratton in fact was in London attending his brother's wedding – so we just did as we pleased, at least until our shore leave was up.

"Look at all those lovely diamonds," said Alice, pointing through a particularly grimy shop window where the lovely diamonds in question were gamely doing their level best to glitter in the weak sunlight filtering down between the surrounding buildings. Even to my diamond-loving eye, they looked pretty sad.

In the diamond district on this Saturday in late March of 1930, barely five months after the stock market crash, few people were holding shopping bags, and even fewer had the cash to be interested in gems. While we were definitely interested, neither of us had the cash, so we stood with our faces close to the jewelry store glass like children at a confectioner's shop, intent on the gemstones laid out enticingly on the worn black velvet on the other side. After a moment I sighed and adjusted the shell-blue cloche on my head, a nice change from my regular nursing cap.

"Never in my lifetime," I said firmly. "Not even from a fly-blown store like this, not as long as I'm a sea-going nurse for the Stoddard Lines."

"You'll have to marry up a doctor, that's what you'll have to do," Alice replied, her South African accent lilting. I gave her a sidelong glance.

"Doctor Bratton's not really my type," I replied.

"Oh, 'coo, I was talking about Doctor Harper."

"Him, either. I have to work with them on board the Victoria, I can't imagine life with them on land." Well, I could with Harper, if he and I could ever properly cross paths without a corpse in the way.*

Alice took me by the arm. "Oh, pish, a doctor on land is the same as one at sea." She gestured at the window. "Haven't you always said you wanted to drip in diamonds, ever since you were a little girl? Let's go inside and have a closer look, shall we? Doesn't cost anything."

"Fine, all right, fine." I tried to check my make up in the window reflection but gave up as Alice pulled me to the door.

The silver bell over the entrance tinkled as we entered the dimly lit interior of the store. A gaunt, hollow-eyed man of indeterminate age, immaculately dressed in a neat if thread-worn black suit, came out from behind a dusty counter. He looked, I thought, like a cadaver.

"Good afternoon, ladies. How may I help you?" Yep. The melancholy voice matched the appearance.

"Good afternoon," said Alice. She put a delicate hand to her jet-black hair, coiffed in the vamp style made popular by Theda Bara, then gestured at the window. "The ring over there – might we see it, please?"

"Certainly, madam." The man walked with deliberate care to the display, produced a key from his vest pocket and opened the case. He gazed down at the assortment laid out on the velvet, then looked back at Alice. "I'm sorry, but could madam point out which ring in particular she was thinking of?"

"The marquis cut," said Alice. I rolled my eyes.

"Very good, madam. An excellent choice." The salesman bent for a moment, then straightened, the ring held delicately between his thin fingers. He walked slowly to Alice, holding the ring out for her inspection.

"It's beautiful," she said. "May I?"

"Of course, madam." The cadaver gingerly allowed Alice to take the ring from him. As she turned it in her fingers he spoke. "From one of the Kimberley mines in South Africa," he said. "A full five carats. It's pre-war; 1908, I believe. One of a few Mr Isaac has in stock, from his personal holdings. The setting is eighteen karat gold, of course."

"Of course," breathed Alice. The man gave us a considered look, appraising our dress from shoes up to hats with the finicky care of someone used to assessing a customer's ability to spend.

"You're English, aren't you?" he asked Alice.

"My sister is," lied Alice with a practised smoothness that always awed and scared me in equal parts. "I was born in South Africa. Our parents separated and we grew up apart from each other."

I fought hard to keep from rolling my eyes. Alice had always been unable to resist letting go a corker, and yes, she really was from South Africa, but the rest — "We're from the Queen Victoria," I added.

Alice nodded in assent. "And we're sailing home tonight, so we thought we might put in a bit of shopping before we leave New York."

"I see," said the man, a bit frostily. "Stewardesses?"

"Oh, no," I blurted, my professional feathers ruffled. "We're not stewardesses at all, we're - "

"First-Class passengers," said Alice smoothly. She handed the ring back into the man's willing hand. "And we've still more shopping to do today, don't we?" she pointedly said to me.

"Yes. More shopping," I said, giving her a look. "At Tiffany's," I directed at the cadaver as I took Alice by the arm and headed for the door.

"Tiffany's," said the man. He gave us a forced and icy smile. "I hope their luck is better than mine."

"I doubt it," Alice replied as the bell above the door jangled. A dour man leaning heavily on a cane entered the store, a man easily seventy plus years old, with a dried-up face and bushy black eyebrows shot through with gray. A battered bowler was jammed down onto his drawn skull head and a black scarf was wound around his neck. A jeweler's loupe hung from a delicate gold chain beneath the scarf. His stooped shoulders and outward thrust head gave him the appearance of a myopic and bad intentioned turtle, yet his build indicated that he had once been a powerful young man. A neatly suited man who looked to be in his early twenties was with him, courteously holding the door open. I felt Alice's hand close over mine. I glanced at her, but she was gazing intently at the young man. The salesman gave them a preemptory nod.

"Good afternoon, Mr Isaac, Mr Singer." He indicated Alice and me. "These two young ladies are also sailing on the Queen Victoria tonight." The clerk gave Alice a meaningful look. "In First-Class as well, I'm told, but first they have more shopping to do at Tiffany's. Perhaps they'll join you both for dinner one night at sea before you reach Cherbourg."

The older man gave us no more than a cursory glance. "Hmph," he grunted, then turned to the young man with him. "You can close the door, Joel, you're letting the heat out, or do you want me to run the furnace for all of New York?" he said with a surly tone.

"Yes, Uncle," said the man as he looked at Alice with wide-eyed interest. I pulled myself free from Alice's hand.

Isaac frowned, his face sour. "Don't 'yes, uncle' me, young man," he said to Joel. He glanced disdainfully at us, then back at Joel. "In front of customers, these shiksas, such as they are, I'm always addressed as Mr Isaac. Family has nothing to do with it." He looked at the clerk again. "Typical of these young people, Jenkins," he said. "Modern easy living has made them all meshuggeneh." A sharp rap of the cane on the floor and Isaac scowled. "Joel," he barked, "if these young ladies don't want to buy anything, then we are closed." He jerked his head toward his salesman. "Jenkins, see them out." He lifted the cane and used it to part the curtains at the back of the shop, then disappeared through them.

Joel shrugged at us. "I'm sorry," he said, still looking at Alice.

"It's fine," I began, but Joel's attention was focused elsewhere.

"You look like a movie star," he said to Alice.

"No – that's very kind – Mr - "

"Singer." Joel put out his hand. "Joel Singer." He glanced toward the curtains. "The disagreeable man is my uncle; he runs the place. I must apologize for his behavior."

"Mr Singer, really," Jenkins said disapprovingly.

"He is disagreeable, Jenkins," Singer replied. "You've been here long enough to know that."

Jenkins gave a short "hrmph" and moved away. Joel turned back to Alice. "Are you a movie star?"

Alice allowed herself a smile. "I've been told I look like Pola Negri."

"Pola Negri. One of my favorites."

"And you look like Douglas Fairbanks," said Alice. "He's one of my favorites."

"Mine, too," said Joel. I finally gave in to the eye roll.

"I didn't know English girls knew the movies like American girls." Joel smiled, showing even white teeth. "You are English, aren't you? I mean, the accent and all."

"Oh," said Alice disarmingly, "I'm not English. I'm South African. As far as the movies, my sister and I go to a lot of them, and I know all the big stars. We're in America a lot."

"And this is your sister?" Joel asked, finally deigning to look at me.

"Yes," said Alice, glancing at me like I was a bug on the wall. "She's – "

"Maeve Chandler," I said brusquely, tapping my foot before Alice could imbellish her cock and bull story about me. "And yes, I'm English." I gave Alice a hard stare. "Our parents separated and we were raised in different countries. Alice and I travel a lot. Speaking, of, you've got to excuse Alice, we were just leaving." I took Alice by the arm, but Alice pulled away.

"Is there a chance I'll see you on board the Victoria, Miss Johnson?" Singer asked. "We can talk about the movies – or maybe see one."

"Yes, I understand the Queen Victoria has a very nice cinema on board," said Alice as I once again took her arm and began steering her toward the door.

"I'm sorry, but we've really got to go," I said, with no little irritation.

"I'll find you," Joel promised Alice as I opened the door. "I'll see you on board."

"Only if you hurt yourself," I said, keeping a firm grip on Alice and marching her out as the door closed behind us with a sharp tinkle of the bell.

Dear Reader –

You reached this page, so I'm guessing you survived your journey on the *Queen Victoria*. I hope you'll come along on book two, *Queen of Diamonds*, featuring a young Harry Winston teaming with Maeve to solve the murder of a diamond dealer found locked in his First-Class cabin with the key turned from the inside, suffocated by having his mouth stuffed with a fortune in diamonds and no sign of a struggle.

If you enjoyed this book, thank you! Please consider recommending it to a friend (or more!). Your word-of-mouth in person and on social media is not only a terrific compliment but also the best advertising in the world.

Speaking of social media, please visit the *Queen* website at www.voyagesofthequeen.com for all sorts of surprises. Doing a costume party for 1929 and the '30's? Find out what fashionable men and women were wearing, head to toe. Need a vintage cocktail recipe? We have them! How about some period artists to ask Alexa to play? There's a list! If you're hungry, come to the Captain's Table for luxury liner recipes. Preview the published *Queen* books on Amazon, and get a look at upcoming titles in the series. Go to the Radio Room and sign up for the *Queen*'s own blog, or just drop a line, either on the site or here: scott@voyagesofthequeen.com.

You can also learn about the men and women who crewed the great ships and the tasks they performed, as well as get a deeper understanding of the *RMS Queen Victoria*, what she carried, when she was built, how large she was and what her decks looked like. Find out more about the Golden Age of the trans-Atlantic liner, and there's a hand-curated list of websites with even more information.

Again, thank you for booking passage on the *Queen Victoria*. Who knows, I may see you on your next voyage (I'll be hiding behind the tall potted palms in the First-Class salon).

Bon voyage
Scott Finley

Reader's Group Guide

Shadow of the Queen

By Scott Finley

Questions and history to augment your club's reading of Shadow of the Queen.

1)   Maeve enjoys reading gossip columnist Walter Winchell in the *New York Daily Mirror.* Do you have a guilty pleasure you indulge in that frees you from everyday life for a while?

2)   Maeve vacillates between celebratory and feeling like she shouldn't be there for her dinner with Harper at the Captain's Table. Have you ever had conflicting emotions about an event you were attending and how did you resolve them?

3)   Agatha Christie remains the world's bestselling author with sales of an estimated two to four billion copies worldwide. Have you read one of her works? Seen a movie, tv show or theatre performance based on a novel?

4)   Agatha tells Maeve that sometimes the best tool for a woman is to just brazen it out. Would you agree or disagree?

5)   Could you have kept Maeve's secret about Agatha's identity? Have you ever had a secret that you knew was going to be hard to keep?

6)	Maeve ranks the days when she felt the belle of the ball as her wedding day, graduation day and day she got her first job. What were your belle of the ball days and why?

7)	Clara is in an abusive relationship but plans to end it once in New York. What advice would you have given her?

8)	Maeve tells Agatha she's tired of having doors closed in her face because she's an intelligent woman. She tries to keep her anger in check, because, she says, no one likes an angry woman. Have you experienced this? Why do you think men are more likely to express anger than women?

9)	When Maeve is trapped in the chain locker, is she keeping her courage up for herself, for Bradley, or for both? How would you have reacted?

10)	Circumstances seem to always prevent Maeve trying to light a spark with Doctor Harper. From your point of view, is Maeve better off letting nature take its course, if it will, or trying push it along?

There are many references to period products, people, ships, places and more within the story. For anyone born in 1901, this knowledge would have been as familiar to them as Ryan Reynolds or Brad Pitt is to you. Here's a quick dictionary.

Products

PROCAINE - Developed in 1905 with the trade name of Novocaine. You probably get a shot if you have dental work done.

LIFEBOUY - Brand of soap first manufactured by Lever Brothers in Great Britain, 1895. Still in production.

VINOLIA - Brand of soap first manufactured in 1910. Provided to First-Class cabins on the *Titanic*. Remains in production today.

L'OREAL - French company specializing in cosmetics, hair color, make up, etc. Founded 1909 and still going strong.

People

THEDA BARA - Movie actress and early sex symbol. 1885-1955.

LON CHANEY - Movie actor and makeup master known for grotesque characters. 1883-1930.

AGATHA CHRISTIE - Worldwide best-selling author of 66 detective novels and 14 collections of short stories. Her incalculable impact continues to be felt in the mystery and detective genre to this day. 1890-1976.

DOUGLAS FAIRBANKS - Movie actor and co-founder of United Artists pictures and founding member of the Motion Picture Academy; hosted first Academy Awards in 1929. 1883-1939.

CLARENCE HATRY - English financier whose massive company business failure based on forgeries paved the way for the New York Exchange crash of 1929. 1888-1965.

HARRY HOUDINI - World-renowned magician, famous for his escape tricks. 1874-1926.

MIR SULTAN KAHN - Chess master from what would later become Pakistan. One of the world's top chess players in the 20's and 30's. 1903-1966.

CHARLES LINDBERGH - First to fly Atlantic Ocean alone in 1927. 1902-1974.

KARL MARX - German philosopher, author of The *Communist Manifesto*. 1818-1883.

AA MILNE - Creator of *Winnie-the-Pooh*. 1882-1956.

TOM MIX - Top-grossing movie cowboy appearing in 291 films, most of which were silent. 1880-1940.

EDDIE RICKENBACKER - Race car driver, automobile and aircraft enthusiast. America's top scoring fighter ace in WWI, downing 26 enemy aircraft. 1890-1973.

MARY ROBERTS RINEHART - Popular American mystery writer. 1876-1958.

DOROTHY SAYERS - Popular English mystery writer. 1883-1957.

RUDOLPH VALENTINO - Movie actor and sex symbol. 1895-1926.

CHARLES DUDLEY WARNER - American essayist, coined the phrases "Politics make strange bedfellows" and "Everybody complains about the weather, but nobody does anything about it." 1829-1900.

WALTER WINCHELL - Popular and powerful American gossip columnist. 1897-1972.

ZIEGFIELD GIRLS - Named for Broadway producer Florenz Ziegfield, these chorus and showgirls were the Radio City Music Hall Rockettes of their day. Active 1907-1931.

Newspapers, magazines, movies

THE COCOANUTS - First Marx Brothers film in theaters, starring Groucho, Harpo, Chico, and Zeppo. Released 1929.

COLLIERS - American general interest magazine, also serialized novels and published short stories. Active 1888-1957.

LANCET - Highly respected and peer-reviewed English medical journal. Active 1823-present.

NEW YORK DAILY MIRROR - Popular tabloid newspaper. Active 1924-1963.

THE SON OF THE SHEIK - Wildly popular silent film starring Rudolph Valentino in his last role before his death. Released 1926.

Contemporary Passenger Ships and Aircraft

ADRIATIC - British-flagged passenger liner. In service 1907-1934. Scrapped 1935.

BRITANNIC - British-flagged passenger liner. Sister ship to *Titanic* and *Olympic*. In service 1915-1916. Struck German mine and sank in 1916 with 30 deaths.

GRAF ZEPPELIN - Successful and popular German passenger Zeppelin. In service 1928, retired 1937. Scrapped 1940.

LEVIATHAN - German and American-flagged passenger liner. Began life as *Vaterland*, was seized in New York in 1917 after America entered World War One. Renamed *Leviathan*, served first as a troop ship then reverted back to a luxury liner. In service 1914-1934. Sold for scrap in 1938, scrapped in 1946.

LUSITANIA - British-flagged passenger liner. In service 1907-1915. Struck by German torpedo and sank in 1915 with 1,198 deaths.

MAURETANIA - British-flagged passenger liner. In service 1907-1934. Scrapped 1935.

OLYMPIC - British-flagged passenger liner and sister ship to *Britannic* and *Titanic*. In service 1911-1935. Scrapped 1935-1937.

SPIRIT OF ST. LOUIS - Single engine custom built monoplane flown by Charles Lindbergh in his Atlantic crossing. In service 1927-1928. Currently on display in Smithsonian Air and Space Museum, Washington, DC.

TITANIC - Sister ship of *Olympic* and *Britannic*. Struck iceberg on maiden voyage in 1912 and sank with loss of over 1,500 passengers and crew.

Places

BELLEAU WOOD - WWI battle near Marne River in France, June 1-June 26, 1918. Primarily U.S. Army and Marines, along with some British and French, fought German forces for nearly a month before securing the area.

JOHN BROWN & CO. - Shipyard Scottish shipbuilding firm that built the *Lusitania*, *Queen Mary*, *Aquitania* and others. 1851-1986.

JUTLAND - WWI naval battle between Britain and Germany, May 31-June 1, 1916. Approximately 25 ships were sunk from a total of about 250 ships on both sides during the battle with over 9,800 casualties. Both sides claimed victory.

YPRES - Any of five battles fought in and near the Belgian town of Ypres in WWI, from 1914 to 1918. Historians believe total casualties of the five battles may have passed one million.

Slang

HORSEFEATHERS - American slang word of the 1920's, meaning nonsense.

SHEDS - British slang word believed to refer to cabins under a steward's watch aboard a passenger liner. "I've got ten sheds to look after."

Miscellaneous

BEAUFORT SCALE - Named for Sir Francis Beaufort, it is a scale that relates wind speed to the observed conditions at sea. First used in 1805 it has undergone many modifications since. Zero means calm and non-windy seas. At the opposite end, 12 means hurricane force.

BLUE RIBAND - An unofficial award, but competed for with vigor, for the fastest crossing of the Atlantic by a passenger liner. 35 liners held the Riband; the last (and presumably final) holder is the *SS United States*, currently laid up in Philadelphia. She won the award in 1952.

WEAR THE PURPLE - Ship's engineering staff wear a purple stripe to commemorate the *Titanic's* engineering staff, who died to a man keeping power and lights up on the sinking ship until the final plunge. The story may be apocryphal, but it's a good one.

About the Author

Scott Finley's fascination with the golden age of luxury liners began with Walter Lord's *A Night to Remember* and continued through a career as a multiple award winning and Lone Star Emmy nominated news producer.

His hobbies include electric trains and restoring radios from the 1930's and 1940's.

He lives in Dallas, Texas.

http://voyagesofthequeen.com